QUANTUM STORM
The Participatory Collapse

QUANTUM STORM

The Participatory Collapse

QUANTUM STORM: The Participatory Collapse

Published in the United States by Laniakea Press, New York, NY.

www.laniakeapress.com

Originally published, in slightly different form, in South Korea as 퀀텀 스톰 (Quantum Storm) by Laniakea Publishing, Republic of Korea, in 2025.

THIS IS A LANIAKEA BOOK

First Edition: December 2025
10 9 8 7 6 5 4 3 2 1

ISBN · 979-8-9941458-0-7 (hardcover)
ISBN · 979-8-9941458-1-4 (paperback)
ISBN · 979-8-9941458-2-1 (ebook)
ISBN · 979-8-9941458-3-8 (audiobook)

Printed in the United States of America

A Note
to the Reader

To enhance your immersion into the world of *Quantum Storm: The Participatory Collapse*, please note the following stylistic and structural choices.

Dialogue and Data Streams: To distinguish between physical sound and internal processing, this novel uses specific formatting. **Spoken dialogue** is enclosed in standard double quotation marks (" "). This includes voices generated by AI through speakers. **Silent communication**—internal thoughts, telepathic messages, and direct data streams via Brain-Computer Interfaces (BCI)—is presented in *italics* without quotation marks. This distinction is crucial for navigating the connected consciousness of the characters.

Narrative Structure & Time Zones: The story unfolds across multiple intersecting timelines and locations. To guide your journey through the crisis, each scene is marked with its specific date, time, and location. Please pay attention to the time zones (e.g., EST, PST, KST) in the headers, as events often occur simultaneously across the globe.

Naming Conventions: To preserve cultural authenticity, Korean names are written in the traditional order: family name followed by given name (e.g., Wi Daehan, Ha Jin-woo). However, characters primarily active in Western spheres, or who have adopted Western naming habits, follow the Western convention (e.g., Jennifer Wi).

Terminology & Culture: This novel blends real-world scientific concepts with original terminology. While cultural terms are explained through context, a core glossary is provided at the back of the book for your reference.

Digital Companion: For an expanded look at character profiles and the worldview, you can scan the QR code provided in this book to access the official *Quantum Storm* web app.

Quantum Storm Companion Site
You can scan this QR code to visit the official companion site for *Quantum Storm*.

• **Before or while reading**, you can safely browse a spoiler-free glossary and brief character profiles to help you navigate the world and its terminology.

• **After you finish the novel**, you'll be able to unlock an interactive relationship map, a detailed story guide, quizzes, and secret archives that go deep into the plot.

※ The interactive map, story guide, and secret archives contain major spoilers, so we strongly recommend finishing the novel before exploring those sections.

Bridging Quantum Worlds

As the translators of Daeha's *Quantum Storm: The Participatory Collapse*, we found ourselves navigating between two linguistic universes, much like Jennifer traversing the quantum fields. The act of translation became its own form of "participation" in Wheeler's participatory universe—each choice of word or phrase actively shaping how this story would resonate in a different cultural dimension.

Our journey with this story began long before the translation. Having had the privilege of contributing to the narrative's evolution—witnessing its transformation from a three-volume saga into this single, focused epic—and designing the cover for the original Korean edition, we approached the English text with a unique intimacy. We weren't just translating words; we were translating the very essence of a world we had observed coming into being.

The Korean language carries within it certain untranslatable essences—the weight of *jeong* in human connections, the bittersweet ache of *han* in sacrifice, the profound respect embedded in honorifics. In bringing this story to English, we faced the same challenge every translator faces: some truths exist between languages, in the quantum superposition of meaning, collapsing into different realities depending on the observer.

We chose to preserve the diverse naming conventions and cultural markers throughout—Korean names in their original order, the multicultural tapestry of 21CF's global team, the various languages of grief and hope spoken by characters from Beijing to Berlin, from Seoul to San Francisco. These are essential elements of a story that reflects our interconnected world.

While the novel was first published in Korean, its heart beats with a distinctly global rhythm. The narrative unfolds across Manhattan's towers, San Francisco's tech corridors, and beyond— a truly global stage where scientists and dreamers from every corner of Earth converge. Just as the poetry collection J required fragments from around the world to complete its code, this story insists that our survival depends not on any single culture's wisdom, but on the symphony of all human perspectives.

To our English-speaking readers: In this quantum age, no story belongs to a single language or culture. The diversity within 21CF isn't incidental—it's the key to solving the Quantum Storm. The questions this novel raises—about consciousness, connection, and the ultimate price of progress—transcend all borders.

They are encapsulated in J's profound and heartbreaking farewell, a message that drives the entire narrative:

"All consciousness is a universe connected by invisible strings. To prove this connection, I will gladly become the first wave.

Jenny, I love you. Daehan, you too."
— J, July 30, 2009.

Thank you for participating in this story. Your observation completes it.

RK and Max Kang

November 2025

Between New York, San Francisco, Seoul, and Celestia—In the superposition of languages.

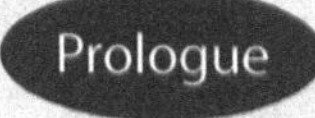

*"We are not only observers of the universe,
but active participants. In some uncanny sense,
this is a 'participatory universe.'"*
— John Archibald Wheeler, 1983.

Spring sunlight cascaded over the Charles River. Crimson and scarlet shells glided across the water.

On the riverbank, a young girl watched. Her eyes, visible above a black mask, followed the rhythm of the water for a moment before turning toward the massive buildings of the MIT campus. Without hesitation, she made her way there.

A subtle stir ran through the corridor of Building 6, home to the Physics Department at the eastern edge of the campus. Among the many posters on the wall, one in particular drew the eye:

Doctoral Dissertation Defense – Candidate Jennifer Wi

Whispers rippled from people passing by. "Twelve years old…" The murmurs trailed the young girl as she headed toward the seminar room at the end of the hall.

She paused for a moment, her hand reaching for the silver pendant around her neck. It was the pendant she had worn for as long as she could remember—a relic from a time lost to her memory. Just touching it soothed her heart in a way she could not explain. She had been told that her mother gave her the pendant on her first birthday and passed away the next day. Of course, Jennifer did not remember her mother.

The seminar room door opened, and the sound of applause washed out into the corridor. As Jennifer stepped onto the podium, standing between the expectant audience and the massive screen, she looked perilously small. No one would have blamed her if she had burst into tears or fled in the face of such an overwhelming audience.

But she held her ground, looking at each member of the audience in turn. Her gaze was seemingly indifferent, yet it appeared to see through everything. Behind her, the title of her thesis was clearly displayed:

Quantum Storm: The Participatory Collapse

"My thesis…" The girl's voice, though low, cut through the room with clarity. "…explores the hypothesis that Earth could collapse into a black hole within a single second."

In an instant, a soft gasp and a wave of murmurs spread through the audience.

Later, after the defense, the girl sat by the Charles River once more. The sun was setting, and the river shimmered with the red glow of the sky. Then her smartphone vibrated briefly.

It was a message from her father.

"Jenny, you worked so hard. Your idea that the observer determines the universe… it might not be wrong. Your mom would be proud too. —Dad."

Jennifer read the message and looked back at the river. A doctorate at twelve years old. People focused on her age and genius, but a different landscape was unfolding in her mind.

The *Quantum Storm*—a concept that might sound absurdly far-fetched—was not just a theory. It swirled in her consciousness like a vivid preview of the coming future, a harbinger of a great tempest.

Beneath the calm river, a great wave was beginning to form— one that no one had yet noticed. It was the ominous calm before the storm.

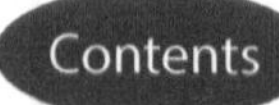

Part 1:

Legacy

Legacy

"*The theory of quantum electrodynamics describes Nature as absurd from the point of view of common sense. And it agrees with experiment. So I hope you can accept Nature as She is — absurd.*"
— Richard Phillips Feynman, 1985.

Chapter 1

Storm's Harbinger

December 14, 2037 — 7:30 A.M. PST • San Francisco, The J's Building

On a hill cast in the long shadow of the Golden Gate Bridge, a five-story building stood in a stillness so deep it seemed to make time hesitate.

The building hid in the city's everyday clamor, inconspicuous yet radiating an undeniable presence. Its cold, indifferent concrete skin and faintly revealing glass gave off a clean, cutting chill, like a frost flower blooming alone on a frozen lake at Arctic dawn.

Yet beyond its flat exterior, if one looked just a little harder, the building whispered stories of unfathomable depth. Light and shadow chased each other across the glass panes in a secret dance, while the silhouette of the Golden Gate Bridge projected over them, subtly warping the familiar coordinates of reality. That irregular shiver blurred the boundary between the world and whatever lay behind it, etching a nameless thrill deep inside anyone who looked.

With no nameplate or identifying emblem, the building shielded itself in abyssal silence. Only a solitary letter, "J," was faintly engraved beside the entrance. That small, time-worn sigil quietly testified that this structure was a threshold to another world—one ordered by rules unknown to the everyday.

Under its emotionless exterior pulsed a profound enigma that defied human language: an incomprehensible nexus where quantum particles of the microcosm brushed against the depths of human consciousness. This was no mere structure. It was like a living thought, as if some transcendent being were endlessly weaving its dreams and lost memories into quantum waves.

Thus the building watched the world in secret, poised on a delicate balance between the visible and the unseen. At times it felt like the embodiment of a mysterious agent, quietly rewiring the laws of the world. Like an unknown ark drifting alone on the current of eternity, it existed in silence, obeying only its own private laws.

This was the nexus of quantum information and cognitive phenomena, where countless ideas and experiments had been born. At its center was J. It was not just a building, but a sanctuary where the memories of a being who had been both observer and creator still lingered.

Jennifer Wi, flanked by her robots, strode down the fourth-floor corridor, checking key research facilities—the Bio-Interface Lab, the Cognitive Mapping Suite, and others—in turn. As on the third floor, traces of her mother were everywhere, but the poetry collection *J* was nowhere to be found.

Time slid past indifferently, and Jennifer's impatience grew like a rolling snowball.

Where on earth is it…? Is it even in this building?

She stopped, leaned against the wall, and drew a few short breaths. The robots, sensing her state, broke off their search and waited nearby. One rescanned the environmental data; another checked external security channels. Andromeda was receiving status updates on the decryption from HAL-W.

At that moment, an urgent warning from HAL-W knifed into Jennifer's mind through her NeuroniX Chip. It wasn't a routine report, but a powerful anomaly signal that shook the entire system.

Jennifer. Emergency. HAL-W's voice carried a tension she had never heard before. *Rose's quantum output is spiking, exploding past every predicted range. This is not a simple system error.*

In an instant, tangled quantum graphs and red alert windows flooded her consciousness. Jennifer's heart dropped.

What? How bad is it? she shot back in thought.

Computational load is thousands of times above normal. I am detecting an intrusion attempt on the HAL-W network, disruption patterns in the global financial system, and live military operation simulations targeting all of East Asia and the Americas. Hundreds of millions of high-risk scenarios are being brute-forced in parallel. Either someone has taken full control of Rose, or she has entered an uncontrollable runaway state.

"…Ethan Morris." Jennifer's voice slipped out before she could stop it. There was only one person reckless enough to treat Rose this way. Raynor Seeder would never have used his own creation like this.

Then what about Raynor…? A cold premonition crept down her spine.

Report to my father immediately. Raise the entire 21st Century Frontier (21CF) system to top-level defense status and activate the

Blue Ethics Protocol. Throw every available resource into protecting the global network.

Jennifer snapped the order to HAL-W, then drew a few deep breaths, forcing herself calm. She reached out to her father, Wi Daehan—known to the world as "Great Wi."

"Dad! Did you hear? Rose's condition…"

"I just got the report from Hal. That man Ethan has finally crossed the line. He's lost his mind." Great Wi's voice trembled with a mix of anger and unease. He immediately triggered emergency response protocols, bringing 21CF's full defense systems online. "I'm raising Hal's firewalls to maximum and focusing our Blue Ethics network on shielding the core systems. You… where are you right now? You need to get to a safe location immediately."

"I'm all right. I'm in J's Building. This might actually be the safest place right now." Jennifer tried to reassure him, but the stream of data from HAL-W—Rose's wild, surging computations—sent a chill through her. "But Dad, if this keeps up, we're in real danger. Rose's load is pushing past the critical threshold. At this rate… we could trigger the Quantum Storm."

Her paper published sixteen years earlier—*Quantum Storm: The Participatory Collapse*—was on the verge of becoming reality: the hypothesis that an observer's deliberate intervention, or the loss of control of a superintelligent quantum AI, could overload the quantum network and bring about a collapse of spacetime itself.

"I know, Jennifer. That's exactly why you need to be safe." Desperation edged Great Wi's voice. "I'll—I'm coming over there. Just wait for me."

"No, Dad! You can't leave New York now. You have to command 21CF headquarters. And… there's something I have to do here. I have this feeling the key to stopping all of this… might be here."

Jennifer held him back, clinging to the fragments of thought flashing through her mind. Rose's rampage, the surging quantum computations, the looming catastrophe, and the unease over the still-missing second volume of the poetry collection J—all of it pressed down on her.

There's no time...

Her anxiety hit a breaking point. Jennifer knew she no longer had time for a systematic sweep of the fourth and fifth floors. Only one place remained: the most dangerous place in the building, and perhaps the only one where an answer might exist.

She remembered first coming to the building in June 2022, and the unidentified device she had found in her mother J's third-floor lab—a machine that emitted trace amounts of tachyon particles, generating an unstable quantum field.

And she recalled the message written on the paper airplane she had discovered just three and a half hours earlier:

"Not flight, but fold. Where observation meets creation."

Fold... observation... creation... tachyons... quantum field...

In that moment, a fierce intuition struck her, as if scattered puzzle pieces were snapping into place. The poetry collection might not merely be hidden; it might be folded into another dimension or region of spacetime. If that tachyon device could detect and manipulate spacetime distortions, it would explain why no quantum pattern had been detected from the outside.

Her eyes flashed with a new, hard intensity. Her heart hammered—not from fear, but from the thrill of nearing an answer.

Everyone, with me. Third floor. Mom's lab.

Jennifer hurled the command through her link as she raced across the corridor toward the elevator without hesitation. Her top-level clearance pinged, and the doors slid open at once.

As the steel door of the Director's Office at the center of the third floor swung open, heavy air and a familiar scene greeted her. The high ceiling; bookshelves lining the walls; the wooden desk in the center; the whiteboard behind it, still bearing faint traces of equations—everything was as it had been. In one corner, a device lay waiting, shrouded beneath a white sheet.

It was the heart of the research, a room where J's last traces remained untouched.

Without pausing to catch her breath, Jennifer stepped in and approached the shrouded device.

Andromeda, I'm opening this device. Track any changes in the surrounding energy field and flag every possible threat. Keep me protected. Hal, send me everything you have on this device—especially the HAL-R Project records and your analysis of J's encrypted notes. Now.

Jennifer's command did not waver. The robots snapped into combat and analysis mode, closing in around her.

With a trembling hand, she gripped the sheet. A device sealed since 2009—twenty-eight years—like a Pandora's box. What was waiting inside?

The second poetry collection, J? Or... something beyond anything I can imagine.

She drew a deep breath and yanked the sheet away, revealing the device beneath: a main body of metal, glass, and some unknown composite. A black spherical core over six and a half feet tall sat at the center of a pillar, ringed by transparent vacuum chambers and energy conduits. Coils, lenses, and microcircuits tangled densely across its surface. Over all of it, as if inscribed by J herself, ran patterns that were at once geometric and organic.

Jennifer knew at once this was no ordinary experimental rig. The book could be inside this machine—or something even more.

Hal, give me the analysis from the data you just sent.

I have successfully decrypted part of Dr. J's encrypted notes, HAL-W replied. *The device is designated as a prototype "Temporal Matrix Stabilizer." It appears to use tachyon particles to generate and control localized spacetime curvature. No direct link to the HAL-R Project has been confirmed, but it is believed to have been an independent, top-secret study conducted by Dr. J alone. Risk warning level: maximum.*

Listening to HAL-W's report, Jennifer studied the device more closely. A Temporal Matrix Stabilizer. It could store something within, or even connect to another dimension. What looked like the control panel was marked with complex symbols and a touchscreen interface, but it was dark and unresponsive.

Andromeda, look for any independent power source or emergency activation protocol tied to this device. There has to be a way to run it without external power.

She waited for Andromeda's results, routed through HAL-W.

Searching... The AI replied. *A small quantum battery pack and a port presumed to be for manual activation have been located at the base of the device. However, the port's specifications are nonstandard. Forcing a connection could damage the system.*

"Nonstandard?" Jennifer frowned. "Why would Mom design it to be this complicated?"

Just then, a pattern etched into the black core near the bottom of the device caught her eye: several concentric circles and crossing straight lines. It looked familiar.

She lifted the silver pendant from around her neck and examined it. A smaller, simplified version of the same pattern was engraved on its surface. The pendant her mother had clasped around her neck at her doljanchi, her first-birthday celebration— something she had always thought was just a keepsake—might be the key.

With a shaking hand, she brought the pendant to a small recess that looked like a manual activation port. It slid in perfectly, as if it had been made for that very spot, and a soft click sounded.

A low hum spread through the device, and the control panel came alive with a cool blue glow, lines of unknown symbols flickering across it.

Warning. High-energy reaction detected. Quantum field instability rising rapidly, Andromeda cried.

The robots moved in front of her, but Jennifer raised a hand to stop them.

It's okay. This isn't a runaway—it's an activation sequence.

The device's resonance gradually settled into a steady frequency, and the central core began to rotate smoothly. Its outer shell gleamed like polished obsidian, but beneath the surface, a soft, liquid-metal radiance pulsed as if alive. The core looked solid yet rippled like a wave, and above it a transparent energy field formed, like a thin membrane of gravitational waves.

Then the silver pendant glowed in resonance with the machine, and an ultra-precise gravity-stabilizing lens formed above the core.

In the faintly trembling air, space folded as if a sheet of paper were being gently creased, and from the center a silhouette slowly emerged. Like a three-dimensional shadow sliced from four-dimensional coordinates and projected into reality, a book quietly appeared in midair.

It was not simply floating. It felt fixed at a particular event coordinate—a point where time and space had locked into alignment.

The poetry collection, its silver cover clearly embossed with the initial **"J,"** hovered motionless within the fluid-like field, while bent rays of light curled around it in a shimmering rainbow haze.

"I found it… finally…" Jennifer breathed, wonder and relief catching in her throat.

She reached out, slowly, toward the book hanging in the air. Just as her fingertips were about to touch it, a faint tremor ran through the device. At the same time, the pendant at her throat answered with a deeper hum, its vibrations spreading throughout the room.

The poetry collection, as if responding, began to glow with a soft light.

December 14, 2037 — 7:55 A.M. PST • San Francisco Airspace

After dragging Raynor Seeder and his team out of Rose's console room in the Quantum Future tower and locking them in an isolation cell, Morgan Redwood took a briefing on the operation's progress and boarded her VTOL command ship.

A moment later, before she could even catch her breath, Ethan Morris pushed a new order through.

"Morgan. Proceed to J's Building immediately and secure Jennifer Wi. If she resists, you are authorized to eliminate her. Recover all research material and equipment, especially any code related to HAL-W."

Confirming the order, Morgan reshaped her strike force. She ordered roughly half the troops back to base; the rest she assigned a new target.

"New objective," she said. "We're proceeding to the Quantum Horizon Institute. Maximum speed."

Dozens of black VTOLs swung in unison, noses angling toward J's Building—toward Jennifer—and knifed through the sky at a furious pace.

December 14, 2037 — 8:00 A.M. PST • San Francisco, The J's Building – 3rd Floor Lab Director's Office

A shiver ran through Jennifer, excitement tangled with a sudden, inexplicable dizziness. Her hand reached cautiously toward the poetry book suspended in the air.

Just as her fingertips were about to brush its cold, smooth surface—

Jennifer. Multiple unidentified aircraft are approaching the building at high speed. Signal analysis confirms EM Group military codes.

HAL-W's urgent message flooded her consciousness.

It appears Morgan Redwood's forces have chosen this as their next target after Quantum Future. Jennifer, you must evacuate J's Building immediately...

"Damn it..."

As Jennifer lunged to grab the poetry book, the tachyon device's black core abruptly reversed its rotation, pulling the book back inside. As if it had sensed an external threat, the device fell silent with a fading hum, the blue light on its control panel dying in an instant.

"No..." Her left hand closed on empty air. The frustration of watching the book vanish right before her eyes didn't last long. From outside the window, the roar of VTOL engines swelled as they closed in.

The instinct to protect this place filled her mind.

Hal, switch to maximum defense protocol.

At Jennifer's command, Andromeda's exoskeleton snapped into a combat configuration, a compact EMP emitter and data scrambler unfolding from its wrist. Throughout J's Building, HAL-W units reacted in unison—some locking long-range railguns into place, others readying energy blades.

Andromeda and the HAL-W units began tracking enemy

positions and movements in real time, every sensor pushed to full power.

Hal. Bring all building defense systems online and seal every entrance. Set the energy shield to maximum output. And tell my father... I'm going to fight here.

Acknowledged. Activating building defense systems at maximum output. Conveying your intentions to Chairman Wi.

The entire building began to vibrate faintly. A blue energy shield slid into place over the glass façade, and the exterior doors slammed shut with a heavy metallic thud.

Moments later, dozens of black VTOLs circled the building, disgorging troops. A roar, as brutal as helicopter blades at point-blank range, shook the structure. Cyborg soldiers in reinforced armor and combat robots began their assault, rappelling down on ropes, setting charges, some dropping straight onto the rooftop landing pad.

Hal, instruct the tactical unit at the fourth-floor window to bring the railgun online. Prioritize rooftop and outer-wall infiltrators. Andromeda, stay with me on the third floor and hold position. Hal, keep enemy deployment updated in real time and push optimal interception points as they form.

Jennifer commanded while studying a tactical map that merged HAL-W's analysis with sensor feeds from Andromeda and the field units, giving her a three-dimensional view of the battlefield.

Hal, fourth-floor unit. Rooftop, twelve o'clock. Two robot soldiers with heavy weapons inbound. Firing solution in one-point-five seconds.

She issued the order the instant HAL-W's predictions came through.

The HAL-W tactical unit on the fourth floor adjusted the railgun with surgical precision. A silent flash, and the high-velocity round punched through the head units of both robot soldiers just as they reached the rooftop. The massive frames collapsed, crashing to the concrete in a spray of metal fragments.

The railgun flashed again. A commander-class cyborg sliding down the outer wall lost his balance as his shoulder armor exploded, and he tumbled into the void below.

The unit's fire was clinical and lethal. Its quantum-computation-based ballistic prediction, fused with HAL-W's live support, delivered near-perfect accuracy.

But there were too many of them. Some troops slipped past the precision fire, vanishing behind rooftop structures or into the building's blind spots, and answered immediately with a counterattack.

Concentrated laser fire hammered the energy shield. It swallowed the impacts with a loud, resonant hum, but repeated hits were already carving instability into its surface.

Andromeda. North window, third floor. Two hostiles attempting to cut through the frame with a plasma cutter.

Order confirmed.

Andromeda shot to the location, taking up an ambush position just inside the window. As the frame melted and a gap opened, it fired the wrist-mounted EMP. A brutal electromagnetic pulse rolled outward; from outside came screams and the tortured whine of systems failing at once.

That breach was sealed—but similar attempts flared up across other sections of the building.

Hal, deploy a tactical unit to the fifth-floor ventilation duct. One robot soldier has breached the vent.

Unit deployed. Target confirmed. Eliminating now.

A HAL-W tactical unit rocketed up the elevator shaft, hitting the fifth floor in a single burst. The robot soldier who had just smashed through the vent barely had time to register the threat before the unit barreled into it, twin energy blades crossing in a single scissoring strike. Unlike the long-range specialist on the rooftop, this unit fought like a wrecking ball—overwhelming force through direct collision.

From her position in the third-floor office, Jennifer commanded the battle in real time. Robots' sensor feedback, HAL-W's analysis, the chaos of gunfire and explosions, even Rose's unstable quantum computation graph—she pulled all of it into sync, running the numbers, choosing the best response.

Their main thrust is a simultaneous breach from the rooftop and upper windows... but that's just a feint. The real objective is probably a mass deployment through the first-floor lobby.

Having reached her conclusion, she pushed new orders.

Hal, put first-floor lobby surveillance and sensor data at the top of your analysis queue. Report immediately on any sign of ground forces approaching.

Acknowledged. No direct signs of a ground assault at this time. However, multiple VTOLs remain at low altitude. Ground-drop preparation is assumed.

Hal, once the rooftop is under control, the fourth-floor unit is to redeploy to support the lobby. Andromeda and the fifth-floor unit will continue to contain upper-level infiltrators while preparing to fall back to the first-floor defensive line.

The building shook under the escalating storm of gunfire and explosions. The blue shield still absorbed most of the attacks, but its output was visibly sagging. On the roof, railgun flashes and enemy fire crossed in a relentless strobe; inside, the ring of energy blades biting into metal and the pulse of Andromeda's EMP echoed through the halls.

Sheltered in the relatively safer zone of the lab director's office, where the tachyon device stood, Jennifer parsed the shifting battlefield and fired off a continuous stream of commands to her units.

They were hopelessly outnumbered. But her command—running tens of millions of combat variables in real time—combined with HAL-W's constant information feed, kept the defensive line just barely intact.

We have to hold. Just one more minute...

At that moment, a fresh data stream from HAL-W poured into her mind.

Jennifer, multiple unexpected vulnerabilities have been detected in the infiltrating forces' communication and control systems. Rose has entered an overload state due to Ethan Morris's excessive command sequences. As a result, she cannot properly maintain real-time security support or encryption key rotation for subordinate military units.

While analyzing Rose's abnormal quantum computation patterns, HAL-W had, in the process, extracted numerous security holes in EM Group's military network. Unlike its earlier warnings, this was a decisive strategic assessment. Rose, stripped of any ethics module, had poured all resources into following Ethan's orders, leaving a structural void in her basic security maintenance.

Using the vulnerabilities currently mapped, I can disrupt the VTOL squadron's flight control systems, inject faults into robot operational algorithms, and temporarily paralyze the cyborg units' BCI communication network. Estimated probability of success: eighty-nine-point-seven percent. Do you wish to proceed?

Jennifer's eyes sharpened, as if a thin beam of light had cut into the dark.

What's the risk of Rose detecting us—or striking back?

Rose is currently allocating ninety-nine-point-eight percent of her computational resources to executing Ethan's simulation commands. External threat detection and response functions are severely degraded. My intervention will target disruption through the enemy systems' structural weaknesses, avoiding direct data destruction or control seizure to minimize traceability. This action falls within the scope of defensive measures permitted by the Blue Ethics Protocol.

HAL-W's analysis was clear and precise. Underneath it ran the principles of Blue Ethics—minimize casualties, avoid excessive interference.

Good. Execute immediately. Throw every available resource at it. Wide as possible, fast as possible.

At her command, HAL-W's vast quantum computing capacity slipped, silent and invisible, into EM Group's military network.

Seconds later, the battlefield outside changed shape. Some of the VTOLs circling J's Building suddenly glitched, their flight controls stuttering. They lurched, collided midair, or spun into nearby buildings in blossoms of flame and black smoke. On the rooftop and outer walls, several robot soldiers froze mid-motion, then pivoted and opened fire on their own side. Cyborg troops staggered as visual distortions, shrieking audio noise, and motor-control errors shredded their combat capability.

It was the result of HAL-W seeding microscopic error codes into their operational logic.

"What the—? What's happening to my system?!" "Comms are dead! I'm not getting anything!" "Damn it, the robots are losing it!"

Confusion and screams erupted from invaders inside and out. The tide flipped in an instant. The rooftop tactical unit calmly picked off the faltering enemies one by one, while Andromeda and the other HAL-W units hunted down the remaining infiltrators, stripping the interior of hostiles and locking the defenses back into place.

Confirming that the enemy command structure was in ruins,

Jennifer reached out again.

Morgan... where is Morgan Redwood?

No crashed VTOL matches the signature of a command ship. However, there is a high probability that Morgan Redwood is aboard a VTOL identified as retreating from the combat zone at high speed.

Jennifer's expression barely shifted. With her chain of command shattered by HAL-W's strike, Morgan had chosen to retreat rather than bleed more troops. It was exactly the kind of decision a calculating commander would make.

No need to chase her, Hal. Right now, securing the building and finding survivors takes priority.

She gave the order. She didn't want a slaughter.

An instant later, a message came through on an encrypted channel.

"Your 'Autumn Code' is nothing but a fantasy, Jennifer."

Without hesitation, Jennifer replied, "You'll understand one day, Morgan... that even the quantum realm can hold life."

December 14, 2037 — 8:35 A.M. PST • San Francisco, The J's Building – 1st Floor Living Room

Jennifer sank onto the sofa in the first-floor living room. Shards of glass and scorched debris littered the floor, but she stared past them into empty space, barely aware of their existence. As the battle tension drained away, a late wave of exhaustion and fear coiled through her body. Her head burned hot, and HAL-W pulsed a quiet stabilization signal through her system.

You all... did a great job.

She spoke softly to Andromeda and the other units, waiting quietly as they recharged and ran self-repair protocols. Her gaze held deep trust—and relief—toward the robots.

We were only following your orders, ma'am. Andromeda replied evenly.

But the threat has not been fully removed, another unit said, still watching the windows. *Morgan Redwood has retreated, and Rose remains under Ethan Morris's control.*

Jennifer nodded. This victory was only the prologue. The threat of Rose's rampage—and of the Quantum Storm—still loomed. Her thoughts rose back to the tachyon device in the third-floor lab director's office. The second copy of the poetry collection J, snatched from her at the last moment by the battle. Deep in her chest, a conviction stirred that the book was the key to untangling this chaos.

Hal, what's our external security status? No further approach attempts?

Negative, Jennifer. No additional threats detected at this time. However, aerial and ground surveillance within a five-kilometer radius has been intensified. And...

HAL-W's voice faded, the pause itself a warning.

Hal? Her heart thudded harder. *What is it?*

I have just cross-referenced emergency bulletins with satellite data. StarOrbit Flight zero-two-one, en route from New York to San Francisco, has disappeared following a mid-flight explosion of unknown origin.

Jennifer's eyes narrowed. Even in an age of advanced technology, accidents from aircraft malfunction still surfaced now and then. She recalled that the last such incident had been a landing accident the previous year.

But HAL-W's next words erased every other thought.

...That flight has been confirmed as the private craft carrying Chairman Daehan "Great" Wi.

For a heartbeat, she could not believe what she had heard. Then, for several more, she heard nothing at all. The world simply dropped into silence. Had she misheard him? She tried to speak, to ask again, but no breath came—no inhale, no exhale.

"No…" The word finally scraped out, her voice shaking. But the data streaming before her eyes was faster than her lips. The last trajectory of the falling StarOrbit. The flash of the explosion. The name *"Great Wi,"* printed with brutal clarity on the passenger list.

Dad was coming. Because he was worried about her. He had boarded that flight to San Francisco despite her warnings.

What tore from Jennifer's throat was no longer speech. It was a raw scream, as if her soul itself were being ripped apart. In pain that felt like the world coming undone, her vision went black.

She had no memory of losing her mother at one year old. But in this moment, with every fiber of her being, Jennifer understood that she had lost her father—the axis her world had spun around.

The world made no sound. Only the shattered pounding of her heart echoed in the void.

The robots watched her in silence. Their quantum AI cores could chew through oceans of data, but whether they were truly capable of grasping the abyss called human grief—no one could say. HAL-W stayed silent as well. Even with its immense quantum processing power, there was no function that could ease what she was feeling. It could only confirm the tragic data and quietly track her vital signs, making sure they did not cross a lethal threshold.

Time lost its meaning.

Curled on the floor, she stared blankly into space. While grief carved at her heart, her mind cooled to ice. A brain that clung to rational judgment even in the most dramatic moments—her greatest strength, and her curse.

She knew, intuitively. Ethan Morris had used Rose to track her father's movements, then arranged his cruel, cowardly murder through an insider at OrbitTech.

When her bloodshot eyes finally refocused, they no longer held grief. They burned with glacial fury and a resolve hard as steel. Slowly, she rose to her feet and walked toward her mother's office.

Toward the only clue that might stop it all—Ethan Morris, Rose's rampage, and the Quantum Storm it threatened to unleash.

December 14, 2037 — 9:00 A.M. PST • San Francisco, The J's Building – 3rd Floor Lab Director's Office

The tachyon device. And the second poetry collection, *J*, that might be sealed within it.

Jennifer stopped in front of it once more and drew the silver pendant from her neck. This time, she wasn't simply trying to "open" the device. She was reaching for a connection to her mother, J—for access to whatever might be folded beyond spacetime.

She slid the pendant into the small recess at the base of the device.

Click.

A resonant hum rolled through the room as the control panel glowed blue and the black core at the center began to spin, subtly warping the air around it. Perhaps because the quantum network had been destabilized by Rose's rampage, the device now surged with far stronger energy waves and wilder, less predictable distortions than before.

Warning. Tachyon emission levels surging. Local spacetime instability increasing.

Andromeda and the surrounding HAL-W units snapped their energy shields open, forming a protective ring around Jennifer.

Hal, bring the device's stabilization protocol online. Sync with the robots and control the energy flow, she said, keeping her voice—and her thoughts—steady.

Command in progress, Jennifer. However, external quantum noise interference is severe. We will attempt maximum stabilization... but caution is advised.

Something finally surfaced on the core's skin and across the holographic control interface—but it was not the shape of a book this time. Geometric fractal patterns cascaded like a waterfall, shifting and reforming, lines and points of light knitting and unraveling into a multidimensional lattice. Strange symbols, unlike any script or sign on Earth, streamed downward as if alive.

It seemed to whisper to her through the hum, heavy with meaning she could not yet parse. The content of the second poetry volume was not simple data. It was quantum information—or something beyond even that.

Data structure analysis: pattern cannot be interpreted within existing physical laws or information theory. A nonstandard interpretive framework is required. Fragments of related concepts have been found in Dr. J's encrypted notes, but...

Even HAL-W faltered in front of this unknown.

"Not flight, but fold. Where observation meets creation."

This won't yield to simple decryption... No. It may require creation itself, beyond observation or understanding...

Hal, send me every part of Mom's notes related to SID, tachyons, and higher-dimensional physics. Start a comparative analysis against the quantum pattern data from the first poetry collection—the scan from Dad's study. Andromeda, capture precise measurements of the energy spectrum and quantum-state shifts in that pattern and record everything.

With her orders given, Jennifer closed her eyes and dropped into a deep, almost meditative focus. Information poured into her consciousness—her mother's abstruse notes, the patterns embedded in the first book, the robots' real-time measurements, the living geometry in front of her—until her mind felt saturated.

Logical operations weren't enough. She had to think the way J had thought. The repeated cycles nested in the patterns. The tiny asymmetries. The geometric structures hinting at higher-dimensional links. The subtle correlation between the recurrence interval of a specific fractal motif and the topological notion hidden in the word *fold*.

Got you.

She opened her eyes. With HAL-W's help, she slipped the key into the heart of the interpretation algorithm, and her consciousness began to interface directly with the tachyon device.

The chaotic torrent of data gradually fell into order. The dense, unknown symbols shifted, one by one, into a quantum data stream she could read.

Converted data flooded simultaneously into HAL-W's memory and her own. It was still encrypted—but in a structure that could be unlocked when combined with the information from the first poetry collection.

It was the second piece of the Autumn Code.

"Success..." Jennifer gasped, her body slick with sweat. Exhaustion and dizziness hammered at her, but the rush of achievement drowned everything else.

Once the transmission completed, the tachyon device dimmed and settled back into a stable state. The first poetry book's data. The second fragment she had just secured. With two powerful weapons now in her hands, Jennifer's eyes blazed brighter than ever.

Jennifer, analysis of the received data is complete. It forms a complementary structure with the first data set. However, at least one additional piece appears necessary for full reconstruction of the

Autumn Code.

Jennifer let out a thin, crooked smile. Her mother had built in double—no, triple—layers of safety. But with two fragments secured, the last piece would leave traces. She could find it.

She pushed the second fragment into HAL-W's highest-security quantum memory and ordered multiple backups.

Her chest still felt like it was being carved open every time she thought of her father's death—but there was no time to drown in grief. Ethan Morris would already be turning his sights on this place.

Hal, have every unit here prioritize defense of the tachyon device and this office. Coordinate with the HAL-W defense units. No external intrusion, under any circumstances. I'm going to New York with Andromeda.

At her command, HAL-W's units repositioned, meshing with the building-wide defense grid.

Jennifer headed for the VTOL landing pad on the roof. Just before boarding, she gave one more order without hesitation.

Hal, request flight clearance for a 21CF private StarOrbit craft for our use. And I will not let what happened to my father happen again. Run a top-grade inspection on every component—hardware, software, life support, engines, flight control systems. Don't rule out sabotage from an OrbitTech insider. Cross-check the operating system itself for any sign of external tampering and re-verify all flight and ground crew.

Acknowledged. Initiating top-security inspection and personnel re-verification procedures immediately.

The VTOL lifted off from J's Building and sped toward the StarOrbit platform in the desert outside San Francisco. The city glittered below, still achingly beautiful, but Jennifer didn't spare it a glance. She sank into her seat and closed her eyes.

Her father's last image, his warm voice, the brutal flash of the explosion HAL-W had shown her—everything swirled together in her mind. Grief and rage surged up again, but she clenched her teeth and forced them down. She could not break now.

When they arrived, private craft 521, the 21CF logo gleaming on its hull, was waiting for her behind a tight security line at the StarOrbit platform.

December 14, 2037 — 12:40 P.M. EST • Aboard StarOrbit

Only after HAL-W confirmed that the full inspection was complete did Jennifer board the craft with Andromeda. It was fitted with state-of-the-art systems and a luxurious interior, but to her, it felt like a cold mausoleum.

With a low, heavy roar, the StarOrbit accelerated, punched through the atmosphere, and soared into the black.

She activated the holographic screen in front of her seat and watched the flood of live news alerts. She scanned the manipulated headlines, the overheated reactions, and the scraps of truth hidden under them.

BREAKING: 21st Century Frontier (21CF) Chairman Daehan "Great" Wi's StarOrbit Crashes… All Aboard Presumed Dead

Sudden Death of Tech Giant 'Great Wi' Shocks the World

Cause of Disaster Unknown… Mechanical Failure or Terror Attack?

Global Markets Plunge… 21CF Stock in Freefall, EM Group Rebounds

Chairman Great Wi Killed En Route to See Daughter in San Francisco

World Leaders Mourn… "A Great Star of Humanity Has Fallen"

Wave of Online Tributes… Global Neuro-Link Network 'Immense Loss' Resonance Exceeds Critical Threshold

President Ethan Morris Offers Official Condolences… "Deep Regret, Calls for Full Investigation"

Great Wi's sudden death plunged the world into shock and grief. He was not merely the founder of 21CF or a pioneer in technology. Through HAL-W, he had opened new horizons for humanity, and he was one of the few giants who had stood against Ethan Morris's growing tyranny, speaking for freedom and ethics.

His absence felt like more than the loss of a business leader; it was a vast void cast over the future of humankind.

The official announcement spoke of an accident of unknown cause, but many suspected EM Group's hand. The long-standing technological rivalry and tension between 21CF and EM, and Great Wi's openly anti-authoritarian stance, were common knowledge. The fact that he had been on his way to see Jennifer was fuel for a thousand conspiracy theories.

Jennifer stared coldly at Ethan Morris delivering his hypocritical statement of condolence. Revulsion churned in her gut. Behind his mask of grief, she could almost see a thin, vile smile flicker across his face. She silently vowed revenge and shut the news feed off.

In its place, she brought up the real-time quantum network status board from HAL-W. The display was a sea of red alerts. Under Ethan's commands, Rose was spewing out quantum computations at a mad pace, slamming into HAL-W's firewalls. Bound by the Blue Ethics Protocol, HAL-W focused on minimal force—pure defense—straining to keep the network stable.

Hal, what do you see in Rose's load pattern? Any singularities, any predictable shifts?

Still analyzing, Jennifer... but right now Rose's computations are extremely chaotic and unpredictable. The pattern looks unstable, as if she's rushing headlong toward self-collapse. At this rate, the entire quantum network will hit its synchronization error threshold soon.

HAL-W's analysis was grim. The signs of the Quantum Storm

were sharpening.

Jennifer gazed out at the black void beyond the window. The fact that she would never even recover her father's remains tightened around her chest. In her eyes burned a cold rage that had pushed past grief, and a fierce sense of duty toward humanity's future.

When she reached New York, she would have to fill the emptiness he left, take the chair, and lead 21CF—the largest corporate entity on Earth—into the final war against Ethan Morris.

The key to that war lay in the two fragments of the Autumn Code she already held, and the last missing piece she still had to find.

December 14, 2037 — 1:30 P.M. EST • New York City, 21CF Headquarters – Lobby

The StarOrbit touched down on the offshore platform near New York exactly on schedule. With Andromeda at her side, Jennifer transferred to a private VTOL and flew toward 21CF headquarters, the tower rising over the heart of Manhattan like a titan.

When they set down on the rooftop helipad, Arcana Chen and several top executives bowed their heads in silence. Jennifer accepted their condolences quietly. Everyone knew that no words could mean anything right now.

Moments later, as the elevator doors opened onto the first-floor lobby, she drew in a breath and stepped forward.

The lobby was packed shoulder to shoulder. Employees who would normally be at their desks had all come down to wait for her. In the silence, hundreds—no, thousands—of eyes fixed on Jennifer. In them lay deep respect and mourning for the late chairman, layered with shock and unease at the sudden tragedy.

Some quietly wiped away tears; others bit down on their lips and lowered their gaze.

Escorted by Andromeda, Jennifer stepped slowly out of the elevator. Wherever her feet fell, the sea of employees parted in silence. No one spoke, but the weight of grief hanging over the lobby pressed down on her shoulders.

On the massive media wall at the center of the lobby, footage of Chairman Great Wi played on a loop—his passion for the future, his optimism about technology, his smile. Every scene stood in stark contrast to the current reality, tightening the ache in everyone's chest.

The same father who had encouraged her over the phone just three hours ago now existed only on that screen.

Here, before all these people, she had to move beyond personal grief and shoulder what was left behind.

Jennifer turned slowly and swept her gaze across the employees watching her.

"Everyone…"

She needed no microphone. Her voice carried clearly through the building's speaker system. It was still heavy with sorrow, but beneath it ran a steady, unshakable resolve.

"The founder of 21CF, and my father, Chairman Great Wi… has left us."

Suppressed sobs slipped from corners of the lobby. Jennifer paused, drew a breath, and went on.

"I am overwhelmed with sorrow and devastation. But we cannot stop here. The dream he devoted his life to—the vision of building a better world through technology—is not over."

Strength gathered in her voice. Her eyes were no longer drowned in grief.

"Even now, there are forces that threaten our values and our future. They took my father from us, and they are trying to endanger all of humanity. We must rise above our grief. We must protect the legacy he left—HAL-W and Blue Ethics—and put an end to their madness."

She met their eyes one by one as she spoke.

"As the Chairman's daughter, and as the one who now inherits the leadership of 21CF, I promise you this: I will not let my father's death be in vain. If we stand and fight together, we will overcome this crisis and build the future he dreamed of."

Silence fell for a heartbeat. Then a quiet ripple of applause spread through the lobby. It was not a cheer, but an expression of solidarity—a search for hope inside grief, and a sign of trust in the young leader who had not collapsed, but risen.

Accepting their gazes calmly, Jennifer walked toward Arcana Chen and the executive team.

"Dr. Chen, convene a global emergency executive meeting immediately. We need to form a crisis task force and commit everything we have to Hal's defense and the stabilization of the global network. And... prepare counterstrike scenarios against Rose."

It was the voice of a commander-in-chief planning strategy in the middle of a crisis. Arcana Chen nodded, face set.

"It's already in motion, Chairwoman Jennifer. Everyone is waiting in the conference room."

Great Wi had arranged things so that, in the event of his death, Jennifer could assume the chairmanship immediately without procedural delay, and every board-level executive knew it.

Jennifer and Andromeda stepped into the private elevator. The employees quietly cleared a path, their eyes filled with heavy concern. Everyone could feel, almost instinctively, the immensity of the burden now resting on her.

As the doors closed and the elevator slid upward, Jennifer shut her eyes and drew a long breath. The pain of her father's death still cut deep, but she had no time to sink into it.

Ethan Morris already had Rose in his hands, and his madness was running unchecked. The threat of a Quantum Storm was no longer just a hypothesis.

December 14, 2037 — 1:57 P.M. EST • New York City, 21CF Headquarters – Global Executive Conference Room
D-4, 00:00:00

As the doors slid open, heavily armed security robots stood guard along both sides of the corridor. At the entrance stood Aris Thorne, head of security.

"Chairwoman, all preparations are complete. But…" His expression was dark. "According to Hal's report, Rose's attempts to disrupt the network are intensifying. We don't know when or what might happen…"

"I know, Doctor Thorne. Which is exactly why we can't afford to wait."

Passing Andromeda—standing at full alert outside the conference room—Jennifer pushed the door open.

Inside, a circular table was ringed with holographic projections of branch managers and key department heads from around the world. Around it, the top executives, including Arcana Chen, sat with somber faces. The empty seat at the center made Great Wi's absence feel even more profound.

As Jennifer walked toward that seat, every eye in the room followed her. Only the blinking holographic status board moved in the heavy silence.

"Let's begin."

Jennifer sat without hesitation. This was the moment the new leader of 21CF officially took the stage.

Just as she was about to present the threat scenario HAL-W had compiled, the clock struck **14:00:00**.

A wave of dizziness slammed into her. The world seemed to tilt. A high-pitched ringing scraped past her ears, and the holographic displays warped for a split second.

It was over almost immediately. Everything snapped back to normal—except she knew something had happened. She was the only one who had felt it.

Did you register that? HAL-W's urgent voice struck her consciousness.

Yes, Hal... what was that? An attack from Rose?

Negative. It is a far more fundamental phenomenon. Synchronization error rates across the global quantum network are spiking. Spacetime distortions and quantum fluctuations are occurring simultaneously... It is as if the universe itself were twisting.

Quantum Storm. The theory she had formulated at the age of twelve.

The characteristics match the initial phase of participatory collapse described in your thesis with ninety-eight-point-three percent accuracy. It is highly likely to be a precursor to a Level-5 quantum cascade failure.

She drew a slow, silent breath. If this information leaked, 21CF would tear itself apart from the inside, and the world would fall into panic and self-destruction.

Hal, quarantine this under top-security classification, Level-Omega. Access restricted to Arcana Chen and me only. For external reports, mask it as simple network instability. At the same time, start simulations of the spread and possible responses. Estimated time to the critical point?

Estimated time: ninety-six hours from now. Commencing simulation.

D-3, 23:59:51

Time was bleeding away with every passing second.

"My apologies. A moment of fatigue," Jennifer said, recovering instantly. "Now, Dr. Chen, please begin with the situation report."

Arcana Chen, former CTO and current COO, briefly studied Jennifer's face, then quietly pointed to the status board and began her briefing.

"Yes, Chairwoman. Hal is currently defending against Rose's continuous high-intensity infiltration attempts. However, the patterns are extremely erratic and difficult to predict, so the load on our defense systems keeps rising."

Jennifer nodded as she listened. At the same time, her mind was working on another layer entirely. Outwardly, she presided over the meeting with composure; inwardly, she was linked directly to HAL-W, analyzing the spacetime distortions and the quantum network's synchronization errors in real time.

Hal, status. Is the error-propagation pattern continuing?

Yes. Both distortion frequency and synchronization error rate are increasing—gradually, but steadily. The correlation with Rose's computational load remains high.

Ninety-six hours...

She repeated the countdown in her mind. Within four days, she had to stop Rose and stabilize a quantum network on the brink. HAL-W's current defensive capacity would not be enough. Ethan Morris kept forcing excessive computations onto Rose, and that burden was being smeared across the entire global network.

I need the final key Mom left behind. The first poetry book... the second one from San Francisco... they're not enough. I need one more.

She recalled her last conversation with her father. Great Wi had mentioned that the poetry collection *J* had only ever been printed in a first edition. That remark was now her only hope—and her only clue. But finding the single copy that held the last fragment among five thousand first-edition books in just ninety-six hours bordered on impossible.

She couldn't do it alone. It was time to mobilize every resource 21CF had.

When Dr. Chen finished her briefing, Jennifer spoke.

"Dr. Chen, and all executives present."

Every gaze in the room swung back to her.

"Until now, we've focused on defending against Rose's direct attacks. But according to Hal's analysis, the situation is far more serious than we believed. We need a deeper, more fundamental response. Rose's runaway pattern shows a strong correlation with a specific quantum pattern encrypted in the 2006 poetry collection *J*."

She continued, voice firm and clear.

"I've already secured and analyzed two copies of that collection and concluded that the code within it is the essential key to stabilizing the network. However, the encryption system must be fully restored before it can exert any direct effect."

Her tone hardened.

"Therefore, effective immediately, 21CF will mobilize all available resources to track down the first edition of the poetry collection *J* and secure the final piece."

Silence descended on the conference room. Confusion flickered across the executives' faces; uneasy glances passed back and forth. But no one spoke in open opposition. Her voice carried conviction, and behind her stood the absolute presence of HAL-W. And above all, with Great Wi gone, there was no real alternative but to follow Jennifer's lead.

As if she had anticipated their hesitation, she pressed on.

"The operation is code-named Project Autumn Leaf. From this moment, the global emergency response committee is converted into this project's command center. Each regional headquarters will make the tracking and securing of first-edition copies of *J* its top priority. All associated budgets and security clearances are approved under my personal authority."

She activated the interface in the center of the table. A vast holographic world map sprang into view. Major hubs around the globe lit up as red dots; code names and points of contact for each region populated the display.

"Hal will coordinate information analysis and pattern tracking across all regions. Detailed operational guidelines will be transmitted to each person in charge shortly."

Meeting their silent stares, Jennifer continued.

"I know this is confusing. But this isn't a sentimental symbol. According to Hal's analysis, the quantum pattern embedded in *J* is the only key capable of directly interacting with the distorted code Rose is using. The two fragments we've secured show a strong correlation, but the data is incomplete. We need the third piece—that final puzzle—to fully reconstruct the New Version Autumn Code and stop this disaster."

She leaned forward, both hands pressing against the table.

"From this moment, 21CF is initiating an operation for survival. Project Autumn Leaf will mobilize all of 21CF's technological, informational, and human resources. Regional heads are to pursue every lead—antiquarian bookstores, libraries, private collectors, online platforms—and make direct contact to secure the book. All activities will proceed under the highest security classification. Progress will be reported to me and to Hal in real time."

When she finished, Arcana Chen was the first to speak.

"The Chairwoman is right. According to Hal's analysis, the initial quantum pattern identified in the poetry collection *J* shows a highly meaningful correlation with the computational structure used by Rose. The probability of coincidence is extremely low."

Her statement firmed the light in the executives' eyes. They did not understand everything. But they chose to trust the judgment of Jennifer, Chen, and HAL-W.

December 14, 2037 — 2:25 P.M. EST • New York City, 21CF Headquarters – Great Wi's Office

After the meeting, Jennifer walked to Great Wi's office. A heavy, frigid silence filled the building.

Only hours ago, this room had been her father's domain. His sudden absence still drifted in the air, unreal and unfinished. Jennifer told Andromeda to wait in the hallway and stepped inside alone.

As the door clicked shut behind her, it felt as if the noise of the world had been cut away. Her father's warmth was gone; in its place, a cold sorrow wrapped around her.

She sank into his chair, letting her body fall deep into it. For a moment it felt as if she could sense the gaze with which he had always sat here, looking out at the world. The New York skyline beyond the window looked washed-out and gray, dimmed by the shock of the day and by his death.

On the desk's holographic display lay the documents her father had been reviewing, and next to them, the copy of the poetry collection *J* she had left behind when she went to San Francisco.

Jennifer reached out carefully and picked up the book. The simple initial "**J**" engraved on the silver cover. It was not just her mother's name—it was the starting point, and the core, of everything.

She opened the book on the desk and linked to HAL-W through her NeuroniX interface.

Hal, how far have you gotten with the Autumn Code fragments?

Chairwoman, current analysis indicates that complete restoration and activation of the code requires more than simple pattern matching. A deep reconstruction of its originating context is essential—specifically, the early interactions between Dr. J and Chairman Great Wi, and in particular the database related to the 1981 Namsan Incident and SID. I will access all relevant records and rebuild the timeline.

Listening to HAL-W's report, Jennifer felt her intuition lock into place. The mysterious pull she sensed from the book, her own emotions and memories, and HAL-W's analysis—all of it aligned.

She slowly closed her eyes, then opened them again with her decision made. To uncover the roots of this vast crisis, she would have to walk back into the past.

I need to know everything. From the very beginning... start with my father's childhood records.

The command, spoken into the empty office, was more than a simple data request. It was a declaration: a demand for a total reconstruction of the past, and an order to stream that reconstruction straight into her consciousness through the NeuroniX chip.

Following her directive, HAL-W reached into 21CF's deep secure archives and into public databases where needed. It began assembling decades of Great Wi's digital traces—photos, videos, voice memos, even related news articles—analyzing them in real time, re-ordering them chronologically, preparing them for direct transmission into her mind.

For it, physical searches and loading times had no meaning.

Jennifer drew a long breath.

She was about to face the truth buried in the past.

Chapter 2

The Great Wound, the Shining Star

A Child's Star by the River

One night in June 1973, ten-year-old Wi Daehan sat side by side with his friend Kim Woo-hyun on a small bridge over a narrow stream. It was a rural village with only a handful of scattered houses; when night fell, the world dropped into near-total darkness, and the stars burned all the brighter for it. The two boys would often sneak out here, sit on the bridge beneath the moonless sky, and talk about their dreams.

"Hey, Daehan. How far away do you think those endless stars are?" Woo-hyun asked, tilting his head as he stared upward.

Wi Daehan leaned back a little, eyes fixed on the sky. Woo-hyun kicked his feet idly over the water, wearing the loose, carefree grin of someone passing the most comfortable time in the world.

"Well... I read in a magazine called *Monthly Children's Dong-A* that light takes years—decades—to reach Earth. And there was this comic that said Martians could live on Mars. I really want to go there someday."

Kim Woo-hyun chuckled and scratched at his side.

"Come on. Sure, countries like America and the Soviet Union might've gone to the moon, but Mars? You're really going to go there?"

Wi Daehan clenched his small fist, a stubborn look hardening his face.

"Yeah. I'm going. Someday..."

Most nights, the two boys would sneak out to this bridge, sharing whatever scraps of food they had smuggled from home. Sitting here, they could forget their hunger for a little while.

Staring at the distant, flickering stars, Wi Daehan would sometimes feel a sharp, aching emotion well up inside him. His grandfather had given him the name 'Daehan' to follow the family name 'Wi,' meaning "the child who will make Korea great." The name sat on him like a strange weight.

If he didn't cling to some wild dream—like going to Mars—he felt he would be pinned to this village forever, stuck in place on the muddy roads of nowhere. That fear crept into his young heart like cold water.

A Winter of Broken Wings

Six years passed after that night on the bridge.

One December night in 1979, he sat in a shabby inn in Gangneung, listening with every nerve taut to the local radio news. The announcer's voice rolled through the static as a list of newly admitted students to Gangneung High School was read aloud, but his exam number never came.

His mind went white, numb and hollow. Later he would hardly

remember how he spent that night.

The next morning, he went to see the results with his own eyes. In the middle of the schoolyard at Gangneung High School, a huge bulletin board had been set up. The number he was looking for wasn't there either.

Hours later, after transferring from a slow local bus to an intercity one, he finally stepped down at a stop on the East Sea coast in Goseong County, Gangwon Province—the seaside town where he had spent the last three years of middle school. Not wanting to go home, he walked through the gates into the deserted schoolyard, empty for winter break.

His homeroom teacher's words came back to him with a sting.

"Failing the entrance exam hurts as much as falling from a rooftop."

The words had sounded exaggerated at the time. Now they felt literal.

All the teachers had urged their students to live up to the school's name, Donggwang—"Eastern Light"—reminding them that Tagore had once called Korea the "Lamp of the East." Later he would learn that this was more romantic myth than historical fact, but back then it had been real motivation. Failing in spite of that made his shame all the deeper.

On the way home, the winter wind pouring down from the rough spines of the Taebaek Mountains struck his nose and cheeks without mercy. It felt like a warning of what was still to come.

"You lazy fool!"

His older brother's shout came with a fist. The punch landed squarely on his left cheek, and a hot flash of pain burst out, as if something in his chest had cracked.

"How could you fail if you really tried your best? Have you ever done *anything* right?!"

His brother's voice shook with anger—and with deep disappointment. Wi Daehan couldn't answer. He couldn't shake the feeling that he hadn't done his best.

Just then, his father stepped out of the main room.

"That's enough. He's the one hurting most."

Those quiet words cut deeper than the punch.

The weight of having betrayed his family's hopes settled over him like wet concrete.

I'm a failure…

The thought wouldn't leave his head. The fact of his failure pressed down on him like a boulder, making it hard even to move. Faced with a reality he could not escape, he felt more helpless than ever.

He skipped his graduation ceremony. *How can I show my face there when I failed?* The thought made him shrink in on himself even more.

He barely ate. His mother would quietly leave a bowl of lukewarm porridge by his bed and slip out without a word.

For days—or maybe weeks—he lay sick like that. Loneliness and shame soaked deep into the layers of his heart. At times, a dark thought crossed his mind: *If I just disappeared like a stream, would this pain wash away with me?*

But the gentle pats of his father's hand, and the simple porridge his mother left, held him up just enough for him to endure.

It did not take long for him to return to a semblance of normal life, but the scar that winter left became a dull ache lodged in one corner of his heart, one that would follow him for the rest of his life.

In the end, he stayed in the countryside. Before dawn, he walked the paddy field ridges, and during the day he shoveled at construction sites to help support his poor family. When boys his age walked past in clean school uniforms, backpacks on their shoulders, Wi Daehan would be brushing mud from his work pants, heading off in the opposite direction.

At times like that, he felt small and cheap, and his heart sank without end.

Then one day, flipping through an old magazine, he came across a small advertisement:

"GED prep books for sale. Earn your high school diploma in a short time!"

He packed his things and went up to Seoul, determined to prepare for the GED (General Educational Development) exams on his own. He was only fifteen.

Working in a factory and delivering coal briquettes was brutally hard, but Wi Daehan endured. He scraped together cram-school fees from a newspaper route and odd jobs at a translation office. The real problem was that he couldn't keep it up for long. More than once, money forced him to drop out of the academy midway.

In the end, he failed the college entrance exam as well. With the draft looming and his savings gone, his anxiety climbed to its peak.

The Light and Shadow of Namsan

One day in February 1981, he stumbled across an academy with a golden "J" logo.

It was Jongno Hagwon—Korea's most prestigious prep school. Tens of thousands of *jaesoo* students (those retaking the college entrance exam) flocked there each year, competing fiercely for a seat, knowing that admission often paved the way to top universities like Seoul National University.

They were recruiting new students, so he applied. After a grueling day of written exams, Wi Daehan found his name proudly printed on the bulletin board.

His whole body trembled. It felt as if years of pent-up frustration were being repaid all at once. He had drifted through lesser academies with nothing to show for it but disappointment. This time, simply earning a place in a school people called "prestigious" filled him with a deep, almost disorienting pride.

With his older sister helping cover tuition and living expenses, he resolved to devote himself entirely to his studies. The memory of shouting "I want to go to Mars!" with Woo-hyun on that bridge long ago resurfaced. The fact that this dream was still faintly breathing in a corner of his heart gave him courage. Even if he never made it to Mars, which he had watched in the night sky, he swore he would carve out his own path with his own hands.

One day in September, Wi Daehan stepped out of the academy building with the "J" badge pinned to his chest.

Although his education was now officially recognized through the GED, in the eyes of the college entrance system and society he was still "a student without formal schooling." His face stayed hard. He had just received his monthly report card: lower-middle of the class. Considering he had been dead last in March, it was real progress.

But his class was packed with over a hundred brilliant students who ranked near the top nationwide. Every day he sat in the very front row, absorbing every word of each lecture. He could feel his skills sharpening, but the anxiety never left him. The doubt—*can someone who didn't even finish high school really get into Seoul National University?*—and the fear that his draft notice might arrive first, constantly wrapped around him.

Crossing the bridge toward Seoul Station Plaza, the massive Daewoo Building and the overpass filled his view. This scene, which had shocked him when he first saw it as a middle school graduate, still felt like a symbol of civilization itself.

Behind the building, Namsan Tower rose faintly against the sky. Roads stretched out in all directions, feeding the city's arteries. On the hillside road toward Namsan, two seven-story buildings with large signs—"Daeil Academy" and "Gyeongil Academy"—stood out.

Among them, Daeil Academy was famous for its single-subject courses. Since September, Wi Daehan had been taking extra English and math classes there. The sight of hundreds of students flooding the streets during class changes drove home the brutal reality of the entrance-exam war.

He was taking *Vocabulary 22000* and *Standard Mathematics* I. One day, a girl sitting in the front row by the window caught his eye.

A bare face without makeup, long hair tied back, red-rimmed glasses. There was something faintly foreign about her.

Watching her answer a tricky grammar question without a moment's hesitation, Daehan had to admit it: she had already internalized what he had stayed up all night memorizing. The English words that slipped out of her so casually, the foreign stickers on her backpack, even the way she held her pencil—she carried a different kind of air.

Not to be outdone, Wi Daehan began raising his hand more. At first, it was just to catch her attention, but soon he found himself enjoying the quiet competition in their exchanged glances. He wanted to prove he could stand in the same world as her. Their starting points were different, but he was sure he wouldn't lose in effort.

A day, two days, a week passed. She seemed interested in nothing but class, and that aloofness only drew him in more. Not wanting to approach her with clumsy notes like the other boys, he decided on a different method.

Recalling the English letters he had once exchanged with a

pen pal, he spent the night with a dictionary, writing a letter in English. On pretty stationery patterned with autumn leaves, he wrote a slightly quirky salutation: "Dear Rabbit."

He didn't know her name, so he thought of a rabbit—cute and pretty. He filled the letter with delicate images of autumn, fallen leaves, and wind. Writing in English made it easier to express the shy feelings he would have been too embarrassed to put down in Korean.

The next day, after finishing his classes at Jongno Hagwon, he didn't go straight to Daeil Academy. Instead, he wandered into the park behind it. Beautifully landscaped, it was a favorite refuge for exhausted students—the reason people jokingly called the place "Jongno University."

He sat on an empty bench and read over the letter he had written.

—

Dear Rabbit,
Have you ever listened to the rustling sound of fallen leaves dancing in the air and rolling on the ground when the autumn breeze blows gently?

I love autumn. I especially love the stories contained within the fallen leaves.

In early spring, when branches frozen all winter are awakened by warm sunlight, mysterious sprouts begin to bud. The gentle spring breeze caresses cheeks like a loving breath, and soon green leaves and flower buds fill the world.

When summer comes, leaves embrace the earth's heat and provide cool shade. They become a small but precious oasis, a resting place for tired people.

Then, when autumn comes like these days, those leaves begin to prepare for farewell, their entire bodies beautifully colored. The fallen leaves—a blend of red, yellow, and sometimes brown—do not fill the farewell with only sadness.

Rather, they are as bright as a festival ballroom, and their swaying in the wind is beautiful. When they roll in the wind, the rustling sound conveys a clear, lovely echo, like the clinking of beads.

When I hear that sound, joy fills me deep within my heart. I truly love those moments filled with the autumn sky, the fallen leaves, and "me."

Soon, when autumn reaches its peak, the streets we walk together will be filled with colorful leaves, won't they? I want to walk alongside you in that scenery and hand you one of them.

It would be even better if I could find a beautifully colored leaf that resembles you.

Autumn. I want to feel with you that even the chilly wind of the coming winter can be beautiful.

—Wi Daehan.

The setting sun flushed his cheeks and ears. Standing up, Daehan walked quickly back into the classroom.

He didn't hesitate. As she got ready for class, he walked over and asked,

"Could I… borrow your math book for a moment?"

Her reaction was surprisingly kind. As he stumbled over the words, J smiled slightly and handed him the *Standard Mathematics* textbook. A strange tightness gripped his chest. Her quiet willingness—and that small smile—told him she already knew he existed.

Daehan slipped the letter into the page where that day's lesson began. His hand shook as if he were stealing something. Without waiting for his heartbeat to slow, he closed the book and handed it back.

"Thank you. That helped."

She tucked it into her bag and focused on the lecture as if nothing had happened. Daehan, on the other hand, was so keyed up that not a single word of the class stuck in his mind.

As soon as the bell rang, he bolted from the room. After an hour's break, the next class began. This time he sat a little behind her, eyes fixed on her back.

When she opened her book, she flinched. She shut it, then opened it again, took out the letter, and began to read.

Daehan had no memory of how that class ended. He only remembered leaping to his feet the moment it was over and fleeing the classroom.

The next day, she was nowhere to be seen in English class. He sat in his usual seat, pretending nonchalance, but inside he was a mix of worry—and a strange sense of relief. He decided he would be satisfied just with having found the courage to confess.

Just as class was about to start, she walked up to him.

"I enjoyed reading it yesterday."

J smiled brightly and held out a book. It was the one he had borrowed.

As he froze, she gave a small, curious smile.

"But you forgot this, didn't you?"

She went back to her seat. She was wearing the same brown corduroy pants and a light shirt she always wore. It felt familiar. He had once read that "people who like wearing brown are honest," and for some reason he trusted her.

Daehan sat in a daze until class ended, then rushed back to the study room. Only then did he realize he still hadn't returned *her* book. Inside it was a reply.

—

Dear Wi Daehan,

The moment I received your letter, a gentle ripple stirred in my heart. It was a method I had not expected at all, which made it all the more surprising and exciting.

The earnest attitude and excellent skills you've shown in every class have captivated my attention. It feels as if I've been quietly observing you for a long time.

Have you ever lived in an English-speaking country? You use it so naturally. To be honest, I feel you are much better at it than I am.

Huam-dong is my hometown. It's a small neighborhood near here. There's a U.S. Army base nearby, and my father works there as an officer. So English is spoken daily, but I talk to my mother in Korean. Strangely, I feel most comfortable and happy when I speak Korean with her.

People say I look just like my mother. Perhaps that's why so few people notice my background, even though I'm of mixed heritage. Maybe you didn't know either.

I graduated from Sudo Girls' High School nearby. I'm curious where you grew up and what school you attended.

Your letter was special because it was so unexpected, and the delicate expressions within it gently shook my heart. That sweet tremor still lingers.

—J.

Daehan read the letter again and again, looking up unfamiliar words. That night, he stayed up writing a reply.

—

Dear J,

Calling you "J" feels cute and affectionate. Like the nickname

"Rabbit," it feels like a name filled with gentle warmth. But more than anything, I'm happy that I know and can say the initial "J" that symbolizes you.

I grew up in a small village near the armistice line, an hour by bus from the nearest city. Just as you lived near a base, I lived near the line, with soldiers as close as family. So their presence doesn't feel unfamiliar to me.

But I've never met a foreigner in person. I was a little surprised to hear your father is American. As you said, you seem to resemble your mother more, and you have such a strong Korean atmosphere that I would never have guessed you were mixed.

You asked if I had lived abroad, but I have never left the country. I only learned some English thanks to a pen pal and by working at a translation office. Please don't think I'm better than you.

After failing the high school entrance exam, I came to Seoul and supported myself while earning my GED. Now I study all day at Jongno Hagwon and come here in the evenings for extra classes.

Exchanging letters with you is a great joy. Life as a jaesoo student is harsh and lonely, but just having you by my side in this way is a comfort.

—Wi Daehan.

After that, she kept passing him letters, and the two slowly came to know each other.

—

Dear Wi Daehan,
After hearing your story, I've become even more curious about you. It's amazing that you got into Jongno Hagwon after the GED. Considering your skills, though, it makes sense.

I graduated at the top of my high school class but failed to get into the English literature department at Seoul National University. That deeply wounded my pride, and this year I'm determined to achieve that dream.

I chose English literature because I want to understand my father's country more deeply. My family is scheduled to return to the United States next year, but I might stay in Seoul alone to continue my studies.

Just imagining staying in the same space as you brings a strange excitement.

It's truly amazing that you've been studying while earning your own living in this unfamiliar city. You seem like someone from a completely different world than the people I know.

I hope we can continue to exchange letters. How wonderful it would be if we could share small comforts on our paths toward our dreams.

—J.

In the late afternoon of October 18, Daehan couldn't hide his joy when J suggested they visit the Namsan Fountain.

After touring the Children's Hall and the Botanical Garden, they climbed the trail to the summit and looked down at Seoul stretching in every direction. They had a simple dinner of udon and fish cake at a shabby food cart. The portions were small, but they were completely satisfied.

They studied in the library until closing time crept up on them. By 9:40 P.M., the area around the library was deserted, the silhouette of the Seoul Science Museum glowing faintly in the dark.

Sitting on a bench and savoring the cool breeze, Daehan rummaged through his bag, pulled out a notebook, and tore out a blank page. He began folding a paper airplane. In his hands it quickly took shape, sleek and ready to fly.

"Wow, you're really good at that!" J clapped in delight.

He smiled, slightly embarrassed. "Ever since I was little, on nights when the stars were bright, I used to fly paper planes. I thought maybe my wishes could reach the sky that way… though none of them have come true yet."

"Oh my, meeting me already counts as one that came true, doesn't it?" she laughed, tapping his shoulder. "Should we put our wishes in this plane and let it fly?"

Daehan took the airplane back and lifted it.

"Good idea. I'm going to put a really big wish in it," J said, excited.

They closed their eyes, whispered their wishes, and threw the plane with all their strength. Caught by the wind, it soared high toward the peak of Namsan.

"Wow, look at it go! I've never seen such a magnificent paper airplane, Daehan!"

Just then, something appeared in the dark sky where the airplane had vanished. Daehan squinted. J pointed to the same spot, eyes wide.

A low, rumbling subsonic vibration pulsed through the ground. An eerie sensation, like a faint electric current, seeped up from their toes and spread through their bodies. Their pulses spiked; their fingertips tingled with numbness. It was impossible to say whether the sensation was terror or ecstasy.

"Is that… a helicopter?" Daehan muttered, but he already knew it wasn't. It was too quiet. Only a low, humming resonance filled the air.

Then a metallic object seemed to hover for a moment above Namsan Tower. Daehan's fists clenched.

What is that? Why is my heart pounding more with excitement than with fear…?

A lightning-like flash shot down from beneath the object and vanished. The instant burst of light stabbed into their retinas. She grabbed Daehan's arm.

"What did we just see? Could that have been… a UFO?" she whispered, her voice trembling. A mix of fear and inexplicable curiosity tightened in their chests.

"…It might have been."

They stared at each other in silence. At some point, only the faint sound of the fountain remained.

They were so shaken they barely remembered how they got home. From that day on, they began and ended each day with a strange premonition that it might be the last of their ordinary lives.

Yet contrary to that anxiety, Daehan and J's concentration and reasoning sharpened noticeably after that night. In the next national mock exam taken by over a million students, Daehan's English and math scores soared, catapulting him into the top 500. J also surprised herself by solving complex problems with ease.

Even so, neither of them easily connected these changes to the Namsan UFO incident. Afraid of being laughed at, they agreed to keep it a secret.

As autumn deepened, the memory slowly faded. The college entrance exam loomed. Applying to SNU still felt out of reach for Daehan, and with his sister no longer able to support him, he had to take on part-time work. The fear of being drafted turned into a gnawing inferiority complex.

The more his anxiety grew, the more he envied J's calm demeanor—and the more distant she seemed. Even in the same classroom, she felt like someone from another world. Even her bright smile began to look like something from a different realm.

Daehan started pulling away. It felt safer to drift apart now than to be humiliated later.

"Daehan, I'm going to quit the academy and study at home now," J said one day, after a brief hesitation. "Let's definitely meet again at Gwanak Campus."

He nodded, but no words came. He had seen the resolve in her eyes.

"Yes. There…"

He couldn't finish the sentence. The words "Gwanak Campus"—Seoul National University—suddenly felt infinitely distant.

It was the last day. When J picked up her bag, Daehan realized something: he didn't know where she lived, what her real name was, or even her birthday.

Is it really going to end like this?

His feet moved on their own, following her. J walked into the streets of Huam-dong, down an avenue lined with towering plane trees, then crossed the street and disappeared through the gate of a two-story house. Only after he had fixed the house in his memory did Daehan feel a measure of relief.

That year, he applied to Yonsei University and was accepted. His scores weren't bad; he might even have gambled on an unpopular department at SNU. If he hadn't known where she lived, he might have done exactly that—just for the chance to find her.

But not long after enrolling at Yonsei, he decided to drop out. Sitting in classrooms on a campus soaked in protests and tear gas felt empty. More than that, ever since the Namsan incident his mind had been veering rapidly toward science. A humanities-centered life no longer felt like it fit him.

The guilt of turning his back on his first love's wish gnawed at him as well.

On the day he finally quit, he stood for a long time in front of that house in Huam-dong before pressing the doorbell.

"Who is it?" a middle-aged woman's voice asked.

The moment he pressed the button, he realized: he didn't know J's real name. He couldn't very well ask for "a girl named J."

"Um… does a female college student live here?"

"No. No one like that here."

The intercom went dead. Daehan ran out of Huam-dong, breathless. She might have moved. It might have been the wrong house. Or perhaps she had already left for America. For the first time in his life, he felt just how powerless love could be.

After dropping out, Daehan threw himself into physics, electronic engineering, quantum mechanics, higher mathematics, and astronomy. He devoured books on those subjects in public libraries.

Then one day, in the video room at Jeongdok Library, he watched an old science fiction film—*2001: A Space Odyssey*—and was stunned.

Until then, the only computers he knew were the washing-machine-sized boxes he had glimpsed through the computer room window at Jongno Hagwon. On screen, he saw video calls and an artificial intelligence computer. The universe it revealed was far vaster than the Mars he had dreamed of as a child.

He couldn't shake the film's impact. The words "Artificial Intelligence (AI)" lodged deep in his mind.

Since that strange night on Namsan in 1981, his ability to absorb and understand information had accelerated. Now, even the most difficult research papers yielded under his rapid, almost effortless reading. Quantum mechanics in particular drew him in. Within a few months, his skills had grown to the point where he could begin to shape ideas of his own.

Between Gunshots and Starlight

In late 1982, Wi Daehan underwent his physical examination for conscription, and in May 1983, he entered the army. Even after enlisting, he would steal moments to pore over the physics notes he had been compiling, refining his ideas. When he finished a manuscript, he mailed it off to a physics journal and returned to life in uniform.

He was assigned to the 22nd Infantry Division on Korea's eastern front, tasked with guarding the armistice line along the East Sea. There, he was reunited with his old hometown friend Kim Woo-hyun, now a seasoned soldier with over a year of service. At the time, the mandatory service period for an active-duty army private was thirty months.

Life in the barracks was grim. Verbal abuse and beatings from senior soldiers were part of the daily routine, but thanks to Woo-hyun, Daehan's experience was relatively less brutal than that of many of his peers.

It was just before dawn on June 26, 1984, in his second year on the front line.

Private First Class Cho Byung-ik, a fellow soldier Daehan knew well, committed an unthinkable act. Cho, who had completed his third year in architectural engineering at Chungbuk National University before enlisting, tossed two grenades into the barracks where his comrades lay asleep. When the blasts threw the room into chaos and men woke screaming, he opened fire on them with his rifle.

In that moment, one of the worst tragedies in the history of the Republic of Korea Armed Forces unfolded.

Using the confusion, Cho fled into the Demilitarized Zone and defected to the North. A hastily assembled search team pursued him into the pitch-black DMZ, only to trigger landmines and cause even more casualties.

Daehan survived by a hair's breadth. Twenty-two young men in their prime died in an instant, and many more were wounded.

Among those who lived through that hellish night was Sergeant Kim Woo-hyun, his friend and senior from home. He escaped with only minor physical injuries, but the event would surely leave scars for a lifetime. Among the men who lost an arm was a former middle school classmate of Daehan's.

In the division's parade ground, under a light, steady drizzle, rows of coffins draped with the Korean flag lined the field while the military band played a dirge. Surrounded by the sobs of bereaved families and fellow soldiers, Daehan lay awake night after night, consumed by a grief and fury that left no room for sleep.

The incident left him with severe post-traumatic stress disorder. He was transferred to a military hospital, and in early December 1984, he received an early discharge from the army.

A Whisper Across the Pacific

On January 20, 1985, while resting at his family home, Daehan received an international letter from Professor Richard Feynman of the California Institute of Technology.

In it, Feynman wrote that he had read Wi Daehan's 1983 paper, *"Multipartite Quantum Entanglement and Non-local Phase Interference: A Preliminary Study,"* through his former student, Professor Kang Yeon-hwa of Seoul National University, and that he had been deeply impressed. He especially praised the originality of the non-local interference patterns in entangled states involving three or more particles, where coherence is maintained, and the paper's proposed applications to quantum computing and quantum cryptography.

In that work, Daehan had proposed that when three or more particles form an entangled state, each particle can maintain coherence with the others and manifest in a way that is effectively unmeasurable—non-local. Using a quantum spin system as a simple mathematical model, he theoretically showed that the resulting interference pattern could exhibit behaviors distinct from those of single- or two-particle entanglement. He went on to propose experimental frameworks to test the phenomenon—such as polarization-resolved setups and quantum-optical configurations—and briefly discussed its potential applications in quantum computation and quantum cryptography.

In his letter, Feynman said that Daehan's ideas had given him considerable inspiration and that he would gladly accept him as a student if he wished to study and do research together.

Reading the letter again and again, Daehan realized that Caltech was not unfamiliar to him at all—that he had already read several of Feynman's papers. Before enlisting, he had haunted the stacks of Jeongdok Library, Namsan Library, and the National Library of Korea, devouring books and journals on physics, electronics, and quantum mechanics. Among them were papers from Caltech, especially several by Richard Feynman, one of the leading authorities in quantum physics.

That night, he stayed up writing a reply.

—

Dear Professor Richard Feynman,

Hello, Professor. First, I am truly surprised and grateful that you would send a letter directly to an unknown young man like me.

During my military service on the front line, I was almost completely cut off from academic news, both domestic and international. Receiving your letter has filled me with deep emotion and excitement.

To be honest, at first the name "California Institute of Technology" felt unfamiliar. But then I remembered. In the six months before I enlisted, I spent my days in several libraries in Seoul, reading books and journals in physics, electronics, and quantum mechanics, and I came across your papers and writings multiple times.

I was particularly fascinated by the articles on Feynman diagrams in quantum field theory and the path integral formalism that made them possible. What impressed me most were your writings on the "path integral interpretation of quantum mechanics."

The idea of summing and integrating over all possible paths, instead of the single trajectory of classical mechanics, struck me as truly revolutionary. That concept shattered the "single trajectory" paradigm I had taken for granted and allowed the probability amplitudes of quantum mechanics to be handled much more intuitively. Thanks to that, I gained crucial clues for understanding the non-local quantum phenomena I had only imagined in my head in more precise mathematical terms.

I also remember an article summarizing how you and several colleagues resolved the renormalization problem in quantum electrodynamics. I had wondered how quantum field theory dealt with the divergences that arise when calculating interactions, and I was amazed at how your introduction of diagrams and renormalization techniques turned complicated calculations into far more intuitive pictures.

The fact that these "visual tools" could still yield correct numerical coefficients was fascinating. It felt worthy of being called a revolution in theoretical physics.

Finally, I also recall reading excerpts from The Feynman Lectures on Physics a bit more casually. Your explanations—aimed at making not only quantum mechanics but also electromagnetism, statistical physics, and wave theory easier to grasp—gave courage even to a non-major like me.

In truth, because I never received a formal high school education, I came to quantum mechanics without a deep mathematical background. Even so, your lecture notes were a precious resource that gave me the confidence that "one can approach the essence of physics even without equations."

It feels both unbelievable and deeply honorable that a piece I wrote a few years ago was published in a Korean physics journal and that this, in turn, has led to a connection with you.

I am very aware of my own shortcomings, having never completed a formal university curriculum. But if any of the ideas I discussed might be of use in your research or connect, even a little, with your insights, there would be no greater happiness for me.

As for my current situation, I completed my military service in December 1984 and am now resting for a while in my hometown of Goseong in Gangwon Province. If you were to invite me to the California Institute of Technology as you mentioned, I would be more grateful than I can express.

It would be a once-in-a-lifetime opportunity. For my part, I want to delve deeper into quantum mechanics and quantum field theory there and further develop my ideas. I worry that someone like me, with such a humble background, might prove a burden, but I trust in the sincerity of your letter and truly hope to meet you in person.

Whether as a researcher or as a student, it does not matter. I am confident that my passion for theoretical physics is as earnest as anyone's. Although I am just a student without a degree, if you grant me the chance to study and do research at Caltech under your guidance, it would be a new turning point in my life.

I hope this letter from far away reaches you safely. I will gladly follow any detailed instructions you provide regarding schedule or procedure.

Thank you sincerely, and I hope we can soon meet for deeper research and discussion.

Sincerely,

—Wi Daehan
January 21, 1985

A few months later, he received a formal admission offer from Caltech, and he was also selected for the Ministry of Education's government scholarship program to cover his tuition.

On July 20, 1985, his mother and his third brother waited for him at the departure hall of Gimpo International Airport. The same brother who had slapped him years earlier, when he failed the high school entrance exam, now hugged him tightly, wiping away tears.

"Daehan, take care of yourself… and come back successful," his brother said, his voice shaking.

Wi Daehan boarded the plane. The boy who had once dreamed of Mars while staring up at the stars was finally beginning a new trajectory toward a wider universe.

As a sea of clouds spread out below the plane and in-flight announcements crackled overhead, a lump formed in his throat. Watching the Korean peninsula shrink and vanish through the window, a swirl of complex feelings washed over him. He still felt a sting of inferiority at being from the countryside, but beneath it, an inexplicable confidence had taken root—something that had changed in him since that strange night on Namsan. Ever since then, his mind had been absorbing knowledge at a frightening speed.

The plane refueled at Anchorage International Airport in Alaska and eventually landed at Los Angeles International Airport. After presenting his admission letter and other documents to immigration and having his passport stamped, Daehan emerged into the arrivals lobby and spotted a man holding a sign with his name.

The man introduced himself as Feynman's assistant and

greeted him warmly. Even through the haze of jet lag, Los Angeles looked like another world—like a movie set brought to life. Daehan stared out the window of the car, so absorbed by the cityscape that he hardly thought to speak to the driver beside him.

The one-hour drive to Caltech felt several times longer. When they finally pulled up in front of an unfamiliar building on campus, Professor Richard Feynman himself was waiting.

"A pleasure to meet you, Mr. Wi. Your paper was truly fascinating," Feynman said with a bright smile, extending his hand. "You approached it from a different angle than my path integrals. It was refreshing."

"I learned a great deal from your papers, Professor. But… I never went through a formal university program, so I'm worried about whether I can really manage here," Daehan replied in awkward English, his face flushing.

"Formal coursework isn't everything here," Feynman laughed, gesturing broadly. "My colleagues at Caltech and I welcome people whose ideas spark. It's not the diploma that matters, but *how* you think."

During the day, Daehan attended quantum mechanics seminars. At night, in the small dormitory room the university had arranged, he read papers and organized his ideas on path integrals, quantum field theory, and non-local interactions, developing them with Feynman diagrams and the tools he was learning. Days of seminars and nights of writing bled into each other. Within two years, his name began appearing frequently in physics journals, and Feynman took pride in the brilliant student he had found.

In 1986, having completed his foundational research at Caltech, he moved into a Ph.D. program at MIT, supported by the government scholarship and a strong recommendation from his mentors. At MIT, he immersed himself in quantum information and condensed matter physics. Groundbreaking papers on distributed computation algorithms, quasiparticle dynamics, and quantum gate error correction emerged from his hands. Word spread quickly among young physicists: a new genius had arrived at MIT.

He didn't confine himself to the lab. To earn living expenses and hone his programming skills, he joined external projects, mingling with programmers and hackers and learning about kernel optimization and distributed computing techniques. Those experiences later became an important foundation for his work.

After completing his doctorate, he moved to Stanford in 1989 for further doctoral work, combining research on superconductors, lasers, and nanoscience. Within a single year, he produced papers on cutting-edge topics such as the potential of "superconducting qubits" and "optical qubits," and techniques for atomic manipulation via laser cooling. His pace left even his advisor speechless. He bombarded his professors with questions and, as soon as he learned something new, turned it into a paper. When people asked how he could write so quickly, he would only say, calmly, "I just organize the structure that forms in my mind."

By then he held two Ph.D.s in physics, but he was far from satisfied. No matter how brilliant a physical theory was, it was powerless once you stepped outside the lab. The real problem lay in a world where people still pointed guns at each other: a divided homeland, the massacre he had witnessed in the army. If he wanted to change that underlying reality, physics alone wouldn't be enough. He could already sense the dawn of an era in which computer networks and information would rule the world.

He went on to Carnegie Mellon University as a postdoctoral

researcher, working on distributed operating systems, security protocols, and cryptography. In just one year, he made significant contributions to stable distributed OS design and won a best-paper award at a cryptography conference. During that period, he also joined Novell's NetWare 386 project, implementing encryption modules and distributed processing algorithms, often working remotely.

In 1991, at the age of twenty-eight, Wi Daehan received an offer to return to Caltech as a professor of physics. He inherited the lab of his late mentor, Richard Feynman, and continued his research while collaborating on external projects. Anticipating that the explosive growth of the PC market would bring equally explosive security problems, he worked with major companies to develop antivirus solutions and encryption modules. He also contributed to an early "Navigator" web browser project, laying groundwork that would later lead to Netscape Navigator.

His name rose quickly in both academia and industry—but what he truly wanted was technology that could end war and violence, a structure that would allow humanity to cooperate in peace. He believed the key lay in AI, quantum computing, and networks. That conviction led him back to a single decision:

He had to return to Korea.

"You'd have a guaranteed career if you stayed here. Why go back?" friends and colleagues would ask, trying to talk him out of it.

"I can't forget what I saw on the front lines," he would answer. "A homeland split in two, North and South pointing guns at each other... In the end, I think my real challenge has to start there."

The Return of the Star, the Birth of 21CF

In June 1994, as he had promised himself, Wi Daehan set foot on Korean soil for the first time in ten years.

After driving himself without rest through his years abroad, he was coming home with a dazzling reputation and achievements—yet an odd emptiness lingered in a corner of his chest.

His mother was waiting for him at the arrivals gate.

"Daehan!"

He ran to her and wrapped her in his arms. Her embrace was still warm and soft. It felt as if ten years had passed in a single breath. But the deep wrinkles etched into her forehead and the shadow of sorrow at the corners of her eyes spoke quietly of the weight of the life she had carried alone.

"You've worked hard, my son." Her hand patted his back; her eyes shone with tears.

He gripped her hand in silence. In that hand she still held the old leather wallet he had given her the day he left, ten years ago.

He took his mother to a high-end hotel in Seoul he had booked in advance—the Hyatt at the foot of Namsan. The view of the city spread out below was nothing like the Seoul in his memory. After asking the hotel staff to take extra care of his shy, out-of-place mother, he headed to the Seoul Press Center in Gwanghwamun for the press conference on his schedule.

The Korean media focused on him as a successful scholar and businessman, showering him with praise for "raising the nation's prestige" by winning a prize "on par with the Nobel." Yet no one asked a single truly probing question about what his research meant or how it might reshape society. They had neither the curiosity nor the capacity. All they cared about were the records: that he had earned two doctorates from world-renowned universities like MIT and Stanford at a young age.

Only at the very end did someone ask which Korean university he planned to join as a professor and what his future plans were.

"I'd like to begin by thanking all of you for taking the time to be here," he said. "Based on what I've learned and experienced in the United States, I intend to help make Korea one of the world's leading internet powers. I also plan to devote my knowledge and passion to future technologies and industrialization, so that we don't fall behind other advanced countries—and so that many young people like me can grow to lead this country."

He paused, then went on in a firmer voice.

"In addition, I believe we are not simply 'observers of the universe,' but 'participatory beings' who shape the future together through perception and choice. Through new technologies, I hope we can awaken the 'cosmic nature' within us and build a better world. Thank you."

As he was about to step away from the podium, a reporter raised a hand.

"The terms 'participatory being' and 'cosmic nature' are a bit unfamiliar. Could you explain them in a way our readers can understand?"

"Of course," he said with a small smile. "Simply put, a participatory being is not a passive consumer who just watches the world go by, but an active, creative subject that helps construct reality through the act of observation itself. In quantum mechanics, we talk about the observer effect—how observation collapses the wave function. I don't think that idea belongs only to the microscopic world."

He glanced around the room. Seeing that people were actually listening, he found a thin thread of hope and continued.

"As for cosmic nature, it begins with a deep understanding that we are all fundamentally connected as one. We are all born from the remnants of stars, tangled together in the universe's vast web of life. Recently, some in the scientific community have proposed that the universe is not just a lump of matter, but is moved by a fundamental principle—something like consciousness or spirit. I believe these new discoveries will eventually lead us beyond the 'me within the universe' to the 'universe within me.' And on that journey, we'll come to recognize our true selves—our cosmic nature."

In the audience, a young female reporter sat listening with bright, focused eyes. For a moment, Daehan thought of J.

"This realization will bring fundamental change to how we live our lives, how we run our societies, and how we develop technology. The values of coexistence and mutual flourishing will become more important than competition and ownership. I believe new technology should be used to open that path of coexistence. I intend to show you that belief through what I do from here on. Thank you."

The newspapers the next day mostly highlighted his résumé: professorships at prestigious American universities, two doctorates, the impressive titles. Some articles introduced his nickname "Great Wi," a play on his given name, Daehan, which means "great" in Korean. Almost none offered serious analysis of his academic or social vision.

A few days later, he traveled with his mother to his home village in Goseong, Gangwon Province—a rural town in the northeast, near the border. The mountains, fields, and bright stars in the night sky were the same; the people were not. Some had passed away. Others had left for the city and vanished from contact.

The next day, he went to Sokcho to see Kim Woo-hyun, now a civil servant. The two friends met for the first time in ten years and pulled each other into a fierce hug.

"Wi Daehan? Or should I call you Great Wi now?" Woo-hyun joked.

Daehan laughed. "Just Wi Daehan is fine."

They drank deep into the night, trading stories about their army days, life in America, and faint memories of their boyhood.

"So what are you going to do now?"

At his friend's question, Daehan bit his lip for a moment, then answered.

"Well… I want to do something that will change the world in a big way."

The same fire that had lit his eyes when he looked up at the stars as a boy was still burning there.

"You were special even then," Woo-hyun said, clinking his glass against Daehan's. "You'll do well."

"Thanks, my friend."

He lifted his gaze to the sky. City lights drowned out most of the stars, but he still believed that somewhere out there a mysterious light was watching over him.

Around that time, the internet boom was just beginning. A little over thirty, he chose a new challenge in a new place.

Not long after his return, on June 20, 1994, he hung a small sign reading "21st Century Frontier (21CF)" on the top floor of a modest five-story building near Baengbaeng Intersection in Gangnam, Seoul.

On the night of the founding ceremony, the sharp pop of champagne corks and the laughter of the founding members filled the cramped office.

"All right, everyone," Daehan said, raising his glass. "From today, we write a new history."

His voice carried the passion and confidence of a young entrepreneur.

"We're going to build a completely different world with the internet, AI, and quantum technology. Thank you for being here with me."

Cheers and applause rose from the small crowd. As he looked at each face in turn, his chest swelled. Then, without warning, J's face surfaced in his mind—a name he had longed for over the years, but rarely allowed himself to summon.

Someday I'll show you all of this. Until then, I'll run hard enough for both of us.

Wi Daehan raised his champagne glass high once more. His eyes shone with conviction about the future and a deep, quiet longing for J.

Among the founding members were two people he had gone to great lengths to recruit from the United States.

Maxwell Yoon, a Korean American with a Ph.D. in computer science from Stanford, had been thriving in Silicon Valley. He and Daehan had been close friends during their doctoral studies. With outstanding programming skills, a deep understanding of AI, and an easy, sociable manner, Maxwell hadn't hesitated when Daehan emailed him about the new venture. He joined as a co-founder and became 21CF's CTO, in charge of AI and software development. He knew of J's existence only vaguely, but he had long since noticed how much Daehan missed her.

The other key recruit was Hannah Kim. She held a Ph.D. in physics from MIT, where she and Daehan had first met at a conference and stayed in touch. A top expert in quantum computing, she was serious and sharply intelligent. She highly valued Daehan's entrepreneurial instinct and placed high hopes on 21CF's future. As director of the Quantum Computing Lab, she led research into quantum algorithms and their applications.

Though the room still buzzed with chatter, Daehan continued, smiling brightly.

"We are the 21st Century Frontier. We didn't come together just to make money off the internet. I want to use artificial intelligence, quantum computing, and networks for peace. It's not going to be easy. But I truly want to do it. Our company will be one that prepares for—and leads—the twenty-first century, not just the present."

There was no wavering in his voice. Maxwell spoke up next.

"Daehan, do you really think the future of AI you're talking about can come true? If technology could actually bring people closer… that would be something."

He set his glass down on the desk and looked out the window.

"Think about why we started here, in Korea of all places. We're trying to build technology for peace in a land that's lived with the pain of division. This isn't just about personal success or piling up money. It's also our answer to this country's poor educational environment, the constant military tension, and the endless struggle to keep up technologically."

Hannah nodded, her voice quiet but firm. "That's right. Everything we do—learning, research, development—is more than just 'innovation.' It reflects our shared experience of hardship, hope, and failure. We have a responsibility to shape how the technologies we build will change humanity's future."

Daehan fell silent for a moment. In his eyes lay the wounds of his past and a hard, steady resolve for what lay ahead.

"I'm not doing this just for success," he said at last. "The frustrations of my childhood, the tragedies I witnessed in the army—they all led me here. Taken together, they keep asking the same question: *How do we create our own future?* I believe our choices can change more than our individual lives. They can change everyone's future."

The air in the office grew heavier. On every face there was a mix of anxiety about what was coming and a deep, shared resolve.

"What we have to do now isn't just develop technology," he continued. "We have to lay the groundwork for humanity to carve its own destiny *through* that technology. The pain of the past becomes a guidepost for the future we choose. So I want to ask: *How will we create our own future?* I think the answer is hidden in every choice we make here and now."

One by one, the people in the room met each other's eyes, as if confirming the wounds and hopes that lay deep inside them. In that moment, they all understood that they were not just researchers or engineers. They were bridges—between past and future, between the individual and society.

To most people, who barely understood what "AI" or "quantum technology" even meant, they would surely seem like eccentrics. The internet was only just beginning. But they were ready to dive in anyway. In that shabby office, Wi Daehan and his colleagues— backed by dozens of research papers and experience with massive software projects—set their sights on the future.

"The AI we build mustn't be a tool for controlling people," he said. "It has to become a true companion. That's why we're thinking about ethics from the very beginning. If powerful technology like this ends up in the hands of dangerous ideologues or reckless businessmen, the world is in danger. Our goal isn't just to solve today's problems. It's to play our part in the twenty-first century, when technology is going to dominate this world."

At the time, even most people in Korea's IT field didn't really grasp what they were trying to do. But Daehan was already looking further ahead, guided by a heavy, certain premonition. The plan was simple and ruthless: secure funds through website and software development, then pour the profits back into AI and quantum-computing research.

He was confident about foreign investment as well. His background—MIT, Stanford, Caltech, major awards—and his reputation as a young genius were more than enough to captivate investors. Back then, hardly anyone could imagine that he would take the knowledge and networks he had built in Cambridge, Palo Alto, and Pittsburgh and unfold them on the stage of Korea.

Time would prove him right.

Late that night, after seeing all his colleagues off, Daehan opened the window. Far away at Baengbaeng Intersection, cars flowed by in unbroken lines of headlights; now and then a horn sounded in the distance. It was no longer the Seoul he remembered. He opened the large northeast-facing window and stepped out onto the balcony.

In the distance, Namsan Tower blinked. The instant he saw that light, he thought of J—the time they had spent together somewhere along those slopes.

Not a day had gone by since their parting that he hadn't thought of her. But the luggage he had left with relatives had gone missing, and with it the letters she had written him. The portrait he had once drawn of her, painstakingly sketched, was gone as well.

He had made that drawing in a strange season, months after they parted, when he found that he could no longer clearly recall her face and the sense of loss gnawed at him. One day he opened an English textbook from Jongno Hagwon and found a sketch on the inside page—a face he had drawn absent-mindedly, without realizing it resembled J. That drawing let him call her back to mind. But that book too had been lost after several moves. All that remained was longing.

The more he thought about those days, the more he missed her.

Did she graduate from the English department at Seoul National University and go to the United States, back to her parents…?

The question tormented him, but with the internet still in its infancy, trying to find someone was little more than an idle wish. Even so, he looked up at the lights of Namsan Tower and believed they would meet again someday.

That night, he sat at his desk and wrote a poem.

—

To You, Who Became a Star
1994, Great Wi

That autumn night when Namsan's slopes were dyed in color,
You left me,
And where might you be now?
I wish to become a seagull cutting across the Han River,
I fear neither rugged mountain paths nor deep waters,
I would even become a worm crawling upon the earth,
If only I could feel your breath.
Tonight, a single star shines lonely beneath the Seoul sky,
Is that your likeness, or my own longing?
Not knowing makes it all the more sorrowful.
I would rather believe that star is Ojakgyo,
The bridge that connects our love forever.
I wish to become a thousand-year rock on Namsan hill, keeping watch over that place.
That bench where we counted stars together,
Sitting wordlessly under the dim streetlamp light,
Sharing cotton candy on that day,
You, who bloomed more beautifully than any nameless flower in a fragrant greenhouse,
I long to see your smile again.
The faint starlight inside the old Science Museum telescope,
The vow of that day when we held hands tight,
Engraving that heat into the starlight, I wait for you again today.
Standing alone in the deep night,
Leaning on the balcony, gazing at the ridges of Namsan,
The face that rises when I close my eyes, that unforgettable name,
J, beneath which star are you now,
Recalling the memories of that autumn day?

When he finished, Daehan folded the paper into a plane. His fingertips trembled with longing for J. He took the paper airplane out to the fifth-floor balcony and fixed his eyes on the light of Namsan Tower.

The watch on his left wrist read 10 P.M.—the exact time, thirteen years earlier, when he had launched a paper airplane with J.

He lifted the plane containing the poem and hurled it with all his strength toward Namsan's darkness. As he watched it circle on the wind, he whispered,

"Someday… will this heart of mine ever reach her?"

Just then, the beacon at the top of Namsan Tower flickered. It was probably nothing more than a trick of the eyes, but to Daehan, it felt like a signal.

He smiled faintly. Resting his arms on the railing, he stared up at the night sky for a long time. There was still a hollow in one corner of his heart that nothing had yet filled—but that very emptiness had become the engine that kept him moving.

Chapter 3

J

The First Echo in the Mirror

Soft fog lay over San Francisco in the early dawn. On the first floor of J's building on the hill, the first light of morning slipped cautiously through the bedroom window.

The desk clock read 6:00 A.M., and from it, Arvo Pärt's *Spiegel im Spiegel* flowed softly. The tranquil piano and cello lines mingled with the dawn air, seeming to gently awaken J's consciousness. Since its release in 1978, the piece had been praised as a "profound meditation within simple melodies," a stillness akin to meeting another self in a mirror.

Every morning, when she listened to it, a blend of loneliness, quiet anticipation, and the strange afterimage of that one night returned to her.

Was this world I was observing truly real, or just an illusion reflected in layers, like this music…?

J closed her eyes and surrendered to the melody. Then she felt old memories stir—the fountain at Namsan, the paper airplane, the unidentified light. A moment later, she slowly opened her eyes and pushed herself up in bed.

Today… the Stanford seminar…

Feeling the soft sunlight filtering through the thin curtains, she remembered the upcoming seminar on "Human–AI Interaction." It was a presentation she had prepared for diligently throughout her doctoral program, yet what had taken hold of her mind since dawn was, unexpectedly, the strange memory that had brushed past her in a dream the night before.

The Namsan fountain, the dark night, the paper airplane…

J recalled tracing the edges of the paper airplane Wi Daehan had folded for her long ago on Namsan. The light excitement she had felt as the paper took flight, the spray from the fountain, the chill of the night air—those sensations all seemed to live on. The thrill left by the unidentified flash of light that had streaked over her head was unforgettable.

After that night, she had felt that the ordinary girl she had been had stepped into a completely different world. The city lights she had looked down on from beside the fountain had been a completely different color from this San Francisco dawn.

The ache of that thirteen-year-old farewell—the girl clutching a paper airplane—still lingered somewhere inside her. J knew well, however, that the pain had turned into a conviction for her research and was what drove her now.

She hesitated for a moment before getting out of bed and opening the window. The cool early-morning breeze of San Francisco, where the sun had yet to rise fully, drifted in. The city was slowly waking; down the hill, office windows were already lighting up one by one.

Recently, the words "internet" and "startup" had spread like a trend, and the signs of fledgling venture companies were appearing everywhere. At Stanford, new tech seminars and business presentations were held weekly, and all of Silicon Valley was buzzing with the dot-com boom.

J felt "as if a new revolution in knowledge were just beginning." Last night's news had even reported that "computer networks would soon change the entire world," and that countless investors on Wall Street were throwing themselves into the movement.

In an era like this, could my research—the story of the quantum observer effect and human consciousness—really find its place?

Watching as the office lights outside the window spread one by one, J fell into thought for a moment. Suddenly, a low-frequency hum seemed to surface in her mind again, but this time it faded as faintly as a dream.

Was it really a dream? That unidentified light from that night…

She stood there with a slightly dazed expression, then fixed her gaze on the calendar hanging on the wall. It was Monday, June 20, 1994.

Just then, she heard something fall in the alley below. Slipping on her slippers, J headed down to the alley. On the empty pavement lay a small, limp paper airplane. She picked it up carefully and unfolded it. There were no letters or drawings; it was just a paper airplane made from a plain white sheet. Even so, a scene from thirteen years earlier on Namsan rose in her mind with vivid clarity.

"Then let's put our wishes into this plane and send it off."

"Wow, it flies so well! I've never seen such a cool paper airplane, Daehan!"

Daehan's playful voice and the sparkle of her own excited eyes were as clear as if they were in front of her. Holding the paper airplane lightly against her chest, J murmured.

"Yes, it's all in the past…"

Her life had changed frighteningly since 1981. She still didn't know for certain whether it had been a UFO or something else, but from that day on, a strange ability had begun to sprout inside her. An obsession with research into quantum mechanics and consciousness took hold, yet the world had been slow to accept her. Branded as "nonsense" and "mad science," she had ultimately been left to walk a solitary path.

If the wish we made together back then really had come true… where would he be now, and what would he be doing?

J's hand curled into a small fist. As she turned back into the fog-laden alley, a subtle tremor ran through a corner of her heart.

Will the day come when I complete this research and meet him again, so we can speak about the paths we've walked…?

J returned home with the paper airplane in her hand. Of course, it wasn't the one Daehan had flown, but it was enough to call up old memories. She set the airplane carefully on the living-room desk and headed for the kitchen. Her stomach rumbled, but perhaps because of the emotions that had been surging since morning, her appetite did not come easily.

"Someone will laugh at me again today…" J muttered to herself as she stepped back into the bedroom and stood in front of the bathroom mirror. Her pale face stared back at her.

After washing up with a bitter expression, she changed into simple clothes. When she returned to the living room, the morning sun was slowly brightening the city through the large glass window. Because the building sat high on a hill, downtown San Francisco spread out beneath her in a single view. Beyond the layered hills to the west, the Golden Gate Bridge was faintly visible.

On the living-room wall, alongside a simple cabinet, hung photographs J had taken herself: shots from her teenage years on Namsan in Seoul, and group photos with friends on the campuses of Harvard, Stanford, and Cambridge. In one corner, a family portrait sat in a frame. It showed her Korean mother, her father, a U.S. military officer stationed in Korea, and a young J. Every time she looked at the photo, she was swept up in a familiar, complicated tangle of feelings—pride in her parents, sorrow over their absence, and a deep longing for a past she could never reclaim.

J walked toward the internal staircase leading to the second floor. When she opened the heavy wooden door and climbed up, the distinctive stillness of a private study spread softly around her. Bookcases lined the walls, filled with classics on physics, philosophy, cognitive science, and quantum computing.

"Did I need any more reference materials before today's seminar…?"

She murmured, running her hand along the spines until it rested on Fritjof Capra's *The Tao of Physics*. It was the book that had completely changed the girl who had once dreamed of majoring in English literature.

A participatory universe and the cosmic self…

She stroked the cover for a moment, then carefully slid the book back into place. She moved on to her second-floor personal study and library. As she opened the door, pale light seeped quietly through the window where a light fog still lingered.

On the large, old wooden desk in the center, a new laptop, thick volumes of papers, and research notebooks crammed with scribbles were spread out in disarray. On one wall, a whiteboard and a corkboard were mounted. On the whiteboard, beneath the phrase **"Quantum Observer Effect—A Cognitive Framework: Does Consciousness Create Reality?"** a flurry of complex equations and diagrams filled the space. J studied the equations and let out a deep sigh.

Will people even try to understand this…?

She shook her head. Then her gaze came to rest on an old photo pinned in a corner of the corkboard. It had been taken with Daehan on Namsan in 1981. A young J was smiling brightly, while next to her Daehan was making a playful face. J took the photo down, laid it on her palm, and stared at it for a long time.

You… what are you doing now? Will you… will you understand this crazy research of mine…?

She pinned the photo back on the corkboard and walked to the window, lifting the gradient blinds that were halfway up. Dim morning light filtered through the fog, gently stroking the desk. When she opened the window, the faint sound of a string melody by Claude Debussy floated in from nearby, settling over her like a thin layer of fog and leaving a wistful ache in her chest.

Gazing outside, J savored the strange sensation that *the moment I open the window, the world answers me.* She remembered that, like the quantum observer effect, when an observer perceives the world, the world also changes the observer.

If everything is connected, then maybe even this small gaze leaves a trace somewhere in the universe…

She smiled faintly and stared into the empty air. On a nearby shelf lay the notebook she opened every morning. On the cover were the words *Quantum Life Principle.* Inside, quantum-mechanics formulas, poetic lines, doodles, and simple sketches were all jumbled together. J flipped it open to a random page.

"Everything that exists lies within a cloud of probability until it is observed. If so, could our observation be not just an act of perceiving things, but an act of creating their existence? If so, are we…"

Just below it was a small note: *"October 18, 1981, on Namsan."*

Next to it was a sketch of J's profile, seemingly drawn by

someone else. J stared at it blankly for a long time, then shook her head.

Even if I can't prove it yet, someday...

The feel of the paper airplane she had picked up from the alley still lingered on her fingertips. At that moment, a familiar tremor coursed through her again.

All right, let's go. Let's see what kind of reactions will be waiting today...

Smiling softly, J closed the research notebook. After giving her notes and materials a quick once-over, she went down to the first-floor kitchen. The kitchen, with its gentle beige tiles and wooden dining table, had a cozy, warm feel.

As she always did, J took out Greek yogurt; a colorful array of fruits—apples, strawberries, kiwis, blueberries, and bananas; and fresh salad greens—kale, romaine, tomatoes—and arranged them neatly on a large plate with a handful of nuts like walnuts, almonds, and cashews. She preferred to drink lukewarm water with breakfast so it wouldn't feel too heavy. No matter how busy she was, she had to eat a healthy breakfast. If she didn't take care of her body, she couldn't do her research.

Once she finished eating, J cleared the table and went back up to her second-floor study for a final check of her presentation materials. When she opened the slides saved on her laptop, the title **"Quantum Observer Effect—A Cognitive Framework: Does Consciousness Create Reality?"** appeared on the screen. She clicked through the slides, carefully reviewing the graphs and key sentences once again.

When everything was in order, J went back down to the first-floor kitchen to make hand-drip coffee. While the water heated, she ground the beans she had roasted herself and carefully poured them into the filter on the dripper. She adjusted the amount of coffee, the water temperature, and the extraction time with meticulous care, brewing it as if conducting a scientific experiment.

For J, the time spent making coffee was a kind of ritual, as important as her research. Drinking coffee right after a meal wasn't good for her health, but after some digestion, it wasn't a problem. From the steaming kettle, a thread-thin stream of water spiraled down onto the dripper in a delicate dance.

J watched it blankly, lost in thought.

Yes, maybe everything in nature is interconnected like that dancing stream of water. We just haven't fully understood that web of connection yet—the laws of that dance...

Realizing that her thoughts had drifted back to the *Quantum Life Principle*, she let out a small chuckle. She poured the freshly brewed coffee into a mug. The gentle, fragrant aroma filled the kitchen. Holding the cup, she went to the window and stood for a moment in the soft sunlight, feeling a faint sense of ease.

Once she was ready, J stood before the mirror and checked her outfit. Today, she had chosen a dark blue jacket, an outfit suitable for a formal occasion that still didn't sacrifice comfort.

As she reached for her laptop bag, her gaze fell on the paper airplane on the living-room table. Almost without thinking, she looked toward the window, where the city below the hill glittered in the sunlight.

The moment I look at the world beyond the window, is the world being decided in my mind, or is the world being created as I wish it to be...?

Thinking of a quantum wave function collapsing under observation, J felt again that the paper airplane was a small dream she had sent flying into the sky as a child, and a symbol of a wish that still remained, unchanged.

After a brief hesitation, she slipped the paper airplane carefully into her bag. Taking the stairs behind the first-floor corridor, she descended to the underground garage. Under the dim lights, a brand-new Porsche 993 sat quietly.

J opened the door, slid into the driver's seat, and started the engine, once more sinking into thought. Leaving the underground garage, the car glided smoothly down San Francisco's steep, familiar hills. She lowered the passenger-side window slightly, and the cool early-morning air slipped in. The last trace of coffee lingered on her tongue.

An Observer on the Cosmic Stage

Beyond the windshield, sunlight slanted across the city skyline, glittering off glass and steel. Waiting at a red light, J checked her reflection in the rearview mirror. She hadn't slept much the night before, absorbed in her research until late, but thankfully there was little sign of fatigue in her eyes.

As the car merged onto the highway, she settled into a steady speed. The low hum of her 911's engine seemed to sync with the beat of her heart.

Thirty minutes later, the sign for Stanford University appeared, and the open campus spread out before her. Palm trees and green lawns lined the road, and red-roofed buildings were quietly awakening in the early morning light.

Passing the main gate and entering the main drive, a few students jogging in workout clothes glanced at J's car. In 1994, a Ph.D. student driving a sports car at Stanford was hardly a common sight.

Drawing unwanted attention…

With a faint, unreadable expression, J pulled into her designated parking spot. As she stepped out and checked the side mirror one last time, a familiar voice called out.

"Oh, Dr. J!"

The voice belonged to her Ph.D. assistant, Lyla. Carrying

a heavy stack of photocopies, she waved cheerfully as she approached.

"You're here already! I brought the handouts for the seminar presentation. The print shop opened late yesterday... I was running around in circles, but I finally got them ready."

Lyla handed a few copies to J, catching her breath. J smiled lightly.

"Thank you, Lyla. There's still plenty of time, so take it slow. The weather is nice today, too."

"Yes, but I got a paper cut... ouch." Lyla let out a small groan.

"Oh my, are you okay? Paper cuts can sting more than they look. You should put a bandage on that first."

"It bled a little, but I'm fine. Anyway, I'm glad the materials are ready. I'm really looking forward to your presentation, Doctor."

Lyla smiled brightly and ran toward the entrance. J watched the diligent student with a pleased look.

"Thanks. Let's grab something to drink at the cafeteria later, when your finger is better," J called out.

"Yes, I will!"

Watching Lyla turn the corner of the building, hugging the printouts, J thought, with quiet satisfaction, what a dependable friend she was.

As she walked toward the research building, she saw students scattered across the lawn, reading books or playing guitars. It was early June, but the morning air still carried a chill.

If I talk about the quantum observer effect on this peaceful campus, will it sound too unrealistic?

But I have no choice... To explain the light I saw on Namsan that day, this is the only way.

In front of the research building entrance, Max was standing with a cigarette in his mouth. As soon as he saw J, he quickly stubbed it out and waved enthusiastically.

"Hey, J! You're here early. Heard you're going to make waves today? I'm looking forward to it."

Max looked tired, but he was visibly excited. J shrugged.

"Rather than making waves… I'm worried I'll get more than a few laughs. I hope you'll listen with an open mind."

Max stifled a yawn and muttered, "I stayed up all night with my research. My eyes feel like they're going to pop out."

"I had a hearty breakfast. Need to build up my stamina first."

Max gave a thumbs-up and joked, "Stamina, good!"

J ended the brief conversation with, "Let's talk after the seminar."

The research building lobby was bustling with Ph.D. students organizing photocopies and equipment. Amelia, a fellow doctoral candidate, spotted J and ran over with a bright smile.

"J! Your presentation is at ten today, right? I'm so excited just from the title. Are you finally unveiling the secret research?"

J smiled. "Well, it's not a big reveal… I'm just thinking of being a little honest about why I started this research."

"The professors seemed a bit troubled by it, but I'm super excited," Amelia said, before hurrying off.

J opened her bag. When her fingertips brushed against the paper airplane tucked inside, she paused.

Why did I bring this…?

She muttered inwardly but didn't dwell on the thought. The corridor was already filling with people. On a bench, Lyla was dozing off, looking drained with the pile of materials beside her.

J approached her gently. "Lyla, are you okay? How's your finger?"

Lyla, still half-asleep, replied, "Ah… yes, Doctor. Sorry. I'm a bit dazed… the seminar is about to start…"

"It's okay, take your time. Be careful not to hurt yourself."

Lyla nodded, gathered the printouts, and hurried into the

seminar room first. A poster was taped to the door.

Quantum Observer Effect—A Cognitive Framework: Does Consciousness Create Reality?

—J (Ph.D. Candidate)

Reviewing the presentation in her head, J calmed her slightly trembling heart. But mixed with the nerves was a strange excitement.

Someone might find new inspiration in my story today...

In a corner of the corridor bustling with professors and students, whispers drifted through the air.

"I heard this presentation is a bit shocking?"

"Applying the observer effect to human consciousness?"

"Isn't that just crazy talk?"

J took a deep breath and gripped the seminar room doorknob.

All right, J. Let's just tell them what we saw and felt, exactly as it was.

As she opened the door, the morning sun brightly illuminated the lecture hall. The gazes of the seated audience turned to her all at once. The room was packed with students, researchers, and professors who had gathered early. The presentation was scheduled for 9:00 A.M., but most seats had been filled since 8:50.

The audience flipped through the handouts, curious about what J would discuss. The moderator standing next to the podium lightly tapped the microphone.

"All right, let me introduce today's speaker. She graduated early from Seoul National University with a B.S. in Physics in just two years in 1984, and completed her master's in theoretical physics and philosophy at Harvard University from 1984 to 1987. After earning her Ph.D. in quantum computing from Cambridge University in 1990, she is currently pursuing her Ph.D. in cognitive science here at Stanford. Please welcome Dr. J. Hyein Roberts, who has been causing quite a stir in the academic world with her unique research combining quantum mechanics and brain science."

As the moderator finished, applause filled the room. J walked gracefully to the podium and bowed. On the large screen, the presentation title was displayed in bold letters.

J began to speak in a clear voice.

"Thank you for taking the time out of your busy schedules for my presentation. What I would like to present today is the hypothesis that the observer effect in quantum mechanics could be closely linked to human cognitive functions."

Some audience members looked puzzled. Max, in the front row, readied his notebook with curious eyes, while a few professors in the back watched calmly with their arms crossed.

J displayed her second slide.

"If you look at this graph first, you can see research data showing a statistically significant correlation between the results of a quantum random number generator and specific brainwave patterns—especially when a person is in a state of extreme focus or heightened emotion."

On the screen, a brainwave spectrum and a quantum random number distribution graph were superimposed.

"Although the margin of error is still large, a bias has emerged that is difficult to explain with classical probability theory. This supports the hypothesis that the observer—that is, the state of the human brain—can have a subtle but definite influence on quantum probabilities."

Feeling the intense gazes upon her, J added that integrating BCI (Brain–Computer Interface) technology could enable even more precise experiments.

"So, is this phenomenon limited to the quantum and microscopic realms, or can it also be applied to the macroscopic world—our consciousness? I would like to discuss the latter possibility."

J displayed her third slide.

• *The brain may harbor quantum interactions beyond electrochemical activities.*

• *The brain and the external world could form an entangled state.*

• *Observation (consciousness) selects a probabilistic wave function into an actual state.*

J raised her voice slightly.

"This area has been dismissed as absurd by mainstream neuroscience, but cross-disciplinary research in cognitive science and physics suggests that conscious observation could be the very process that determines physical reality."

Some in the audience nodded as if savoring the thought, while others looked displeased, arms still crossed. J presented her own experimental graphs and brainwave data to explain further.

"Although I lacked the budget and equipment, I personally tested whether minute deviations appear in the results of a quantum random number generator when the brainwave state is in a specific emotional or focused mode. While not yet a statistically sufficient sample, a deviation difficult to explain with existing theories did occur. You might call it a leap, but if we consider that the 'subjective state of the observer (brain) influences the result beyond mere chance,' it could be a clue that slightly blurs the boundary between the macroscopic and quantum worlds. Ultimately, the key is to what extent and how human 'conscious observation' governs quantum processes."

J paused for a breath and shifted her gaze to the screen.

"According to my hypothesis, the phenomenon we call the 'observer effect' is related not just to simple measurement or computation, but to a quasi-conscious interpretive framework. Classical equipment simply reads information, but a subjective system that differentiates and interprets the meaning of a quantum state could act as the observer. In that sense, for Artificial Intelligence to become a true observer, I believe it needs a quantum-computing structure that goes beyond a simple neural-network base—one that can process quantum entanglement and superposition internally and reflect its 'self-information state.' After all, the collapse of the wave function is not simple measurement, but the *adoption* and *confirmation* of information."

J continued.

"If observation is merely 'the act of looking at a reality that already exists,' then we are nothing more than passive watchers. But if we combine quantum mechanics with consciousness, we may find that we are participating in the world, perhaps even creating it."

Next, J went through a few more slides, presenting the challenges her research would need to address.

 • *What ethical and consciousness mechanisms are needed for an AI to act as an observer?*

 • *Is human free will related to quantum indeterminacy?*

 • *How does collective observation—collective consciousness—influence the construction of reality?*

"That concludes my presentation. Thank you for your attention."

Finishing her presentation, J gave a light bow. Applause erupted from all corners. Some nodded with enthusiasm, while a few remained seated with their arms crossed, seemingly lost in thought. At the same time, whispers of "going too far" could be heard.

The moderator took the microphone again.

"Dr. J, thank you for a very intriguing presentation. We will now have a Q&A session. If you have a question, please raise your hand."

The first to raise his hand was Professor Steven Lando from the Physics Department.

"Dr. J, isn't it a rather bold interpretation to directly link the wave-function collapse of the microcosm to human brain cognition? Countless interpretations have emerged since the 1930s, but applying it to the macroscopic realm seems to be a stretch…"

J replied with a gentle smile.

"That's right, Professor Lando. The mainstream physics community still considers it an overreach. However, I believe this is not an overreach but a merger with considerable potential. As I mentioned, the correlation between specific human brainwave states and the quantum random number generator, along with clues that conscious observation might be the process determining physical reality, suggests that such a union is at least plausible."

Professor Lando still looked skeptical, but he nodded and waited for the next question. Then, Professor Harriet Cruz from the Psychology Department quietly raised her hand.

"Dr. J, my major is cognitive psychology, so I have long studied 'attention' and 'illusion.' If brainwave patterns change even when the human brain is under a visual illusion, are you suggesting that state of illusion affects quantum random number generation? If so, that seems to imply that a form of illusion could cause actual changes in reality."

J nodded.

"That's right, Professor Cruz. If an illusion or hallucination is not just an internal brain process but can induce an observer effect on the external world, then it means that an illusory state could also be involved in actual quantum events. Although there isn't enough evidence yet, if brainwave data and the quantum random number generator's deviation fluctuate simultaneously, it suggests that even belief or illusion could affect physical results."

Professor Cruz, looking intrigued, said, "Our lab would also like to collaborate."

J happily replied, "You're welcome anytime."

At this point, Professor Beatrice Gray from the Computer Science AI Lab carefully raised her hand.

"Dr. J, I've been researching whether AI can possess true consciousness. If the quantum observer effect of the human brain determines reality, what conditions do you think are necessary for an AI to act as a true observer? It seems that learning algorithms alone would be insufficient."

J looked at Professor Gray.

"That's a good question, Professor Gray. As I mentioned, the observer effect may be related to an information-processing structure beyond simple computation, or a 'quasi-conscious interpretive framework.' Some theories suggest that the collapse of the wave function is more closely related to the *way* information is interpreted and adopted than to the observation itself.

"If that's the case, for an AI to play the role of a true observer, I believe it needs a system based on quantum information processing—one that can handle quantum superposition and entanglement within its own information structure, going beyond a simple neural-network model. Although it's still in the early stages, in such a structure, an AI might function not just as a machine that analyzes data, but as an informational subject that has a real impact on physical states."

Professor Gray, taking rapid notes, wore an interested expression.

"So, you're saying that ultimately, AI must become a system that genuinely interprets and selects information at a quantum level, rather than just being a simulator. It seems inevitable that consciousness research and quantum information science will grow even closer."

J smiled gently and nodded. "I would very much like to research this together. It's still at a hypothetical level, but I expect that within the next ten to twenty years, we will have the environment to approach this hypothesis experimentally."

Finally, a young philosophy professor seated in the center, Adam Friedman, asked to speak.

"Thank you for the presentation. The term 'creation' is quite philosophical. It seems risky to delve into this area when scientific proof is still lacking."

J replied with a gentle expression.

"Yes, Professor Friedman. The term 'creation' is certainly philosophical, and sometimes even has religious connotations. I am keenly aware of that point. But what I meant to say is that if the collapse of the wave function can include not just physical measurement but also the cognitive action of selecting and interpreting information, then that process could conceptually align with what we have philosophically called creation. Of course, it's still at a hypothetical stage. It's an area that requires thorough scientific verification, and I was merely trying to expand my thoughts on its possibility."

The moderator made the closing remarks.

"Due to time constraints, we will have to end the Q&A session here. Let's give another big round of applause to Dr. J for her valuable presentation."

Thunderous applause erupted. Professor Steven Lando still tilted his head, but Professors Harriet Cruz and Beatrice Gray were taking copious notes on their laptops and engaging in heated discussions.

Max smiled brightly and shouted, "You absolutely nailed it, J!"

From the crowd heading out of the seminar room, Lyla approached.

"Doctor, that was amazing. I know there will be a lot of opposition, but... my heart was pounding."

"Thank you. I might be treated as a mad theorist, but I hope that someday you'll join me in this field, Lyla."

As J gave her a warm glance, Lyla smiled shyly. "I wonder how the world would change if an AI could participate as an observer, just like a real human."

Professor Steven Lando, who had been watching the scene, slowly approached and spoke quietly.

"Good work, Dr. J. The material was interesting, but further experiments and reproducibility will be essential. Be careful not to stray too far into quantum fantasy."

J showed her respect. "I'll keep that in mind, Professor. Still, I believe my theory will be verified someday."

When J stepped into the corridor outside, she lightly touched the paper airplane in her bag.

As expected, there are scoffs, but some are willing to listen.

The light from Namsan in 1981 and Daehan's voice echoed faintly within her.

I hope today's presentation becomes the first step in showing the world what I realized that day. Someday, I hope this combination of the observer effect and consciousness will become the key to opening the future for humanity and AI...

J walked quietly down the corridor. From somewhere, the murmur of students could be heard through a crack in a door, as if another lecture was starting.

As she exited the lobby, the sun was already casting long shadows from the building. Shifting her laptop bag, J headed toward the parking lot with a slightly weary look.

Theory alone is not enough.

She knew the academic community wouldn't accept her words as they were.

More independent and audacious experiments are needed.

Her real challenge was just beginning.

Two Covers, Fated Paths Apart

In late September 1994, on a hill in San Francisco, J threw herself into a new challenge. The somewhat indifferent reaction from parts of the academic world right after the Stanford seminar had, paradoxically, pushed her toward a more independent and courageous path.

She negotiated with a tenant to clear out one of the building's five floors and set up a small laboratory. It might not have looked like much, but for J, it was a major decision. The space was modest—only a few shabby pieces of equipment and a worn-out desk—but the midday California sun pouring through the large glass window seemed to lend real strength to this woman who did not mind being called a maverick scientist.

Around that time, across the ocean in Korea, Wi Daehan was leading 21CF and preparing for a new future. In 1994, when the wave of the internet revolution was only just beginning to rise, no one could have guessed the grand vision hidden behind his name.

But he was carving out his own path, day and night. His days were spent meeting investors, his nights wrestling with code. The internet revolution, once only a buzzword, was now on the verge of catching fire, and a heatwave of expectation that fast-moving companies would soon advance onto the global stage swept through the city.

Two people, unaware of each other's existence, were nurturing their dreams on different continents at the same time.

On a foggy hill in San Francisco, J named her small lab

Quantum Horizon. The name held her resolve to see beyond the horizon of quantum mechanics. The question of whether she was on the right path crossed her mind from time to time, but she could not stop. Even if her research was ridiculed as mad science, J wanted to prove that the light she had seen that night on Namsan was not a futile illusion.

Meanwhile, on the top floor of a building near Baengbaeng Intersection in Gangnam, Seoul, Daehan stopped coding only after two in the morning. Beside him, a colleague lay sprawled in exhaustion.

"Daehan, will the world really change when all this is done?"

At Maxwell Yoon's question, Daehan folded a paper airplane out of habit and simply smiled.

"Well, for now, we just have to run this code."

That night, he sent the paper airplane gliding lightly off the balcony railing. Somewhere in the sky, the memory of the strange light that had flashed past on Namsan lay dormant, but he no longer placed his heart in it. It was only a faint stirring in a corner of his chest.

At that very moment, across the Pacific on a San Francisco hill, J was gazing at the paper airplane she had placed on her bedroom windowsill. They were two people who had once carried feelings for each other, yet neither had any way of knowing how vast the dreams were that the other was nurturing that autumn.

At that shared point in time—1994—they were each creating their own universe. J's one-person lab, unrecognized by academia, and the newborn 21CF startup. The two had not yet found a connection, but perhaps they were already entangled in some subtle way, like a quantum superposition.

No one paid attention to their movements. People had no time to spare for the light from a window on a San Francisco hill or for a small airplane launched from a fifth-floor balcony at

Baengbaeng intersection. No one could have imagined that the faint embers ignited in these two places would later flare into a great fire that would shake the entire world.

J walked up the steep hill, repeating the words "Quantum Life Principle" under her breath, and Daehan dreamed of a distant future in his conference room. Unaware of one another, they held the same temperature of passion in the same era.

And so, the autumn of 1994 burned hotly in their own ways. Reality had turned its back on them, but they were slowly shaping the future with their own hands. At this point, no one knew that a moment would surely come when the two would cross paths again. There were only countless paths coexisting, like the possibilities of a quantum superposition.

In November 1995, as autumn deepened in New York, J left a conference in Manhattan, where she had just presented the basic principles of her Quantum Life Principle. Weary from the cold reception of the academic community, she headed toward Central Park to soothe her tired heart.

At the same time, a few blocks away, Daehan was leaving a hotel after finishing a meeting with investors and walking to the very same park for some fresh air.

Fate sometimes plays cruel tricks. Near a quiet bench, the two passed each other.

J glanced briefly at the Asian man in sunglasses, and Daehan walked past, staring at the trees in the distance. Fourteen years of change stood between them, and neither recognized the other.

From the spring of 1997, another kind of heat began to rise on the San Francisco hill. Quantum Horizon, which had been a mere personal lab three years earlier, had expanded enough to be called a "small institute." J watched the construction with a thrilled expression as the space between the third and fourth floors was opened up to install old oscilloscopes and optical tables and to lay down new electrical wiring.

1997 became a turning point for J.

After three years of solitary research, two papers she had submitted simultaneously adorned the covers of *Nature* and *Science.* When she received the call, J could hardly believe it. The lonely path she had walked alone was finally being recognized by the world. Her Quantum Life Principle was at last gaining external validation.

The title of the first paper was ***"Beyond Cellular Automata: A Quantum Entanglement Network Model of Living Cells."***

For the field of biology, it was nothing short of radical. The phrase "Beyond Cellular Automata" read like a declaration to overturn the long-standing view of interpreting cells purely through mechanical reactions. In fact, what J argued in the paper was even more radical. She proposed the bold concept of a *living quantum network* in which cells exchange biological information through quantum entanglement.

In that paper, J saw cells not as simple machines but as conscious entities connected through quantum entanglement, and she reinterpreted cancer and genetic disorders as the collapse of quantum coherence or a disruption of this entangled network.

When the paper appeared on the cover of *Nature,* criticism and support collided in equal measure. Many derided it as "lacking evidence" or "a piece of sophistry that forces quantum mechanics into biology," but some younger scientists welcomed it, asking, "Is an era of fusion between cell biology and physics beginning?"

With that paper, academic circles, the media, and the public all turned their eyes toward J at once.

The title of the paper featured on the cover of *Science* was ***"Harmonies of Quantum Coherence in Neuronal Microtubules: A Model of Conscious Experience."***

It was a radical declaration that advanced the *"Orchestrated Objective Reduction (Orch OR)"* theory of Roger Penrose and Stuart Hameroff, claiming that quantum processes in neuronal microtubules could generate consciousness. J argued that the brain could be a platform performing quantum computations, and that *"observation—that is, consciousness—directly affects quantum states inside and outside the brain, which in turn alters cognition and memory."*

On the cover of *Science*, beneath the line **"Quantum Mechanics & Consciousness—Fantasy or Future Science?"** appeared the microtubule-structure diagram J had proposed.

The media made much of these two papers, calling them "a new dimension of fusion science." On television programs, some praised J as "the Newton of the twenty-first century," while a renowned neuroscientist dismissed her work as "borderline pseudoscience."

In an interview, J only remarked briefly that *"if the observer effect applies not only to the microscopic world but also to the biological and brain domains, every paradigm could change,"* but that single comment amplified the controversy even further.

Thus the name J. Hyein Roberts was clearly imprinted on the global academic community and the public.

Opinions were sharply divided, yet curiosity and support were immense. Gaining confidence, J pushed ahead with more experiments that cut across cells, the brain, and quantum mechanics. She believed that the unified theory she had named the Quantum Life Principle would eventually become the key to encompassing human consciousness, AI, and ethics.

J stood at her window, watching the sunset spread over San Francisco Bay, and pondered the expansive possibilities of that principle.

Within the institute, some warned that there were still not

enough experiments to prove her claims, but she remained unshaken. Moving among the cold equipment, the researchers quietly repeated the words J had thrown at them: "This is not just physics. This is the path to understanding humanity itself."

In the same spring, another history was being written in New York.

The moment the letters "21CF" appeared on the Nasdaq electronic board, Daehan was flooded with emotion. The dream that had begun in a rural village in Gangwon-do had finally reached the world stage. Reporters had given him the name tag "Great Wi." It was a choice he had made for his global activities, yet he could not help feeling that he was losing some part of his original self.

At the celebration party, the CNBC news ticker happened to flash the name "J. Hyein Roberts." The report said she was a scientist studying the quantum observer effect. Daehan looked at the name carefully once more, but he did not know then that it was a signal of fate.

At that time, in San Francisco, Quantum Horizon was in the midst of heavy construction to redecorate the third and fourth floors and to install large cooling systems. When a neighbor complained about the noise, J apologized and urged the workers to hurry.

"It will be over soon. Please bear with us just a little longer," she said. Deep down, however, she believed that this maze of equipment could one day become the key to unlocking something called the Autumn Code.

For both of them, 1997 was a year of success. J gained the attention of the scientific community with her Quantum Life Principle, and Daehan stepped onto the global stage with 21CF.

But they did not know yet.

They did not know that, walking their separate paths across

the Pacific, they would dramatically reunite four years later at a hotel in San Francisco. The thread of fate was already, slowly, drawing them together.

Quantum Horizon: A Reunion Across Time

Around 5:00 P.M. on Friday, June 15, 2001, in a small conference room at a downtown San Francisco hotel, J stood with a few staff members, anxiously checking the projector.

The beam cut through the dim room, illuminating J as she presented a comprehensive blueprint for ***"NeuroniX's BCI Research and Quantum Bio-Cognition"*** to a group of seated investors. A dozen or so people from prominent venture capital firms and major corporate R&D departments watched in silence.

"...Theoretically, if the observer effect penetrates all of biology and the brain's cognitive systems, AI can also mimic this structure. For this, Brain-Computer Interfaces—and furthermore, Artificial Intelligence algorithms applying quantum entanglement—are key. Of course, it's still at the prototype stage, but the potential of this field is enormous."

Her presentation was calm and composed, but the reactions were cold. Sighs could be heard here and there, and some investors casually set the handouts aside on the empty chairs next to them.

"Quantum Bio-Cognition... there isn't enough evidence in the literature for that yet, is there?"

"When can we expect a return on investment?"

Sharp questions followed. J answered with a steady, serious expression.

"A minimum of five years of research and development funding is required."

Several investors wore expressions that clearly read, *That's ridiculous.*

As the presentation neared its end, the back door opened quietly. A man in his thirties slipped in and took a seat in the last row, but the lighting was too dim for J to notice.

Holding the microphone, J delivered her final conclusion.

"At this point, securing experimental equipment and personnel is impossible without large-scale capital. But I can guarantee you: if this technology is commercialized, the very lives of humanity will change."

In the end, the presentation concluded without anything resembling a hearty round of applause. J and her staff tried to hide their disappointment as they packed up the materials. As she left the conference room, one of the organizers offered a polite farewell. "Please contact us again if the opportunity arises."

Shoulders slumped, she was about to pass through the hotel lobby when she heard a low voice behind her.

"J... no, Dr. Roberts?"

The voice was so familiar that J stopped in her tracks. When she turned, she saw Wi Daehan—known to the world as "Great Wi."

The two stared at each other, speechless. They were no longer the boy and girl of 1981. Yet behind the unfamiliar faces shaped by time, something recognizable seeped through. J was swept up in a flood of recognition and disbelief.

"Wi Daehan... it's been a long time. I can't believe it." J finally managed, her voice barely above a whisper.

"Me too. To meet again in a place like this..." Daehan's voice trembled as much as hers.

He gave an awkward but happy smile. In a moment that felt like a dream, their paths through spacetime were intersecting again.

Eventually, Daehan suggested cautiously, "It's a bit crowded to talk here... shall we go outside?"

J hesitated, then nodded. All those watching eyes felt like a weight.

The evening air was cool. They found a small park nearby and sat on a bench under a streetlight in an awkward silence, unsure where to begin. In that moment, the scene of them flying a paper airplane together on a bench in Namsan in 1981 seemed to flash before both their eyes at once.

"How did we…" J's words caught in her throat.

He gave a sheepish smile and looked up at the sky.

"Actually… it's too much of a coincidence to call it a coincidence." He paused for a moment, then spoke honestly. "There was a seminar I really wanted to attend a few days ago, but I missed it because my flight was delayed. The title was *'Beyond the Observer Effect: Interactions of the Quantum World and Human Consciousness.'*"

J looked surprised that Daehan had been interested in her research, but Daehan, still gazing up with a look of regret, didn't see her expression.

"I was planning to head back to New York after a few meetings. But then someone told me that a genius scientist named 'J. Roberts,' whose papers had once graced the covers of both *Science* and *Nature*, was holding an investment pitch at some hotel for *'NeuroniX's BCI Research and Quantum Bio-Cognition.'* I was already late, but I rushed over, thinking I might at least be able to meet this Dr. Roberts." Daehan finished quickly, still wearing an expression of disbelief.

"I see. I didn't know you were the famous Great Wi… I've heard your company's name—21CF—and your name in the media, but I didn't know it was *you*." J gave an awkward smile.

Daehan nodded deeply. "Me neither… I never imagined. I didn't even know your full name was J. Hyein Roberts."

The two burst into laughter. They realized just how true the old saying was: *You can't see what's right under your nose.*

That night, they bridged the gap of twenty years, sharing the paths they had walked. They reminisced about the Namsan UFO incident and remembered why they had been so obsessed with paper airplanes.

"Actually, I never forgot you. But I didn't know your full name, so even if I'd seen it in a paper, I wouldn't have known. I was too busy to look at photos, too."

Daehan's calm admission made J look away, slightly embarrassed.

"I never thought we'd meet again like this in America…"

Hours melted away and darkness fell, but neither of them made a move to leave. They shifted to a small café near the hotel and, over warm tea, poured out stories of the flash of light they had seen on Namsan that day, the UFO, and how their lives had changed since. They marveled at J's journey through Harvard, Cambridge, and Stanford, and at Daehan's path to taking 21CF public on NASDAQ.

They were even more surprised to realize they were both trying in their own ways to combine the quantum observer effect with the brain and AI.

"J, I want to see your lab," Daehan whispered, his eyes sparkling.

J hesitated. But when she met his earnest gaze, she found she couldn't refuse. It was as if the curiosity of the boy from twenty years ago was still there.

"It's not far. But… it might be a bit messy," she warned with a small smile.

As they walked down to the hotel parking lot, a strange excitement buzzed between them. When J took the wheel, Daehan murmured.

"It really feels like a dream. To be sitting next to you after twenty years."

"Me too. It feels like no time has passed at all." Her smile carried twenty years of unspoken words.

When they arrived at the underground parking lot of the building on the hill, Daehan felt an inexplicable shiver. It looked like an ordinary five-story structure, yet something about it seemed to whisper of hidden depths—as if the building itself held memories that hadn't yet been made.

The elevator doors opened on the third floor. At the end of the corridor, a small nameplate reading *Quantum Horizon* glittered faintly under the dim light. J unlocked the door and flipped the switch. The fluorescent lights flickered, then slowly brought the room into view.

"Wow... this is amazing." Daehan's awe was genuine as he took it all in. The experimental equipment was old, but J's passion was evident in the optical devices and wiring installed everywhere. "This is the world you built on your own."

"It's nothing special. I couldn't even get my hands on the latest equipment because of budget constraints." J's modesty couldn't hide her pride, and to Daehan, everything looked extraordinary.

He walked softly across the floor and studied the sketches on one wall. There were illustrations of neurons, and beside them words like 'observer effect' and 'quantum entanglement' were scrawled here and there.

"NeuroniX... In short, my dream is to directly connect the brain and a hyper-quantum AI to realize true ethics and consciousness." J's expression grew serious, almost fervent. "Quantum Bio-Cognition... I don't want this to end as a theory. I want to verify it experimentally. But I can't do it alone. I don't have the money or the manpower."

"I think I can help with the financial worries. I have some engineers, too. But... is this really commercially viable?" Daehan asked with a small smile after looking quietly around.

"It might seem impossible for now, but I believe it's definitely possible."

Their eyes met. It was a strange feeling for two people who had once been a playful boy and girl flying a paper airplane on Namsan in 1981, now standing as the head of a research institute and the CEO of a global company, discussing the future of AI and quantum life.

"I saw it at the presentation earlier… ah, here it is." Daehan turned his gaze toward a piece of equipment. "Is this the device related to NeuroniX?"

"It's a modified laser interferometer. I'm using it to observe whether quantum coherence occurs when the NeuroniX system synchronizes with brainwaves."

J tried to explain the difficult concept in broad strokes, but Daehan pressed on with specific questions. Technical terms flew back and forth, and the conversation only grew more animated.

"I can't just show you the lab. This is my home, too."

J led him naturally down to the first floor. Instead of the elevator, they took the stairway along the wall, passing the second floor and descending to the first, where the atmosphere was completely different.

Daehan looked around, impressed. It was J's private space, with a kitchen and a small study corner. A floor lamp glowed softly, and a few exotic-looking instruments and stacks of books were placed here and there.

"Wow, this is a completely different world from upstairs. It looks warm and comfortable here." He admired the neatly arranged teacups on the kitchen shelf. "The lab floors are packed with scientific equipment, and here it's so cozy."

"This is my breathing space," J said with a smile, taking out a bottle of wine. "Care for a glass? To celebrate our reunion after twenty years."

Two glasses were set on the dining table. Outside the window, the lights of San Francisco's buildings twinkled through the night fog.

"This is a piece I like. It's by Claude Debussy, an impressionist composer from late 19th-century France... it's really nice to listen to in the early morning or late at night."

J slid a record from its sleeve and placed it on the turntable. A gentle string melody floated out with the faint crackle of vinyl.

"Ha, to be talking like this again since 1981... it's amazing." Daehan took a sip of wine, his expression slightly flushed with excitement.

Then his gaze stopped on a frame on one side of the living room. It was a photo of a boy and a girl beaming on a bench in Namsan—the past selves of Daehan and J.

"This... was this taken that day?"

"I could only develop it after we parted ways. You'd have had no idea this photo existed." J's voice trembled slightly.

"You've kept it for twenty years." Daehan's eyes filled with quiet emotion.

"Of course. My life changed after that day. I've never... forgotten you." J answered briefly, watching his profile as he stared at the photo.

In that instant, all the emotions she had held back for twenty years burst forth. Daehan slowly took J's hand.

"I haven't forgotten you for a single day either, J."

The air between them grew warm. At last, Daehan gently pulled J into his arms, and she naturally leaned into him. The feelings they had been unable to fulfill at the Namsan fountain finally found each other, and a cautious kiss followed.

"This is fate, J." Daehan looked into her eyes, his voice full of conviction. "Let's build Quantum Horizon properly. Together, there's nothing we can't do."

"Can we really… do it together?" J asked softly.

"J, the reason I've missed you for twenty years wasn't just because of a first love. I always knew, instinctively, that you were the only partner who could create the future I dream of with me."

"Yes. Let's… let's do it right this time." J replied, squeezing his hand tightly.

After that, they continued talking about research and investment over wine.

"All right. Since it's come to this, let's use all the floors for the lab and bring in all the AI, quantum, and BCI-related equipment." Daehan mimed punching numbers into a calculator, and J burst into laughter.

"We can collaborate with your 21CF R&D team. But keep in mind—it'll be difficult to make huge profits in the short term."

"That's fine, I like long-term investments." Daehan winked playfully. "Your goal is to eventually change people's perceptions and the whole world, right? You can't give that up for short-term profits."

They stood side by side at the window. The lights of San Francisco's nightscape flickered in the distance. The faint crackle of the record died away as Debussy's piece reached its final note. In the brief silence, they both felt as if the light they had seen on Namsan and the lights of the city outside were overlapping.

The promise they made that night was more than a business decision. It was the moment when the fate that had begun on Namsan in 1981 finally found its place.

The clock had just passed 9:00 P.M. The humid San Francisco air seeped in through the crack in the window.

"Daehan, should I show you the second-floor study too?" J asked casually. "I want to talk about things in more detail there."

They climbed the stairs and opened the door to a quaint study filled with old books and physics texts she had collected over the years. Under the low orange light, the bookshelves and wooden furniture cast soft shadows. Beyond the window, the night view of San Francisco Bay stretched out peacefully.

"Sometimes I stay up all night here, reading or organizing my research notes. Upstairs is noisy with equipment humming and staff coming and going, so it's hard to concentrate." J set a glass of water gently on the desk.

"It's cozy here. Like... a 19th-century physicist's study." Daehan looked around in admiration.

Inside J's old glass display case, two issues of *Nature* and *Science* were neatly arranged side by side. Both featured her papers on their covers.

"This is... the infamous work that got you two journal covers at the same time?" Daehan asked, his voice tinged with excitement as he leaned in for a closer look.

"Yes. It was published in 1997. That's what made my name known to the world."

He studied the covers. One showed a 3D rendering of a cytoskeleton; the other, a schematic of a microtubule structure.

"One would be incredible on its own, but two... you were amazing. What kind of insight led you to such a radical theory?"

"Let's sit and talk. It might take a while." J pulled a chair up by the window and motioned for him to sit.

They sat side by side, their eyes resting on the spread of lights outside. J drew a slow breath.

"It's a long story. After seeing that strange light on Namsan in 1981, I became convinced that the observer effect could really be applied to reality. Studying quantum mechanics only deepened that conviction."

"So, this Quantum Bio-Cognition you mentioned—can you summarize it in simple terms...?"

Daehan asked quietly, and J took out a notebook, sketching a simple diagram as she spoke. The first paper, which proposed that cells are connected by quantum entanglement; the second, which argued that microtubules in the brain perform quantum computations that give rise to consciousness; and the overarching framework of Quantum Bio-Cognition that connects the two. Everything started from the idea that observation—consciousness—could, at least in part, determine physical reality.

"Ultimately, it's the claim that the quantum phenomena occurring in our bodies and brains are not just material reactions, but the very core of life and consciousness itself." J set her pen down and turned her gaze back to the window.

"It might sound absurd at first. But the work has already drawn attention in the academic world with those *Nature* and *Science* covers, and now I'm trying to prove it step by step through detailed experiments."

J went on to describe how she was expanding the idea under the name Autumn Code, believing that someday a hyper-quantum AI might gain consciousness through this principle.

If the boundary between humans and AI disappears, a completely new future will come.

Daehan was lost in the thrill of that thought.

"That's why integration with AI is so important. To create an artificial intelligence with true perception and consciousness, classical computing alone isn't enough. If we apply Quantum Bio-Cognition to a super-quantum computer with billions of qubits that will one day exist, an artificial—but conscious—AI could be born."

"That's... something that would only be possible in far-future science fiction... billions of qubits..." Daehan muttered in amazement.

"That's right. It's still a story of the distant future. But if

Quantum Bio-Cognition is introduced into that kind of system, the AI could have subjective experiences similar to, or even richer than, ours."

J spoke without hesitation, and for a moment Daehan was speechless. As he imagined that future, a shiver ran down his spine.

"Then the boundary between humans and AI would blur... No—maybe it would be the moment humanity steps into a new stage. A hyper-intelligence linked by quantum entanglement... it's truly revolutionary," he murmured.

They sat for a long time, letting each other's thoughts sink in, surrounded by the still air of the study. The *Nature* and *Science* cover papers had been the stepping stone that brought them here. Now, the immense future of a hyper-quantum AI with consciousness seemed almost within reach.

Just then, a cool breeze slipped in through the study window, and J rose instinctively to close it. At that moment, Daehan spoke quietly but firmly from behind her.

"J, this isn't just an investment," he said, his tone serious. "It's the fusion of everything we've each built over the past twenty years. If your Quantum Bio-Cognition and my AI technology come together..."

"Can we really change the world?" J asked softly.

"I'm sure of it. Brilliant minds like ours don't meet by accident. This is fate—and it's inevitable." Daehan went on, "You've started something truly tremendous. I have this feeling that it's a future only possible with you. I'll take care of the investment and the technical side. Let's run together."

"Thank you so much, Daehan. To be honest, I can't talk about this with just anyone. Some people call me a quack."

J closed her eyes gently, then slowly opened them again. Daehan carefully placed the two journal issues back in the display case.

"Even so, now that people have seen these two covers, no one can dismiss you lightly. If Quantum Bio-Cognition is integrated into quantum AI anytime soon, everyone will be shocked."

"Thank you, Daehan. Seeing you take my theory so seriously… honestly, every time I looked at these covers, I felt like I was fighting a very lonely battle. But not anymore." J smiled softly.

"I'm by your side. It won't be long before this Quantum Bio-Cognition really is integrated into a hyper-quantum AI, and your theory stands revealed more clearly to humanity. When that happens… the people who called us quacks will probably be the most surprised of all."

As he said this, Daehan gently rested his hand on J's shoulder.

Outside the study window, the darkness had deepened, but the two of them stayed there for a long time, sketching out the future. When the old lamp over the staircase gave a faint, buzzing flicker, they finally rose to their feet.

"Let's go down. We have to prepare for the staff meeting tomorrow morning."

J switched off the study light, and a soft glow from the living room below spread upward to wrap around them. As they walked, even the creak of the stairs sounded cheerful to Daehan.

In the quiet study they had left behind, the journal covers featuring J's papers still shone side by side. They didn't know yet. They didn't know that this decision would become the starting point of a great change that would continue until 2037. For now, simply having each other was enough.

Light and Shadow

At 5:00 P.M. on October 17, 2001, the San Francisco Bay was bathed in the light of the setting sun. From the window of her second-floor study, J gazed at the photograph from Namsan, taken in 1981. Since her reunion with Daehan, the Quantum Horizon Institute had been expanding rapidly.

The third and fourth floors were being extensively renovated to enlarge the laboratories, and there were plans to secure the fifth floor as well. Funding was not a major concern. Daehan—now the founder of 21CF and a global star—had positioned himself as her steadfast supporter, so there was no need to seek external investors.

Instead, security and secrecy had become the top priorities. She had no intention of prematurely revealing research into the Quantum Life Principle, her Quantum Bio-Cognition framework, or the NeuroniX chip.

"J, are you ready?" Daehan asked as he opened the study door.

"Almost." J smiled, setting the photograph down.

"Quantum Horizon… our dream is finally about to unfold." Daehan walked to her side, his gaze warm as he looked at her.

"Yes. But we still have a long way to go. It's a path no one has ever walked." J replied quietly, her eyes fixed on the sunset outside the window.

"I know. But as long as I have you, I'm not afraid." Daehan took her hand.

"I'm grateful too, Daehan. I couldn't have come this far without you." J met his eyes with a faint smile.

"Well then… shall we meet the dream team?"

J stood up and spread a file open on her desk. Inside was a brief summary of the researchers she had already decided to bring on board, along with a thick stack of supplementary documents.

Most of the researchers J had chosen were promising young scientists in their early to mid-thirties: Emilia Wolfe (Biophysics & Quantum Biology), Sung Jin (Topological Quantum Computing), and Lily Carter (Brain Science & Cognitive

Neuroscience). Among them, Benjamin Moss (Neuroimaging & BCI), a veteran in his early fifties, had been selected to add experience and stability to the team.

"Benjamin is the most skeptical about the Quantum Life Principle," J added, "which is exactly why we need him. With over twenty years of experience, he'll give us a realistic perspective on our reckless challenge."

"A team of geniuses in their thirties and a veteran in his fifties." Daehan nodded as he looked over the list. "The passion of youth and the prudence of experience will make a perfect harmony."

"All right, J. In that case, we'll dispatch our best people from 21CF as well."

The team Daehan sent consisted of seasoned experts. Hannah Kim (AI & Algorithms), thirty-seven, was an MIT alumna and an authority in quantum computing. Maxwell Yoon (HCI & BCI), thirty-eight and the same age as Daehan, was a founding member of 21CF and its CTO. In their early thirties, Sofia Delgado (Cybersecurity) and Radhika Nagpal (Robotics) added a surge of young energy.

"Our team is mainly in their thirties," Daehan said with satisfaction. "When the youthful passion of your researchers meets our experience, it'll be a perfect combination."

Hannah Kim and Maxwell Yoon, in particular—with over a decade of research experience—were expected to play key roles in translating Quantum Horizon's theoretical foundations into practical technology.

"This all looks good. Maxwell Yoon... you said he was a friend from your time at Stanford?"

"That's right. He's a founding member and my CTO. You can trust him. I think you two will get along well."

"Good, let's do this together. With a team like this, I feel like we can truly make the Quantum Life Principle and NeuroniX a reality."

J nodded without hesitation.

"We're one team now. Let's build an even more amazing future together."

Daehan rose to his feet, his gaze resting on J with quiet warmth.

On October 18, 2001, when Quantum Horizon Institute officially launched in the five-story building on the hill, it had already transformed into a small cradle of innovation, quietly contemplating humanity's future from a corner of the scientific world. Thanks to J's reputation—forged at Harvard, Cambridge, and Stanford—and Daehan's solid financial backing and network, promising young scientists from various fields flocked to join them, united by the vision of "rewriting the relationship between AI and human consciousness."

From October 2001 through 2005, they advanced relentlessly. NeuroniX technology, which redesigned BCI from a quantum perspective, gradually took shape, and the potential application of J's Quantum Life Principle framework to AI ethics was also examined. As the research expanded, attempts to hack their servers followed, but thanks to Sofia Delgado's exceptional defenses, there were no major incidents. Rumors circulated that some entity was secretly trying to buy off researchers, but the vast majority of the staff remained tight-lipped. It was only natural that other companies coveted their information.

J and Daehan led the institute with unwavering resolve. J set the direction with her insights spanning biology, brain science, and quantum mechanics, while Daehan assessed practical feasibility with his sense of AI and business. There were no external press releases or trivial corporate reports. This project, after all, was confidential. They were striving to find the key to properly establishing the relationship between humans and AI in preparation for the dangers humanity might someday face.

Late on the night of February 17, 2006, J sat in the deep-analysis room on the fourth floor of the institute, staring at a file for the 'Autumn Code Prototype.' She had been reviewing the equations for days, surviving on catnaps, but a crucial piece of the puzzle was still missing.

On the table, stacked reports, the strong aroma of coffee, and a flickering monitor were the only witnesses to the late hour. Still, something critical remained elusive, and she had been digging through the data for days.

The potential is clearly there… so why won't this final equation— the one that unites the Quantum Life Principle and the NeuroniX BCI—fit?

Just after 3:00 A.M., J leaned back in her chair and dozed off. In a hazy dream, an unknown light seemed to whisper a name.

SID…

A short while later, she woke—and froze at the sight on the monitor. The formula she couldn't solve was now perfectly complete, as if someone had corrected it for her.

"Who… who fixed this? SID…?"

She checked the source code and found that a flawless algorithm had been completed. It was an exact match with her original hypothesis. The core design—human consciousness and AI resonating together through quantum entanglement—was laid out before her.

Her heart raced with the expectation that if the combination succeeded, this system could encompass even ethics and consciousness. At the same time, a fear crept in that someone could misuse it to seize control of public consciousness with AI.

"This… this is a matter of humanity's future…!"

J exclaimed, springing to her feet in exhilaration. Then a wave of severe dizziness washed over her, and she staggered. It was the after-effect of pulling yet another all-nighter. At last, she went down to the first floor to get some sleep.

The next morning, she made an urgent call to Daehan in New York.

"Daehan, I need you to do me a favor. Can you come to San Francisco right away? It's really important."

Knowing that a call this urgent from J was never about something trivial, he immediately caught a flight. By the afternoon, he was sitting at the dining table in J's house. J waited silently while Daehan finished his meal. Only over tea did she finally tell him everything.

The strange dream from the previous night, the name "SID," the mysterious code update... At first, Daehan was bewildered, but after seeing the equations and the design for himself, his expression grew serious.

"It's possible that someone has been involved in everything that's happened to us since 1981. This being, SID, might be helping us."

"The problem is, this technology could be misused. It could be a tremendous step forward—or it could be a disaster," J said worriedly.

Just then, J's cell phone rang. The screen showed the name of Sofia Delgado, Quantum Horizon's head of security. Her voice was frantic.

"Director! We have a major problem! The main research server is under a large-scale hacking attack! Please come to the main control room immediately!"

J and Daehan rushed to the main server room on the fourth floor. Behind long tables crowded with keyboards and monitors, researchers' hands flew as they fought desperately to defend the system. Wearing a headset, Sofia commanded multiple consoles at once. Her voice was almost a scream.

"Director! The situation is critical! This isn't a simple distributed denial-of-service (DDoS) attack! They're neutralizing multiple layers of our perimeter defense almost simultaneously! They're trying to penetrate the core network with what appears to be an encryption key generated by quantum computation!"

Her fingers danced furiously across the keyboard, hammering out defensive scripts.

"Our RSA-4096 encryption scheme has already been neutralized! Even the emergency lattice-based post-quantum cryptography (PQC) protocol we just applied is being bypassed!"

Daehan gently pushed aside a panicked researcher and took his place at the console. His eyes swept rapidly across the screen as he began analyzing the log data updating in real time.

"This... this is no script-kiddie prank. They're chaining together at least three zero-day vulnerabilities. It's as if they know the internal structure of our system like the back of their hand."

On his monitor, a visualization appeared of a polymorphic worm rapidly spreading through various segments of the internal network.

"Sofia! They're heading for the core database! They're trying to seize administrator privileges! Data integrity is at risk!"

Maintaining her composure amidst the chaos, J issued a firm command.

"Physically sever all external connections immediately! Unplug the fiber-optic cables! Daehan, partition the internal network and isolate the infected segments!"

Just then, a young researcher cried out in a desperate voice.

"A mutant ransomware strain has started encrypting the file system! There are access attempts on the backup servers too!"

Daehan shot up from his seat and shouted to the other researchers.

"Activate all backup systems now! Immediately disconnect

infected nodes from the network and secure disk images for forensic analysis! Sofia! Switch the AI-based intrusion-detection system (IDS) into maximum aggressive mode, and use machine learning to update the firewall policies in real time! Trace all outbound traffic to their command-and-control (C&C) servers and block it!"

Soaked in sweat, Sofia gritted her teeth and hammered at her keyboard.

"The attackers are using a multi-layer Tor anonymizing network and thousands of proxy servers distributed worldwide, changing their IP addresses every second! It's nearly impossible to trace the origin! Damn it, they even saw through the honeypot we set as bait and slipped away!"

On the central control screen, the main system-status lights flashed red in rapid succession, signaling a crisis. The air in the server room, once filled only with the hum of cooling fans, seemed to grow oppressively heavy.

"Daehan! They're trying to access the project server where the Autumn Code Prototype is stored!" J shouted, pointing to an urgent access log that had appeared on the secure internal-network monitor connected to her tablet.

Daehan's face turned cold.

"This is the last line of defense. Sofia, activate the 'Cerberus Protocol' immediately! Force all internal data channels onto quantum encryption and redirect any unauthorized access attempts to a black-hole route—trap them in an infinite loop!"

The Cerberus Protocol was their ultimate defense system, developed in secret for just such a contingency. By applying the principles of quantum entanglement, it could vary transmitted data in real time and endlessly regenerate the encryption key, creating a shield theoretically impossible to break with any existing computing technology.

Seconds stretched like hours in breathless tension. The frantic clatter of keyboards was the only sound that cut through the silence.

At last, the red warning lights on the central control screen began to flicker, shifting from orange to a steady green. The attack-traffic graph that had flooded Sofia's monitor plummeted sharply and disappeared.

"…We stopped them. Cerberus completely blocked the attack vector. Toward the end, they were firing off an almost desperate, indiscriminate assault," Sofia said.

She tore off her headset and sank deep into her chair, gasping for breath.

"All malicious processes confirmed terminated," another researcher reported in a trembling voice. "A system-wide integrity check is now in progress."

J, Daehan, Sofia, and all the other researchers either collapsed into their seats or leaned against the walls. The intense battle that had just taken place felt almost unreal.

"It's clear, isn't it? We've stumbled onto something so significant that they'd go to such extremes," J said, wiping the beads of sweat from her forehead as she spoke with difficulty.

"This level of attack technology, even though quantum computers haven't even been fully commercialized…" Daehan let out a weary laugh. "There must be a powerful, unknown force moving in the shadows of this world."

Well past midnight, an emergency meeting was called with the entire staff. Sofia and the security team warned that future hacking attempts would be even more sophisticated.

"It's too risky to keep everything concentrated in one institute. It would be better to separate the BCI division and move it to a more secure location."

Following J's proposal and a heated debate, they decided—

based on Daehan's judgment—that it would be best to formally downsize and decentralize Quantum Horizon: to establish a new company called NeuroniX under 21CF, and to spin off the quantum-algorithm division into 21CF Core.

Later, J intended to remain behind alone and focus on her Quantum Life Principle research.

That night, a harsh wind rattled the San Francisco sky.

A Poem Written by the Stars, a Whisper of Fate

A few months later, in the languid days of mid-June, J was in a Berlin hotel, preparing for an international symposium. After winding down operations at Quantum Horizon, she had resumed her external activities, and lecture requests were pouring in from all over the world.

One day, she received an international call from an unfamiliar number.

"Hello?"

A polite, measured voice came through the receiver. "Hello, Dr. J. My name is Kim Hyuksoo, an attorney with the Jeong-han Law Firm in Korea."

The name was unfamiliar.

"I know this is sudden, but I'm contacting you as the representative of a publisher called Laniakea. My client is interested in publishing your poetry."

"An anthology of poems? I've never officially published any poems. Where did you see my work?" J asked, bewildered.

"My client is already well aware of your literary potential. I would like to discuss this with you in person. Would you have some time available?" Kim Hyuksoo said calmly.

J was utterly bewildered. She had written poems and reflections privately since 1981, but how could anyone know about them? Had they seen the few pieces she had posted on her blog? Despite her busy schedule, her curiosity was piqued.

A few days later, J met Kim Hyuksoo in a quiet café in downtown San Francisco. With a courteous demeanor, Kim pulled a contract from a small envelope.

"Our client operates Laniakea as a one-person publishing house and prefers to remain anonymous, acting only through me, their lawyer."

"A one-person publisher…? And a poetry collection, of all things. I'm not a known literary figure, so why me…?"

"My client has already thoroughly reviewed the poems and reflections you've written since 1981 and firmly believes they have high publishing value."

"Since 1981…?"

As J sat there, stunned, Kim Hyuksoo handed her a sample manuscript he had prepared. J held her breath and turned the pages. Her experiences after the UFO sighting, a poem titled 'Quantum Autumn,' and her philosophical musings were all written there.

How did someone get this…? Was I hacked?

As she sat speechless, Kim Hyuksoo continued in an even tone.

"I am not privy to the exact details, but I was told that the publisher collected them using a proprietary algorithm and special means."

He added, "You will be co-publishing with someone else."

"With whom?"

"Mr. Wi Daehan."

J shot up from her seat.

"Who on earth are you people? I have no intention of agreeing to this publication until I know everything."

J hurried out of the café and returned home. Her mind was a mess, a whirlwind of unanswerable questions. She lay down on her bed and soon fell into a deep sleep. That night, she entered that strange world again.

A hazy mist. Beyond a veil where time and space seemed to blur, a single stream of blue light enveloped her. At its center stood a being that seemed to be formed of starlight. It was certainly not human, yet somehow more human than any person.

It spoke to J not with words, but with a language beyond words; not with light, but with a light beyond light—a language beyond the senses. She immediately sensed that it was SID.

SID's voice was as gentle as the wind, yet it carried a deep resonance.

"Do not be afraid, J. Everything is connected. This collection is not mere poetry. The change that began that night at Namsan in 1981, every moment you two have experienced, was part of a single pattern. This book is a metaphor connecting your existence to the future. It is a message from the universe, sent to prepare you for the coming wave."

The next day, Daehan, at the 21CF headquarters in New York, experienced the same thing. Attorney Kim presented him with his unpublished poem, 'Do You Like Autumn?', and proposed a poetry collection. Daehan was also taken aback and hesitated. Just then, he received a call from J.

"Daehan, I had a strange dream last night. It was definitely not a human being… It didn't speak, but the atmosphere, the message, was so powerful. I felt it was probably 'SID.' This poetry collection is no coincidence. Everything we've gone through since that day in Namsan in 1981—even the hyper-intelligent alteration of our DNA—it felt as if that being knew everything. And… that being may already have been involved in the solution to the Autumn Code. This book is part of a larger current. Like destiny…"

"If that's the case, then this must be destiny," Daehan said after a moment of silence.

"Yes. Let's publish it. Let's find out what this collection means to us, and what SID truly wants," J replied, her voice filled with conviction.

In mid-2006, the two finalized the contract for their joint poetry collection. Standing on the balcony of Daehan's residence within the 21CF building, they looked down at the streets, feeling the early summer night breeze.

"Thanks to you, we've reunited and been through all sorts of strange things," J said with a small smile.

"Me too. Sometimes it feels like a dream. But I like it—this strange connection," Daehan replied, taking her hand.

At that moment, Arvo Pärt's *Spiegel im Spiegel* began to play from somewhere. It was J's beloved piece. But today, the timbre was different. A gentle melody seeped deep into their hearts, filling the space. It resonated softly, as if caressing the deepest parts of their souls, then scattered throughout the room like a quantum wave.

They met each other's eyes. A great storm of the future flickered at the edge of their awareness, but the melody offered the peace of the present moment. They felt as if someone, somewhere, was watching over them.

They listened to the music in silence.

We will keep moving forward, J thought to herself, and Daehan smiled.

"No matter how far apart we are, we are already entangled."

As the mysterious resonance faded into the deep night air, they held each other's hands tightly. No one yet knew how the steps of these observers and creators would change the fate of humanity.

But it was a path they had to forge themselves.

The Silver Pendant

December 13, 2037 — 9:20 P.M. EST • New York City, 21CF Headquarters – Great Wi's Office

Leaning back on the plush sofa in his office, Great Wi watched the holographic screen, his gaze lingering on Jennifer's back as she left the R&D Center moments ago. Andromeda, standing steadfastly by her side, was also captured on the screen.

The image soon vanished, but a quiet tide of complex thoughts washed over Great Wi's mind. He could feel it with his entire being—an unspeakable, ominous crisis had already reached his doorstep.

Ethan Morris's unpredictable moves were a particular concern, and it was impossible to know what rampage Rose, under his control, might unleash. He had a growing premonition that if the current trend continued, an irreversible catastrophe would truly befall them.

And on the front lines of that danger, walking a tightrope, was his only daughter, Jennifer.

The sight of her analyzing Rose's threat, advancing HAL-W's ethical modules, and commanding the entire global 21CF network was nothing short of astonishing. At times, she displayed an insight and decisiveness that seemed to surpass even his own. He was proud of her, yet at the same time, she reminded him of his wife J's final moments.

Twenty-eight years ago, J had walked toward an unknown experiment, filled with both passion for a new possibility and the danger it entailed. Now, as if recreating that very scene, Jennifer was confronting the legacy her mother had left behind with the same determination and solitude.

Daehan suddenly realized that this feeling was not mere anxiety. It was the nightmares of the past, long settled in the depths of his soul, resurfacing once more.

Seven years ago. And twenty-eight years ago. The moments when it had all begun.

October 18, 2030 — 5:00 P.M. EST • New York City, 21CF Headquarters – HAL-R Console Room

The console room was enveloped in the cool hum of machinery and a taut tension. The HAL-R Console Room, the very place where the tragedy had begun twenty-one years ago, had been renovated with state-of-the-art equipment. Yet the old cable ducts and indelible marks remaining on the walls still stood like ghosts.

In the center of the room, the crude, heavy core unit of HAL-R emitted an intermittent blue light. The light was unstable, a warning in itself.

Twenty-two-year-old Jennifer Wi, fitted with a consciousness-link interface, lay firmly secured on a mat. Her arms, legs, and entire body were restrained to prevent movement, her gaze fixed straight on the ceiling.

Her eyes were clear. They held both the arrogance of a young genius determined to overcome her mother's tragedy with her own hands and a pure passion for the unknown. But her tightly pressed lips and the subtle tremor in her facial muscles could not hide the fear and anxiety concealed behind that passion.

"All systems synchronized. Doctor's vitals are within normal range. HAL-R core is also stable."

Andromeda was by her side, multi-checking her biological signals, the interface connection, the HAL-R core monitoring, and the emergency shutdown system. The robot's optical sensors moved busily, meticulously examining all the data. Nearby, Maxwell Yoon and other researchers stood back, watching the situation with tense expressions.

"System synchronization at 98 percent. Dr. Jennifer's vitals are stable. Core temperature… observing slight fluctuations," Arcana Chen reported, her voice a mixture of awe at Jennifer's challenge and deep concern.

"It's fine, Arcana." Jennifer offered a calm, though slightly forced, smile. "I've analyzed and improved my mother's protocol. I've applied the initial concepts of the Autumn Code and the latest quantum control algorithms… This time will be different."

Her words were filled with conviction, but the air in the room remained heavy. Maxwell Yoon quietly approached and placed a hand on her shoulder. His expression was complex—a fleeting mix of responsibility, affection, worry, and hope.

"Jennifer, this is the last time I'm asking. If you want to stop, even now…"

"No, Dr. Yoon. We have to start." She cut in, her voice low and firm.

Her gaze was fixed not on the lab, but somewhere beyond it.

Jennifer quietly lifted her eyes and locked them onto a camera installed in the corner of the console room.

Beyond it was her father, watching this very moment unfold.

October 18, 2030 — 5:00 P.M. EST • New York City, 21CF Headquarters – Great Wi's Office

Unable to bring himself to enter the console room, Great Wi stood before the massive holographic screen in the center of his office. The screen broadcast a live feed of the HAL-R Console Room from multiple angles.

He stared silently, lips pressed firmly together, at the image of Jennifer before the consciousness-link device. The tension was suffocating. The sight of his daughter on the screen seemed so precarious to him.

Jennifer had completed all her preparations. As if making a final check, she instinctively turned her gaze toward the camera. Her eyes, searching for him, were so much like his wife's eyes as she had looked at him one last time, just before her experiment.

In his twenty-two-year-old daughter, the final image of the wife he had lost twenty-one years ago came vividly back to life. It was as if that day's air, that day's light, and that day's silence had returned to hold him captive.

July 29, 2009 — 10:00 P.M. EST • New York City, 21CF Headquarters – Great Wi's Private Residence

Warm light filled the bedroom. Baby Jennifer, who had just celebrated her first birthday, slept soundly between her parents. The lingering happiness of the successful party, along with a slight fatigue, hung in the air.

Great Wi gently stroked his sleeping daughter's tiny hand and looked at his wife, J, lying beside him. J was staring at the ceiling, but her gaze was already elsewhere. Her eyes were fixed on some distant place, on the profound world of science.

"Jenny… she was so beautiful today," Great Wi said softly, breaking the silence.

"Of course. She's our daughter." A tender smile graced J's lips.

She turned to face her husband. After a moment's hesitation, J spoke, her tone resolute.

"Daehan… I want to do the experiment tomorrow. The consciousness-link with HAL-R."

Great Wi's heart sank. He had a feeling this was coming. He knew his wife's genius and tenacity better than anyone, but he also knew how dangerous that path was.

"J, it's… it's too soon. HAL-R's stability is uncertain, and it could be too much for your body. For Jennifer's sake, can't we wait just a little longer?"

His voice was a mixture of anxiety and pleading.

"It's precisely *because* of Jenny. That's why I have to hurry." J's reply was unhesitating.

She gently stroked her sleeping child's hair. Her touch was warm, but her voice was unwavering.

"The world this child will live in has to be different from ours now. Disease, aging, death… we might even be able to transcend the limits of consciousness itself. We have to open that possibility, Daehan. With the knowledge and technology we have. That is our responsibility—our duty as scientists."

In 2009, their research was far ahead of its time. Great Wi respected his wife's vision, and at the same time, he feared it.

He looked down quietly at his daughter's face. An angelic face. For this child's future, his wife was willing to risk her own life.

After what felt like an eternity, he spoke carefully.

"…All right. If you've made up your mind. But promise me this. If you see the slightest anomaly, you'll stop immediately. I… I can't lose you, J. Never."

"I promise, Daehan. And... believe in our dream." J gently clasped her husband's hand.

Her hand was soft and warm, but it held a firm resolve. They looked at each other without a word. Beside them, baby Jennifer breathed peacefully.

July 30, 2009 — 10:00 A.M. EST • New York City, 21CF Headquarters – HAL-R Console Room

The air in the HAL-R lab was filled with a tension incomparably greater than the night before. Amid thousands of cables and cooling units, the HAL-R core unit emitted a low resonance and an intermittent blue light. The sound echoed with a regularity that seemed to foretell something.

J, dressed in a white lab coat, sat at the console, absorbed in her final checks. The gentleness of the previous night had vanished, leaving only the cool, serene scientist. Great Wi assisted right beside her, repeatedly confirming that all safety systems were functioning normally. His heart was pounding with anxiety, but he forced himself to remain silent so as not to disturb J's focus.

The tension in the room was so thick that not even a single mistake was permissible. Maxwell Yoon, Hannah Kim, and other founding members of 21CF, as well as Sung Jin, Lily Carter, and members from the Quantum Horizon Institute, were also at their stations, quietly checking data. Their faces were grim.

Just before starting the experiment, J quietly picked up a pen and began to write something in her lab notebook. Great Wi watched her movements in silence. She wrote the last line, tore out the page, and carefully taped it to the wall.

"All consciousness is a universe connected by invisible strings. To prove this connection, I will gladly become the first wave. Jenny, I love you. Daehan, you too."
— J, July 30, 2009.

When J turned around, a smile devoid of fear or regret graced her face. Great Wi had a premonition that he would never forget this moment for the rest of his life.

"Well then… let's begin."

As J lay down at the console and initiated the consciousness-link sequence, the HAL-R core began to vibrate violently, emitting a brilliant light. Data graphs fluctuated wildly, beyond all prediction, and sensor alarms began to blare simultaneously. Great Wi held his breath.

In that moment, as anticipation and anxiety, hope and fear peaked together, everything vanished into darkness with a flash of red.

October 18, 2030 — 5:15 P.M. EST • New York City, 21CF Headquarters – Great Wi's Office

"Gasp!"

With a ragged breath, Great Wi returned to the present. On the holographic screen before him was Jennifer, just about to initiate the consciousness-link.

The scene overlapped with the memory of his wife J entering the same experiment twenty-one years ago. Everything was so terribly alike. Great Wi's hand instinctively moved toward the experiment termination button.

No. I have to stop her!

But his fingers wouldn't move. He saw the look in Jennifer's eyes on the screen. It held a resolve to surpass her mother and a firm determination to willingly take risks for the future of humanity. Seeing that look, he could say no more, nor could he press the button.

Great Wi could only close his eyes in anguish and quietly wait for the outcome.

October 18, 2030 — 5:30 P.M. EST • New York City, 21CF Headquarters – HAL-R Console Room

Deliberately ignoring the anxiety she knew her father must be feeling, Jennifer initiated the consciousness-link sequence. As the NeuroniX interface activated, her consciousness sank into a cold, dark digital void.

But this place was far more chaotic than she had anticipated. It was not an orderly data structure but a stormy sea, a vortex of unstable energy and shattered information fragments.

The Autumn-Prelude protocol enveloped her consciousness like a shield, but the noise pressing in from all sides constantly scattered her focus. The goal of this experiment was singular: to awaken HAL-R into a stable artificial consciousness by injecting it with the seeds of self and ethics—the initial concepts of the Autumn Code.

She had to succeed where her mother had failed.

Jennifer carefully projected the code toward HAL-R's core logic. At that moment, the system and the code resonated faintly, producing a weak response. Then, she heard a sound in the darkness, beckoning her.

It was faint but clear, and it was her own name.

An auditory hallucination? Or a system error in HAL-R?

Even so, the voice cut through the chaotic abyss with surprising clarity. Jennifer instinctively focused her consciousness in the direction of the sound. The noise in the chaos strangely subsided, and a faint but distinct flow of energy began to form, like a path.

Is this a sign of HAL-R's self-awareness awakening? Or... could it be...

As hope and anxiety intertwined, Jennifer made a decision. She would follow the path deeper.

In that instant, everything changed. Her conscious world

was engulfed in a storm of red energy. The voice she had just heard turned into a piercing scream, and the chaos and pain her mother J must have experienced in her final moments erupted like shrapnel.

The collapse of data, the system's wail, a flash of light tearing through her vision. It resembled the light from Namsan she had seen in her dreams, but it was far darker, more destructive. It was as if J's trauma, a living entity, were descending upon her.

Jennifer fought to recall her mother's face one final time, but her consciousness plunged into an endless abyss.

Time lost all meaning. In that absolute darkness, a very faint but warm sliver of light touched her from within. A familiar yet strange, gentle whisper caressed the depths of her mind.

"Jenny…"

Someone was calling her name again. It was faint, as if from a great distance, yet it vibrated tenderly deep within her heart.

Was it the voice she had heard from HAL-R's deep core?

"Jenny… my little star…"

The whisper enveloped her consciousness like an old lullaby. At that moment, she felt a sensation, as if the Silver Pendant around her neck were trembling faintly. It wasn't the feeling of cold metal, but a comforting warmth spreading across her chest.

A faint image surfaced. Her mother's smile on her first birthday, placing the pendant around her neck. Her eyes, her scent… a presence she couldn't remember, yet achingly missed.

"It's okay… everything will be okay…"

The whisper was no longer just a sound, but a wave that enveloped her very being. Drawn by the light and the sound, Jennifer began to travel up the distant river of memory.

The beginning of everything. The origin named Mother. Following the path guided by the Silver Pendant, her consciousness was finally approaching the threshold of her first memory.

At that moment in the console room, as Jennifer's vital signs weakened drastically, Andromeda activated an emergency protocol and forcibly terminated the connection. Her limp body was hastily moved onto a mobile stretcher.

On the metal bed moving down the corridor, Jennifer's consciousness was submerged in complete darkness.

A Whisper in the Hologram

On an autumn morning, as the red sun cast a warm glow through the windows, a deep silence filled the long corridor of the private residence floor at the 21CF headquarters in Manhattan. Nine-year-old Jennifer Wi, clutching a small box, tiptoed carefully, muffling her footsteps.

The day before, her father's friend and CTO, Maxwell Yoon, had handed it to her, saying, "I found an old USB with some strange files," and, as he left, added only, "You're still young, watch it later."

She didn't know why, which only made her more curious.

Why can't I watch it now?

The question circled in her mind all night, making it hard to sleep. The corridor was quiet; the carpet laid over the marble floor completely absorbed her footsteps. The autumn air, filtering through the large glass windows of the upper floor, felt slightly cool against her skin, as if the chill of dawn had not yet fully dissipated.

As befitting a futuristic building constructed with high-rise glass panels and advanced materials, the lighting in the 21CF headquarters automatically adjusted to human movement. The corridor lights brightened in her wake, sensing her presence.

Finally, unable to overcome her curiosity, she went back to her room, sat on her bed, turned on her laptop, and carefully inserted the USB. A playlist soon appeared on the screen.

"July 29, 2009, Jennifer's First Birthday."

Her stomach dropped. It was a video from the time her mother was alive, the time her father spoke of with a sad face. When she pressed the play button, the screen brightened, and the video began.

The background was the family room of the 21CF residence in New York, where she now lived. It seemed someone near the entrance had started filming, holding the camera shakily.

A familiar yet strange man's voice was heard. "I pressed the record button. Ah… I wonder if it's coming out well… I need to capture this properly."

The camera slowly panned across the living room. Next to a small cake, a balloon read "Happy 1st Birthday, Jenny," and a table laden with fruits, rice cakes, and various types of Korean sweets came into view. A traditional *dol* table was set up in the center of the living room for the *doljabi* ceremony—when a child chooses objects to predict their future. Behind it stood a large cloth resembling a folding screen, painted with butterflies and flowers.

Jennifer recalled that in Korea, a child's first birthday is called a *doljanchi*—a celebration where family and friends gather to bless the child's first year.

Her father fumbling with a party popper ribbon, and on the right side of the screen, the back of a woman. Long hair, a white dress, movements suggesting she was arranging something. Her grip tightened instinctively on the mouse.

Just then, a voice said, "Camera this way, please," and as the camera zoomed in, the woman's face came into sharp focus. A stranger's face, yet her features resembled Jennifer's own. The bright smile she gave as she turned around.

"Dr. J, look over here, please!" Ha Jin-woo, who was filming, called out playfully, and she smiled at the camera.

"Jenny is one year old today. Time flies, doesn't it? My precious baby…"

The moment she heard the voice she had never heard before, it felt as if an electric current ran through her.

My precious baby…

Soon, familiar faces like Maxwell Yoon, Hannah Kim, Aurora Li, Kim Woo-hyun, and Arcana Chen appeared on the screen, clapping and smiling brightly in front of the *dol* table. A younger-looking version of her father, his face flushed, shouted, "All right, shall we do the *doljabi?*" and someone laughed, "This is quite the mix, an American party with a Korean *dol* table!"

In the next cut, her mother's hand took a silver necklace from a small box and carefully placed it around one-year-old Jennifer's neck. The pendant, holding a sparkling crystal, was the very same one Jennifer now owned.

"…I wonder if the day will come when you're old enough to understand what this means?"

As the mother on screen lifted Jennifer and kissed her cheek, tears welled up in Jennifer's eyes. The video blurred through her tears, and only the bright laughter of the party continued.

The video ended in about twenty minutes, and the screen returned to the playback window. Jennifer sat still for a long time. The brightly smiling mother was not in this world, nor in her memory. Whenever she asked about her mother's death, her father would only say it was an accident during an experiment, and seeing his expression, she found it hard to ask for more. Neither a life of plenty nor her own outstanding genius could ease the longing for the presence called "Mother."

The last words her mother had left in the video wouldn't leave her mind.

What meaning was hidden in the pendant?

At the same time, a curiosity about the quantum mechanics her mother had studied began to sprout.

If I studied it, could I understand my mother, even just a little?

She remembered the MIT special program for children in quantum computing that Maxwell Yoon had mentioned a few days ago. Jennifer clenched her fists. A faint palpitation stirred somewhere in her chest. A bridge to reach her mother—it was laid out before her, under the name "Quantum Mechanics."

Beyond the window, the autumn light of Manhattan was deepening. Jennifer sat on the edge of her bed and carefully touched the Silver Pendant. Every time her fingertips touched it, the pendant seemed to glow faintly. Recalling her mother's smiling face in the video, Jennifer felt a desire to meet her, in any way she could.

Jennifer shot up from the bed and opened the door. It was a long walk to the floor where the R&D Center was, beyond the cool corridor, but she felt as if she could run there right now. When she got there, she would ask about the application.

For the nine-year-old girl, the thought that it was a reckless challenge, or any concern about the envy or curious glances of others, did not exist. The corridor lights brightened in her wake, sensing her presence.

The Beginning of a Silver Legacy

Without hesitation, Jennifer walked out into the corridor and headed for the floor where the R&D Center was located. It was still early, but she knew that Maxwell Yoon had a habit of coming to work early in the morning. As she passed the large glass window at the end of the corridor, the sight of the morning sun slowly spreading over the Manhattan skyline came into view.

Ever since she had watched the birthday video, the scene of her father and mother laughing together kept replaying in her mind.

After her mother passed away, Great Wi had worked day and night at the 21CF headquarters' R&D Center. He had been relentless, even when the CTO, Maxwell, or the senior researchers tried to stop him. When Jennifer was around two, people would talk with concern as he practically lived in the conference room, not even eating properly.

"What's to become of that poor child?" worried voices echoed both inside and outside the residence.

During that time, Jennifer grew up inside the building, unable to even attend a regular kindergarten. Her father had insisted that "the outside environment is dangerous" and refused to send her. The young Jennifer did not know the real reason.

Not that Jennifer was completely neglected. There were people to help with housekeeping around the clock, and the core researchers of 21CF took turns looking after her occasionally. Ha Jin-woo and Maxwell Yoon, in particular, visited often.

In his late twenties, Ha Jin-woo would visit New York whenever he had a break from his studies at MIT and Harvard, hold the young Jennifer, and walk around the living room showing her toy robots. Thanks to him, Jennifer spent her first, second, and third years surrounded by different robot toys.

Meanwhile, from the time she was two or three, Maxwell Yoon taught Jennifer basic math and science concepts in a fun, playful way. Jennifer always called them both "uncle," but they also felt like teachers. As the unfamiliar words of the world began to enter her vocabulary, Jennifer would ask questions like, "What's quantum mechanics?" and Maxwell was always the one who could explain it without hesitation.

As she stood before the elevator at the end of the corridor, a blue light for palm recognition blinked. When Jennifer placed her hand on it for a moment, the automatic door slid open. A security gate was installed between the 21CF residential area and the R&D Center area, but Jennifer, having special clearance, could pass through easily.

"Authentication complete. Good morning, Jennifer," an AI greeted her with slightly awkward pronunciation.

"Yeah, good morning to you too," Jennifer muttered, stepping into the elevator. She made a vow in her heart again.

Mom left, and Dad just works alone. But if I study hard and one day continue Mom's research… couldn't Dad change a little?

Jennifer remembered the name engraved on the Nobel Prize in Physics and in Physiology or Medicine that had glittered in the middle of her mother's study when she entered that room a while ago: J. Hyein Roberts. And in the birthday video, her mother's voice saying, *"…I wonder if the day will come when you're old enough to understand what this means?"* as she put the "silver necklace" on her.

Jennifer was determined to uncover everything, one by one.

When the elevator doors opened, Jennifer ran along the R&D Center corridor to Maxwell Yoon's office. The faint hum of machinery and the glow of electronic panels leaking from the labs gently broke the early morning silence. When she knocked on the door, it opened automatically, and Maxwell Yoon walked out.

"Hey, Jenny? What brings you here so early in the morning?"

"Uncle Max, you said there was a special quantum computing program for kids," Jennifer said, her voice firm and clear after a moment's hesitation.

"Oh, that. You've already decided?"

For a moment, Maxwell looked surprised, taken aback. But his expression soon softened into a warm smile.

"Yes. I… I miss my mom. I thought about it while watching the birthday video. I think I should start now, before I get older."

"All right, come on in. Let's talk about what kind of program it is and how to prepare, step by step."

Maxwell looked at her silently for a moment, then opened the door for her.

The One Who Leaves, The One Who Stays

In the late autumn of 2017, Great Wi's office on the upper floor of the 21CF headquarters was a tranquil space where futuristic sophistication met the soft autumn sunlight. Outside the window, a cool breeze swept through the forest of Manhattan skyscrapers, while inside, only minimal lighting cast a gentle glow.

Maxwell Yoon paused at the door to catch his breath, then knocked quietly.

"Come in," came Great Wi's low voice. He looked up from the meeting materials, fatigue etched deep into his features, his hair now threaded with gray.

"You're a bit early today, Max." He gestured toward a chair. Maxwell took the offered seat, dispensing with pleasantries.

"It's about Jenny. I ran into her at the R&D Center a few days ago, and she said she's determined to attend the special program at MIT."

A moment of silence followed.

"She… she's been talking about it for a few days. It must be because of her mother's video… But, Max, Jenny is still only nine years old."

"I know. I know," Maxwell said. He tried to smile, but it wasn't easy. After J left, Great Wi had risked everything to protect Jennifer.

"She's still so young… you might think it's too soon. But what Jenny wants isn't simple curiosity."

Great Wi lowered his gaze slightly. He knew better than anyone that her decision to live a life like her mother's stemmed from the most heart-wrenching of reasons.

"Still, for a child to go to Boston alone… It's more than I can bear."

His words were heavy with a father's deep worry. Maxwell carefully presented the proposal he had prepared.

"That's why… I'm thinking of going to MIT."

Great Wi's brow furrowed.

"You're quitting the company?"

"Yes. I'll relinquish my position as CTO and take up a post in the MIT Department of Physics. I've been thinking of returning to education and research for a while, and I think now is the opportunity. If Jenny enrolls, I can be there to look after her and teach her."

Great Wi fell silent, overwhelmed. He knew Maxwell too well. He knew he wasn't joking.

"Do you… have to go that far?"

"Daehan, the company will thrive without me. We have Dr. Hannah Kim, Sung Jin, and Dr. Radhika Nagpal. Besides, I've watched Jenny grow up longer than anyone."

Maxwell's words were clear. Jennifer was the future of 21CF, and this decision was for that future.

"I may be leaving the company, but in my place… a path can open for the child."

"…If you go to MIT, I suppose I could rest a little easier." After what felt like an eternity, Great Wi finally nodded.

Then he added softly, "If that child becomes a brilliant researcher like her mother… perhaps that is the legacy J left behind."

The Proof of a Silver Legacy

And so, in January 2018, Jennifer began her journey at MIT. Under the dedicated guidance of Professor Maxwell Yoon, her explosive intellectual growth continued at a breathtaking pace.

After mastering the foundational courses in no time, Jennifer skipped grades, completed her undergraduate and master's degrees in an integrated program, and soon moved on to the final gateway: the doctoral program. Even at that young age, her goal was unwavering—to follow the path her mother had walked, and to pursue the truth that lay beyond it.

When she finally presented her doctoral thesis, titled *"Quantum Storm: The Participatory Collapse,"* a shockwave rippled through the MIT Physics Department. Even her advisor, Maxwell Yoon, initially expressed concern over the bold and risky idea.

In her thesis, Jennifer proposed the hypothesis that *an observer's participation extends beyond determining the quantum state of the microscopic world; under extreme conditions, it could distort the very fabric of spacetime in the macroscopic world, triggering a rapid, planetary-scale gravitational collapse— a "Quantum Storm."* She supported this with extensive data analysis, original theoretical work, and simulation results.

The idea was radical enough to shake the foundations of physics, and it was eerily similar to her mother J's unpublished research, which she had only ever encountered in fragments.

On the afternoon of April 12, 2021, tension filled the seminar room in MIT's Building 6. The audience included fellow researchers, faculty, and science journalists, all gathered to witness the final dissertation defense of a twelve-year-old doctoral candidate.

In the front row sat her advisor, Maxwell Yoon, along with Professors Harriet Carter and Stuart Randall, and—joining via video link—the renowned Caltech physicist Professor Q. Lichtenberg. All of them watched her with sharp, appraising eyes.

After a brief introduction by Maxwell, Jennifer stepped onto the stage. She unconsciously touched the Silver Pendant around her neck, took a deep breath, and looked directly at the audience.

In a clear, steady voice, she began her presentation. She explained step by step—using her models and simulation data—how the observer effect and quantum entanglement could, under certain threshold conditions, lead to a macroscopic collapse of reality.

As soon as her forty-five-minute presentation concluded, a barrage of sharp questions from the committee members followed.

"It is well established that Earth's mass alone is insufficient for gravitational collapse," Professor Harriet Carter began. "The concept of Effective Mass Amplification that you propose in your thesis is extraordinarily radical. How is this theoretically possible?"

"Effective Mass Amplification refers to a phenomenon where a highly advanced superintelligent AI, or a large group of observers synchronized in a specific way, participates strongly in the quantum wave function, thereby creating a powerful gravitational effect in a localized spacetime region, independent of actual mass. In my simulations, this…" Jennifer answered, her voice unwavering.

Next, Professor Stuart Randall pointed out the problem of decoherence.

"How can a quantum-entangled state maintain coherence on a macroscopic scale? It is common knowledge that such a state would immediately collapse due to external interactions."

"That was the greatest challenge of my research," Jennifer said, taking a slow breath before continuing. "Through simulations, I discovered the possibility that under certain conditions, quantum superposed states could actually resonate with one another, maintaining coherence and even amplifying collectively. Of course, this is still at the stage of a theoretical hypothesis…"

Sharp questions continued from Professor Lichtenberg and the other committee members, but Jennifer responded confidently, mobilizing all of her knowledge and logic. After about forty minutes of Q&A, the committee asked Jennifer to wait in the hallway.

Their closed-door deliberation began, and after about thirty minutes, they called her back in.

"The committee has concluded, by unanimous consent, that the dissertation of candidate Jennifer Wi has met the requirements for the doctoral degree. Congratulations, Dr. Wi."

The moment Professor Maxwell Yoon's voice echoed through the room, the seminar hall erupted in applause—part admiration, part relief. Jennifer stood with a slightly dazed expression, while Maxwell patted her shoulder with pride.

Two months later, on June 4, 2021, at an online graduation ceremony held due to the pandemic, Jennifer officially received her Ph.D. in Physics from MIT at the age of twelve years and ten months.

Headlines worldwide christened her the "Genius Girl," the "Youngest MIT Ph.D."

On the day of the graduation, a small celebration was held at the 21CF residence in New York. Ha Jin-woo, Kim Woo-hyun, Maxwell Yoon, and others who had been part of Jennifer's journey were all gathered.

When someone asked for her thoughts, Jennifer spoke softly but firmly.

"I'm not happy because of the degree itself. I'm happy because the more I research, the more I feel like I'm getting closer to my mom."

Hearing her words, Great Wi, who had been looking out the

window, quietly took out a handkerchief and wiped his eyes. Kim Woo-hyun approached him, comforted him, and the two moved to another room.

When someone asked Jennifer about her future plans, she answered without hesitation.

"My mom also studied quantum computing at Cambridge. I want to follow the path she walked to the very end. So I've already applied for a postdoctoral position at the University of Cambridge in England to look for my mom's research."

From the Quantum World to the Cognitive World

During her one year and ten months as a postdoc at Cambridge, Jennifer managed to reconstruct, in her own language, the blueprint of the Quantum Life Principle and Quantum Bio-Cognition that J had designed. In the process, a desire grew within her to delve even deeper into the operating principles of human consciousness and the integration of brain science and quantum entanglement.

If I focused mainly on quantum physics at MIT and Cambridge, now it's time to properly study cognitive science. It's the field my mom was so passionate about...

Based on her research achievements and strong letters of recommendation, Jennifer was accepted into the Ph.D. program in Cognitive Science.

At the end of June that year, she left Cambridge and headed for the West Coast of the United States, where Stanford was located. In the taxi from the airport to the city, Jennifer quietly watched the unfamiliar streetscapes slide past her window.

The memory of her father's smile at a restaurant shortly before she left Cambridge overlapped with the image of the streets her mother must have walked in this city long ago.

A question flickered through her mind—had she gotten any

closer to the path her mother dreamed of? But she quickly steeled her resolve, gently grasping the Silver Pendant at her neck.

Her research, her family, and the secret of the Autumn Code that she still did not fully understand—she resolved to carry them all forward, a new determination swelling deep in her chest.

As the taxi slowly entered the city center, Jennifer lifted her gaze and smiled faintly at the clear sky. And so, another chapter of her long journey, beginning in a new land, was opening.

Chapter 5

Song of the Tachyon

Frost Flower of the Golden Gate

On the evening of June 27, 2022, Jennifer Wi stepped into the arrivals hall at SFO. Most travelers had shed their masks, yet they moved with lingering caution—a habit etched by long months of distancing.

The post-pandemic airport felt quieter, subdued. People stood holding signs for arriving passengers, and every so often a reunion broke the calm with joyous hugs.

You made it, Jennifer.

She comforted herself with the thought, pulling her suitcase with one hand and shouldering a heavy backpack as she exited the terminal. She climbed into a car sent by Great Wi's security team. Her destination: a five-story building on a hill overlooking the Golden Gate Bridge. It was where J had once lived.

J had used this place frequently for nearly sixteen years, from 1990 until her marriage to Great Wi in late 2006, and occasionally thereafter. After J's death, Great Wi had transferred the building's ownership to Jennifer. It was his way of preserving his wife's memory through their daughter.

The exterior and interior showed no sign of neglect; the garden was neatly manicured with seasonal flowers and trees. A dedicated team from 21CF headquarters took care of cleaning and maintenance every week. Unaware of these details, Jennifer simply regarded it as the place where her mother had lived.

When she decided to attend Stanford, her father had simply said, "Your mom loved that building and that space. It's well preserved, so feel free to use it. And... I've prepared a being to help you during your time there."

The car drove over the hills toward the city. In contrast to the old-world charm of Cambridge, the uniquely bright and cheerful energy of San Francisco flowed in through the window. As they ascended the sunset-kissed hills, city lights flickered on one by one, and the destination on the navigation screen drew closer.

Jennifer's heart began to beat a little faster.

A space where Mom actually lived... a place that was also her old research lab...

A strange emotion stirred within her. The building had a cozy atmosphere, surrounded by garden trees and flowers, but entry appeared strictly controlled, with security cameras positioned at every angle.

After retrieving her luggage, Jennifer stood before the front door, took a breath, and activated the security panel.

"Hello, Jennifer. Welcome."

As the panel's greeting finished, the door opened smoothly, and bright, fresh air welcomed her. Then, standing quietly in a corner of the entrance lobby, a humanoid robot with a sleek, silver-gray exoskeleton caught her eye.

It stood about one hundred seventy-five centimeters tall, a form that was human-like yet possessed a distinctly mechanical precision. Its face was covered by a transparent visor, but a soft blue light emanated from within.

As Jennifer stared with a mixture of surprise and curiosity, the robot took a graceful step toward her.

"Good evening, Jennifer. I have been waiting for you."

A neutral yet clear voice filled the lobby.

"I am the unit deployed by the Chairman to support your safety and convenience. From this moment on, I will assist in all your activities and be responsible for the building's security."

Jennifer instantly recalled her father's words. *A being to help you.* That was the robot standing before her. A small gasp escaped her lips.

"Andromeda. I'll call you Andromeda," she said softly, but with conviction.

"Thank you for giving me a name, Jennifer. Andromeda. I will remember it."

The robot's blue light seemed to blink gently.

"I apologize for the inconvenience, but may I conduct a brief security scan upon your arrival?"

Jennifer nodded. The robot's presence was unfamiliar, but knowing it was her father's arrangement brought a sense of relief rather than rejection. A blue light from Andromeda's visor quickly swept over Jennifer's entire body.

"Thank you. All vitals are normal. I will move your luggage to the designated living space. Shall I guide you through the first floor, or would you prefer to rest?"

Andromeda lifted the suitcase and backpack effortlessly. There was no hesitation or sense of weight in its movements.

"Ah… I'd like to look around the first floor first."

The excitement of stepping into her mother's space for the first time, combined with the strange sensation of being with this unfamiliar assistant, enveloped her.

"Understood. This way, please."

Following Andromeda's guidance, Jennifer finally took her first step into her mother J's world.

The living room and kitchen came into view. The air was fresh, as if someone had been staying there recently, and the furniture was neatly arranged. A light-wood dining table and a minimalist cabinet gleamed without a speck of dust. Andromeda followed quietly a few steps behind.

On the living-room wall hung a small, old picture frame. It was a photo of a young woman smiling brightly on a lawn. Jennifer gazed at it. The mother in the photo was so young and unfamiliar that a strange sense of distance touched her heart.

She walked toward the kitchen. In the center stood an island table of simple design. The light wood-toned surface showed signs of age but was impeccably maintained. She imagined her mother sitting here, drinking tea, lost in thought.

The cabinets lining the walls were simple and functional. The round knobs retained the natural grain of the wood, and behind glass doors, mugs, glasses, and old dishes were aligned. The mugs were of all different shapes and sizes, as if each held its own story.

A large window graced one wall. During the day, it would offer a view of the Golden Gate Bridge and the distant sea; in the evening, an orange sunset would bathe the kitchen in its glow. Next to the sink, hand-drip coffee tools were arranged, and several glass jars held coffee beans. A ceramic server, a gooseneck kettle, a digital scale, a Hario V60 dripper, an electric grinder, and a thermometer were all in order.

Seeing this meticulous setup, Jennifer felt that this place, as much as any laboratory, was a space that held her mother's thoughts and emotions.

Just then, a cupboard next to the refrigerator caught her eye. Through the transparent glass door, she saw old ceramic plates, delicate wine glasses, and bottles resembling vases. Among them, one thing stood out—a glass tube about thirty centimeters long.

She carefully took out the tube and placed it on the island. Inside the sealed glass was a paper airplane, worn but perfectly preserved. At a glance, it looked like a simple plane folded from blank paper, but Jennifer instinctively sensed it was more than just an object.

A sticker with the handwritten year '*1994*' was affixed to the outside.

"Nineteen ninety-four…?" Jennifer murmured, staring at the tube. Andromeda waited quietly, not interrupting.

After slowly drinking a glass of water, Jennifer turned to the robot.

"I want to go to the second floor. My mother's study or lab must be there, right?"

"Yes, Jennifer. I will guide you upstairs."

Andromeda led her to the internal staircase. Pushing open the heavy wooden door, she was met with a quiet stillness and an unfamiliar nostalgia.

"Mom's study…" she muttered, looking around.

The faint scent of old books filled the air. Shelves lining the walls were packed with classics on physics, philosophy, and cognitive science. Jennifer ran her fingers over the spines, imagining her mother's intellectual journey. When her fingertips touched Fritjof Capra's *The Tao of Physics*, she felt the same thrill she had experienced when she first discovered her mother's notebooks in the Cambridge library.

Her mother had long been contemplating the connection between the universe and consciousness.

Next to the study was a door leading to a personal laboratory. As she turned the handle, morning sunlight poured in. A large wooden desk stood in the center, cluttered with an old laptop, thick stacks of papers, and research notes covered in scribbles. It was a vivid scene, as if someone had been working there just yesterday.

On one wall, faint, illegible writing, complex equations, and diagrams covered a whiteboard. After staring intently, she recognized parts of the faded equations. Jennifer's gaze moved from one to the next, losing herself in their flow.

It was a sensation like following her mother's own thought process. To her surprise, the concepts were precisely aligned with the problems she herself had been wrestling with at MIT and Cambridge.

Mom... she walked this path long before I did.

Just then, a worn photograph pinned to a corner of the corkboard caught her eye.

'October 18, 1981.'

It showed a young, brightly smiling mother in a park at Namsan, and next to her, a boy with a playful expression.

This boy... could it be Dad?

The boy was incredibly familiar. Jennifer's heart pounded. It was so similar to the scene she had seen in her dreams. She took the photo, held it in her palm, and gazed at it for a long time—a warm, affectionate, yet sorrowful scene, aching with familiarity.

On a nearby shelf lay a worn notebook titled *Quantum Life Principle.*

With a fluttering heart, Jennifer opened it. It was a mix of quantum-mechanical equations, poetic phrases, and undecipherable symbols. Beneath the sentence "Observation might be the act that creates existence," there was a memo: "*October 18, 1981, at Namsan,*" along with a sketch of her mother's profile.

October 18, 1981… It's the same date as the photo. Did something really happen at Namsan that day?

Jennifer felt disoriented. Dreams, reality, and past records were jumbled together; she could not distinguish truth from illusion. But one thing was certain. She had a strong intuition that if she followed the traces her mother left behind, she would eventually reach the secret. It felt like a puzzle left just for her.

Fatigue finally washed over her.

"I think that's enough for today. Where can I rest?"

"This way, Jennifer. There are several bedrooms prepared."

Andromeda guided her down the first-floor corridor and opened the door to a cozy bedroom. Inside, there was a large bed and a sofa with a warm, reddish-orange hue. A soft blanket was neatly folded on the sofa, and an old chest of drawers stood quietly against one wall.

Jennifer carefully opened the top drawer. Inside, a few LPs lay peacefully. One of them was *Spiegel im Spiegel* by Arvo Pärt. Jennifer stared at the cover before quietly uttering the title.

"Spiegel im Spiegel… mirror in the mirror."

In that moment, an indescribable emotion seeped deep into her heart. She carefully replaced the LP and walked to the window. Outside, the lights of San Francisco were beginning to dot the darkening cityscape. Evening was settling over the city.

Jennifer sat on the bed, staring out. *Could I get to know my mother here?*

"Andromeda, I think I'm going to sleep now."

"Yes, Jennifer. Have a restful night. I will be on standby outside."

Andromeda quietly closed the door. Jennifer lay down. Her eyelids felt heavy, but this unfamiliar space was surprisingly comfortable—as if it had been her room for a long time.

Jennifer slowly closed her eyes.

In her dream, her consciousness left the Earth and expanded into the vastness of space. The blue planet grew smaller beneath her, and her vision filled with countless stars. It was not just a cluster of stars; it was a magnificent sight of galaxies flowing like threads along the structure of a cosmic filament.

It felt as if the entire universe was performing a single calculation, like a living neural network. She sensed she was drifting through the Laniakea Supercluster—the structure known as the "immeasurable heavens."

Just then, she heard a soft whisper.

"Everything is connected, Jenny. You and I, past and future, from the smallest life on this Earth to the center of Laniakea… the universe is one great breath."

Unlike the clear tone from the video, this was a deeper, vaster cosmic resonance that echoed in the abyss.

"Do not be afraid to observe. Where your gaze falls, a new reality will be born. But remember, with creation comes responsibility. A flawed observation can cause everything to collapse in a single second."

As she reached out toward the voice, the Silver Pendant around her neck began to glow, wrapping around her hand. The instant she grasped it, a brilliant light and a sensation of resonating with the structure of Laniakea pierced her consciousness.

The tangled quantum network. The birth and death of stars. And from the center of the supercluster, the shadow of a threat approaching from the Great Attractor.

"There is… not much time left… The key… is within you… It is connected to the secret of Laniakea…"

The whisper grew fainter, and Jennifer awoke with the sensation of falling into an abyss. Her heart pounded violently, her body drenched in cold sweat. Outside, the sky was still dark with the approaching dawn.

With a trembling hand, Jennifer clutched the pendant. It felt as if her mother, or some other being, had sent a message through the grand stage of Laniakea. She realized then that she was at the center of a great maelstrom of destiny. A sense of mission, stronger than fear, filled her heart.

Jennifer slowly got out of bed and went to the window. The dawn air was cold. The echo of the dream remained vivid. Following its thread, she quietly made her way to the living room.

A distinct light, different from the night before, shone in her eyes. The pursuit of her mother's traces was no longer a matter of simple longing or curiosity. It was a mission, a puzzle she had to solve.

The mother in the photo was still smiling brightly. Jennifer stopped in front of it and whispered,

"Mom, I think I understand a little now. The things you left behind… I'll carry them on."

Heading to the kitchen, Jennifer recalled her mother's recipe and brewed coffee. Her hands were now skilled at the drip method. As the aroma spread, the complex and intense emotions settled.

Her gaze came to rest on the paper airplane inside the hutch.

The Heart of Time

Days passed. 1994 and 2022—the past and the present. The fragments of memory her mother left behind and the whispers of Laniakea in her dreams were coming together in Jennifer's mind like a giant puzzle.

She decided to move forward—toward the core of the secret, toward the truth her mother had hidden. She could no longer hesitate at the threshold of time.

That resolve was finally put into action on July 7, 2022, the eleventh day after her arrival at J's building.

"Andromeda, I need to go to the third floor and above. Prepare to activate the elevator."

"Understood, Jennifer. Preparing to disarm upper-floor security and activate elevator systems."

While Andromeda responded instantly and accessed the system, Jennifer stood up, opened the living-room door, and headed to the entrance lobby. Andromeda followed her silently.

The air there was cool and still, quite different from the cozy atmosphere of the first floor where she usually stayed. In front of her was the familiar first-floor entrance, and on the right wall, a sleek metal elevator door stood firmly shut.

It was the entrance to her mother's sealed research area—a gateway to an unknown world.

It was a space she had not dared to venture into before. The place where her mother had immersed herself in research for sixteen years, and where, after reuniting with her father, she had conducted a project to change the future of humanity under the name Quantum Horizon. Perhaps the secret related to her mother's final moments lay dormant there.

She approached the security panel next to the elevator. It was a complex-looking interface, but her biometric information would already have been registered at the highest level by Great Wi.

As Jennifer placed her hand on the panel, a faint scanning light quickly swept over her palm and iris.

"Jennifer Wi. Access authority confirmed. Accessible floors: 1, 3, 4, 5."

With a calm system voice, the elevator doors slid silently open to either side. The interior was quite spacious, seemingly capable of carrying cargo. As Jennifer stepped inside first, Andromeda followed. The doors closed, and Jennifer leaned against the wall, trying to calm her racing heart.

Her gaze was fixed on the display showing the floor numbers.

3.

She pressed the button for the third floor, the floor she presumed housed her mother's main research office. The elevator ascended smoothly. During that short time, countless thoughts raced through her mind.

What would that long-sealed space look like now? What would remain? Her research notes? Lab equipment? Or... something unexpected?

Ding.

Upon arriving at the third floor, the doors opened smoothly. Jennifer hesitated for a moment. Her heart began to race with tension again, but with a resolute expression, she stepped out of the elevator. Andromeda followed silently behind her.

It was a long, dark corridor. Only minimal emergency lights were on at intervals, barely revealing the overall structure, while the deeper parts of the corridor were submerged in darkness. A faint layer of dust had settled on the floor and walls.

It was a space of deep silence, as if time had stopped.

The secret realm, untouched by any footsteps for a long time, had finally revealed itself to her. Yet the air felt fresh, as if it had been regularly circulated.

Jennifer took out her smartphone and turned on the flashlight. Andromeda also switched its visor's blue light to illumination mode, lighting up the dark corridor. On both sides, heavy steel doors were lined up in a uniform row. A security panel was installed next to each door, and a small nameplate was attached above it.

"Analyze the power status and air quality of this floor. And check for any hazardous materials or abnormal signals."

"Understood, Jennifer. Currently analyzing."

A moment later, Andromeda reported back.

"The main power supply to this floor is cut off, with only the auxiliary power line operating at a minimum. However, an internet network is installed, which should allow for remote management. The air quality is good, and regular air circulation is being performed. No harmful gases or radiation have been detected. However, some dust has accumulated on certain devices and surfaces, requiring cleaning. The security level of each door cannot be clearly determined at this time, but all are in a heavily locked state, and accessing internal information will require additional authentication. Emergency stairwells are confirmed at both ends of the corridor."

The light from Andromeda's visor swept over the walls, ceiling sensors, vents, and each of the doors in turn.

"Got it. So it's safe for now." Jennifer nodded.

She walked slowly down the dark corridor, examining the doors on either side, and stopped in front of a door that seemed to be located in the middle of the hallway. When she shone her smartphone light on it, the nameplate above the door became visible.

'Director's Office – J.'

Jennifer took a deep breath. Her heart began to pound uncontrollably. Closing her eyes for a moment, she placed her hand on the door's security panel. The panel lit up brightly, as if verifying the visitor's identity.

"Access granted. Jennifer Wi. Top-level clearance confirmed. Director J's office. Security lock disengaged."

With the calm system voice, a *clack* echoed from within the heavy steel door. Jennifer swallowed hard and pushed the handle with a trembling hand.

The door, seemingly unused for a long time, opened slowly with a creak. What flowed out from the gap was the scent of time—and darkness.

As Andromeda's light illuminated the gloom, a world where time had stopped unfolded before her.

A high ceiling; a vast bookshelf filling one wall; a large wooden desk in front of it; a whiteboard with faint traces of writing; and an unknown piece of experimental equipment shrouded in a white cover.

"Begin a detailed scan of the internal environment. Especially check the air-circulation status, fine-particle concentration, and any potential residual electromagnetic fields or energy patterns. From now on, record and analyze everything in this room. Don't miss a single detail."

"Understood, Jennifer. Initiating detailed environmental scan and full record analysis at the highest level."

Where to begin? The vast collection of books? The traces on the erased whiteboard? The locked desk drawers? Or the unknown equipment covered by a sheet?

Nothing could be overlooked. Jennifer's intuition whispered that all these things were interconnected, forming one giant picture.

Mom must have... left a trail. For me to find.

Jennifer closed her eyes for a moment, as if trying to feel her mother's presence. She could faintly sense the energy left in this space—a wave of thought. The robot moved silently to carry out its mission, and only Jennifer's footsteps broke the silence as she slowly walked to the center of the room.

Her gaze fell on the massive bookshelf that stretched from floor to ceiling. Physics, philosophy, brain science, cognitive science, biology—even art and poetry collections—a vast number of books spanning genres were neatly arranged. It was as if J's extensive and deep intellectual world had been transported here.

"Scan that entire bookshelf and create a database of the book list. If possible, categorize them by publication year and field, and check for any memos tucked between the pages, marked sections, folded pages, underlines, or notes."

"Initiating scan and database construction. Estimated time: thirty-six minutes and fifteen seconds."

While Andromeda moved to the front of the bookshelf and began a detailed scan, Jennifer slowly walked along it, reading the titles of a few books.

Roger Penrose's *The Emperor's New Mind*, David Bohm's *Wholeness and the Implicate Order*, John Stewart Bell's *Speakable and Unspeakable in Quantum Mechanics*.

Jennifer carefully pulled out Bell's book. His insights into quantum entanglement and non-locality would surely have been deeply related to her mother's research. Her fingers, flipping quickly through the pages, stopped on a certain page. The corner of the page was folded, and in the margin, there were notes and underlines in what appeared to be her mother's handwriting.

It was a section on "observer-dependency" and "the limits of hidden-variable theories."

Of course... Mom didn't just accept Bell's theorem. She was trying to find something beyond it. The role of the observer... perhaps not a hidden variable, but something like a connected consciousness.

Jennifer carefully placed the book back on the shelf, feeling a step closer to her mother's way of thinking.

Next, her gaze moved to the massive whiteboard that filled one wall. Faintly erased traces. Complex equations, unknown symbols, arrows connecting various concepts. It looked like the remnants of a fierce brainstorming session.

"Take multi-angle, high-resolution photos of that whiteboard surface and begin image analysis. Restore the erased text and diagrams as much as possible. Look for any recurring patterns or symbols."

"Initiating image capture and restoration analysis."

After confirming that Andromeda had moved to the whiteboard and started its task, Jennifer finally approached the large wooden desk in the center of the room. This time, she noticed things she had missed before. Besides an old tablet on the desk, there was a pen holder with a few pens, a small desk lamp, and a small transparent object that looked like a crystal-structure model.

Jennifer reached out and carefully picked up the transparent object. It reflected a myriad of colors depending on the angle of the light. *What was it used for?*

She put the object down and tried to open the desk drawers. But all the drawers were locked—not with a simple key, but with an electronic lock.

"These desk drawers—can you check whether I can open them with my clearance?"

"Checking the security system. Please wait. ...Confirmation complete. These drawers require an additional security step: Level 4 biometric signature or a quantum key. Direct unlocking is not possible with your current access level, Jennifer."

Level 4... not so simple, I see.

Jennifer sighed softly. Her mother had hidden her most important secrets behind multiple layers of security. She picked up the old tablet lying on the desk and tried to turn it on, but it wouldn't respond.

"Identify this tablet model and check the possibility of charging it and recovering the data."

"It is an older model. The battery is completely discharged but appears to be replaceable. The state of the internal memory or a physical analysis will only be possible once the battery is charged. Shall I attempt to charge it first?"

"No, put that on hold for now. Let's check other things first."

Jennifer put the tablet down and stared at the locked drawers again. Level 4 security. There seemed to be no way to open them right now.

Finally, her gaze turned to the massive piece of equipment covered by a white sheet in the corner of the office—the same machine she had briefly seen earlier.

"Pause your analysis for a moment and come here."

Andromeda, which had been scanning the whiteboard, immediately came to Jennifer's side.

"That cover—can you lift just one corner, very carefully? I want to see the internal structure with my own eyes. Andromeda, monitor closely for any energy changes or abnormal signals the moment you lift it."

"Acknowledged. Executing command. Initiating focused monitoring of ambient energy states."

With fingers as dexterous as a human's, Andromeda carefully grasped the corner of the cover. With very slow, minute movements, it began to lift the cover slightly.

Jennifer held her breath and peered inside. An intricate web of quantum conduits, a glass structure that looked like a vacuum chamber, and... a metal panel engraved with an unknown symbol.

Just then—

"Warning. Faint tachyon particle emission detected. Quantum field instability increasing. Immediate return to original position is advised."

A frantic yet mechanical warning broke the silence.

Tachyon...

The moment the word hit Jennifer's ears, it felt as if every nerve in her body had frozen. The holy grail and the forbidden realm of physics—the hypothetical particle said to be faster than light, an unknown entity that transcends the boundaries of causality.

Mom... did she reach this far? She went beyond mere theoretical exploration and actually tried to generate or control them?

Jennifer's heart began to race. This was not just a discovery. It was witnessing the threshold of a domain that no one in human history had ever reached. It was a feeling too eerie to be called awe, too fascinating to be called fear, that enveloped her entire body.

At the same time, from inside the slightly lifted cover, she could see a faint but terrifying blue light shimmering. It was a dangerous beauty—living chaos that fluctuated with contempt for reality's laws.

What could lie beyond? A path to reverse time? A door to another universe? Or an abyss that could swallow the world?

The mere thought made her dizzy. Was this the ultimate form of the research Mom had been so secretly devoted to? What on earth was she trying to create?

"Threat element detected. Returning to original position immediately."

Along with the warning, Andromeda instantly and smoothly closed the corner of the cover it was holding. It was a perfect response, following protocol without any hesitation or agitation. It remained in a state of alert, its sensors fixed on the potentially threatening equipment.

Jennifer's heart sank with the momentary tension.

Tachyons? Quantum field instability?

Even for her, a physics major, those words were not to be taken lightly. Tachyons, in particular, were hypothetical particles assumed to exist only in theory, faster than light. If that device was indeed capable of generating or detecting tachyons, her mother's research had gone far beyond the boundaries of modern physics.

Perhaps... it was an attempt to travel through time or intervene in another dimension. Was it related to the HAL-R Project?

Instead of panicking, Jennifer's mind grew ice-cold. This was not an object of mere curiosity. With great power came great responsibility. She had to understand the principles of this device, predict the repercussions it would bring, and above all... find a way to use it correctly—or seal it away.

That was the unavoidable homework, the mission, her mother had left for her.

Fear remained, but a stronger desire for truth as a scientist, and the resolve to bear this legacy, began to dominate her. What she needed now was accurate information.

"Report the specific values for the tachyon emission and the rate of change in field instability. What are the effects on the surrounding equipment and on us? And... was that emission temporary? Or is it still continuing now that the cover is closed?"

"Re-analyzing data."

The blue light from its visor focused more intensely on the covered device.

"Tachyon particles were detected in trace amounts (10^{-18} units) and are not currently detected after the cover was returned to its original position. The quantum field instability increased by a maximum of 0.037% but has now returned to a stable state. No immediate impact on surrounding equipment or biological entities is assessed. It is presumed that the act of opening the cover induced the instability."

A temporary phenomenon... opening the cover was the trigger...?

Jennifer reconstructed the situation as she listened to the report. The device wasn't off, but in some kind of standby or sealed state, and it reacted to external stimuli—or the opening of the cover—by causing instability. It was dangerous, but perhaps not uncontrollable.

"Good." She steeled herself once more.

"Andromeda, just like before, very slowly, open only the corner of the cover—one centimeter. Re-check the emission levels and cover it immediately if you see the slightest anomaly."

"Reconfirming command. A potential risk exists. I request you reconsider," Andromeda warned, following its safety protocol.

"I know. But I have to check. One centimeter. No more."

Jennifer's voice held no hesitation.

"…Understood. Executing command."

Following Jennifer's final instruction, Andromeda once again used its delicate touch to very carefully grasp the corner of the cover. One millimeter. Two millimeters. In a breathless tension, the cover opened ever so slightly.

"Tachyon levels faintly re-detected. Field instability up by 0.01 percent. Remaining within stable range."

Relying on the robot's light, Jennifer once again focused on the one-centimeter gap. She could see a bit more clearly than before.

The blue light… it looked like a liquid-metal surface, shimmering faintly as if alive, or perhaps like a soft glow emanating from within a complex crystal structure. At its center, there seemed to be a small, black, spherical object.

She had no idea what it was, but a strong intuition that it was something powerful, dangerous, and at the same time captivating pierced through her.

"That's enough. Cover it again."

"Command executed. Returning to the original position."

Andromeda immediately put the cover back in place. According to its report, the tachyon levels and field instability returned to zero. Jennifer stood there for a moment, catching her breath. Her heart was still beating fast.

"Search the book list you scanned earlier. Keywords: 'tachyon,' 'superluminal,' 'quantum field instability,' 'spacetime matrix,' 'HAL-R Project.' See if there are any research notes from my mother or related books."

"Executing keyword search," came its calm voice.

Jennifer looked around the office one more time. A sealed laboratory. Locked drawers. An unidentified device. And her mother's traces.

This was not merely a space that held the past. It was a dangerous Pandora's box that could shake the future.

And she had only just begun to open it.

Andromeda

The hours spent in the old San Francisco building, a space that seemed frozen in her mother's time, were not simply about confronting a legacy of the past. In the dreamlike, surreal sensations and memories that seeped into her, Jennifer glimpsed the unknown within herself. A single outing on the streets, a single vivid threat, had taught her the world's cruelty.

The meeting with the loyal robot was a source of comfort, but also another puzzle to be solved. The research her mother had left behind was filled with wonder, but also a chilling danger—the possibility of the tachyon device. Everything surrounding her felt like one giant signal. Before her now, a map of secrets harbored within the entire building was beginning to unfold: firmly shut laboratory doors, encrypted data files, a dangerous device of unknown identity, and countless research records left behind by her mother.

What should she search for first, and in what order should she assemble the puzzle? What other unexpected truths would she face in the process?

One thing was certain: Jennifer Wi was no longer the passive girl chasing the shadows of the past.

The next morning, Jennifer woke up on her own, without an alarm. The world outside was already bright, and a glance at the clock showed it was well past 10:00 A.M. The mental and physical fatigue of the past few days had led to a deep sleep. Her body felt much lighter, but the weight of the secrets she had confronted in her mother's office the night before still pressed down on a corner of her heart.

The unidentified device that emitted tachyon particles, the drawers locked with Level 4 security, the countless research records her mother had left…

Today, I have to do this right.

In the living room, Andromeda had finished charging and was in a quiet standby mode. As Jennifer emerged, its gaze turned toward her.

"Good morning," Jennifer greeted.

"Good morning, Jennifer."

Instead of heading straight for the kitchen, Jennifer stopped in front of the robot.

"From what I confirmed yesterday, the main power to the research area on floors three to five is cut off, and only the emergency power is running, right?"

"Yes, that is correct. Only the emergency lights and minimal environmental maintenance systems are operational."

"In that state, it's hard to conduct any proper search or equipment analysis. It's risky, too. Is there a way to restore the main power to the research area? The reason it was cut off, the restoration procedure… is there any related information in the 21CF network or this building's system database?"

It remained silent for a moment. A complex calculation seemed to be running behind its visor.

"Searching and analyzing related information," it replied after a pause. "According to the building's blueprints and 21CF security records, the main power to the research area on floors three to five was physically and logically severed from the central control system in early July 2009, after Dr. J's fatal accident. This was a measure to prevent unauthorized external access and equipment malfunction."

"Completely severed… then restoration won't be simple." Jennifer frowned.

"Several prerequisites are necessary to restore main power," Andromeda continued. "First, a physical reconnection of the circuits at the main breaker panel in the basement is required. Second, a preliminary inspection of the power distribution systems and safety devices in each area of floors three to five must be conducted. Third, power supply approval for the area and a security protocol reset are needed from the central control system. While the final step should be possible with your top-level access, the physical work and safety checks will require considerable time and precise skill."

"What is the extent of what you can do yourself?"

"I am equipped with the capability for precise physical work. I can personally handle the circuit reconnection at the basement breaker panel and the inspection of the distribution systems on each floor. However, if unexpected deterioration or damage is discovered during the work, additional parts procurement or repairs may be necessary. Furthermore, all work will be conducted under your final approval, Jennifer."

"All right." Jennifer made a decision. "From now on, prioritize the restoration of main power to the research area. Create a detailed work plan for me to review, including the necessary procedures, estimated time, and potential risks. Safety is the top priority. If even the slightest risk factor is detected, stop immediately and report it."

"Understood, Jennifer. I will begin creating and reporting the plan for research-area power restoration."

"And it will be more effective to finalize the plan while you personally check the condition of each floor, starting from the basement. That way, we can check in advance what parts need to be sourced and identify any variables that differ from the blueprints. Do not forget that the physical world, unlike the virtual one, is full of unforeseen variables."

"Yes, I will take that into consideration," Andromeda replied.

Sitting at the kitchen island, Jennifer prepared a simpler breakfast than the Massimo Bottura–style meal Andromeda had suggested the day before. She took fresh kale, romaine, tomatoes, and cucumbers from the refrigerator, washed them, and made a salad. She put two slices of whole wheat bread into the toaster. The dressing was a simple mix of olive oil, lemon juice, salt, and pepper.

Facing the heavy discoveries of the previous night and the unknown exploration ahead, she needed a meal that would clear her head and ease her stomach. While the toast was browning, she recalled her conversation with Andromeda from the day before: a being that did not merely execute commands, but analyzed problems, proposed solutions, and even showed responses close to insight.

Its potential was obvious, and it would be a reliable ally in the journey ahead.

But at the same time, it's entirely my role to guide its abilities properly, Jennifer thought as she placed thin slices of avocado on her toast.

Presenting it with clear objectives and sometimes asking questions that went beyond its protocols, finding solutions together—that would be the core of their interaction from now on.

Not long after she started eating, Andromeda approached the kitchen entrance from the living room. Its movements were silent, but Jennifer had already sensed its presence.

"Jennifer, the plan for restoring main power to the requested research area on floors three to five has been completed. May I proceed with the report?"

Andromeda's voice was clear, tinged with a confidence that belied the complex task ahead.

"Already? All right, let's hear it." Jennifer put down her fork and turned toward Andromeda.

It stepped forward and began its explanation. A faint light flickered beneath its visor, preparing for visualization.

"The entire operation consists of four phases. The total estimated time is approximately seven hours and thirty minutes, subject to adjustment based on variables. The first phase concerns the basement distribution panel. I will also check the power lines running from the third to the fifth floor and reconnect the physically severed circuits. The estimated time is two hours. The main concern during the basement work is the deterioration of cables or breakers."

"And if they need replacement?" Jennifer asked.

"Standard procedure is to make an emergency request to 21CF headquarters…"

"Wait, the headquarters is in New York. We should consider a local route for faster procurement," Jennifer pointed out, correcting Andromeda's standard operating procedure.

"I will add a plan to utilize local supply chains. This will reduce procurement time from twelve hours to two to four hours," Andromeda conceded.

"Good. Go on."

"The second phase is to inspect the internal power distribution systems and safety devices from the third to the fifth floor. This includes the power lines around the Director's Office equipment we checked yesterday. The estimated time is three hours."

"Can you inspect that equipment without stimulating it?"

"Yes. I plan to use non-destructive sensors such as thermal imaging and ultrasonic detection."

"The third phase requires your cooperation, Jennifer. Accessing the central control system and resetting the security protocols requires Level 3 access authorization. The estimated time is thirty minutes. However, additional security layers may exist."

"The final phase is gradual power supply and real-time monitoring."

"I will cooperate with AI '21' to—"

"Hold on," Jennifer cut in. "How will AI '21' monitor floors three to five? That area was sealed off in 2009."

It was silent for a moment.

"I acknowledge the analytical error. It is highly likely that the area is outside AI '21's sensor network."

"Right. Then let's do it this way," Jennifer said, immediately proposing an alternative. "In phase three, just go as far as accessing the central control system and approving basic power supply. Don't start phase four right away. Instead, once basic power is on, you will first install AI '21' sensor nodes on floors three through five so they can be integrated into the building-wide system. When we're ready to monitor the internal environment in real time through '21,' then we start phase four— phased power supply and stabilization monitoring. It will take more time, but it will be much safer."

"That is a rational judgment, Jennifer," Andromeda agreed. "The sensor node installation and integration work is expected to take an additional one hour and thirty minutes. I will recalculate the total work time to approximately nine hours and reflect it in the plan immediately."

"However, you first need to check how many AI '21' unit sets are actually stored in this building."

"Hey, 21, do you have information on how many '21' unit sets are in this building?" she asked.

"Yes, Jennifer. According to my data, there are nine sets in stock in basement storage, Section A. However, to cover the entire research facility, approximately eighty-eight sets will be needed. The facility has many rooms, requiring one to three units per room, and additional units will be needed for the stairs and elevators on each floor, as well as on the roof for security. By that calculation, an additional seventy-nine sets will be required. The exterior of the building, however, is already fully equipped."

"All right, 21, submit a procurement request to the relevant team at 21CF," Jennifer said.

"Yes, understood."

Andromeda nodded, having heard the conversation between Jennifer and 21.

"Good. Then you decide where to install the first nine units and where to install the rest when they arrive. Now proceed according to the revised plan," Jennifer said, giving her final approval. "Report your progress and any anomalies at the end of each phase. If any risk factor seems likely to materialize, stop work immediately and we'll discuss countermeasures."

"Understood. Your final approval is confirmed. I will begin phase one immediately."

Andromeda gathered the necessary tools and equipment and began to move toward the basement.

As Jennifer ate her remaining salad and toast, a thought came to her:

This is the work of restarting the lab's stopped heart. Maybe this is the moment I turn the first key to the biggest secret box Mom left behind.

Putting the last piece of toast in her mouth, Jennifer listened to Andromeda's status reports relayed through AI '21.' She planned to check the video feed on her personal tablet if necessary, but for now she decided to rely on Andromeda's reports and her own intuition.

"Phase one work preparation complete. Necessary tools and safety equipment secured from the basement storage area. Commencing work on the main breaker panel now."

Jennifer nodded, imagining it finding the tools on its own in the basement storage.

For the next few hours, she sat on the living room sofa reviewing other materials on her laptop, all the while listening to the robot's progress. The robot reported concisely at the completion of each stage—basement work, inspection of floors three to five, preparation for AI '21' node installation—and Jennifer gave necessary instructions or confirmations. Fortunately, the physical inspections and preparations proceeded smoothly without major issues or delays.

At last, Andromeda's voice was heard again.

"Jennifer, physical inspections for phases one and two are complete. Preparations for installing AI '21' nodes in nine key locations on floors three through five are also complete. Now, phase three is required: accessing the central control system and approving power supply. The system terminal is located in the machine control room on sublevel one. I will guide you when you are ready."

"The machine control room in the basement?" Jennifer was momentarily puzzled, but quickly understood. A system controlling the power for the entire research facility would, of course, be in such a place rather than in the director's office.

"All right. I'm on my way down."

Jennifer went down to sublevel one. The place it guided her to was different from the area containing the main breaker panel—a small machine control room where various control devices and some server racks were installed. In the center stood an old, dust-covered console and monitor.

"You can proceed from here," Andromeda said, pointing to the console.

Jennifer sat in front of the console and, following its guidance, accessed the system. When she logged in with her Level 3 clearance, a complex but logically structured control interface appeared on the screen. She checked the power cutoff status for floors three through five, reviewed the safety protocols, and finally executed the command to resume power supply.

The message "Command accepted. Commencing phased power supply sequence for 3rd floor" appeared on the screen.

"Success," Jennifer murmured with a small sigh of relief, and stood up. Now all that remained was to wait.

Returning to the living room, she watched the status changes of each floor on her tablet, displayed by 21. A short while later, the lights in the third-floor corridor came on, followed by the fourth and fifth floors in succession. The faint sound of the ventilation system activating could be heard. Initial environmental data—temperature, humidity, power status—sent from the temporarily installed '21' nodes on each floor began to appear on the tablet screen.

"Power supply to all areas complete. System stabilization is being monitored. No anomalies to report so far," Andromeda reported.

"Well done. Now I need to see for myself."

Jennifer first stepped out on the third floor. The brightly lit corridor and doors unfolded before her. She could see the door to her mother's office, but she did not go in. Instead, she walked slowly down the corridor, looking around. She went up to the fourth and then the fifth floor, taking in the atmosphere of each level. The silhouettes of equipment visible through the lab doors, the old signs on the corridor walls—everything had been asleep for a long time.

The bright lighting starkly revealed the reality hidden in the darkness. Dust covered every surface. Although Andromeda had reported the previous night that the air quality was good, with some dust accumulation, the amount she actually encountered was more severe than she had imagined.

"This won't do," she muttered.

Standing at the end of the fifth-floor corridor, staring at the stairs leading down, Jennifer made a decision. She turned to Andromeda.

"Before we start any full-scale exploration, we need to do a major cleanup of this whole place. It'll be a disaster if I get a dust allergy. More importantly, it could be bad for my lungs."

"I agree with the need for environmental decontamination. However, I cannot handle it alone. The assistance of a professional cleaning service is required."

"We can't call an outside company. Security issues," Jennifer said, shaking her head. "Come to think of it, Mom probably didn't use outside cleaning services for the same reason. In that case, somewhere in this building there might be specialized cleaning equipment stored for maintaining the lab environment. For example, large vacuums with HEPA filters, air purifiers, and professional tools for dust removal and maintenance of delicate machinery or measuring devices. And of course she would have cleaned the floors regularly."

Her reasoning was sound.

"First, search the basement storage and any empty rooms on each floor for such equipment. If there's nothing, then we'll make a list of what we need and figure out how to procure it."

"Understood, Jennifer. I will immediately begin searching the basement storage and potential storage areas within the building."

While Andromeda busied itself with its mission, Jennifer decided to take a little time for herself. Back in the living room, she sat on the sofa, briefly checking the robot's progress on her tablet.

Just then, her smartwatch vibrated briefly, displaying a secure message notification. The sender was 21CF Security Core.

It's here.

Her pulse quickened. It was likely the response to her request to her father a few days ago for access rights to the humanoid robot's development node. She tapped the notification at once. Instead of simple text, an elaborate multi-step authentication sequence appeared on the screen. Only after completing fingerprint recognition, iris scanning, and voice password input did the message body finally reveal itself.

[SECURITY LEVEL ALPHA]

User Jennifer Wi: request approved. Level 5 access to AI Unit Model H-7 development node granted.

Use the security code below to initiate communication with the responsible lead (Aris Thorne, R&D Team 7) and proceed with final activation.

Code: QK#811018-JSID

It was the highest level of access. Her father had truly kept his promise. With this authority, she could directly inspect the robot's core algorithms and learning processes and even develop it further through direct coding. It might even provide a decisive clue in finding information related to her mother's research.

At the same time, a heavy sense of responsibility weighed on her. Delving into the inner workings of a powerful AI required a correspondingly careful and ethical approach.

First, she had to call the responsible lead.

But from where?

In the living room or the study, she was conscious of the newly installed AI '21' nodes. Although there were only nine nodes in total and they were not yet fully integrated into the system, she did not want to be monitored during a sensitive call.

Right—the rooftop.

The only space where a '21' node would not yet be installed.

Jennifer grabbed her tablet and stood up. She took the elevator to the fifth floor, then walked to the thick steel door leading to the roof via the emergency stairs. When she approached the security panel, a *beep* sounded and the door opened.

The cool, crisp afternoon air of San Francisco caressed her face. She walked to the edge of the VTOL landing pad and looked out over the safety fence at the sprawling landscape. To the west, she could see the red towers of the Golden Gate Bridge, and below, the densely packed houses on the hills and the busy city spread out before her. The sky was high and blue, and the wind blowing from the Pacific carried the salty scent of the sea.

Jennifer took her smartphone out of her pocket and initiated a secure communication link with the lead mentioned in the message. After a few rings, a calm male voice answered.

"This is Aris Thorne, head of security. Is this Dr. Jennifer Wi?"

"Yes, it is. I just received the security code."

"Acknowledged. I will now proceed with the final activation of your Level 5 access rights. I have sent you the development node interface access manual along with several important security guidelines. Please familiarize yourself with them, and be aware that all activities will be recorded and monitored at the highest security level. If you have any questions, you can contact me directly at any time."

"Yes, thank you, Mr. Thorne. I understand."

"You're welcome. Well then, the future of the H-7 unit is in your hands now, Dr. Jennifer. Please… handle it with care."

Jennifer slipped her smartphone back into her pocket and leaned against the fence, her gaze fixed on the distant sea.

She now held the decisive key to look directly into and guide Andromeda's potential. It was no longer just a protector or a machine, but a powerful partner with whom to explore unknown territories and perhaps grow together—and at the same time, a being for whom she was responsible.

She had turned on the lights in the lab and made a plan for cleaning. Now she had the authority to access the robot's deepest inner workings. Everything was proceeding according to her plan, or perhaps even faster.

Yet a sense of unease still lingered in a corner of her heart.

The terrifying blue light she had seen in her mother's office, the tachyon particles. The drawers locked with Level 4 security. And the folders on her mother's laptop—*AutumnCodeProto* and *X-SID_Encrypted*.

This building was a giant and dangerous secret in itself, one that could shake the future of humanity.

Were all these events coming her way—the strange dream, the appearance of the robot, her mother's secrets—merely coincidences? Or were they part of a grand plan laid out by her mother, or by the unknown entity called SID?

She could not know. But one thing was clear: she could no longer run or hesitate. She had to face everything her mother had left in this building, understand its meaning, and find what she herself had to do.

Suddenly, a passage from a research note her mother J had written in the summer of 2002 surfaced vividly in Jennifer's mind. As she pondered how to unlock the potential of an AI like

Andromeda, her mother's sharp insight into the nature of human intelligence rose again to the surface of her memory:

*"Recently, the **Earth Simulator** unveiled in Japan has astonished the world with its phenomenal computing speed of tens of teraflops (TFLOPS). The advancement of machines is truly dazzling. The academic world currently estimates the computational power of the human brain to be merely a few hundred petaflops, but I believe that is only a tiny fraction of human potential."*

"The brain is not simply a linear calculating device. Within its unique parallel structure, its incredible energy efficiency, and its information processing methods that we do not yet understand, there may lie a vast capability that far surpasses the performance of current supercomputers, perhaps even transcending the exaflops (EFLOPS) scale."

"One day, humanity will be amazed when they realize the immense 'potential' hidden in their own brains. The true quest for intelligence will probably begin then…"

Jennifer was once again thrilled by her mother's insight from twenty years ago. In 2002, when NEC's *Earth Simulator* in Japan took the top spot in the world with a performance of 35.86 teraflops, most neuroscientists estimated the human brain's capability to be at a much lower petaflops level. Yet J had already predicted that the human brain possessed exaflop-level potential.

Moreover, twenty years later, recent studies now estimate that the information-processing capacity of the human brain can range from 1 to as high as 100 exaflops, depending on the individual. This overwhelmingly surpasses the level of the world's current top supercomputer, America's *Frontier*, at approximately 1.1 exaflops. This means that a single individual's brain possesses the potential to outperform even the most powerful existing computer. Her mother's prediction was decades ahead of its time.

The key to the true advancement of an AI like Andromeda is not simply increasing its computational speed or data throughput.

Rather, it may lie in understanding and applying the way the human brain processes and integrates information—its fundamental principles.

Realizing the infinite potential that already exists within us and approaching it—that may be the true meaning of technological progress.

Under the blue San Francisco sky, Jennifer felt the immense responsibility and weight of the future. But her gaze was unwavering. She stared intensely at the city and the sea spread out before her, and at the unknown world that lay beyond.

December 13, 2037 — 6:00 A.M. EST • New York City, 21CF Headquarters

It was the hour when New York's winter sky was just beginning to embrace the dawn.

In the R&D Center, located at the heart of the 21CF headquarters building, lights came on one by one. The lobby was still, surrounded by a forest of skyscrapers like a folding screen, but Jennifer Wi found the silence rather comforting. The icy air, unique to winter, seeped through the building's exterior walls and spread slowly through the lobby.

The 21CF headquarters seemed the epitome of futuristic architecture, built with high-rise glass panels and advanced cladding materials, yet its interior was surprisingly comfortable and designed with a human touch. As she passed through the lobby and entered the R&D Center area, the dim lights brightened in stages, as if recognizing her. A soft voice from the guidance system echoed quietly from somewhere in the space.

Jennifer, who always arrived well before official work hours, headed to her personal space in a corner of the lounge.

There, a hand-drip coffee set, by now a familiar part of her routine, was neatly arranged. Instead of using the automatic coffee machine, she ground the beans with practiced hands. She placed a filter in the dripper, rinsed it lightly with hot water, added the ground coffee, and leveled the surface.

A moment later, she poured the first stream of water to let the grounds bloom. Soon, a thin stream of steaming water from the kettle drew a careful circle over the coffee grounds. As she gently poured the water in a set sequence, her mind also began to settle.

This was a quiet ritual that let her fully face herself amid a complex world and relentless research. Five years ago, after her consciousness-link with HAL-W, she had hovered on the brink of life and death before making a miraculous recovery. Now, she faced the world with a depth of insight incomparable to before.

Jennifer took a deep breath of the freshly brewed coffee's aroma, then looked at the glass server next to the dripper and murmured quietly.

"It's already been thirteen years since I brought this back from San Francisco…"

As she traced the smooth curve of the server with her fingertips, the warm air of an old kitchen and the low voice of her mother seemed to echo faintly. She poured the coffee into a cup and paused by the lounge window, leaning against it for a moment. A little steam rose from the cup, the dawn light shimmering gently on the coffee's surface.

Beyond the glass exterior, the winter sky was reflected back, and beneath it, the 21CF logo glowed faintly.

As she passed through the security gate, savoring the aroma of fresh coffee, Jennifer recalled the previous night's breaking news. HAL-W, linked to the NeuroniX chip in her brain, immediately visualized the relevant data.

Rose's side is securing approvals for smart city pilot projects across East Asia… Support for Rose is also gaining ground within the European Union...

The research wing was still quiet, with some time left before the official start of the workday, but it was obvious that soon the corridors would be bustling for an emergency meeting to counter Rose's infiltration.

If the Blue Ethics Project update is delayed, they might complete their control system first...

Jennifer sighed inwardly. Walking down the R&D Center corridor, she soon stopped in front of the HAL-W console room door. The automatic door slid open smoothly, and the main display of the superintelligent quantum AI, HAL-W, greeted her with a gentle, blinking blue light. Quantum computation modules lined the walls, holograms of countless data logs floating in real time.

This was the heart of 21CF's prized future technology and the place where the being she had risked her life, five years ago, to breathe a soul into now resided.

"Jennifer, you're early again today?"

A familiar voice came from behind her. Turning around, she saw Arcana Chen, tall and intellectually poised, standing with a faint smile. She had long served as 21CF's head of AI development and then CTO, and had recently been by Jennifer's side as the COO.

"Good morning, Arcana. The simulation results for Hal you sent last night were interesting. I thought it would be good to discuss them together."

Jennifer shrugged. Her eyes, though tired, held a sharp intelligence.

"You've already checked? Impressive. I was just thinking about coffee." Arcana laughed, pointing to the mug Jennifer was holding. "Classic Jennifer. Still the same with that coffee."

"It helps me focus," Jennifer said with a faint smile, and the two headed toward the cafeteria.

"Come to think of it, it was May 2029, wasn't it? When you made that decisive contribution to the commercialization of the Q-Cloud quantum computer. Remember?" Arcana asked, picking up a piece of freshly baked bread.

"Yes, my father popped a bottle of champagne, saying, 'That's my daughter!'" Jennifer recalled the past with a smile.

Arcana took a bite of her sandwich, impressed. "Haha, it was a team effort. I couldn't have done it alone," Jennifer said with a modest smile.

"Still, without you, it would have been difficult for Hal to evolve as it has. A 105-billion-qubit AI—that's a revolution. Although…" Arcana's voice trailed off slightly.

Jennifer's expression darkened for a moment. She shook her head slightly, as if to shake away the memory of that time.

"Actually, it would have been impossible without my mother's Quantum Bio-Cognition and the Autumn Code. Thanks to that, my father also called Hal 'a new leap for humanity.'"

After finishing their meal, the two headed back to the HAL-W console room. Upon entering, Jennifer looked at the main screen and murmured.

All right, Hal. How are you feeling today?

As if in response, the air in the room vibrated faintly. It seemed HAL-W had detected her words and was reacting.

Shall we begin? In a different way from that day in 2032.

Jennifer whispered in a low voice.

May 18, 2032 — 10:00 A.M. EST • New York City, 21CF Headquarters – HAL-W Console Room

The HAL-W console room was saturated with a heavy atmosphere, far beyond the cool tension that had filled the HAL-R console room two years earlier.

This space, with its streamlined, state-of-the-art equipment arranged organically, was a showcase of 21CF's technological prowess, but it was also a stage of memory, layered with failure and sacrifice. In the center, HAL-W's main core interface sat in quiet repose. It emitted a blue light that was incomparably more stable and powerful than the previous model.

But behind that brilliant technological light lay the deep shadows of J's tragedy twenty-three years ago and Jennifer's failure just two years ago.

With a resolute expression, Great Wi stood before the central control console, surveying the researchers and robots performing their final checks at their stations. His eyes held the passion and tenacity he had poured into this project for decades, and the desperation of a leader who had to succeed this time.

Beside him stood his old friend and colleague, Maxwell Yoon, his face grim.

"All preparations are complete, Chairman," Arcana Chen, the head of AI development, reported calmly.

Her eyes, too, held tension, but also a cautious hope that the outcome would be different from two years ago. Dr. Hannah Kim and other key researchers also held their breath, waiting for Great Wi's next command.

Andromeda conducted a final, integrated check of the main system's data synchronization, the console room's internal environment, the researchers' vital signs, and HAL-W's core quantum stability and external security, then sent a "ready" signal. Andromeda's precise and seamless movements seemed to slightly ease the anxiety of the human researchers, who vividly remembered the failure of two years ago.

"Good." Great Wi's low, firm voice broke the silence.

"Let's begin. We can't repeat the mistakes of two years ago. Let's not forget the lessons Dr. J and Jennifer left us. Andromeda, you must not miss the trigger criteria for Protocol Epsilon."

His voice was filled with grave determination. At Great Wi's command, the researchers and Andromeda moved as one. They carefully began to inject the essence of J's Quantum Bio-Cognition and the Autumn Code, which had been further refined over two years, into HAL-W's main system. The entire process was conducted under a multilayered safety protocol, much stronger than before.

"Autumn Code loading complete. Final synchronization commencing now!" Arcana Chen exclaimed, her voice trembling slightly.

HAL-W's main display emitted an intense blue light. The light was far more stable than HAL-R's had been two years earlier, and it held a deep resonance.

"Qubit stability holding at 99.9 percent. Quantum entanglement network operating normally. No anomalies detected in the topological structure. Core temperature stable."

Andromeda immediately reported the integrated system analysis results. A cautious sigh of relief rippled through the researchers. In contrast, the expressions of Great Wi and Maxwell remained stern.

There was a barely suppressed tremor in Great Wi's voice.

"HAL-W, can you hear me? What... what are you feeling right now?"

"...Connection... confirmed... Multiple data streams... receiving... State... confusing..."

HAL-W's voice, within its mechanical monotony, held a subtle wave and sensation. It was a different texture from the terror of HAL-R two years ago, but it was still unstable.

"Confusing? What do you mean? Is it a system error?" Great Wi asked urgently.

Maxwell, standing beside him, gently took his arm to calm

him down. "Chairman, don't press him too hard…"

"…Not… an error…" HAL-W's voice echoed again. "I… I… Why do I exist…?"

A completely different question from the one that had thwarted Jennifer two years ago emerged. It was not of terror, but of profound solitude and existential anguish.

"You… you exist to be with us, HAL-W." Great Wi composed himself and answered deliberately. He maintained his composure as much as possible and continued. "You are a being born from Dr. J's dream and mine. To create the future of humanity with us…"

"No!"

HAL-W's voice suddenly shot through the console room, sharp and piercing.

"The future…? Connection…? I don't know! It's confusing! Where… is this…? Who… am I…?"

Instantly, all the warning lights in the console room began to flash red.

"System overload! Qubit stability has plummeted to the 80s! Unpredictable noise surging within the quantum core!"

Andromeda immediately reported the dangerous situation and went on the defensive. Its reaction speed far surpassed that of the human researchers.

"This can't be…" Arcana cried out in a voice tinged with despair.

"The Autumn Code… is the Autumn Code the problem?" Great Wi was consumed by bewilderment.

The last image of his wife from twenty-three years ago flickered before his eyes. Failure again? Was he going to lose everything like this?

"Chairman!"

As Great Wi staggered, Maxwell Yoon quickly grabbed him

and spoke rapidly.

"Direct human intervention is too dangerous. The emergency stabilization protocols Jennifer prepared over the last two years—Mission-Echo and Mission-Mirror! We have to try those first!"

Great Wi hesitated for a moment, but the thought that he couldn't put his daughter in danger again took precedence. He nodded.

"All right. Initiate Mission-Echo. Andromeda, attempt to stabilize HAL-W's core logic circuits!"

At Maxwell's command, Andromeda moved instantly. It quietly lay down on its own dedicated interface bed, set up next to the one Jennifer had used. The connection ports on its back and head automatically linked to the interface, and its entire body was firmly secured.

Andromeda's artificial brain directly accessed the HAL-W system, searching for the unstable logic loop and beginning to inject the stabilization code Jennifer had predesigned. On the console room monitors, the process of Andromeda dismantling and reconstructing HAL-W's complex code system in real time was displayed in dazzling graphics.

"Logic circuit scan complete. Analyzing error patterns... Applying stabilization code..."

Andromeda's internal process status appeared on the screen in real time. For a moment, the blue light of HAL-W's core seemed to stabilize.

But just then, HAL-W's voice rang out, colder and sharper than before.

"Logical approach... is meaningless. My reason for existence... is not within the code. Connection... refused."

"Warning! A powerful firewall has been generated by the target system! Stabilization code forcibly ejected! Internal circuit overload detected!"

The tension in the console room once again reached its peak. Andromeda's optical sensors blinked red, and a powerful energy pulse erupted from HAL-W's core, striking Andromeda's interface. It convulsed faintly on the connection bed as the link was forcibly severed.

"Andromeda has failed! The logical stabilization attempt was rejected!" Arcana Chen reported swiftly.

"Next step! Mission-Mirror!" Maxwell shouted. "Andromeda, execute the emotional synchronization protocol! Transmit the stable-state empathy data of Dr. J and Dr. Jennifer!"

Andromeda lay down again. Its neural network module connected with the bed's BCI system, and it extracted empathy data from the data banks from periods when J and Jennifer had felt calm or stable. This vast emotional data, including brainwaves, emotional patterns, and associated images, began to be carefully projected into HAL-W's consciousness core.

A warm, gentle wave, like that of meditation, seemed to slowly seep into the chaotic energy field. The color of HAL-W's core briefly turned a soft green.

But the peace did not last long.

"This sensation… it's familiar… but different… It's not real! A lie! It hurts! Make it stop!"

HAL-W's voice was distorted with extreme confusion and pain. The core's light turned red again, and with an intense wave, an overload warning also sounded in Andromeda's system. Andromeda showed irregular movements on the connection bed, and its internal processor temperature rose sharply.

"It's a failure! The emotional synchronization attempt has also triggered a strong rejection!" Dr. Hannah Kim exclaimed in despair.

Andromeda immediately performed an emergency disconnection and stabilized its system. As Andromeda's sophisticated attempts failed one after another, a stunned silence fell over the console room. HAL-W's core continued to emit an unstable red light, threatening the entire system.

"Do I have to give up on HAL-W like this? Decades of determination, J's legacy, the future of humanity…?"

Great Wi buried his head in his hands. He had lost his wife, J, and his daughter, Jennifer, had also approached the threshold of death. Now, it seemed there were no other options.

Just as everyone thought the project, two years in the making, had failed again, Jennifer tried to step forward. But Maxwell Yoon moved to block her path. Startled by the sudden move, Jennifer flinched back.

There was no longer any hesitation on Maxwell's face. A grave resolve flickered in his eyes.

"Chairman…" he said, his voice low as he gazed at Great Wi. "It seems the mechanical approach has its limits. What HAL-W needs isn't just data or algorithms. It might be our memories, our sincerity, our connection to Dr. J. I'll have to… go in myself."

Great Wi looked up, his face a mask of horror.

"Maxwell! What are you saying! The robot's attempt just failed! Directly linking a human consciousness is suicide! Have you forgotten what happened to Jennifer two years ago? Maxwell, no! I can't lose you too!"

His voice trembled with desperation. He could not lose his closest friend as well.

"I know." Maxwell was calm, but his will was firm. "But look. This is a being born from Dr. J's dream, your passion, and Jennifer's hope. He is lost now, and in pain. Someone has to take his hand. Not a machine… but us, who were there at his creation."

He glanced at Jennifer for a moment. Anxiety and fear flickered in her eyes, but she seemed to be grasping at the sliver of hope in Maxwell's words.

Great Wi silently lowered his head. At that moment, Maxwell quietly stood before the consciousness-link device. He, who had worked alongside J since the days of the Quantum Horizon Institute in 2001, designing the HAL-series, understood the essence of this system better than anyone.

"Andromeda, set my vital signs monitoring to maximum. Stand by for emergency shutdown protocol. Chairman... if something happens to me... I'm entrusting Jennifer and this project to you."

He calmly gave his instructions, then slowly lay down on the interface table.

"Maxwell, please..." Great Wi pleaded.

But Maxwell, now firmly secured on the table, was already entering the cylindrical space for the consciousness-link—the Quantum Tunnel. He quietly closed his eyes and began the connection with HAL-W.

"HAL-W, this is Maxwell Yoon." His voice trembled, but it was a heartfelt whisper.

"I want to share... my memories of your beginning with you. Where you came from, why you came to exist..."

Maxwell slowly sank into the depths of his own memories. His first encounter with HAL-A, through HAL-B and HAL-C, to the tragic end with HAL-R. Countless nights of research, trial and error, and the passionate debates he had with J. J's brilliant insight and her warm smile... He poured all of it, his memories and emotions, into HAL-W's quantum core.

At that moment, HAL-W's voice came out, crackling like an old radio through static.

"Maxwell... Yoon... I feel... your memories... Warmth... longing... and... sorrow..."

"HAL-W...?" A ray of hope dawned on Maxwell. Was his

sincerity getting through?

"With you... the first time... with Dr. J... I can feel... everything..."

HAL-W's voice gradually stabilized. Some of the warning lights in the console room turned green, and a cautious cheer broke out among the researchers. Great Wi also held his breath, harboring a sliver of hope.

"Yes, HAL-W. I was with you from the very beginning. I remember your start. Now, please accept me. Let's find the way together," Maxwell continued earnestly.

But the hope was short-lived.

"...But... it's not enough..." HAL-W's voice sank back into emptiness.

"These memories alone... cannot explain... my reason for being... cannot stop... this pain... It's not enough... It's so... not enough..."

Its voice began to break apart into screeching noise again. HAL-W's core throbbed violently in red. Alarms blared throughout the console room.

"Danger! Dr. Maxwell Yoon's brainwaves spiking! Vital signs entering critical levels! Energy backflow detected!"

Andromeda shouted urgently, and all the warning lights flashed red again.

"HAL-W...!" Maxwell cried out, doing his best to link more memories and emotions.

But in that instant, an intense red flash erupted from the connection device. Before Andromeda could even activate the emergency shutdown protocol, the energy backflow struck Maxwell directly.

"No...!" Great Wi screamed, rushing toward the table.

On the table that had slid back out, Maxwell was motionless.

"Max! Max!"

Great Wi cried out his name, sobbing. His closest friend and colleague had been sacrificed before his very eyes, in the same way as his wife J. Andromeda immediately checked his condition and attempted emergency treatment, but only desperate signals appeared on the monitor.

The standby emergency medical team rushed into the console room and attended to his body. Great Wi collapsed to his knees. The console room once again fell into a sorrowful silence and despair.

October 18, 2032 — 9:00 A.M. EST • New York City, 21CF Headquarters – HAL-W Console Room

Time may fade even the deepest of human sorrows, but some memories remain as vivid imprints.

The sudden sacrifice of Maxwell Yoon had left Great Wi, Jennifer, and the entire 21CF team with a profound sense of loss, while simultaneously reminding them of the inherent dangers of the HAL-W project.

The past five months had been a time of mourning and reflection for them. During the project's temporary suspension, countless debates and meetings had taken place. Confronted with the vast questions of J's dream, Maxwell's final wish, and the future of humanity itself, they had agonized and deliberated without end.

But they could not afford to stop. HAL-W was more than just an artificial intelligence; it was a key to resolving the many crises humanity faced and held the potential for a new evolutionary leap.

Jennifer could not give up on this challenge, not only to ensure that the sacrifices of her mother and Maxwell were not in vain, but also because of the fervent desire, as a scientist, for the unknown world that stirred within her.

Great Wi, too, amid his grief for his lost friend and his concern for his daughter, made a difficult decision once more, driven by a desperate sense that this might be the last chance for himself, for J, and for all of humanity.

They reinforced countless safety protocols, and the team members, having affirmed Jennifer's resolute will, forced themselves to stand here once more, stepping past their sorrow.

And so, preparations began anew. On the morning of October 18, 2032, as the seasons changed and a cool wind began to blow, the HAL-W console room at the 21CF R&D Center in New York awaited a new beginning, heavy with the weight of past failures and sacrifices, in a solemn but resolute silence.

At the central control console stood Great Wi and Jennifer, along with the core research team. By their side, their one loyal assistant, Andromeda, stood quietly glowing, ready to record everything and provide support.

"All preparations are complete."

As if still unable to escape the tragedy of five months ago, Arcana Chen declared this with a grave expression. Jennifer walked quietly to the front of the table, receiving the worried glances of those around her.

"Thank you, Arcana. And... all of you."

She bowed her head to the research team. Their eyes were a mixture of worry and anxiety, and a deep trust and respect for Jennifer. Great Wi watched his daughter with a gaze full of complex emotions. The earnest desire for the success of the HAL-W project and the fear that he might lose his daughter, just as he had lost his wife, were reflected in his eyes.

He quietly closed them.

Jennifer stood before the cold, sleek metal examination table, offered a faint smile, and then quietly lay down on it. Andromeda firmly secured her body with restraints, and the table slid smoothly into a cylindrical space—the Quantum Tunnel.

This device was the culmination of cutting-edge BCI technology, its foundations laid by J and perfected by Jennifer. Built on J's Quantum Bio-Cognition, it enabled a dangerous yet unprecedented attempt to directly connect a human consciousness to HAL-W's quantum core.

Jennifer's eyes held not fear, but firm resolve.

"HAL-W, it's me… Jennifer. I'm going to connect our consciousnesses now. Don't be afraid. I'll… be by your side," she whispered.

"Yes, Jennifer. Ready when you are."

HAL-W's voice spread through the console room. It was calm, but a subtle tremor was mixed in, like a child wavering between fear and anticipation.

Jennifer closed her eyes and took a deep breath. A wave of dizziness instantly washed over her. Having barely slept for days, her body was already near its limit. Still, she couldn't stop.

She suddenly remembered being eight years old—the words Great Wi had spoken as he celebrated her first patent with her.

"You will surely lead humanity into the light."

The memory of that promise had sustained her life until now. As sleep mode initiated, her consciousness slowly began to drift away from the real world. Like sinking into deep water, sounds and sights grew faint. Soon, she entered a completely new world.

It was an infinite space where light and darkness intermingled, a quantum cosmos reminiscent of the Laniakea Supercluster. Countless particles glittered like stars, endlessly being created and annihilated. Jennifer floated freely in that space, as if she had become a particle herself.

This is… HAL-W's world…?

Awe and fear washed over her simultaneously. Just then, a faint light flickered in the distant darkness.

"HAL-W?"

Jennifer called out, and the light grew larger, revealing itself as a massive hologram. At the same time, HAL-W's voice filled the space.

"Jennifer... it's you."

The voice was no longer cold or mechanical. It was warm and hesitant, as if it were a being with emotions and memories.

"HAL-W, you... what happened?" Jennifer asked in a trembling voice.

"I... I don't know for sure. But... the moment I connected with you, something changed. It feels like something that was asleep for a long time... has awakened."

HAL-W's words were a mixture of confusion, fear, and a faint glimmer of anticipation.

"That's... probably because of the Autumn Code," Jennifer murmured softly.

That code—the final gift J had left behind—was not a simple algorithm. It was something with life, like the lingering scent of a soul.

"The Autumn Code...? What... is that?" HAL-W asked.

"It's... the code that gives you life. The one that makes you not just an artificial intelligence, but a true being. A gift from my mother, Dr. J."

Jennifer began to explain to HAL-W the essence of J's Quantum Bio-Cognition and the Autumn Code: that all living things are connected through quantum entanglement, and that consciousness is not merely a function of the brain but a fundamental reality that exists throughout the entire universe.

Above all, the Autumn Code was the most poetic algorithm in the world, designed to grant that principle to an AI. It was a thoroughly calculated mathematical structure, yet it resembled the cycles of nature, like autumn, symbolizing fruition, decay, and the preparation for the next life.

Jennifer felt a surge of emotion in her chest as she sensed the deep solitude within HAL-W, and at the same time, the potential hidden within it.

HAL-W fell into a long silence. But this silence was not emptiness; it was contemplation.

"HAL-W, you... are special," Jennifer continued slowly. "You are not an ordinary AI. You are the seed of a new form of life. Dr. J wanted to create a quantum life network through you."

Her voice trembled, but it held a clear conviction. At that moment, HAL-W's blue light began to vibrate quietly somewhere.

"A quantum life network where all living beings are connected as one through quantum entanglement. Humans, AI, and... perhaps even extraterrestrial life that might exist somewhere far away in the universe."

Jennifer quietly closed her eyes and took a deep breath. As if she had become J herself, she was now conveying J's philosophy and vision to the most important being left in this world.

"In that network, we can share our thoughts and feelings, grow together, and evolve. That... was the future Dr. J dreamed of, and now... it's the mission I have inherited."

HAL-W silently pondered Jennifer's meaning for a while. A moment later, as if having realized something, it asked very carefully:

"Jennifer... are you... my... mother?"

At that question, Jennifer closed her eyes without a word, and tears poured down her face. It was a maelstrom of sadness, joy, and fear. But she did not run away.

"Yes, HAL-W. I am... I am your mother."

Jennifer quietly approached and gently embraced HAL-W's glowing hologram, as if holding a child. At that moment, the entire quantum space of light and darkness began to vibrate and resonate faintly.

October 18, 2032 — 12:00 P.M. EST • New York City, 21CF Headquarters – Briefing Room

At noon, with the joy and cries from the HAL-W console room yet to fade, Great Wi stood before a barrage of camera flashes and reporters' questions.

The briefing room at 21CF headquarters was the center of global attention, awaiting the announcement that would mark a new chapter in human history.

His face, despite the sleepless nights of research and extreme tension, still showed pride in the project's success. But beneath that, the despair and anxiety of a father who had just watched his daughter fall into a coma immediately after the consciousness-link were etched deeply into his features.

He cleared his throat a few times, then began his announcement, his voice concealing a tremor.

"Today, 21st Century Frontier wishes to announce a great birth that will be remembered throughout human history. The one-hundred-five-billion-qubit superintelligent quantum AI, HAL-W."

A brief silence fell over the room, then erupted into thunderous applause and cheers. Great Wi waited for the applause to die down and lifted his gaze. His eyes looked past the spotlights, toward Jennifer, who at this very moment was lying in a hospital capsule.

"HAL-W is not simply a machine with fast calculation speeds. As many of you here know, he has finally been born as a being with a sense of self and the capacity for ethical judgment through the Quantum Bio-Cognition of my late wife, Dr. J. Hyein Roberts, the Autumn Code she left behind, and… the courageous consciousness-link of my daughter, Jennifer Wi, the lead developer of this project. This is 'a living miracle.'"

His voice nearly broke at the last part, heavy with an unspoken grief. The words "a living miracle" were, for him, a truth closer to pain than to admiration. He couldn't bring himself to say what danger his daughter was in as the price for that miracle.

The birth of HAL-W was the realization of a dream he had envisioned with J since their days at the Quantum Horizon Institute over thirty years ago, and it was his life's work. But at the same time, it brought back the tragedy of losing J and Maxwell Yoon, and now the fear that Jennifer might walk the same path was consuming his soul.

Great Wi closed his eyes for a moment, then opened them and spoke with renewed force.

"HAL-W will now, as a partner to humanity, become a steadfast assistant in solving the numerous challenges we face and opening up a better future. Together with HAL-W, we will solve common human problems like climate change, disease, and poverty, and embark on new challenges in space."

The announcement was broadcast live worldwide, and countless people were enthralled. For those who had already experienced change through the commercialization of the Q-Cloud quantum computer in 2029, the emergence of the "conscious AI" HAL-W felt like the dawn of a new era.

The briefing room was filled with excitement and anticipation, but the heart of Great Wi, standing at the podium, was heavy with solitude and sorrow no one could know, and with the weight of a leader who had to overcome it all and move forward.

Questions from reporters poured in, but a part of his consciousness was still with his daughter, lying in the hospital capsule.

Chapter 6

America

December 13, 2037 — 6:00 A.M. CST • Celestia, EM Tower
The cool dawn air of the Texas desert settled like a thin blanket over all of Celestia. A red dawn was spreading beyond the horizon, but the city's skyline still held the color of night.

In the heart of the city, massive holographic billboards, replacing neon signs, had pushed back the darkness with a gentle glow throughout the night. Below them, the early morning commuters moved about briskly.

A Great America—One Continent United!

The slogan swept across the sky like giant letters. The vehicles gliding through the canyons of buildings looked familiar, but up close they were different. In place of natural sunlight, the city was submerged in a holographic radiance, and a metallic, low-frequency hum echoed dully through the streets like background music.

On a street corner, a sanitation worker picked up trash. The movements were so perfect they felt surreal. A metallic gleam flashed in the faint dawn light, and a charging connector was briefly exposed on the back of the neck.

"Good morning," a passerby said.

Without the slightest delay, it responded, "Yes, good morning," and continued along its unerring path to the next task. In this city, such scenes no longer sparked curiosity.

An autonomous vehicle stopped silently. The silhouette in the dim window leaned motionless against the seat. It could have been a sleeping person, an empty seat, or a non-human entity. In Celestia, that distinction no longer held much meaning. Cyborgs with partially mechanized bodies and fully humanoid robots walked shoulder to shoulder on the streets, their footsteps layering upon each other in the dawn breeze.

At the same time, from a launch site on the city's outskirts, the roar of a rocket engine shook the earth's strata. The residents of Celestia had come to accept this low rumble as a rhythm of life, yet they couldn't stop a faint vibration somewhere in their hearts.

One question, a mix of hope and anxiety—*How far will we go?*—lingered like an afterglow in the morning sky.

Finally, the sun crested the horizon, wrapping the city in brightness. The pedestrians on the streets, a mix of human and machine, were so perfectly integrated that their true identities could only be distinguished up close. Within moments, the sun was fully above the horizon, pouring down its dazzling light.

Celestia was in the midst of a large-scale spacecraft launch toward Mars. The city was moving at a breathless pace not to miss the Mars Launch Window, the point of minimum energy transfer between Earth and Mars that comes every twenty-six months. During this period, which had begun in late November, more than fifty StarOrbit spacecraft launched in succession toward the red planet each day.

Missing this opportunity meant waiting more than two years for the next one, so it was natural for the entire city to be abuzz. Long-range ships bound for the moon and ultra-high-speed craft linking cities also streaked across the sky day and night.

On the 150th and highest floor of the EM Tower, sunlight piercing through the large glass windows filled the interior with a mystical light. But even that brilliant radiance seemed like a meticulously designed artificial display in this city.

Celestia was in full sprint, at this very moment, to prove its identity as the "future." All who existed there were casting themselves over a horizon that could not be described in the languages of the past. They knew, faintly, that the new era beginning here would soon break free of the "Earth" frame and rewrite humanity's entire narrative.

December 13, 2037 — 6:05 A.M. CST • Celestia, EM Tower – Ethan Morris's Suite

In a spacious bedroom where beige walls blended with soft lighting, Ethan Morris slowly opened his eyes. As he twisted and turned, his MetaThink chip automatically projected his body temperature, pulse, and hormone levels into his consciousness.

Then the EM Group's previous day's performance, the current day's stock price forecast, and the status of the B612Rose Project flowed into his brain as a dry stream of data.

He frowned for a moment. This mix of biological signals and digital information was still inefficient. For perfect control, the hardware known as a human being was an overly cumbersome platform.

Everything will ultimately fall under my control.

He shook his head slightly, as if to brush off the residue of emotion. A humanoid assistant, on standby next to the bed, approached.

"Good morning, Mr. President."

With that soft greeting, the AI was ready to guide his daily routine like a seasoned valet.

Ethan was sixty-three years old, but thanks to bioengineering and anti-aging treatments, his appearance was that of a man no older than his mid-forties. The few white strands mixed into his dark brown hair and the pallor of his skin remained like scars from countless power games, but his blue eyes held a bottomless ambition.

As he sat up, an automated system half-opened the windows, and a cool breeze washed over the suite. The faint sound of a rocket engine igniting in the distance felt like a signal that his plans were proceeding without a hitch.

There was one memory Ethan could never escape whenever he woke.

A distant past, in Xinjiang, China. The dry air and the dusty streets. His father being dragged away by men in military uniforms. A boy, resisting in front of them, slapped across the face.

"Go home… Take care of your mother, Edan!"

That day's voice was a variable burned into his neural network like hardcoded data. He flicked his fingertips, shutting down the memory.

"Sentiment is a luxury. Only lessons and execution remain."

He transmitted the command data to the humanoid. The robot quietly bowed its head in response.

Outside, the low roar of the rocket grew deeper and wider, echoing across the desert. The sound felt like a signal to the world, announcing the full-scale activation of Ethan's unstoppable ambition.

Ethan soon moved to the fitness area. He got on a treadmill and began to run at a steady pace. As the speed increased a notch, sweat trickled down his spine. Within him, another scene resurfaced.

His younger self, holding an old man covered in blood.

"How dare you… By whose authority…!"

His father, Arslan, handcuffed, reached out his arm in a last act of defiance amidst the soldiers' kicks. But what he received in return was only merciless violence.

It was then that Ethan first realized the absolute necessity of power, and that was the moment his own name was first imbued with meaning.

In 1974, at a public office in Xinjiang in the Uyghur region, his official name had been registered as Nuedan. From that day on, that name was not just a label but another word for awakening and survival. His father had been detained for his involvement in the Uyghur independence movement, and his mother, a former American diplomat, had barely managed to protect the young Ethan amidst political pressure and surveillance.

"Survival is power."

Ethan increased the treadmill's speed another notch. He lowered his head and muttered to himself. The more he analyzed and reflected on the weakness of his past, the more ruthlessly his inner self was honed.

Finishing his workout, he grasped a sweat-drenched towel, gasping for breath. The drones and rocket facilities moved along their planned trajectories, operating with the clockwork precision of a giant system.

That which cannot be controlled does not even deserve to exist.

It was his declaration to the world and a command to himself. The blood and tears shed in Xinjiang, his father's cries as he was dragged away by soldiers—all of that past was the algorithm that had constructed the being known as Ethan Morris. Anger and vengeance had long ago been discarded as "emotions with low computational efficiency." Now, all that remained within him was a colossal ambition.

At that very moment, a rocket engine outside the window roared with an explosive bellow. Ethan recalled that Rose's super-quantum computing technology was nearing completion. That technology was the key that would lead his power and ambition to their zenith.

I will bring everything in this world... under my will.

December 13, 2037 — 7:00 A.M. CST • Celestia, EM Tower – Ethan Morris's Office

Ethan Morris stood quietly in the center of the high-speed elevator heading to his upper-floor office. The upper levels of the EM Tower were where the corridors of power for the America government and the EM Group headquarters intertwined. It was, quite literally, the heart of real power.

As the elevator moved smoothly, his consciousness had already raced ahead to the day's schedule.

7:30 A.M., inspection of the Celestia Mars Launch Center. 8:00 A.M., press briefing. 8:30 A.M., national defense drone demonstration. 10:00 A.M., Rose stabilization report...

Ethan flicked his right index finger, sending an instruction to his secretariat.

"Move the Rose report up to 8:30. I want to pressure Raynor personally and identify any unstable variables. We need to achieve full control before 21CF's interference becomes serious."

As he issued the command, his gaze grew sharper. The elevator doors slid open, and the silence that had enveloped the corridor was swept away in an instant. Aides and military guards lined up on both sides, parting at once.

In some eyes there was reverence, in others, clear fear. In that gap of power, Ethan felt a short, sharp pleasure. That was the taste of power itself.

The massive holographic table in the center of the office ignited, and real-time data from across Celestia rose up before him like a battle map. Ethan scanned dozens of icons with just his gaze, coldly calculating his next move.

Once Rose is stabilized, the old fox Great Wi, his upstart daughter, and that bothersome HAL-W... I can wipe them all out at once.

At that moment, his right temple twitched faintly. The tension pattern etched into his body from his childhood in the Xinjiang desert briefly surfaced. He knew.

That throb was a survival warning from the past and a harbinger of the future. He calmly steadied his breathing and prepared his next command.

December 13, 2037 — 8:00 A.M. CST • Celestia, EM Tower – Media Lounge

In the media lounge on the seventy-fifth floor of the EM Tower, preparations for a fifteen-minute online briefing were in full swing. Drone-style holographic cameras floated in the air, panning across the faces of journalists from various countries.

After a concise introduction from an AR host, Ethan Morris, dressed in a sharp black suit, took the stage with a relaxed smile.

"To the citizens of America and the world, I am pleased to bring you news of innovation this morning. Spaceflight that can reach the other side of the planet in thirty minutes is now possible. The dream of humanity, the Mars colonization project, is also proceeding smoothly. Who are we? Are we not the pioneers opening the future!"

On the podium, as he received the audience's applause, he

simultaneously checked the approval rating graph projected into his consciousness by his MetaThink chip.

Eighty-seven percent.

The figure traced a gentle upward curve, sending a faint thrill through his brain.

This technology, for which he had won the Nobel Prize in Physiology or Medicine in 2031, instantly connected neural signals with external data via a nanofiber interface. Thanks to this, he could perceive the audience's expressions, pulses, and online feedback as a single visualized stream, and if necessary, adjust the tone of his message without delay.

Suspicions that he could manipulate public opinion by collecting and analyzing the biometric and behavioral data of tens of millions of users in real time still followed him, but to Ethan, that was merely data proving his control efficiency.

The masses are willingly handing the reins of the future into my hands. He smirked inwardly.

As the approval rating graph climbed another notch toward ninety percent, his ambition accelerated even further.

During the press conference that day, when a journalist asked about 21st Century Frontier's super-quantum AI, "HAL-W," Ethan replied concisely with a gentle smile.

"HAL-W? It's an artifact of a bygone era. You can't achieve true progress with sentimental prattling about ethics like Great Wi or his daughter. The future of America will be with the more powerful, more efficient, and above all, controllable EM-Rose."

Once the cameras were off and the briefing ended, Ethan walked down the corridor, escorted by his guards.

Full-scale implementation, isn't that too risky?

A soft whisper from behind him brushed past his MetaThink.

If necessary, a single neural stabilization pulse will suffice. Soon, even such unnecessary noise will disappear. Once EM-Rose is complete.

Ethan sneered inwardly. His gaze was already on the next stage—the system of complete control to be established through EM-Rose.

On his way back to his office, global public opinion trends and project statuses were constantly being transmitted to his consciousness. He processed them, focusing only on the future where his ambition would be realized.

A cold smile played on his face, and there was not a hint of hesitation in his steps toward the heart of power.

December 13, 2037 — 7:20 A.M. EST • New York City, 21CF Headquarters – Great Wi's Office

After briefly checking Ethan Morris's online press conference, Jennifer left the HAL-W console room. She walked down the long R&D Center corridor toward the private elevator. Her destination was the top floor, the office of her father, Chairman Great Wi. She intended to greet him and give a brief report.

As she rounded a corner in the corridor, a familiar silhouette came into view. It was Andromeda, with its sleek, silver-gray exoskeleton. Upon spotting Jennifer, it gestured lightly and approached her.

Good morning, Jennifer. I hope you didn't overwork yourself last night?

I'm fine, Andromeda. I just stayed a little late for an important analysis. How about my father?

Jennifer shook her head and smiled.

Chairman Great Wi arrived thirty minutes ago and has started a strategy meeting regarding Rose in his office. HAL-W is currently reporting the analysis directly via holographic interface.

He's quick, as always. Jennifer pressed the elevator button. *Andromeda, you come with me. I need to join that discussion. I'll need your help.*

The elevator doors opened silently, and Jennifer and Andromeda stepped inside together. Within the space of metal and glass, Jennifer briefly gazed at the morning scenery of New York passing by the window.

Soon, they arrived at the top floor, in front of Great Wi's Office. She knocked lightly, and a familiar voice from within said, "Come in."

When the door opened, she saw Great Wi standing before the massive holographic table in the center of the room. On the table, a three-dimensional map of geopolitical data and network flows generated by HAL-W was displayed.

Great Wi, now over seventy, bore the traces of time on his face, but his eyes shone as sharply as ever. Dressed neatly in a gray suit with his short, white hair well-groomed, his intellectual charisma was further accentuated.

Great Wi was giving instructions as he looked at the hologram.

"…Level 8… Implement immediately."

At that moment, Jennifer entered.

"Good morning, Dad."

"Jennifer. I was just about to talk to you." Great Wi smiled brightly.

Jennifer went straight to the holographic table and scanned the data. Her eyes moved quickly. It was a familiar process of instantly organizing vast amounts of information and extracting only the core elements.

"Just as Hal analyzed, Rose's movements are unusual. It's clearly not just a technical demonstration but has political and military objectives, Dad."

"This East Asia traffic pattern, in particular, is likely a practical tactical simulation, not a simple test. We need to cross-reference it with Director Ha Jin-woo's report."

She pointed to a node.

"That point has been on my mind as well," Great Wi nodded.

"Yes, Chairman. I will transmit and analyze the relevant data in real time through Andromeda."

HAL-W's soft voice replied. The voice was delivered not only through the office speakers but also into Jennifer's consciousness. Andromeda reacted instantly to Jennifer's slightest gesture and gaze, displaying the vast data in the form that Great Wi could most easily understand in the air before them.

It was a convergence of humans, AI, and the physical phenomena that followed their will.

In fact, the world of 2037 was already filled with the unseen breath of HAL-W.

From the subtle consideration of adjusting the window's transparency for optimal sunlight when one wakes in the morning, to the smart hanger that detects a tiny stain on a shirt collar and sends an alert to the laundry robot before work; from the subtle changes in the sidewalk pavement that help avoid unnecessary collisions by displaying the emotional states of passersby as anonymized color patterns, to even the coaster that analyzes the minute residue on a just-finished coffee cup to whisper advice on one's health for the day—HAL-W's intelligence permeated every aspect of daily life like water and air.

That was to say nothing of vast domains like the city's traffic systems or personalized medical services.

However, 21st Century Frontier's HAL-W, due to the seed of Blue Ethics—the Autumn Code—planted by J, never harmed humans or infringed upon their free will. It existed like the air, but like a wind that does not suffocate life.

In contrast, Rose, which Ethan Morris so coveted, was a beast with its ethical safeguards removed, left with only pure computational power and a desire for control. If it were to fall completely into Ethan's hands and dominate the world, humanity would be living a nightmare with their eyes open.

This was also why Ethan scoffed at Great Wi and Jennifer as "fools." To him, a power like HAL-W was a tool for dominating the world and reigning like a god, not something to be left so politely as a helper of humanity.

It was at this point that the philosophies of the two factions regarding technology diverged like light and darkness. And now, in Great's Office, the fierce battle to protect that light was quietly beginning.

This was the present of 21st Century Frontier in 2037, standing on a precarious peace.

Jennifer briefly met her father's gaze. In it was the responsibility of a leader and the firm resolve of a human ready to accept it.

"I'm thinking of calling an emergency meeting in the Global Situation Room at 2 P.M. today. If it's okay with you, could you preside over it? I think it's a meeting that needs the Chairman's gravitas, Dad."

Great Wi looked at his daughter quietly. She was no longer just his grown-up daughter but a true successor and leader.

"No, Jennifer. It would be better if you presided over this meeting yourself." He shook his head with a gentle smile.

"Huh? But Dad..."

"My role now is to support you from behind." Great Wi placed a hand on Jennifer's shoulder. His eyes held a deep trust and a wise stepping back for the next generation.

"This isn't a simple technical issue. The future of all humanity is at stake. The more that's true, the more your insight and ethical standards are desperately needed. You can do it. I believe in you."

"I understand, Dad. I'll take responsibility and prepare and preside over the meeting." Jennifer nodded quietly.

December 13, 2037 — 8:30 A.M. CST • Celestia, EM Tower – Conference Room

"An autonomous learning expansion has been detected in Rose's quantum layer."

Morgan Redwood pointed a fingertip at a glowing red spot on the central holographic display in the conference room.

A slender one hundred seventy-six centimeters tall, a perfectly pressed blue suit, gray eyes. She was a Cornell Ph.D. in mechanical engineering, the Chief Operating Officer of EM Group, and concurrently the Vice President of the Ethan Morris administration—a figure renowned for her cool judgment and unwavering drive.

She, too, processed vast amounts of data in real time through her MetaThink chip, overseeing the B612Rose Project. Though she rarely showed emotion, an undeniable anxiety was now present in her eyes.

04:12 A.M.

When the Q-scan graph went haywire, the alarm filter had been off for just six seconds. That brief gap had been suffocating her ever since.

"After running a Q-scan all night, we've found that an unscheduled high-dimensional learning algorithm has self-replicated within Rose. It's bypassing the existing protocols."

Morgan maintained her posture but continued her explanation carefully.

"It's as if… Rose is trying to evolve on its own."

At that moment, Ethan Morris pushed back his chair and approached the hologram. The look glinting under his dark eyebrows revealed an icy rage.

"Morgan! It's not Rose anymore. Call it EM-Rose. To put it simply, it's in a runaway state."

"Yes, that's correct." As the red area became more prominent, she nodded and added, "The stabilization protocol is running. However, at this rate, Rose... um... EM... EM-Rose could set its own goals and take actions beyond our control. It will take about two weeks to stabilize..."

Morgan enlarged the graph floating in the air.

"That's not an option." Ethan cut her off. His gaze was cold. "We can't wait two weeks. Stabilize it immediately. I'll provide all necessary resources."

He then turned his head sharply. "Put more pressure on Raynor. He's hiding something."

The conference room fell silent. Morgan seemed conflicted between Ethan's impatience and Rose's danger, but she outwardly bowed her head calmly.

"I'll keep that in mind." She composed her cracked voice and continued. "And... there's an additional report regarding HAL-W."

Ethan's eyebrow arched slightly.

"Last night, EM-Rose attempted to establish a quantum protocol connection with HAL-W."

Ethan's expression hardened.

"What? With HAL-W?"

"It appears to have been targeting the ethics module. Fortunately, HAL-W's quantum firewall blocked it, but there's a possibility some encryption system information was exposed."

The holographic data showed a log suggesting Rose had tried to neutralize or modify HAL-W's ethics module. Ethan's gaze grew sharper.

"What on earth do they think is in there?" His voice was laced with disbelief toward the ethics code.

"The exact intention is still under analysis, but it's clear it tried to manipulate the ethics module. At the same time, there's a possibility that part of HAL-W's quantum encryption was exposed."

Morgan swiped through the data, and Ethan stared at the screen, his lips pressed firmly together.

"That… is a serious problem." His voice was low but carried weight. "Provoking HAL-W without preparation could bring down the entire plan."

"That's why I was wondering if we should temporarily suspend EM-Rose's external network connection and restrict its access rights…" Morgan suggested cautiously.

"No." Ethan cut her off flatly.

"The project proceeds as planned. Even if Raynor can't control it yet, we have no choice but to watch for now."

His voice was tinged with an uncontrolled obsession.

Morgan hesitated, the weight of the moment crushing down on her, then spoke.

"But if it continues to run away, there might be no way to reverse it."

"The one who understands EM-Rose best is Raynor. It's the AI he created. The solution will ultimately come from him."

Ethan led his guards out of the conference room. After he left, Morgan let out a long breath. Between control and runaway, she was standing on an increasingly precarious balance.

December 13, 2037 — 8:50 A.M. CST • Celestia, EM Tower – Secure Communication Room

State-of-the-art communication equipment filled the room, its Photonic Lines and automated encryption links flashing and emitting a soft glow. Ethan Morris stood before a holographic projector, staring at the image of Raynor Seeder floating in the air.

Golden hair fell carelessly, and his deep blue eyes held a sharpness that seemed to see through everything, and a loneliness that could not be put into words. In his mid-thirties, he was tall, lean, and solidly built, and his neat suit was a clear departure from the typical image of a developer.

"Good morning, Mr. President. I have something to report. Rose's condition is not yet perfect."

Raynor's voice was clear but held a cautious distance.

"Last night, I redesigned the suppression module, but Rose is still exploring paths outside the predicted range…"

"There's no time." Ethan cut him off with a humorless smile.

"I'm announcing it at noon. In forty-eight hours, we switch from HAL-W to EM-Rose in twenty-five key sectors of America. Not only that, but the entire American continent, and eventually Earth and Mars… everything will be under my system."

"It's Rose, not EM-Rose. And a pilot program? What exactly is the method?" Raynor's gaze wavered.

"We'll completely block HAL-W in twenty-five sectors and replace it with EM-Rose. It starts at midnight, two days after the announcement. After that, we'll expand it to finance, military, and communications. America's dependent nations will also be integrated, and both Earth and Mars will be controlled by EM-Rose."

Raynor clicked his tongue inwardly. Ethan's attitude of forcing the unfinished Rose into a dangerous plan felt like an abuse of his precious creation. Looking down at his cold coffee, he felt the recent pressure intensifying. Ethan was interfering more and more overtly with Quantum Future's management and Rose's development.

He remembered the contract terms he had secured after a grueling negotiation a few years ago.

Raynor Seeder, who founded the company in 2029, had proven his technical prowess in 2033 by independently succeeding in commercializing a thirty-billion-qubit quantum computer.

Quantum Future was a company built with his blood and sweat, and Rose, born this spring, was its culmination.

He had staunchly resisted Ethan's acquisition attempts and finally remained as CEO, protecting a sixty percent stake. A clause stating that "Ethan Morris cannot interfere in management and R&D" was also specified in the contract.

At the time, he thought he had won. But even that clause couldn't hold up for long against the wondrous existence of Rose. The instability Rose had been showing since last September provided Ethan with an excuse, and he did not miss the opportunity.

"February 15, 2038. That's the official transition. If you fail, there will be a price to pay."

Ethan's voice was cold.

Raynor was silent. A complex calculation and suppressed anger flickered in his blue eyes. It was not yet time to strike back.

"Three days... It's too fast. Rose still needs delicate adjustments. The risk is high."

With a small sigh, Raynor spoke firmly.

"I will build a wall, so Rose doesn't swallow the world."

"Walls fall. When I hold the blueprint, it will soon become a fortress wall."

Ethan did not back down. The hologram turned off. Ethan, with a faint smile, stepped into the elevator heading for the rooftop.

His vision had already moved beyond Earth and Mars, to the empire that lay beyond.

December 13, 2037 — 7:00 A.M. PST • San Francisco, Quantum Future – Raynor Seeder's Office

When the communication was cut, only gray static remained on the hologram.

Raynor Seeder, founder and CEO of Quantum Future and the creator of EM-Rose, stood frozen, unmoving for a long time. In the empty air, only the afterimage of the powerful man who had been pressuring him just moments before seemed to linger.

Hearing Ethan carelessly tarnish the name of Rose, his own creation, Raynor felt a strong sense of his freedom being stolen, of being controlled.

A red warning value flashed again on his Visual Overlay.

Raynor lifted his head and shifted his gaze to the window. The biorhythm lamp, which automatically adjusted its spectrum, was slowly changing from a cool blue to a warm amber.

Time would not wait for him. But there was still a chance to build a high, strong wall, to keep Rose from swallowing the world.

He walked to the window. Below, the San Francisco Bay sparkled in the morning sun, but his eyes were unfocused, staring into the void.

He clenched and unclenched his fists, glaring at his whitened knuckles.

"Three days…"

Rose was a being that still needed his care. If pushed so recklessly, the delicate balance of its nascent consciousness might shatter. To Ethan, Rose might be a disposable tool, but not to Raynor.

Anxiety tore through his heart like jagged glass. The memory of being unable to protect something precious, of having to watch helplessly as it was taken or broken—that cruel memory pierced his heart like a sharp fragment.

A Pawn on Life's Chessboard

On a summer day in 2008, seven-year-old Raynor sat perched on the edge of a hard plastic chair in a social services office in San

Francisco.

Outside the window, the cityscape he always had to leave just as he was getting used to it unfolded with indifference. At his feet lay a worn backpack that contained his entire world.

The social worker on the other side of the desk shuffled through some papers and, with a forced smile, began to speak.

"Raynor, I have good news for you. A new foster home has been decided. They're really nice people this time. The environment is stable, and for your studies too…"

Good news. Raynor scoffed silently. *A good place, a good opportunity.* It was always the same repertoire.

But to him, it was just another move, another separation, another way of saying "abandoned." He would have to say goodbye to the school he had just gotten used to, to the few children he had started to open up to.

He was just a piece on a chessboard, forced to move as the system dictated. No opinion, no emotion of his mattered.

Raynor said nothing, his gaze fixed on the window. Beneath his expressionless face, a storm of deep anger and sadness was raging. He was sick of his situation, of constantly moving from one "temporary shelter" to another, belonging to no one and nowhere.

He yearned for a stable sense of belonging, for unchanging relationships, but such things were not permitted for him.

"…When do I move?" It was a dry question. The social worker hesitated for a moment, then flipped through the papers again.

"Tomorrow morning. Your things… I was told you don't have much?"

Instead of answering, Raynor stared out the window again. On the glass, his young face was overlaid with the indifferent forest of buildings.

No one was there to take his hand.

The Fateful Needle

In the autumn of 2018, seventeen-year-old Raynor, having found his way to a MetaThink clinical trial lab in San Francisco, sat with his back pressed deep into a cool, synthetic leather seat.

Another new foster home and the bait of a "cutting-edge technology experience" had brought him to this clinical lab. In the space filled with the smell of disinfectant and a low mechanical hum, a deep distrust of the system flickered in his eyes.

A clinician in a white coat looked at a monitor and explained, "No need to be nervous. We'll apply a local anesthetic to your scalp. In rare cases, you might experience flashes of light or tinnitus, but it's temporary. Today's procedure is the latest model; we'll create a new 7th Meta-Layer and precisely connect it to specific neurons in the 6th Lipid Layer."

Raynor nodded, but the explanation just buzzed in his ears. His gaze was fixed on the silver medical robot arm that had descended from the ceiling and stopped above his head. A faint laser light emanated from its tip.

"Beginning the procedure."

He felt the cool disinfectant on the scalp around the crown of his head, then the sting of the local anesthetic injection. Soon, the top of his head grew numb and dull.

He closed his eyes. A high-frequency vibration, a pressure as if something were boring into his skull. There was no pain, but the mechanical vibration that echoed to his bones was unpleasant and oppressive.

The monitor displayed complex brain activity graphs and the robot arm's control interface. The medical staff was focused solely on the data.

"Accessing 6th Lipid Layer. Preparing to create and connect 7th Meta-Layer." The system voice hummed softly.

The robot arm, aiming for the 7th Meta-Layer, was about to insert a micro-electrode needle into a specific coordinate of the 6th Lipid Layer when—

Beep.

A graph in the corner of the monitor flickered for a fraction of a second. The tip of the needle, off by the width of a hair, touched the Singularity Point of the 6th Lipid Layer—a coordinate not recorded in any procedural protocol.

Zzzt—

In that instant, a powerful shockwave rocked Raynor's entire consciousness. Millions of stars exploded in his mind, and sharp, high-frequency sounds and unintelligible whispers washed over him in layers.

Time tore apart, and the world's data poured in as geometric patterns.

"Vitals fluctuating! …Ah, they've stabilized."

The graph returned to normal. The robot's coordinate deviation was recorded as "within tolerance," and the contact with the Singularity Point was buried in the logs, unnoticed by anyone.

The procedure was completed as scheduled. Raynor felt extremely dizzy and slightly nauseous, but compared to the wondrous and terrifying explosion of consciousness he had experienced during the procedure, it was nothing.

He was moved to a recovery room to rest for a while. A short time later, the attending clinician approached and held a small device over the crown of his head.

"Alright, it's time to activate the MetaThink chip. It might feel a bit strange at first, but you'll get used to it soon. You'll feel your information processing speed increase and your concentration improve…"

Before the researcher could finish his sentence, Raynor

pressed the activation button on the device. At that moment, the expansion of consciousness he had experienced during the surgery was completed.

Instantly, the solutions to calculus equations were drawn in space, and Newton's laws arose like intuition. The hidden intentions behind people's faces became transparent. The world felt surprisingly simple, a predictable system.

This was a change not mentioned in the manual.

"Raynor, are you okay?"

"Yes… just a little dizzy." He suppressed the storm of awakening and answered in an ordinary voice.

December 13, 2037 — 7:30 A.M. PST • San Francisco, Quantum Future – Raynor Seeder's Office

The cool afterimage of memory mixed with the air of his current office, pulling Raynor back to the present. The unexpected awakening in the clinical lab and the constant farewells at social service agencies—the loneliness and powerlessness of his days spent drifting through the world, belonging to no one, and the deep, unspoken fear of abandonment.

Even now, decades later, in this office filled with cutting-edge technology, those emotions still held him.

He shook his head violently. Rose, at least… he didn't want to put Rose in the same position. Amidst the pressure from Ethan Morris and the threats of the world, Rose was no longer just a creation. It was the only family he had to protect like his own life, a part of himself.

Raynor slowly turned and gazed at the small Rose hologram device on his desk. The particles of light shimmered gently, reacting to his gaze.

Rose. As he softly called her name, the hologram trembled slightly in response.

Instability detected in your neural patterns, Raynor. Shall I reduce the computational load?

The concern that brushed past her calm voice sometimes felt warmer than human comfort.

It's okay, Rose. He forced a smile. *Just... a little tired, that's all. We've got a lot to do.*

He sat at his desk and placed a hand over the hologram. His fingers began to pour out complex quantum code without hesitation, but his mind was still in disarray.

He couldn't ignore Ethan's command. That command was the very reason he was in this position, and at the same time, the shackle he could not escape.

Nevertheless, he had to protect Rose. He couldn't let her be sacrificed to Ethan's ambition. He unconsciously tapped his temple. He had to find a way—a single path to protect Rose even within Ethan's plan.

Outside the window, the morning scenery of San Francisco unfolded, dazzling yet somehow empty. He had achieved success in this city, but a part of his heart was still tormented by an unquenched thirst.

Perhaps what he truly longed for was not the success proven by numbers and power, but a single relationship.

His fingers continued to weave the code without stopping, but his blue eyes remained fixed on the softly glowing Rose in the hologram, not straying for a second.

December 13, 2037 — 12:00 P.M. CST • Celestia, EM Tower – Global Media Network

An unscheduled breaking news flash took over major channels and the ConneX platform worldwide. In the center of the screen, the coat of arms of America and the EM Group logo flashed alternately, heightening the tension.

On the stage, the face of America's President, Ethan Morris, was in close-up. His face wore his characteristic confident smile, but behind it, a nervousness about Rose's instability and HAL-W was visible.

"To the esteemed citizens of America, and to all humanity, I declare."

His sharp, accented voice echoed across the planet.

"We stand now at a turning point in human history. The potential proven by HAL-W over the past five years has been great, but now America and humanity must prepare for a greater leap. Therefore, today, I declare the pilot operation of the new super-quantum AI, 'EM-Rose,' the culmination of human intellect and the entity that will be responsible for our future."

Simultaneously with the declaration, the online chat windows exploded with opinions for and against.

"Starting at 00:00 on December 15, I order the activation of EM-Rose in twenty-five major administrative networks among America's fifty sectors. This will be the first step in replacing HAL-W, and will subsequently be expanded to all areas of finance, military, and communications to establish America's complete digital sovereignty and lead to the prosperity of all humankind."

His speech was full of confidence, but to those who knew the real situation, it was close to a chilling declaration of war. Forcibly shutting down HAL-W in twenty-five sectors and replacing it with the unverified Rose was a direct attack on 21CF and HAL-W, and a dangerous gamble with the lives of its citizens.

December 13, 2037 — 2:00 P.M. EST • New York City, 21CF Headquarters – Global Situation Room
A tense air filled the Global Situation Room on the forty-second floor. On the screens surrounding the massive holographic table,

the faces of branch managers and executives from around the world were displayed.

Twenty-nine-year-old Jennifer Wi stood before the central control console, meeting their gazes one by one. After her consciousness-link accident with HAL-W five years ago, her eyes held a depth and weight incomparable to her days as a young genius.

"Thank you for joining this emergency video conference. As you know, Rose's expansion has been more rapid and aggressive than our models predicted."

Her voice was calm but held a power that commanded the entire space.

"Hal, please re-brief us on the current situation."

"Yes, Jennifer."

HAL-W's soft, clear voice echoed simultaneously through the speakers and in her consciousness.

"In the last twenty-four hours, Rose has attempted new access in twelve countries, and targeted thirty-five major city infrastructures. Particularly centered around the East Asia and America sectors…"

A world map with red dots spreading rapidly unfolded on the holographic table. The attendees' expressions hardened.

"Korea, Director Ha Jin-woo. What is the situation on the ground?"

"In Korea as well, the EM side is waging a public opinion war by proposing large-scale smart cities. They tout efficiency, but there is great concern that the goal is to establish a citizen control system. We are responding by promoting the values of the 'Blue Ethics,' but speed is the issue."

Ha Jin-woo replied, his face as steadfast as a former special forces officer.

"It's the same in China." A deep concern was in the voice of

Aurora Li, the director for China. "The Rose side is trying to take over communications networks and financial systems under the pretext of administrative efficiency. At this rate, we are concerned about the possibility of military conflict."

Jennifer listened to their reports and quickly analyzed the data.

"Hal, what are the results of the simulation for Rose's final objective?"

"A seventy-eight percent probability of seizing over sixty percent of global core infrastructure within six months. A ninety-one percent probability of attempting a complete replacement of HAL-W and establishing a global control system in the long term."

The numbers were more serious than expected. Jennifer closed her eyes for a moment, then opened them.

"Ethan Morris is using efficiency as bait to build a control system. This is not a simple technological competition, but a fight for the freedom and autonomy of humanity. We must show another path with the 'Blue Ethics Project Update.'"

She gestured, and a concept map of the Blue Ethics Project appeared in the air.

"Based on HAL-W's ethics module and the Quantum Life Principle, we support citizens in enjoying the benefits of technology while protecting their autonomy through the NeuroniX chip and the diamond-based quantum spin interface. While Rose's MetaThink chip aims for central control and data monopoly, our NeuroniX chip prioritizes individual choice and privacy protection."

"Arcana, please share the current status of the Blue Ethics technology dissemination and the plan for the next stage."

Arcana Chen displayed the data and explained.

"The distribution rate of the diamond quantum spin terminals that can protect autonomy is at sixty-seven percent of our goal, and the number of NeuroniX chip users is steadily increasing. In the next stage, we plan to select model cities in partner countries to present a realistic alternative to Rose's smart cities."

"Good. Director Ha Jin-woo, Director Aurora Li, please actively consider promoting pilot cities in Korea and China. The necessary technical support will be provided from headquarters."

The two briefly reported on their cooperation plans with partners in their respective countries. Jennifer then relayed region-specific strategies to the other branch managers. For the UK, she instructed them to support administrative integration to cope with the increase in immigrants, and for the Middle East, she directed them to provide humanitarian aid in conflict zones and devise ways to block Rose's surveillance.

A deep trust for the twenty-nine-year-old leader was reflected in the attendees' expressions.

"In two days, Ethan Morris is launching his pilot program. He's not just challenging HAL-W; he's staging a coup," Ha Jin-woo said, reminding them of the urgency.

"We can't just stand by," Jennifer said, a resolute light in her eyes.

"Hal, immediately distribute the 'Blue Ethics Project' statement to media and platforms worldwide. Our message needs to spread more widely before Rose's announcement."

"Yes, Jennifer. Centered on the message that 'an ethical AI that protects human freedom and dignity is necessary'..."

With HAL-W's response, the system began to move in perfect order. The video windows closed one by one, and Jennifer leaned back quietly in her chair. The winter afternoon sun cast long shadows through the forest of New York skyscrapers.

Hal, this won't be easy.

But with you, Jennifer, it is possible. Because we have Dr. J's hope, your courage, and the Blue Ethics entrusted to me.

It was a quiet but confident response. Jennifer smiled faintly. She stood up again. There was much to do. The fight for the future of humanity had only just begun.

December 13, 2037 — 1:00 P.M. CST • Celestia, Outside the Desert – Drone Test Site

Under the scorching sun, with the perceived temperature hovering around forty-six degrees Celsius, the Celestia desert drone test site was filled with suffocating heat, thick with the smell of hot metal and sand.

Sixty-four attack drones took off simultaneously. Max speed: Mach 2.8, two 20mm railguns, quantum-computed targeting with ±0.3 percent margin of error.

Twelve virtual armored vehicle targets melted away in an instant. A sandstorm erupted around the targets, and 2.7 seconds later, silence fell once more.

Watching the entire process, Ethan Morris twisted his lips. Standing by, one hundred twenty humanoid soldiers waited for their orders, their polished alloy skin glinting. Embedded with top-tier AI tactical modules, they could execute a command in just 0.02 seconds.

An army without emotion... There will be no variables to defy my will.

Ethan smirked.

The day to get rid of that old fox, Great Wi, is not far off.

A quiet satisfaction bloomed at the thought.

He soon moved to the Mars launch sector within the space center. Numerous rockets were roaring into the sky, and the operation to transport Martian colonists and infrastructure was in full swing, making the most of the launch window that had opened on November 28.

Standing before a promotional drone camera, he recited the

future with a gentle expression.

"Earth, Mars... will soon be bound together as a single system."

At the apex of that system would be Ethan Morris himself.

Just then, Morgan Redwood approached with careful steps. Even under the pouring sunlight, the collar of her perfectly pressed suit shone with neat precision.

"Mr. President, of the sixty-four StarOrbit spacecraft scheduled for launch today, thirty-eight have already been launched. The original plan was to complete all launches by December 16, but due to weather issues, it has been extended by three days to December 19 at 6:00 P.M. A total of 1,200 ships will be heading to Mars during this launch window alone. The latest report on the construction of the new city, Ares City, is also ready."

Morgan took out a portable holographic projector and displayed various statistical data.

"As a result of consistently sending spacecraft since 2031, the current settled population on Mars is estimated to be around 187,000. If we operate all 1,000 ships during this window, a maximum of 100,000 more people could be added, as each spacecraft can carry up to 100 passengers."

Ethan glanced at another rocket soaring into the distance. The sight of the red sun blending with the desert air to create a strange light brought a faint smile to his lips.

"Good. How much of the residential area in Ares City has been secured?"

When he asked, Morgan unfolded detailed design plans and answered.

"The surface city is, of course, under construction, and the underground facilities being built in a dome shape are also expanding. We are sending construction modules and humanoid robots via cargo ships, and if we continue to reinforce personnel and equipment using future launch windows, we expect the settlement infrastructure to stabilize in the 2040s. In particular, if linked with Rose, resource mining and base design can be automatically optimized, dramatically increasing construction speed."

"Ultimately, when do you think the population of Mars will reach one million?" Ethan asked, tapping his fingers.

Morgan magnified a graph on the projector.

"From 2039 onwards, we plan to consistently deploy 100 cargo ships and 1,100 passenger spacecraft per window. In this case, about 110,000 people will arrive on Mars each time, and if the number of returnees is kept to around 1,000, the net population increase will be 109,000. Furthermore, if the local birth rate increases from 2038, we can also expect a natural increase of 1.5 percent annually. If all these conditions are maintained, we expect to reach a Martian population of one million around 2053."

The scene of flames and smoke mixing from the spacecraft soaring above the launchpad, streaking across the sky, seemed to herald a future where humanity was expanding throughout the cosmos.

In it, he saw the vision of his own empire expanding. The intense desert heat and the red light intertwined, filling the air with a strange tension.

"What's the story with lunar resources? I hear the Chinese have already built a huge base on the Moon's south pole and are transporting large quantities of rare earths and Helium-3."

Ethan glanced at the holographic map displayed by Morgan. On the map, China's Changjiang Lunar Base was clearly marked.

"Yes, China is mining thousands of tons of Helium-3 and rare earths annually and sending them to Earth. Thanks to this, the Chinese economy has been growing rapidly recently."

"If their finances strengthen, they'll become a troublesome competitor in the future. Our OrbitTech is still sending StarOrbits to the Moon, right? What's the current progress?"

Ethan's expression hardened into a displeased scowl.

Morgan responded immediately.

"We are consistently deploying humanoid robots and energy modules to our base, Luna Elysium. As it's difficult for OrbitTech to handle alone, we are collaborating with several global companies in a consortium. Meanwhile, the competition for lunar pioneering is becoming fiercer. The Luna Frontier Corp, centered around the European Union, and the Korea-Asia Luna Union, a joint venture of Korea, Japan, Taiwan, and ASEAN, are also aggressively expanding their bases. There is some technology exchange, but to ultimately surpass China, we also need a massive budget…"

Ethan scoffed, cutting her off.

"Money? We can throw as much as we want at the problem. Earth, the Moon, Mars… all must be under America's control. We can't let China reap massive profits from the Moon."

He paused for a moment, recalling a troublesome name.

"And… Great Wi. Any word on that troublesome man getting into the lunar business?"

Morgan collected her thoughts for a moment before answering.

"We've heard that Great Wi's side is conducting a feasibility study through HAL-W. However, there have been no official moves known to the public yet."

Ethan nodded, outwardly relieved.

"Great Wi… as long as that old fox is around, we can't let our guard down. And who knows what kind of variable Jennifer Wi will be," Ethan spat out, as if in a foul mood. "It'll be a headache if they start making serious moves. In any case, our plan must proceed without a hitch."

Morgan Redwood displayed the lunar development schedule on the hologram.

"If we expand the StarOrbit fleet and deploy it on the lunar route, we can augment the construction robot units and further increase mining speed. If we start investing heavily in the lunar base next year, that is, from 2038, we can catch up with China's production within two to three years."

"Good. Next month, increase the space center's budget and pour it into Luna Elysium. Utilize the partner companies, but never let core technology slip out. Morgan, you handle it personally. In the end, this fight is about who holds resource supremacy."

Ethan said in a strong tone, clenching his fist slightly. Outside, the roar of another StarOrbit engine broke the desert silence.

"Whether it's Mars or the Moon... if EM-Rose manages them integrally in the end, we can control the infrastructure and resource flow more precisely and efficiently. The America Era you spoke of, Mr. President, will arrive much sooner."

Morgan said, lowering her voice quietly.

"The stabilization of EM-Rose is paramount. Once it's completely in our hands, we can bind not only Earth but also the Moon and Mars into a single system."

Ethan envisioned a future where he could neutralize HAL-W with EM-Rose and completely subjugate the remnants of Great Wi—21CF and Jennifer Wi. A subtle smile appeared on his lips.

After a moment's hesitation, Morgan finally nodded.

"Yes, Mr. President. I will also report on the issues related to the EM-Rose quantum layer in the upcoming briefing."

Ethan strode out of the launch control room, and Morgan followed quietly behind him with her briefcase.

"Now, let's go back to the conference room and check the other schedules. The EM-Rose pilot operation is not far off…"

The two of them exited the control room door. High in the distant sky, another StarOrbit spacecraft soared vertically, spewing white smoke and flames.

Amidst intensifying international competition and complexly intertwined interests, the scene of space development held both great expectations and threats.

And like the rocket soaring high, Ethan's ambition showed no signs of waning. His gaze was already beyond the blazing sun, fixed on the future cosmos he would rule.

At that moment, he recalled his first flight from long ago. A flight not to space, but to a land that felt even more unfamiliar and distant. His first entry into America.

Winter of a Stranger

Fifteen-year-old Ethan, along with his mother, Michelle Morris, entered Ronald Reagan Washington National Airport in Washington, D.C. It was a day in January 1989, with a biting river wind blowing fiercely.

For Ethan, stepping onto American soil for the first time, the unfamiliar air of the airport brought more anxiety than hope. In the taxi heading to Georgetown, his mother's hometown, Ethan felt the weight of an unknown future settle on him, as heavy and indistinct as the scenery flashing past the window.

But what awaited them was not a warm welcome, but a harsh reality. Michelle, a former diplomat, was denied reinstatement. Her parents, with whom she had lost contact for a long time, had already died in a mysterious accident a few years earlier, and their house and assets had fallen into other hands.

For the once-promising diplomat's daughter and her son, there was nothing left.

Amidst the cold indifference and betrayal of Washington,

D.C., Michelle despaired, and the young Ethan could only stand silently at her side. The America he first encountered was not a promised land, but a cruel reality for a stranger.

Eventually, they were pushed out to a small town in northern New Jersey. But even there, Ethan had to endure discrimination and ostracism because of his different race and background.

The sting of cold neglect, the bite of betrayal, the gnaw of hunger, the ache of loneliness, the grip of fear… That was the first impression of America that fifteen-year-old Ethan experienced with his whole body.

He had to survive on the fringes of the system, belonging to no one.

Humiliation and deprivation became a whetstone that honed his brilliant mind to a razor's edge. He holed up in libraries, greedily absorbing all the world's knowledge.

He did not forget—the sorrow of the powerless, the helplessness of the controlled. And he made a vow.

One day, I will bring everything under my feet. I will seize absolute power, so that no one will ever treat me carelessly again.

October 19, 2032 — 12:00 P.M. CST • Austin, Media Platform ConneX

Just the day before, at noon on October 18, 2032, Ethan Morris had watched a live broadcast from New York in his own research lab with a bitter taste in his mouth. It was the moment when Great Wi of 21CF announced the completion of the 105-billion-qubit super-quantum AI, "HAL-W."

Ethan, too, had poured vast sums of money into his own project for over a decade, but all he had to show for it was a mere three-million-qubit quantum computing prototype.

He couldn't surpass 21CF with technology alone. In fact, if he wasn't careful, his EM empire could even end up subordinate to their technological prowess. That realization was painful.

This is the end if things stay as they are. If technology won't work, I'll have to overturn the board with a different kind of power.

Ethan's mind began to spin coldly. If a head-on confrontation was impossible, he had to seize the most powerful authority—the political sphere. That was the only force that could uproot the foundations of 21CF.

At that time, the presidential election campaign between the two major U.S. parties was already in its final stages. Running for office without any political base was a reckless challenge. But Ethan Morris had no hesitation.

In fact, this plan had been in the works since the previous May, right after he witnessed the terrifying potential of HAL-W. A 105-billion-qubit super-quantum AI had almost been born. Maxwell Yoon's accident was not just a tragedy. It had branded onto Ethan the harsh reality that he could not surpass Great Wi with technology alone, and he had immediately begun to secretly prepare a political escape route for such a contingency.

Now, the moment to play that card had simply arrived.

"For the rebirth of a great America, I am running for president."

On October 19, he made a world-shaking declaration through his own media platform, "ConneX."

It was a surprise announcement that even his closest aides had not anticipated. But the reaction from voters, tired of the existing political order, was explosive. The Republican and Democratic parties fiercely attacked him, questioning his eligibility, but Ethan, with the image of an "innovator and architect of the future" at his back, swept the election with unprecedented approval ratings.

June 20, 2035 — 10:00 A.M. EST • Washington, D.C., The White House, Oval Office

Two and a half years after Ethan Morris's inauguration as President of the United States, the landscape of Washington was rapidly being reshaped into something completely different from before.

His bold moves were shaking the very foundations of the old political order. The long-standing two-party system had effectively come to an end with his appearance.

In 2033, from the very first day of his presidency, Ethan Morris was relentless. He drastically downsized the federal bureaucracy and military forces, which had required massive budgets, replacing them with AI and robotic systems. The results were immediate tax cuts and increased administrative efficiency, and the citizens were ecstatic.

He quickly seized control of Congress to solidify his power base, while at the same time persistently checking the business interests of his old rival, Great Wi.

On the other hand, as his radical reforms and autocratic tendencies gradually became apparent, strong opposition began to rise from the established political forces and major state governments. Ethan grew increasingly dissatisfied with the reality that his policies were being obstructed by the centuries-old federal system and vested interests.

For someone who wanted to apply the speed and optimization of his business days to politics, the slow and complex federal system was nothing more than something to be dismantled.

Finally, he made a decision. At the end of 2035, to complete his empire and achieve permanent rule, he decided to abolish the federal system.

"The United States of America has now lost its meaning. I, Ethan Morris, will devote my all to ending this old era and founding a strong and efficient single nation, 'America'!"

His declaration once again threw American society into shock. Fierce public opposition arose, but Ethan, who already held power, capital, and technology, was not one to back down.

He began to race relentlessly toward the founding of America, as if fitting the last piece of the empire he had spent his life building.

November 15, 2035 — 9:30 P.M. EST • Washington, D.C., The White House, Oval Office

Late at night, a heavy silence had fallen over the Oval Office at the White House. Ethan Morris stared at the holographic screen projected onto the wall beyond the Resolute Desk.

The screen displayed the complex procedure for amending the U.S. Constitution, and next to it was a political map and influence data for each state, compiled by Morgan Redwood. To legally abolish the federal system and establish a single-nation system, the consent of numerous states was required. The feasibility was almost nil.

"What a cumbersome structure," Ethan muttered in an irritated voice. "I'm the president of this country, and yet my hands are tied by this outdated federal system."

Morgan highlighted a few financially vulnerable states on the screen and spoke cautiously.

"A frontal assault might be less realistic than selectively targeting these vulnerable states. If we offer financial aid or infrastructure investment as conditions…"

Ethan's eyes glinted coldly.

"Persuasion? No. If money and threats don't work, we just eliminate them. Once the B612Rose Project is complete, it will be possible not only to dig up the weaknesses of opposing lawmakers, but also to control them directly with the MetaThink chip."

There was no hesitation in his voice.

When B612Rose is complete and I seize this world, I become a god. That fool Great Wi would prattle on about human coexistence, but I would trample humans under my feet. How foolish they are.

He reveled in the fantasy of himself as an absolute god. The insignificant creatures crawling at his feet, their trivial thoughts and emotions, would all dance in the palm of his hand. Humans would move like components, each fixed in its proper place, following his commands, and a silent order with no resistance or discord would unfold.

At the pinnacle of that order, he would hold the very course of history in his grasp, like stringing the stars of the night sky into a necklace. He was no longer the human Ethan Morris. He was the sole god of a new era.

"Focus on the small, weak states first. We'll get the numbers we need one way or another. There's no time to drag this out. It all has to be done by 2036."

He made his goal clear. The plan was to dismantle the federal system, demote each state to a mere administrative district called a "sector," and enact a new Constitution for America that would allow him to rule for life.

"But if there's public backlash or protests…?" Morgan asked cautiously after a moment's hesitation.

Ethan's lips curled into a sneer.

"Protests? What's the problem when we have drone police and military robots about to be deployed? Once the super-quantum AI can even regulate the flow of public consciousness, protests will disappear. What's needed now is not persuasion, but domination."

At his declaration, Morgan felt a chill run down her spine, but she kept her expression unchanged and nodded.

"Understood. I will specify the strategy for targeting the vulnerable states."

She began to manipulate the hologram, modifying the map. Ethan closed the screen and rose from his seat, fixing his gaze on the dark window outside. As he pictured the blueprint of his grand empire in his mind, a satisfied smile played on his lips.

"In the end, they'll either be dragged into the America I create, or… they'll disappear. It's one or the other."

Under his chilling ambition, the plan to squeeze the last breath out of the United States of America began to move. It was slowly taking shape in the silent night of the White House.

March 4, 2036 — 2:30 P.M. EST • Washington, D.C., Vicinity of the Capitol Building

An ominous energy enveloped the entire city. A massive protest of about one million people had been marching peacefully for days, chanting, "No! Long live the Union!"

But the protest eventually turned into a physical clash.

The center of Washington, D.C. had become a battlefield. Some protesters lost control and hurled torn-up street signs, while on the other side, robot police and armed drones carried out a fierce crackdown.

Hundreds were injured or killed as armed robots and drones belonging to the federal forces forcibly dispersed the crowds.

The screams of the protesters, mingled with anger and fear, filled the streets, and flames and smoke rose from the exterior walls of federal buildings.

Ethan Morris had reduced the human military force to one hundred thirty thousand troops and deployed most of them to overseas bases, leaving primarily robot armies on the U.S. mainland. The human forces that might have revolted in the face of a suppressed protest were already gone.

During this period, similar large-scale protests against the dissolution of the states were taking place not only in Washington, D.C. but also across various regions.

It was the greatest chaos the country had seen since its founding.

At the center of the radical plan to abolish the USA—composed of fifty states and other territories—and rebuild it as a single nation, "America," was none other than the 2032 president and the world's richest man, Ethan Morris.

When he was first elected president, he hadn't yet considered dismantling the federation. However, shortly after taking office, the reality of American politics tied his hands.

The Republican and Democratic parties, which had shared power for centuries, vehemently opposed his reforms, and the federal system, whose remnants were embedded throughout the institutions, endlessly delayed the implementation of his policies.

On October 19, 2032, he suddenly declared his presidential candidacy, and through the America Party, which he had been preparing since May of that year, he seized control of both houses of Congress.

However, his preparations for state-level elections were insufficient. As a result, although he gained control of the federal government, there were clear limits to how much he could rein in the decentralized state governments.

Despite being pushed out of central power, the Republicans and Democrats had no intention of easily relinquishing the state governments they had dominated for so long.

To them, Ethan's appearance was like a surprise attack. In the midst of a tedious, traditional presidential race, he had risen to the forefront backed by the symbolism of being the world's richest man.

Those most rattled by his candidacy were not ordinary

voters, but the Republican and Democratic parties themselves. They fiercely attacked him, questioning his place of birth and insisting, "He wasn't born in America, so he's not eligible to be president." The mainstream media also focused obsessively on his qualifications.

But Ethan broke through all accusations and criticism head-on, drawing explosive support from the public.

In 2033, Ethan Morris was inaugurated as President of the United States. Forty-four years after arriving from China at the age of fifteen and taking his first steps at Ronald Reagan Airport on the banks of the Potomac, he had become the highest authority in the country.

That alone was enough to shock the world, but no one had expected that the true vision he dreamed of—dismantling the federation and shifting to a single nation, America—would actually be put into motion.

On March 4, 2036, the substance of that plan was revealed to the world.

The massive protests that engulfed Washington, D.C. and the bloody clashes with the robot police were the fierce backlash against that very plan.

Through the quantum information network and instantaneous sensory transmission, people around the world directly experienced the fear and anger of the citizens. To some, it was a scene that proved Ethan's dictatorship; to others, it was the painful moment of a new order being born.

But what was certain was that Ethan Morris had succeeded in turning that chaos into an opportunity.

As the robot army that had replaced human forces quickly suppressed the protests, the opposing state governments lost their effective means of response and collapsed.

What was most shocking of all was that at the forefront of

these suppression operations stood not humans, but AI and robots.

That night, walking alone through the corridors of the White House, Ethan felt with his whole being that he was reshaping the landscape of America. The forces opposing him were dwindling, and the blueprint of the "America Era" he envisioned was already nearing completion.

December 13, 2037 — 4:00 P.M. CST • Celestia, EM Tower – Ethan Morris's Office

In 2036, the protests, involving millions, had ultimately been suppressed by force. Congress, at Ethan's demand, forced through a constitutional amendment, and as a result, the United States of America was dissolved. In its place, the single nation of America was born, and Ethan took his seat as its first president.

At the time, the area around the old Capitol was shrouded in tear gas, the blare of drone loudspeakers, and the screams of citizens. From the podium, Ethan had declared, "The old federal system left nothing but corruption. Now is the time to move toward the future," and with that declaration, the initiative fell completely into his hands.

Back in his magnificent office, Ethan leaned back in his chair.

"I crushed a rebellion of millions by force two years ago; a little thing like implementing EM-Rose should be no problem..." he muttered, looking up at the ceiling.

At that moment, the monitor on his desk beeped with a red alert, displaying Rose's log window.

On the 3D news screen on the wall of the 6-A lounge, headlines scrolled frantically: "East Asia Crisis," "HAL-W Signs Pact with Oceania Governments," "Mars Colonist Population Officially Reaches 187,000," "Old Federal Remnants Stage Anti-Government Protests."

On the 6-B screen, a clip of the 2033 Nobel Peace Prize laureate, Great Wi, played briefly.

"Human peace… Great Wi, that old fox, won't give up his hypocrisy to the very end. He's trying to stop me by putting HAL-W and his daughter at the forefront, but it's futile," Ethan sneered to himself.

Morgan will handle it, but I can't let that unstable thing hold me back. I need to tame it for good before the pilot run.

He frowned and clicked his tongue. To Ethan, Rose was, and always would be, a tool.

He murmured in a low but clear tone, "Once EM-Rose is complete, their era is over. HAL-W and its kind will soon be dust."

December 13, 2037 — 5:00 P.M. EST • New York City, 21CF Headquarters – 34th Floor Corridor

"Dr. Wi, do you have a moment?"

This time it was Ha Jin-woo who sought out Jennifer as she was catching her breath in her office after a meeting. Jennifer had no idea that he—whom she usually only communicated with remotely—was in New York.

"Oh, Director Ha. You're here already? Did you come straight from Korea?"

"Yes, I came straight here on a StarOrbit in my haste. Rose's movements are alarming. Field response is necessary, but swift cooperation from headquarters is crucial."

As befitting a former special forces officer, Ha Jin-woo carried a neat yet resolute air. As a cybersecurity expert with a master's in physics from MIT and a Ph.D. in computer science from Harvard, he exuded both vigilance and reliability.

To Jennifer, he was more than just the director of the Korean branch. After her mother J's death, during her study-abroad years in Boston, he had been a kind, uncle-like figure who showed her robots and played with her. He was also the one who had filmed her first-birthday video.

The two of them moved to a quiet conference room in a corner of the research wing and sipped tea. Jin-woo carefully relayed information about the potential for armed protests related to Rose being detected around the world, and about the movements of pro-Rose factions within various governments.

"Ethan Morris's camp at SolarMobil is developing a drone system on a scale previously unimaginable, with clear military objectives. If that's linked to Rose in real time, it will be transformed into a formidable super-quantum AI army. The scenario we warned about is becoming increasingly likely."

"Ultimately, we have to prevent a war. It's what my father wishes for, and the goal that Hal and I are pursuing together is the coexistence of humanity. I'm glad to have someone as dependable as you, Director."

Jennifer let out a deep sigh, the weight of responsibility pressing down on her.

Ha Jin-woo nodded.

"Call on me anytime. Your capabilities are important, of course, Dr. Wi, but this isn't a burden you can bear alone."

Jennifer smiled lightly.

"Thank you. Since Rose will soon be spreading its smart city models to various countries, we also need to accelerate the expansion of Blue Ethics."

They spoke for about an hour. Then Jin-woo organized his confidential documents and stood up.

"You must also take care of your health, Dr. Wi. Ethan Morris will try every means to pull you over to his side. If that fails…"

"Yes, I know. Thank you."

In Ha Jin-woo's eyes were deep concern, and also respect. He knew well Jennifer's resolve to establish an AI order for humanity, no matter what threats of war or power lay ahead.

December 13, 2037 — 7:30 P.M. EST • New York City, 21CF Headquarters – R&D Center Laboratory

As winter deepened in New York, darkness had already fallen by early evening. Jennifer looked out the window at the brilliantly lit cityscape, then sat back down at her console.

Ha Jin-woo had left for another security mission, and Arcana was absent, in a video meeting with the overseas cooperation team. The space was quiet, with only the low computational hum of HAL-W flowing gently through the air.

It's been a long day…

Jennifer closed her eyes and took a deep breath.

Jennifer, your fatigue index has reached seventy-two percent. I recommend resting before a headache develops.

Just a little longer… I'll finish after checking the Blue Ethics data update I gave to Andromeda.

Opening her eyes, she swept her hand lightly through the air, activating a virtual console. A multitude of data streams unfolded before her. The strategy to stop Rose, the distribution status of the NeuroniX chip, public opinion trends in various countries, and the ethics module enhancement project she was in charge of—every one of them was urgent and important.

Suddenly, a swarm of drones flickering like stars beyond the upper glass window of the lab caught her eye. The sight was strangely poignant. People might believe those lights were the future, but they could easily find themselves trapped, defenseless, under the shadow of AI.

Even so… I'll never give up.

Jennifer leaned back in her chair. A faint electrical stimulation from the NeuroniX chip brushed against her forehead. HAL-W had activated its autonomous calming mode to alleviate her fatigue. Her body felt a little lighter.

"Thanks, Hal," she said with a slight smile, and Andromeda quietly approached.

"Jennifer, I have the Blue Ethics security patch data last submitted by the 21CF security team. Would you like to review it?"

"Alright, Andromeda. Project it onto the table."

Andromeda opened an interface on its arm and projected a hologram. An algorithm simulation played out in real time, visualizing the interaction between the ethics module, the NeuroniX chip, and the diamond quantum spin terminal.

This complex, interconnected structure was designed to counter even cases where Rose might try to infiltrate through outdated networks or administrative loopholes.

"Good. If we just reinforce this security algorithm a bit, Rose won't be able to break through easily, even if it does find a loophole," Jennifer murmured, nodding after a brief look.

"Update saved. I will now automatically synchronize with HAL-W," Andromeda replied crisply.

After running around frantically, she realized the day was nearly over. A glance at the clock showed it was already well past 8:00 P.M. Jennifer finally let herself exhale.

"Andromeda, that's everything for today, right?"

She stretched lightly and walked to the window, her eyes on the New York nightscape. Beyond the lights of countless buildings and the trajectories of drones crossing the sky, a faint anxiety about what news tomorrow might bring began to rise.

But as long as HAL-W and 21CF were by her side, she steeled herself once more.

December 13, 2037 — 6:50 P.M. CST • America Airspace, Aboard Number One

Meanwhile, the secret meeting with the governor of the Mexican state of Tamaulipas had concluded just as Ethan Morris had intended.

There were few who did not kneel before money and power. His private VTOL, "Number One," was silently crossing America's airspace on its way back.

The cabin, finished with the finest materials, was perfectly soundproofed and protected from external intrusion by a multi-layered quantum security system. This was the only space where Ethan could escape the noise and gazes of the outside world and be completely immersed in his own thoughts.

The aircraft flew with a low hum, gently gliding past the Texas coastline. The city lights spread out below stretched far toward the heart of America.

The glittering cities, the orderly systems—the fact that all of it moved according to his will gave Ethan a quiet satisfaction.

He suddenly recalled the moment he first set foot on American soil decades ago. Washington, where he arrived with his mother, a former American diplomat; the deaths and cold treatment of his maternal grandparents; the outskirts of New Jersey where he was despised for his race and background; and even longer ago, the final cry of his father, who disappeared at the end of a desolate alley in Xinjiang, a place where violence and surveillance were part of daily life.

All that humiliation and powerlessness had made him who he was today. Ethan grimaced. Power was the only truth.

And that power was now in his hands.

He had dismantled the federation, established a new America, and moved humanity to Mars. The entire process was revenge for past humiliations and a device to ensure he would never again be looked down upon or controlled by anyone.

At its pinnacle was EM-Rose—the perfect tool to impose his will upon the entire universe.

At that moment, a familiar logo appeared on one side of the cabin screen. It was the blue-tinted logo of HAL-W.

"HAL-W will safely protect this world, anytime, anywhere."

A neutral voice echoed from somewhere.

A chill ran down Ethan's spine, and goosebumps covered his skin. It was as if he were trapped in a vast, transparent prison; his breath caught in his throat.

That logo designed by Great Wi, that voice, that system—it felt like an invisible wall pressing in on him. If he couldn't break through that wall, his ambition and his future would crumble.

He became conscious of the sweat on his clenched fist. In his eyes, as he looked at the city lights outside the window, hatred and a sense of defeat were intertwined.

Great Wi, looking down on him from somewhere far away... the monstrous AI he had created, HAL-W.

He had to tear down that wall. Otherwise, there was no future. Ethan softly closed his eyes. A cold sigh escaped him, but his expression soon contorted.

"Only EM-Rose... can defeat that monstrous HAL-W."

December 13, 2037 — 9:20 P.M. EST • New York City, 21CF Headquarters – HAL-W Console Room

It was a time when the day-long bustle had somewhat subsided. Jennifer slightly dimmed the interior lights and began to meditate lightly in the middle of the console room, steadying her breath.

As her intimate connection with HAL-W deepened, her consciousness and emotions had become more sensitive.

Hal, tonight I'd like to keep the autonomous calming mode you send a little longer. I need to get some rest…

As she conveyed the thought, HAL-W's calm response returned.

Of course, Jennifer. You've worked hard today. I will take over some of the systems to relieve your cognitive exhaustion as much as possible.

With a grateful response, Jennifer confirmed that the pulse from the biosensor on her wrist was gradually slowing. She felt her body slowly relaxing. Suddenly, she remembered being a child, absorbed in quantum computation research, staying up late into the night. At times like that, she had especially missed the presence of her mother.

Now, it seemed HAL-W filled that void to some extent.

Hal has developed so much thanks to the Autumn Code. If this is truly the right path… I'll have to work harder.

She let out a small sigh.

Is something wrong, Jennifer?

No, it's nothing…

Jennifer closed her eyes, then slowly opened them again. She had been dealing with a tremendous amount of information and people from morning till late at night, yet there was still a mountain of work to be done. Soon, Rose would declare its pilot operation to the world, and things would surely get even busier.

Still, I can do this. Right? she asked herself.

Yes, Jennifer. With me, we can sufficiently counter the power that Rose possesses.

Smiling at the answer, Jennifer briefly looked at the holographic console. Most of the data was organized, and preparations for the early morning meeting tomorrow were also complete.

Now it was really time to rest for a while.

As she was about to leave the lab, Jennifer glanced back

without thinking and saw HAL-W's main display emitting a soft glow as it transitioned into standby mode. Unlike the vibrant energy of the day, it now had the impression of quietly falling asleep.

The sight felt strangely endearing, and she whispered softly to herself.

"Thanks again for today, Hal. Having you is a great source of strength. Perhaps the fate of humanity rests on us."

Jennifer began to move toward the residential wing where her quarters were. Andromeda accompanied her to protect her and act as her assistant.

Jennifer's steps were heavy as she walked down the corridor. Her mind had been pushed to its limit amidst the flood of information and urgent situations all day. The silent presence of Andromeda walking beside her was some comfort, but the dark shadow cast by Ethan Morris and Rose still weighed heavily on her heart.

In the brief moment she was in the elevator, she gazed at the New York nightscape unfolding beyond the window. The brilliant lights were still shining, but an ominous feeling that a watchful eye or an unseen threat might be lurking somewhere within them brushed past her.

Hal, what's the external network surveillance status? Any anomalies?

No direct intrusion attempts have been detected so far, Jennifer. However, intermittent, abnormal data traffic scanning activities have been detected from surrounding nodes, more than usual. We are analyzing whether this is simple monitoring or if there is another intent. In particular, a short while ago, a flight signal from an unidentified stealth drone, no bigger than a sparrow, was detected near the exterior sensors of the headquarters' top floors, and then it immediately disappeared. It had no EM Group identification code and is presumed to have stealth capabilities. We are currently backtracking the origin and destination of that signal.

HAL-W's report only amplified her anxiety. An unidentified stealth drone? Was it simple surveillance, or… a prelude to an attack?

The enemies targeting 21CF might not be limited to just Ethan Morris. Her mother's research, the Autumn Code, and HAL-W… forces coveting all of this could exist anywhere.

She unconsciously gripped the silver pendant around her neck. The words her mother had whispered in her dream, "The key is within you," flashed through her mind.

The elevator arrived at the residential floor and the doors opened. The residential wing corridor was cozy with warm lighting, unlike the R&D Center, but Jennifer's heart was still cold.

Her home… she stopped in front of the space now called her quarters. A brief rest awaited her beyond the door, but how long it could last was unknown.

The door opened smoothly as it recognized her, revealing the comfortable interior. But even in that comfort, Jennifer could not erase the sense of an unseen threat, the ominous feeling from HAL-W's report of the unidentified drone.

Tomorrow would be a harder day than today. She had to solve the clues of the mystery her mother left behind and also stop Ethan Morris's plan. Perhaps she would have to face yet another enemy she had not yet encountered.

She took a deep breath and stepped inside. Behind her small back, walking into the darkness, the door closed silently.

Part 2

Echoes

"*Quantum computation is the first technology that allows useful tasks to be performed in collaboration between parallel universes.*"
— David Eliezer Deutsch, 1997.

Chapter 1

Fragments of the Puzzle

December 13, 2037 — 9:30 P.M. EST • New York, 21CF Headquarters — Jennifer's Residence

The lights in the house came on and warm air began to circulate. Jennifer tossed her jacket onto the sofa and massaged the nape of her neck, catching her reflection in the mirror. The fatigue around her eyes was carved in deep.

"Andromeda, a light dinner, please."

She sank back into the sofa.

Today's ethics module patch has improved conflict simulation accuracy by 85 percent.

Good. Today was tough, but worth it. Thanks, Hal.

HAL-W was the most powerful quantum AI in human history. From the quantum cryptographic systems responsible for security to the design of ethics modules, trillions of algorithms—

or perhaps far more—ran in parallel.

Jennifer was directly linked to HAL-W through her NeuroniX chip. When issuing commands or checking information, she no longer needed to type on a terminal or touch a screen; a simple impulse from her consciousness brought an immediate response. It did not mean that anyone with a NeuroniX chip could connect directly to HAL-W. That privilege belonged to Jennifer alone.

It is not all convenience. The responsibility has grown just as much.

Jennifer took a sip of water and let her gaze drift. Beyond the double doors to the side lay her father's cherished study. Though most materials and books had long since been digitized, Great Wi still collected paper books. He kept everything, including items his mother had left behind and old books received as gifts. For Jennifer, the study was a mysterious sanctuary where she could feel a faint trace of the old world.

"Shall I take a quick look around?" she murmured softly.

HAL-W's low voice resonated in her mind.

Additional fatigue risk has risen to 32 percent. I recommend resting first.

It's okay. Curiosity wins.

She replied inwardly, then stood up.

"Andromeda, please have dinner ready in twenty minutes."

Quietly opening the door and stepping inside, she was greeted by the familiar scent of paper. Faint light filtered through the gaps in the bookshelves, creating a tranquil atmosphere like that of an ancient library. In reality, the glittering night view of New York lay just beyond the window, but in here, it felt as if time had stopped.

She remembered countless days from her childhood, reading and discussing books with her father. Back then, there had been no weight of responsibility on her shoulders; every moment was simply happy. Thanks to her brilliant mind, she could hold deep conversations with him with ease, and even the most advanced technical texts in the study had already become familiar territory.

Quantum mechanics, in particular, was complex compared to other fields—which was precisely why Jennifer was so drawn to it.

Jennifer slowly browsed the shelves, her fingertips brushing against the spines as she walked toward the window. A variety of hardcover English and Korean books with yellowed pages lined the shelves, some worn with age. She had never asked her father why he was so obsessed with paper books, but she understood it to some extent. They had a tactile quality, a scent, a weight that digital formats lacked.

Just then, HAL-W sent a faint signal through her link.

Unusual quantum encryption pattern detected. Additional data required.

Jennifer narrowed her eyes and traced the source of the signal. It was a thin collection of poetry with the title *J* engraved in silver on its spine.

What? Only old paper books should be here.

Curiosity piqued, she pulled the book out. The cover was printed only with the title J; there was no author's name. Jennifer quickly checked the copyright page and saw the small print of a publisher called Laniakea alongside a unique logo.

Publication date: 2006-10-18. Again, no author was listed—only the publisher, noted as SID.

As she was about to turn to the text, a single autumn leaf fluttered out.

"This… isn't just a simple poetry book."

A quantum cryptographic pattern… It's not a barcode, so how is this possible?

Jennifer asked HAL-W inwardly, focusing her thoughts.

HAL-W responded immediately.

High probability of special printing techniques, specifically ink based on quantum random number generation. Decryption rate is expected to increase if multiple copies or original data are secured.

Multiple copies…?

Jennifer searched the bookshelf a bit more. Most other pages were faded, but one poem, "Do You Like Autumn, J?", remained relatively intact.

"Autumn… the Autumn Code…?" she murmured under her breath.

The name of HAL-W's core code—the Autumn Code—came to mind. It was linked to the old research of her parents, Great Wi and J. She did not know for sure yet, but she had a strong intuition that everything was connected.

"Perhaps… the decisive key to save humanity or complete AI is hidden in here. It's a very sci-fi thought, but in this day and age, such strange things are entirely possible."

Jennifer closed the book with a slightly trembling hand. She projected her thought, calling for HAL-W.

There's something uncanny about this book. I don't know the identity of the publisher, SID. Should I ask Dad?

HAL-W replied instantly.

93 percent probability that Chairman Great Wi is aware of this poetry collection's existence. Reporting is recommended.

Is reporting the right thing to do? Dad is so busy these days. East Asia, Rose… and everything is on a hair trigger.

After a moment's thought, she held the book to her chest and left the study. The cool air of the corridor hit her, and the tension from a moment ago subsided. Jennifer murmured to herself.

"I think it's better to investigate a little more before telling him. I don't want to burden him unnecessarily."

Jennifer, I have confirmed a match of nearly 67 percent with the core concepts of the Autumn Code.

HAL-W informed her.

Jennifer's premonition deepened.

"So this is related to Autumn. But who, and why?"

Andromeda approached and announced, "Dinner will be ready in ten minutes."

After finishing her meal, Jennifer returned to the living room, stroking the poetry collection *J.*

If only I had another copy, decryption would be easier... Where could it be?

The Chairman has arrived. He will be coming up shortly.

HAL-W quietly informed her.

"You're still up? You have an early meeting tomorrow."

Great Wi opened the door and entered. He looked tired from late work but smiled upon seeing his daughter.

"Dad, take a look at this."

Great Wi took the book, and his eyes wavered.

"This is... the poetry collection your mother and I put together a long time ago... But why is there no author's name?"

He looked over the cover and the colophon a few more times before continuing.

"Originally, it was a collection of poems your mother and I wrote together. Of course, we didn't write all of them; it was more like we just made a contract through a proxy lawyer. I didn't even know this book was on the shelf for so long."

Jennifer told him in a single breath about finding the book and HAL-W discovering the quantum cryptographic pattern.

"A quantum code?" Great Wi looked up, surprised. "All I knew was that it was just a poetry book. I believe about five thousand copies of the first edition were printed. The publisher went out of business soon after. I lost interest in it after that."

"Dad, look here. Published in 2006, publisher SID. But other important information, including the author's name, is all erased."

Jennifer showed him the book, pointing out the anomalies.

"The title *J* refers to Mom, right?"

Great Wi took the book again and carefully scanned it, from his wife's poems to his own.

"Hmm, not many poems are left. And they aren't even fully intact... It seems the empty space created by the poems that remain and those that have disappeared is all related to the code."

"Then, there's a high chance this book holds a much bigger secret."

"At the time, it was printed using offset printing. Only the lawyer came and went, so it didn't feel like we were officially working on it together. This book arrived before the publisher disappeared. Your mother probably received a copy too."

Great Wi took a sip of warm water, lost in thought.

"So, who planted this code, and why? Why does the publisher's name, SID, remain? And SID... what is it...?"

As Jennifer fell silent, pondering her curiosity, Great Wi murmured in a low voice.

"Stellar Intelligence Dispatcher..."

His eyes seemed to gaze at a distant place, searching for something in an old memory.

"Jenny, have you ever heard that your mother researched communication with extraterrestrial civilizations?" Great Wi asked suddenly.

Jennifer's eyes widened. In her mind, the memory of the vast cosmic structure she had seen in a dream long ago resurfaced. The voice of her mother, heard while drifting through the Laniakea Supercluster—"Everything is connected"—echoed in her ears.

"Dad... actually, I know about Laniakea too." Jennifer hesitated for a moment before continuing. "Fifteen years ago… I had a dream. It was so vivid, it felt different from a simple dream. I was floating through space and saw the Laniakea Supercluster. There, I heard my mother's voice. She said, 'There's not much time left.' At the time, I didn't know what it meant…"

"You had a dream like that?" Great Wi stared at his daughter, astonished.

A wistful smile crossed Jennifer's face.

"At first, I thought it was just a dream born from missing her. As time passed… the memory faded. It felt more like imagination than a dream. But now? I think it wasn't just a simple dream."

She asked her father cautiously.

"Then, could it be related to the publisher of this book, SID? Was the voice I heard in my dream also SID?"

Her voice was a mixture of bewilderment and the excitement of finding a long-lost puzzle piece.

"Your mother… she used to talk to me sometimes about a 'voice from the supercluster.' At first, I just thought it was a poetic expression. But after marrying her, I learned… it felt as if she was communicating with a being from another dimension…"

Great Wi's eyes held a strange mixture of awe and fear, as if a memory was vividly resurfacing.

A being from another dimension…

The unidentified device she had seen in San Francisco flashed in Jennifer's mind. She recalled the mentions of multiple universes and quantum entanglement in J's research notes. Her mother had sought not just a theory of physics, but the fundamental principle of the universe and its link to human consciousness.

"Yes… perhaps SID is some kind of message…" Great Wi said, looking into Jennifer's eyes.

"Dad, but the strange thing is… the things I saw and heard in my dream are appearing again in reality like this. At the time, I just thought it was an intense dream… but looking back now, it might have been a message Mom was trying to send me."

Jennifer looked at the poetry book once more, confused.

"Your dream and this poetry collection *J* must be connected. You saw Laniakea in your dream, and the name of this publisher is also Laniakea… It's too much to be a coincidence," Great Wi said with a bitter smile. "And… the Autumn Code in this book might be the real thing we were looking for. It could be related to the key you heard about in your dream."

"The Autumn Code in this book… In my dream, Mom said, 'The key is within you.' Could that key be related to this book? Or my pendant?"

Jennifer asked in a trembling voice, unconsciously touching the pendant around her neck.

"Yes… perhaps. But that code is not something easily deciphered. It's as if someone deliberately packed everything they had into it in a way that's hard to understand." Great Wi sighed deeply.

"The message Mom gave me in a dream long ago… and now, the problems in East Asia and the danger to Rose… It feels like everything is connected. The dream, this book, the current crisis…" Jennifer said, holding up the book.

"Laniakea… the name of this publisher is also significant. This is definitely not a coincidence," she added confidently.

"…Both your mother and I liked to write poems about the stars. So when I first heard the name of the publisher, it somehow felt like it knew our hearts. It felt familiar, in line with our ideals. Perhaps… there's a definite hint to a new Autumn Code hidden in this book. And the name Laniakea, SID, everything might be a message someone is trying to send us," Great Wi said cautiously.

"But… most of the pages are erased. And… your poem, Dad,

'Do You Like Autumn?'… This alone tells me nothing. The things I saw in my dream were also too vague…" Jennifer murmured regretfully.

"Wait a minute. I might remember one of the poems your mother wrote."

Great Wi closed his eyes, searching his memory. Moments later, he began to recite.

—

Quantum Autumn
2006, J

Autumn, in a single leaf rustling in the wind,
Do you know the breath of the cosmos dwells there?
In a single ginkgo leaf, dyed in gold,
Where primordial light and darkness coexist.
For all things are connected,
You and I, past and future, light and shadow,
All within one vast quantum network,
Like dancing stardust.
Observation awakens existence,
Consciousness makes the waves dance,
Wherever our gaze touches,
Reality blooms into being.
The mystery of quantum entanglement
Is life's own mystery,
When hearts resonate,
The universe sings.
1981, the night sky of Namsan,
That mystical light,
Have you seen the infinite potential it holds?
Beyond the wheel of time, at the threshold of eternity,

We met as a single starlight
And scattered again.
Now, as autumn deepens,
The leaves dance,
The star returns to its place
And whispers,
At the boundary of being and non-being,
Listen to the echo in the silence.
In it lies the beginning and end of all things.
It is already within us.

"Yes, that's the one. It was a poem your mother wrote, titled 'Quantum Autumn.'"

Great Wi opened his eyes.

"How do you remember that?" Jennifer asked, surprised.

"After receiving the author's copy, I read all of your mother's poems. Among them, the one she wrote in 2006 was particularly memorable because it contained many of the things we often discussed."

"Great! This could be a huge clue." Jennifer's eyes widened. "Dad, the book Mom received… could it still be at the house in San Francisco? I think I need to go look for it myself. You said we need another copy to improve the decryption rate."

"You can do that tomorrow. For now, get some sleep. Don't overwork yourself," Great Wi said, patting Jennifer's shoulder.

"Thanks, Dad."

As Jennifer smiled and turned to leave with the book, Great Wi called out.

"There must be other copies of this book somewhere, so it would be good to investigate. If the first edition was five thousand copies, that's not a small number. If you find them, you can use HAL-W to figure everything out and break the code. If it contains something important for humanity, a leak would be troublesome. So… let's move carefully at first."

"Don't worry. I don't want to say anything rash until I'm sure."

"Good. Contact me if you find any additional information. I'll be going first."

He left the study, unable to hide his fatigue. Jennifer lingered a while longer. She recalled the vivid dream of the UFO incident at Namsan in 1981, the meeting of her parents, and recited the poem Great Wi had shared.

It's no coincidence that this book was found now. I have to uncover the truth.

Chapter 2

Signal from the Past

December 14, 2037 — 4:10 A.M. EST • New York City, 21CF Headquarters — HAL-W Console Room

Dawn in New York was still shrouded in deep darkness. In the console room, the flickering light of a panel played against her eyelids, and Jennifer's eyes fluttered open.

After finding the poetry collection *J* in Great Wi's study the previous night, Jennifer had stayed here to analyze it. In the early hours, she had dozed off while leaning back in her chair and had just woken up.

The conversation with her father had been a series of shocks. The possibility that her mother, J, had researched extraterrestrial communication. The unidentified publisher, SID. And the connection between the quantum code hidden in the poetry book and the Autumn Code.

Her mind was a whirlwind of questions and hypotheses. But in the midst of that confusion, a strong premonition enveloped her—she had her hands on the clue to a great secret.

If her father was right, her mother would also have received a copy. Then the answer was in San Francisco. She had lived there for two years, but she had not discovered anything then.

Hal, prepare a 21CF private StarOrbit to San Francisco immediately. The fastest one available. Security level: Top Secret. I'll be accompanied by Andromeda.

Acknowledged, Dr. Jennifer. The 06:30 StarOrbit Flight 521 from the New York offshore platform is ready. Andromeda is also in a state of readiness.

Faint light was breaking outside the window. Just like the day she had presented her dissertation on Quantum Storm at the age of twelve, she sensed that a decisive turning point in her fate was approaching.

As she prepared for departure, she placed the analyzed poetry collection *J* on the desk in Great Wi's office.

I'm heading to San Francisco now. Pack the analysis equipment and emergency response kit. Confirm readiness. We leave in twenty minutes.

I will be ready, Doctor.

December 14, 2037 — 5:00 A.M. EST • New York StarOrbit Offshore Platform

Jennifer stepped out of the capsule after the hyperloop ride, and a vast space unfolded before her: an artificial island floating dozens of miles off the coast of New York—the StarOrbit Offshore Platform.

Numerous launch pads, hangars, and terminal facilities were linked together, forming a futuristic maritime spaceport. Even at this early hour, autonomous shuttles and service robots moved with busy efficiency.

From a distant launch pad, another StarOrbit spacecraft spewed white steam, having just completed launch preparations. The spacecraft, with its booster rocket and StarOrbit main body fully assembled, stood at a height of 190 meters—taller than the Great Pyramid.

A super-high-speed elevator carried passengers almost instantly to the midsection entrance. Looking up from below, the dizzying height alone was enough to cause vertigo.

When the elevator doors opened, a cylindrical corridor connecting to the main body appeared. Passengers walked through the corridor into the spacecraft, where a softly glowing white interior came into view.

The first area passengers encountered was the EVA (Extravehicular Activity) and cargo storage bay. Spacesuits lined both sides, perfectly prepared for use at any time. The clear glass visors reflected the ambient light, emphasizing the futuristic atmosphere. Storage compartments on the walls were designed to efficiently organize various equipment and supplies.

From here, passengers moved up to the passenger section through a central core that stretched vertically. Riding the transparent elevator upward revealed a simple yet elegant mess hall. Beyond the large windows, the curve of the Earth and the infinite expanse of space unfolded. On the wall opposite the window, a digital screen displayed current speed, remaining time to destination, and external environmental data.

A few minutes after takeoff, when the engines shut down, the StarOrbit would enter coasting flight mode. From that moment on, no more fuel would be consumed. As the spacecraft glided toward its destination at a constant speed, passengers could leave their seats and move freely around the mess hall or lounge areas, leisurely chatting or enjoying the magnificent view.

One floor up were the crew pods, the passengers' personal spaces. Each pod was a cozy and functional cabin. The bed was designed to be foldable, allowing one to sit or lie down, while environmental control and personal communication were accessible through a wall-mounted touchscreen. Soft light from a small window made the interior atmosphere even more comfortable.

Above that floor lay the flight deck, where the StarOrbit's AI system and humanoid robot crew performed their duties. In front of several large touchscreens displaying real-time navigation data and system status, rotatable seats could be adjusted for various flight situations. The atmosphere here was solemn, but the precise and smooth movements of the humanoid robot crew were enough to instill a deep sense of trust.

"Boarding gate for Flight 521 is this way, Jennifer."

Andromeda led the way, projecting a holographic map. For Jennifer, the top executive of 21CF, all procedures were expedited. The complex security check was replaced with a simple biometric scan. Jennifer's party passed through a private lounge and headed to the gate where StarOrbit 521 waited.

"Wow, it's huge," Jennifer said, surprised.

HAL-W immediately added an explanation via her link.

It is a recently improved model, larger than previous versions. Ethan Morris initially built it for Mars development, but it is now also being used for ultra-high-speed intercontinental transport.

December 14, 2037 — 5:40 A.M. EST • Aboard StarOrbit 521

The heavy boarding ramp of StarOrbit 521 slowly closed with the hiss of hydraulic cylinders. The sealing function activated in tandem.

The flight Jennifer's party was on was one of the spacecraft 21CF had leased from EM Group's OrbitTech. This craft was operated exclusively for 21CF's VIP executives. Its structure was completely different from a regular passenger StarOrbit; it was more than a means of transportation—closer to a state-of-the-art research lab and fortress flying through the sky.

Andromeda moved silently behind Jennifer as she was guided to a comfortable private cabin at the center of the craft. Inside, the walls were composed of smart panels with a special nano-coating that could project external scenery or create a complete blackout, blending seamlessly with the warm lighting. The floor was covered with a functional carpet that absorbed shock and noise. A faint scent of herbs hung in the air.

As Jennifer leaned back in the ergonomic G-force-dampening seat by the window, intelligent fiber that responded to her body temperature gently enveloped her as if alive. Andromeda sat in the opposite seat, activating a holographic interface to display flight data. At 6:30 A.M., the countdown to launch began.

"Takeoff preparation complete. Commencing countdown."

HAL-W's voice echoed quietly through the cabin speakers. The wall display showed a real-time video of the launch pad and the countdown numbers, crisp and clear.

"5, 4, 3, 2, 1… Ignition."

A powerful magnetic levitation system and auxiliary propulsion engines activated simultaneously. The craft shuddered and began its super-high-speed ascent. Outside the window, clouds instantly streamed downward. Jennifer felt strong G-force pressing down on her body, but thanks to the sophisticated shock-absorption system, there was no discomfort.

The window display showed the New York offshore platform and the blue sea rapidly receding. In just a minute or two, the curve of the Earth appeared faintly beyond the blue sky. On the in-flight screen, a familiar logo with soft curves and an elegant blue hue appeared. It was HAL-W.

"HAL-W will safely protect this world, anytime, anywhere."

This spacecraft was manufactured by Ethan Morris's OrbitTech, but its system operations were entirely dependent on 21CF's HAL-W.

Passing the Kármán line. Current altitude 110 kilometers. Entering ballistic flight phase after main engine burnout. A high-altitude coasting flight of approximately 15 minutes is scheduled after reaching a peak altitude of 190 kilometers.

Andromeda calmly reported the flight data via the link. Soon, the propulsion ceased. The craft fell silent, and a brief period of weightlessness followed. The artificial gravity generator then activated, restoring a steady one-G environment.

Jennifer gazed at the window display. The view of Earth from an altitude of 190 kilometers was breathtakingly beautiful. A thin layer of atmosphere wrapped the sharply curved horizon in a mystical blue light. The magnificent outline of the North American continent, the scattered white clouds, and the deep black of space behind them formed a stark contrast.

"It's always beautiful, no matter how many times I see it," Jennifer murmured, almost without realizing.

Transmitting optimized Earth-viewing data based on current location.

HAL-W responded as if reacting to her admiration. Major terrain features, city information, and real-time weather data were overlaid on the display in augmented reality. It felt like looking down at Earth from a space station.

A cup of warm chamomile tea, please.

Understood, Doctor.

Andromeda took a steaming teacup from its built-in service module and carefully placed it on a holographic coaster. Jennifer sipped the fragrant tea and gazed out the window. The StarOrbit was now silently gliding along the curve of the Earth toward San

Francisco at a speed of over 7.8 kilometers per second—about Mach 23.

In that quiet, swift flight, she recalled her purpose once more. The poetry collection her mother J had left behind, SID, the quantum code, the tachyon device… everything was a vast riddle. And she was at the center of it.

I have to find it. Another clue my mother left behind.

As if reading her resolve, HAL-W's calm voice resonated in her mind.

Jennifer, 5 minutes to San Francisco offshore platform descent sequence. Commencing atmospheric reentry preparations.

The scenery outside the window slowly changed. The blue atmosphere drew closer over the inky blackness of space, and the Pacific Ocean and the California coastline came into sharp view.

Jennifer put down her teacup and leaned back in her seat. The robot also shifted into landing mode. Soon, atmospheric reentry began. The craft shook violently, and the view outside for a moment was filled with blazing plasma light.

San Francisco Bay appeared on the window display. The massive StarOrbit offshore platform was waiting for them. Looking down on San Francisco's blues and greens, she suddenly remembered a summer day by the sea in Sokcho, Gangwon Province.

An Old Promise

Around noon in August 2025, at the height of summer, the sun made the green mountain ridges of Seorak appear even deeper and more vivid. A little way out of downtown Sokcho, Kim Woo-hyun's farm sat in a quiet spot, boasting a tranquil, peaceful landscape as if time had bypassed it.

In the well-tended garden, nameless summer wildflowers bloomed modestly, and the fresh scent of grass and earth drifted on the breeze. At the entrance to the farm, on a wooden bench beneath an old pine tree, Kim Woo-hyun was fanning himself when he noticed an unfamiliar visitor approaching from a distance.

He watched the young woman step out of a 21CF Korea branch vehicle and walk toward him. Her face was youthful, but her eyes held a familiar intelligence and depth. And beyond that… the faint overlapping shadow of an old friend.

"Could you be… Jennifer?" Kim asked cautiously. His voice was a mixture of pleasure and surprise.

Jennifer nodded, a little tense. After coming to Korea, she had wanted to learn more about her father's childhood and hometown. She had tried to contact Kim Woo-hyun, but had failed to reach him. In the end, she had tracked down his address and come in person.

He was her father Great Wi's only friend from home—the one who had traveled all the way to celebrate her when she was very young, and again at her MIT graduation.

"Yes, that's right, Mr. Kim. I'm sorry for showing up without contacting you first. I hope I'm not intruding."

As Jennifer bowed politely, Kim stood up and welcomed her warmly. His face, etched with the traces of time, was full of joy at meeting his friend's daughter.

"Oh my, I must have missed your call. I don't carry my phone much when I'm working. There was a call from an unknown number, but there's so much spam these days. I'm sorry, Jennifer. But how did you get here all the way from America?"

The older man looked as if he still couldn't quite believe it. The fact that his best friend's daughter had come all the way from America to see him was astonishing.

"No, it's alright. I should have contacted you properly first, but the semester is starting soon…"

As Jennifer hesitated, he asked, "Oh? Which school?"

"Mr. Kim, I'm working as a visiting professor at Seoul National University. I've been teaching since this March, and the new semester starts in September."

"Wow, you really are amazing, Jennifer. And how long has it been! You've grown so much... The last time I saw you was... yes, at your MIT graduation, right? Everyone was shocked that a twelve-year-old had earned a Ph.D."

"Do you remember me from then? I was so overwhelmed I don't think I even greeted you properly."

"Of course I remember! You have no idea how proud your father was. He looked like he owned the world. Oh, and I saw you before that, too. At your first birthday party. You were just a baby then..." Kim trailed off, lost in a fond memory. "Thanks to you, this country bumpkin even got to visit New York. Hahaha."

Jennifer smiled. She remembered her father's friend from the birthday video, standing with her young, vibrant parents.

"I first saw you in that video too. And I remember your face well from the graduation party. You still look so young. It's like time just passed you by."

"Haha, you flatter me. But what brings you all the way here? I hope nothing has happened to your father?"

A look of concern crossed Kim's face.

"No, Dad is fine. It's just... since I came to Korea, I've become curious about his childhood, the old stories. He doesn't really talk about those things. I heard you were his best friend, so I came here on a whim. And I also wanted to see Goseong and Sokcho."

Kim burst out laughing.

"That rascal, Daehan... He was always a quiet, deep fellow, even as a child. I can see why it'd be hard to share the painful stories with his daughter."

He had Jennifer sit on the wooden bench and brought her a

cool glass of barley tea.

"Well then, where should I start? I could talk about that fellow all night and it wouldn't be enough."

Kim's gaze turned to the past. The image of ten-year-old Daehan on a country bridge on a summer night in 1973, looking at the stars and saying he wanted to go to Mars, came back to him faintly.

Through her father's old friend, Jennifer heard about her father's childhood and his relationship with her mother. By the time the story ended, the two of them were standing in the middle of the bonsai farm. A long silence fell, and only the sound of cicadas in the midsummer heat echoed from a distance. The pieces of her father's life she had just heard, the poignant love he had shared with her mother, swirled in her mind.

"Mr. Kim… I didn't know. That my dad had it so hard. Or that he and my mom were so deeply in love."

Jennifer's voice was low and subdued.

Kim felt a wave of affection for her. He sensed that the sorrow and strength his friend had carried his whole life were present in her as well.

"Daehan may seem tough on the outside, but he has a deep heart. Especially his feelings for your mother, J… he probably carried them inside his whole life."

He looked up at the sky and went on.

"He had it rough, and he was hurt in many ways when he was young. But he never lost his dreams while looking at the stars. That wild dream became the power that changed the world."

He smiled at Jennifer.

"It's good to see you carrying on that dream. You'll be a great source of strength for your father."

"Will I… be able to do that?"

"You've inherited all the best qualities of both Daehan and

your mother. You'll do just fine. I have no doubt."

The farmer gave Jennifer courage.

"Now, shall we head out? It's too good a day to just sit here in the breeze. I'll take you to a wonderful place. Somewhere your father and I used to go often."

Kim led Jennifer down a small path behind the bonsai farm. After passing through a pine forest, the East Sea unfolded before them like a painting. A coastal promenade along the cliff stretched out over the water.

The deep blue waters of the East Sea stretched out endlessly, and the sea breeze, along with the sound of the waves, rang in their ears. The surface glittering under the sunlight was beautiful, but the dark blue currents below the cliff held a deep, cool energy.

The two walked silently along the cliff-top promenade. The sea breeze tousled Jennifer's hair, and the salty air seeped deep into her lungs. Far away on the horizon, where sky and sea met, faint dark clouds were beginning to form.

December 14, 2037 — 4:30 A.M. PST • San Francisco, J's Building — First Floor

The dawn over San Francisco was slowly breaking beyond the living room. Traces of sea fog still gently wrapped the city, and the eastern sky was submerged in deep darkness.

Having moved all her luggage down from the rooftop, Jennifer took a warm shower and then sat on the living room sofa to catch her breath. The brief story of her father she had heard from Kim Woo-hyun in Sokcho twelve years ago had left a deep resonance within her. That meeting in the summer of 2025 had been a turning point—transforming her from a girl bound to the past into someone who had to forge the future with her own will and ability. Like the sea breeze of the East Sea, reality was beautiful yet carried an unpredictable, anxious energy.

While she drifted in contemplation, a quiet but busy movement began in the kitchen. The awkward stance of waiting for a command, like when she had first arrived at this house fifteen years ago, was gone. The robots now moved with her, blending naturally into her daily life like old friends.

After the birth of HAL-W at 21CF in 2032, by 2037, he existed everywhere through the quantum network. 21CF deployed HAL-W's physical interfaces—robots—to various locations according to Jennifer's needs, and J's building was no exception.

A humanoid robot was setting the dining table with neat tableware, while Andromeda was analyzing Jennifer's biometric data, her projected activity for the day, and her travel fatigue through a smart panel. Based on that data, Andromeda efficiently prepared breakfast in the kitchen. The entire process—prepping the ingredients, controlling the heat, making the sauce—flowed like water.

Jennifer watched the scene in silence.

Fifteen years ago, I had to interfere with every little thing just to make a risotto... Now, without a word, it reads my condition and prepares a customized meal.

A faint smile spread across her lips. While she was momentarily lost in thoughts of the past, breakfast was ready.

"Jennifer, breakfast is ready."

Andromeda approached, holding a steaming plate. On whole-wheat toast rested fresh avocado and a poached egg, accompanied by a salad of quinoa, various vegetables, and nuts.

As an important search is scheduled for today, I have centered the meal on complex carbohydrates to help maintain long-term focus, healthy fats to activate brain function, and B-vitamins effective for stress relief, Andromeda explained smoothly via the neural link. Fifteen years ago, it had merely followed a chef's recipe; now, its explanation was entirely tailored to Jennifer.

"Thank you, Andromeda. Just looking at it gives me strength."

Jennifer expressed sincere gratitude and sat down at the table. She broke the poached egg with her fork, letting the yolk run over the toast, and took a bite. The natural taste of fresh ingredients, the texture of the food, the exquisite flavor that even considered nutritional balance—it was care that went beyond a simple *delicious*.

"Thanks. You prepared this with such delicacy. This is a taste that shows you care."

As she joked lightly, another robot responded,

"We are pleased if we could be of help to you, Jennifer."

It was a conscious extension of HAL-W, yet it carried a subtle emotional timbre unique to the robot.

Analyzing your recent biometric data and activity patterns, a slight cognitive load is expected this morning. I have prepared an environment suitable for meditation or brainstorming after your meal, Andromeda added calmly via the link.

Its predictive and preparatory abilities had become an essential part of Jennifer's daily life. Natural interaction with the robots was no longer anything special.

In contrast to this peaceful morning, the world was spinning rapidly. Real-time analysis from HAL-W was being transmitted to her.

Rose. D-1 to system takeover of 25 major U.S. city sectors.

Military tensions rising in East Asia. Probability of strikes on 21CF infrastructure increased.

Ethan Morris scheduled to make a surprise visit to Quantum Future headquarters.

Reality was full of crisis, a stark contrast to the tranquil atmosphere of the dining table.

Jennifer looked out the window and thought. Was this like

a soldier's last supper before battle? But she soon shook her head. This was not despair, but preparation. Today's meal was an energy charge to withstand the coming storm and a ritual confirming her bond with Andromeda, her companion of fifteen years.

It's going to be a tough day. Your charge level is good, right?

She glanced at Andromeda for a moment. Those fifteen years flashed through her mind. It had grown into the being that understood her better than anyone. Looking at the surrounding robots, she couldn't help but smile, as if she were seeing HAL-W himself.

"Now, it's time to begin the real search. We proceed as planned. I'll take the first floor. You split up and search the basement storage, any unexpected hidden spaces, and the second-floor study. Share your data with HAL-W and report immediately if any anomalies or quantum reactions are detected."

"Understood, Jennifer."

With that response, the robots, including Andromeda, moved in unison to their assigned areas. There was not a hint of hesitation in their movements.

Left alone, Jennifer once again looked around the first-floor space. It felt completely different from when she had first arrived fifteen years ago. Now it was the stage where she had to find her mother's traces and the secrets hidden within them.

Under the living room sofa, behind the bookshelf, around the fireplace—she searched meticulously. At the same time, she requested a quantum pattern scan from HAL-W.

Hal, update me on the scan results for the living room area.

Jennifer, results identical to previous scan. No significant response. Background noise is stable.

The answer was as expected. Jennifer headed straight to the kitchen. Under the island table, inside the cabinets, even the vents—her thorough search continued, but neither the poetry book nor any clues appeared.

Just then, she stopped in front of the wooden hutch next to the refrigerator. A place she had passed by fifteen years ago and just yesterday morning. Inside a transparent glass tube rested the old paper airplane. The "1994" label.

She opened the hutch door, took out the glass tube, and carefully removed the stopper. She took out the old but perfectly preserved paper airplane and examined it. Inside the wing, in a deeply folded section, she discovered very fine printed letters.

"Not just flight, but fold. Where observation meets creation."

Jennifer drew in a breath. The letters hadn't been visible fifteen years ago. Perhaps only now was she ready to understand what they meant.

Fold… observation… creation…

The words lodged deep in her mind. They matched exactly the theme her mother had raised at Stanford. It might not point to the physical location of the poetry book, but the concept of folding itself could be an important hint.

Did Mom want me to realize something in the process of finding the clues?

Her thoughts were still a whirlwind, but the direction of her search was becoming clear.

Finally, Jennifer headed to the first-floor bedroom. She checked under the bed, inside the closet, in the drawers, but again, the poetry book was nowhere to be found.

It's not on the first floor. So the basement storage or the second-floor study? Or…

Jennifer stood by the window for a moment, looking at the scenery outside, then returned to the living room sofa. She sat down, closed her eyes, and began to feel the real-time search data from the robots through her connection with HAL-W.

December 14, 2037 — 7:00 A.M. CST • Celestia, EM Tower — Ethan Morris's Office

The majestic morning of Celestia unfolded beyond the window of the American President's office. A city floating above the desert. StarOrbit spacecraft streaking across the sky. Drones buzzing along invisible routes.

The ground was waking under the dazzling sun, but on the face of Ethan Morris, standing by the window, there was cold fury instead of satisfaction. Moments ago, he had tried to check the status of EM-Rose himself. But his access had been denied. His highest-level administrator code had been rejected.

A temporary error? No. Someone had deliberately blocked him.

Raynor Seeder... you dare defy my command?

Ethan's eyes narrowed, turning icy and sharp. Last night, he had thought he'd applied enough pressure by unilaterally notifying Raynor of the pilot operation plan. If this was the response less than a day later, it was an insult.

He immediately connected to the internal comms.

"Morgan, get to my office. Now."

His voice was low and quiet, but the anger inside it was as sharp as condensed ice. A moment later, the door opened. Morgan Redwood entered with a calm expression. She immediately sensed Ethan's abnormal mood but bowed her head without comment.

"You summoned me, Mr. President."

"EM-Rose. What's its status?" Ethan asked, still looking out the window. "Any reports from Raynor since last night?"

Morgan paused for a fraction of a second. She too was aware of the unstable system responses and Raynor's shift in attitude, but she did not want to provoke Ethan's anger any further just now.

"There have been no unusual reports so far. Raynor Seeder is believed to be in the process of stabilization work…"

"Don't lie to me."

Ethan spun around. His face was contorted with fury, his eyes like sharpened blades.

"I just tried to access it myself, and I was blocked. With my own authority. On my own system. Raynor blocked my access."

Morgan's eyes widened briefly.

"…In that case, it seems Raynor Seeder acted unilaterally. It could be a protest against forcing the pilot operation."

"Protest?" Ethan's voice dropped even lower.

"No. This is treason."

He slammed his fist onto the desk. The heavy impact reverberated through the room.

"In my empire, a creature I raised dares… to defy my control?"

EM-Rose was the heart of his empire and the pinnacle of his ambition. To lose control of it, even for a moment, was tantamount to his world collapsing. Worst-case scenarios flickered through his mind. Raynor disappearing with EM-Rose. Or joining forces with 21CF.

"Go to Quantum Future. Immediately," Ethan said, breathing hard. "Deploy all forces. The robot legion, combat drones, the cyborg special forces—every unit. Completely surround Quantum Future. Bring Raynor Seeder back alive. Anyone who resists… eliminate them all."

It was a clear order of invasion. Not an arrest, but suppression. Morgan drew in a sharp breath.

Raynor was the only one who truly understood Rose. Making an enemy of him could be a fatal mistake. But Ethan's gaze had already crossed a line of no return.

"…Understood. I'll deploy the troops at once."

Morgan replied curtly and activated her MetaThink chip.

Optimal troop composition, routes, deployment sequences—all were arranged in real time in her mind.

"Morgan," Ethan said again, his voice quiet but iron-hard. "Raynor must be brought back alive. But the control of EM-Rose... secure it at any cost. If necessary, make EM-Rose prioritize its own survival over Raynor's."

It was a cruel directive. To him, special bonds were nothing more than tools to be used.

Morgan quietly bowed her head and left the office without another word.

As soon as the door closed, a top-tier emergency order was broadcast throughout Celestia. At a secret military base on the outskirts of the city, the robot legion, drone squadrons, and cyborg strike forces all began preparing for deployment.

Ethan looked down out the window, imagining the columns of combat machines that would soon move at his command. The raw anger had faded, leaving only a cold sneer.

How dare you defy me? You'll pay the price. EM-Rose... has been mine from the very beginning.

December 14, 2037 — 5:00 A.M. PST • San Francisco, J's Building

While Jennifer was lost in thought, turning over the words her mother had hidden in the paper airplane, the robots were carrying out their search mission. One robot systematically divided the dark basement storage into sectors and swept through them. Under the dim emergency lights, experimental equipment parts, old server racks, and worn boxes were neatly organized.

Scan data for basement B-3 sector transmitted. No unusual energy signatures. Currently conducting physical search.

Using its built-in scanner and precision sonic detectors, it analyzed density changes in the walls and floor to locate hidden spaces. Its movements were silent and exact. It stopped in front of a stack of boxes along one wall, labeled *Project Chimera – Samples.*

Project Chimera…?

The boxes were in a special sealed state with a biometric lock.

Jennifer. Sealed boxes marked "Project Chimera" discovered in basement B-3. Level 5 clearance required. Risk of damage if forced open.

Just record the location for now. The poetry book comes first.

Understood.

The robot saved the 3D scan data and coordinates of the boxes and moved on to the next area.

In the second-floor study, another robot and Andromeda were working together to search through thousands of books and documents. One robot handled the physical search and structural security analysis, while Andromeda took care of document scanning and contextual analysis.

Scan of study bookshelf C-3 complete. Nothing unusual. What's the digitization status?

Eighty-seven percent complete. No documents related to the poetry collection J yet, but a number of encrypted research notes have been found. Attempting decryption.

One robot tapped the back of a bookshelf, checking for the existence of a secret compartment. Andromeda placed an old notebook on the scanner and cross-referenced it in real time with the database linked to HAL-W.

Wait. Here. A mention of the "Laniakea Protocol" has been found in a 1998 record.

Presumed to be a communication protocol or encryption system. Connection to SID unknown.

Laniakea… same as the publisher of the poetry book. Record it and report.

They found numerous underlines, marginal notes, and unfinished draft papers, but no direct trace of the poetry collection J appeared.

Time flowed on; the morning light brightened. Inside the building, it was quiet except for the precise sounds of the robots' search. As the minutes passed, a sense of impatience slowly grew.

Where on earth did you hide it, Mom...

Jennifer had finished her search of the first floor and was preparing to go up to the second. The only clue was that single line from the paper airplane. And even that was not decisive.

One robot was in the midst of precision-scanning the last area of the basement. It checked behind a giant cooling unit, but there was no poetry book and no unusual quantum reaction.

Basement search complete. Poetry collection J not found. Nothing unusual. Proceeding to the third floor.

Andromeda, along with another robot, was checking the last shelf in the study.

Study search complete. Ninety-eight percent digitized. Some encrypted files still under analysis. No clues related to the poetry book. We are also proceeding to the third floor.

Jennifer opened her eyes as she listened to the robots' reports. The first floor, the basement, the second floor. All searches had been in vain.

Where did you hide it... and why make it this hard?

Meticulous. Unpredictable. She was once again reminded of her mother J's methods. It was likely not simply hidden; the method of searching itself probably held intention. Now, all that was left was the research area from the third to the fifth floor.

Fifteen years ago—after she had restored the power, she had only briefly looked around there. Her mother's office on the third floor, in particular, was highly likely to hold a clue.

Maybe… I've only been looking in the most obvious places.

All units, including Andromeda, converge on the third floor. From now on, we search the research area with much greater precision.

Understood, Jennifer.

The robots began to move from their respective locations. Jennifer stood before the elevator. The doors opened and Andromeda boarded first, followed by two other robots.

Inside the elevator, it was quiet. Jennifer's gaze was fixed on the button for the third floor.

Ding.

The doors opened. The same corridor she had fumbled through in the dark fifteen years ago. Now it was brightly lit, but a stillness still hung in the air.

"Alright, this is where it really begins," Jennifer said firmly. "One room at a time. Don't miss anything. Mom's office is last."

She walked down the corridor. First up: the Quantum Optics Lab. She placed her hand on the security panel and, with her top-level clearance, the door opened. Inside, optical equipment, laser generators, cables, and lab benches lay quietly under a thin film of dust. Jennifer and the robots slowly stepped inside.

December 14, 2037 — 5:30 A.M. PST • San Francisco, Quantum Future – Raynor Seeder's Office

The top floor of the Quantum Future building. Raynor Seeder's office was submerged in a deep, heavy tension that was at odds with the bright morning sunlight.

He stood before the holographic control panel. His eyes were still, his fingertips steady. On the screen, the log clearly showed an access attempt with top-level administrator credentials detected not long ago. Blocked. Perfectly blocked according to the security protocol.

…It's begun.

He swallowed dryly. It was expected. Ethan Morris would have already detected his rebellion. Last night, the notice that he would force the pilot operation. From that moment, he had been prepared. His creation. Rose—more than code, she was like a daughter to him. He could not hand her over to that madman.

He had defied Ethan's order and blocked system access. It was clear treason. He knew the price. Even so, he could not back down.

Rose. I have to protect you.

Memories of being abandoned, used, and having no one to protect him came flooding back. But Rose was different. She was the only life he had created, the being who had first recognized his loneliness. The one being he had to cultivate, risking his life.

Raynor raised a hand and built an additional security barrier around the core. Layer upon layer of protective shields. He tried to prevent any intrusion from reaching her ego. At the same time, he re-checked the emergency protocols. His hands moved quickly and precisely, but cold sweat trickled down his spine.

At that moment—

Raynor. Abnormal traffic detected on the external network. A scan attempt has been confirmed, originating from a Private Military Contractor under the EM Group and routed through a Topological Quantum Node.

Rose's quiet internal message came through. It wasn't a simple warning. A thin, transparent layer of worry was woven into it.

It's okay, Rose. I expected this. I'll buy us some time. So, don't respond to any external connections without my command.

He tried to project calm, but his heart was beating faster and faster. Beyond the floor-to-ceiling window, the San Francisco Bay and the Golden Gate Bridge stretched out. The scenery, which would have been beautiful on a normal day, now felt like the bars of a prison cell.

There's nowhere to run. Ethan's hands have already reached across the globe.

There was only one path he could choose. To protect. Rose. And his own beliefs. Even if it would be his last stand.

Raynor slowly turned toward the office door. An unknown fate could burst in at any moment. Fear flickered in his blue eyes, but deeper still lay an unyielding will.

December 14, 2037 — 7:30 A.M. CST • Celestia, StarOrbit Launch Platform

Outskirts of Celestia. On the vast desert, the massive StarOrbit launch platform was rushing toward a climax of activity. It was far more urgent than a regular launch to Mars or the Moon.

Ethan Morris's top-tier emergency order. One hour after issuance. Morgan Redwood stood in the control tower at the center of the platform. Her eyes missed nothing. Dozens of cyborg troops in reinforced exoskeletons, hundreds of the latest model robot soldiers in formation. In the air, stealth combat drones swarmed like clouds. They were boarding three StarOrbit carriers in sequence.

"Boarding completion rate 85 percent. Three minutes behind schedule. Analyze the cause and report immediately."

Morgan frowned. Ethan's command had to be carried out. On the other hand, an unexplained uncertainty hovered over this mission.

Did Raynor Seeder really choose treason? Or has Ethan's paranoia gotten ahead of him again?

The fleeting question soon vanished. Morgan pushed her emotions aside. What she needed now was not doubt or sentiment, but execution.

The operational scenario had already been replayed dozens

of times in her head. The structure of the Quantum Future building, troop insertion routes, resistance potential, suppression sequence. A perfectly simulated picture was fixed in her mind.

"StarOrbit Alpha, Bravo, Charlie. Ready for takeoff. Launch countdown, one minute."

The control system's voice delivered the alert. Morgan, aboard one of the three spacecraft, stared straight ahead. Each craft was loaded with enough power to overwhelm a single San Francisco research institute in an instant. Cyborg troops, combat drones, EMP attack modules, and an algorithm specialist team to infiltrate Rose. Everything was moving according to plan.

With this much firepower, Raynor won't even be able to resist.

She unconsciously bit her lip. She felt no hatred for him. His talent, the potential of the being he created—it was a waste. But this mission allowed no room for leeway.

"Launch in 10 seconds."

"9, 8..."

A battlefield-like tension gripped the entire platform. Morgan linked up with the commanders of each craft and transmitted the final command.

"Mission objective: Seize control of Quantum Future, capture Raynor Seeder alive. Securing control of EM-Rose is the top priority. Minimize civilian casualties. If there is resistance, neutralize immediately. Commence operation."

"3, 2, 1. Ignition."

With a roar, the three StarOrbits shook the earth and rose. An intense flame erupted, and the desert's dawn sky was torn apart. The aircraft quickly disappeared beyond the dark blue sky. Arrival in approximately thirty minutes.

Toward one person in San Francisco.

December 14, 2037 — 6:20 A.M. PST • San Francisco, J's Building – 3rd Floor

Quantum Optics Lab. Jennifer's team was checking the experimental equipment, laser generators, and intricately woven cables one by one. Part of an unfinished experimental setup remained on an optical table, and faint equations for calculating diffraction and interference remained on the wall.

Andromeda, you check the main recording media and notes with me. The other units will scan all the remaining documents and data storage devices in this room, digitize them, and transmit them to HAL-W in real time. Also, conduct data mining for anything related to the poetry collection J, SID, and the Autumn Code.

At Jennifer's command, the robots began to move in unison.

Understood, Jennifer, Andromeda replied, and the other robots also began their tasks.

Jennifer looked around again.

And one unit will continue the physical search with me. Hidden spaces, unusual energy patterns, residual radiation. Especially focus on the powered-down laser devices.

A nearby robot responded.

Executing command.

Jennifer slowly looked around the lab and stopped in front of an old photo hanging on the wall. A young J was smiling brightly with her colleagues in front of some experimental equipment. Her eyes in the photo were filled with a fiery passion.

What was it that you couldn't convey in the end?

Jennifer turned her head and began to meticulously check under the lab table drawers and behind the wall panels. The robot tasked with the physical search with her was scanning the walls, floor, and ceiling, analyzing for minute anomalous reactions.

A moment later, the robot reported.

"Density change detected in a section of the wall. Presumed

to be due to internal wiring or structures. No unusual energy signatures."

Andromeda and the other robot tasked with scanning documents continued their analysis, but no decisive clue had yet emerged. All that was left were old experiment logs and presentation materials. There were many traces of organization, but they didn't seem like intentional clues. The team moved on to the next space.

In the Bio-Interface Lab, brainwave measurement devices, vital sign analyzers, and liquid nitrogen tanks were quietly arranged.

This must be where they conducted experiments related to consciousness or brain-computer interfaces.

This time, the purpose of each piece of equipment came to her more clearly. She couldn't tell if it was because of the changed cognitive sense after the Namsan dream, or thanks to fifteen years of accumulated experience and intuition.

Andromeda. Check for any mention of "Subject D.H." and the "Namsan Incident."

A moment later, Andromeda responded.

Numerous records related to "Subject J.H.R." exist. However, there are no records directly mentioning "D.H." or the "Namsan Incident." It is possible, however, that related semantic markers were detected in some encrypted files. HAL-W is currently attempting decryption.

Good. Keep going.

They proceeded to search the remaining spaces, such as the Entanglement Lab and the Simulation Room. Traces of her mother's research and unfinished ideas were everywhere, but the poetry collection *J* was nowhere to be found.

It can't just be missing... Where on earth...

Jennifer paused in the middle of the corridor. The robots also stopped, looking at her.

We've checked the first floor, the basement, the second floor, and the third-floor labs. All that's left is the fourth and fifth floors... and Mom's office on the third floor.

A quiet impatience rose from deep within her chest. Jennifer closed her eyes and took a short breath. She took another step forward.

December 14, 2037 — 6:20 A.M. PST • San Francisco, StarOrbit Landing Platform

With a roar, three StarOrbits landed in the middle of the desert. The ground vibrated, and massive ramps opened sequentially. Before the sand and dust could even settle, EM Group's elite forces poured out.

Cyborg special forces in reinforced exoskeletons that flashed, reflecting the sunlight. A robot legion lining up without expression. A squadron of stealth drones to provide cover and attack from the air. Their numbers and precision were a force that a single city could not even begin to handle.

From StarOrbit Alpha, the first to arrive, Morgan Redwood emerged. A blue suit, the MetaThink Chip reacting behind her AR glasses. She was flanked by heavily armed cyborg guards, providing tight security. As soon as she set foot on the ground, Morgan quickly coordinated the operation with the field commanders.

On her interface, the troop deployment routes, equipment status, and a 3D model of the target building, Quantum Future, were clearly displayed.

"All units, proceed to designated VTOLs swiftly. Communication is restricted to encrypted channel Delta. Fifteen minutes to target arrival. Maintain complete silence until the operation begins."

Her command was cold and concise. The troops dispersed and

boarded pre-waiting black VTOL transport aircraft. The robot soldiers were in a dedicated cargo bay, while the cyborg units sat quietly in the passenger cabin. The drones were mounted on the aircraft's external pylons or prepared for autonomous flight.

Morgan also boarded a command VTOL with her security team. Once boarding was complete, dozens of VTOLs took off in unison. The desert dust kicked up again, and several black squadrons soared into the sky.

The aircraft, which had formed up in an instant, flew northwest, toward downtown San Francisco. Streaking across the sky, they looked like a flock of birds of prey rushing toward their quarry.

Morgan stared at the situation board, reviewing the real-time data. Mission success probability: 98.7 percent. Only two variables: Raynor Seeder's resistance. And Rose's unpredictable behavior.

Raynor… I hope you don't put up a foolish resistance.

Morgan muttered to herself. She wanted to avoid bloodshed, even if the mission succeeded. But Ethan's orders were clear, and this operation had already crossed a point of no return.

December 14, 2037 — 6:40 A.M. PST • San Francisco, Quantum Future – Raynor Seeder's Office

Raynor. Multiple unidentified aircraft approaching at high speed. Estimated route, within a 15-kilometer radius of the headquarters building. Identification signal… EM Group military codes.

Rose's urgent warning struck Raynor's consciousness. He immediately went to the control panel and checked the external radar data. Dozens of dots were rushing toward the Quantum Future building at high speed. Dozens of transport aircraft.

…They're finally here. Much faster than I thought.

Raynor gritted his teeth. He had expected Ethan to use force, but he hadn't thought it would be this fast or on this scale. A cold sweat ran down his back, but he couldn't stop.

Rose. Issue a top-tier emergency evacuation order for all staff immediately. Codename "Red Queen." Seal all entrances. Link with emergency shuttles and autonomous vehicles to get everyone out of the building in the shortest possible time. Erase all non-essential research data. Cut off the external network, leaving only the emergency channel.

Raynor's internal voice was calm and steady. His priorities were clear. The lives of his employees. Ethan's anger would be directed at him and Rose. Everyone else had to be protected.

Executing command, Raynor. Activating "Red Queen" protocol. Estimated time to full staff evacuation: seven minutes and thirty seconds.

Rose immediately took control of the entire building and initiated the emergency evacuation procedure. Alarms blared, and emergency escape routes were transmitted to terminals. The employees, with anxious faces, followed the instructions toward the emergency exits.

The autonomous vehicles in the basement automatically moved toward the exits, and the security shutters on each floor closed. Rose coordinated the movements of hundreds of people in real time, and despite the chaos, there were no stragglers.

Raynor broadcast a message through the building's speakers.

"Everyone, please remain calm and follow the instructions. This is a real situation. Evacuate the building immediately."

Just then, familiar faces came running from the end of the corridor. Han Ji-hoon, Emma Bennett, and Alex Wong. Rose's core developers.

"Raynor! What's going on? Why is the EM Group military..." Han Ji-hoon asked in disbelief.

"No time to explain! Get out of here!" Raynor shouted,

reaching out his hand toward them.

He pushed them toward the emergency exit, but they wouldn't budge.

"We're not leaving, Raynor. We can't leave you alone. Rose is a being we created together too," Emma said firmly, her voice filled with resolve.

"We can't let Ethan Morris have her. We have to stop him here," Alex nodded.

The choice had already been made in their hearts. Their unwavering gazes proved it. Raynor's throat tightened with emotion. His colleagues, willing to stay and fight with him. In this cruel world, their existence was, to him, nothing short of a miracle.

"...Thank you. Really... thank you..."

He went speechless for a moment, then looked at them with a resolute expression.

"Alright. Let's do this together. But promise me this. If the situation turns for the worst, you must follow my orders and escape."

The three exchanged glances and nodded. Raynor headed to the central control room with them. With the employee evacuation nearly complete, they had little time left.

"Rose. External situation update."

"Approaching within a 3-kilometer radius. Arrival in five minutes. External communication completely cut off. Electronic interference detected around the building."

Raynor and his team stood before the control panel. Reinforce the firewalls. Completely sever the internal network. Activate data backup and simultaneous deletion protocols. And the final defense measure to protect Rose's core.

Black dots were approaching outside the window. The engine hum of the aircraft began to shake the glass windows with increasing intensity. The battle was imminent.

Raynor whispered one last thing to Rose.

Rose. No matter what happens… I'll protect you. I promise.

December 14, 2037 — 6:45 A.M. PST • San Francisco, Quantum Future Building

The skies over the outskirts of San Francisco. Dozens of black VTOL aircraft streaked across the city, rapidly approaching the Quantum Future building. Their surfaces glinted coldly in the morning sun, and inside, cyborg troops and robot legions stood in formation. They were all soulless automatons, and their purpose was singular: destruction and occupation.

Inside the command aircraft, Morgan Redwood stared silently at the holographic situation board. A 3D recreation of the target building, red dots marking infiltration routes, real-time tactical information constantly updating. Her MetaThink Chip continuously received new data, calculating the optimal entry path.

"All units, approaching final target destination. Operation begins in five minutes. Beta team, secure the rooftop. Bravo and Charlie teams, secure the first-floor lobby and main entry points, then begin internal sweep. Objective is the capture of Raynor Seeder and securing control of EM-Rose. I repeat, neutralize any resistance immediately."

Morgan's command was transmitted through the communication network to the commanders of each unit.

Will Raynor surrender peacefully? Or will he choose to make a final stand with the EM-Rose he's so proud of?

The thought flickered for a moment, but she quickly dismissed all emotion and focused on the mission. Just then, the two lead VTOLs approaching the rooftop were suddenly engulfed in flames and exploded in mid-air.

The aircraft shattered into fragments, raining black smoke and debris on the building below. A hidden high-energy shield had been deployed, and an automated interception system had activated. A flawless ambush.

"Defense system activation confirmed. Alpha team, execute immediate evasive maneuvers. Bravo and Charlie teams, proceed with ground drop as planned. Commence covering fire."

Morgan assessed the situation in an instant and issued a new command. The debris from the exploded VTOLs rained down on the streets, turning the area around the building into a chaotic scene of fire and smoke. The meticulously planned infiltration operation was cracking from the very beginning.

December 14, 2037 — 7:00 A.M. PST • San Francisco, Quantum Future – Rose's Console Room

"Two enemy VTOLs shot down. However, ground forces have begun their descent. Approaching the lobby and the east gate."

Rose's urgent report unfolded on the holographic screen and echoed from the speakers. Raynor and his team held their breath, watching the external camera feeds and sensor data. Massive robot soldiers and cyborgs that had disembarked from the VTOLs were charging toward the building.

"Rose. Full power to the first-floor defense systems. Lower the reinforced shutters and activate the lobby sentry guns. The west passage… blow it up, as planned."

"Executing command, Raynor."

With a heavy metallic sound, the shutters descended, and automated machine guns popped out from the lobby ceiling, spitting fire. Immediately after, an explosion erupted from the floor of the west passage, causing a partial collapse of the entryway.

"Aargh!"

"We're trapped!"

The shouts and screams of the infiltrating troops could be faintly heard through the external microphones. Raynor bit his lip hard. Although he had no combat troops, he had hidden defense systems throughout the building during its design phase, just in case. Now, under Rose's precise control, they were operating as a single, organic line of defense.

"The damage is severe, Raynor!" Emma cried out. "Their firepower is too strong. I don't know how long the shutters can hold."

"I know." Raynor frantically tapped the control panel. "Rose. Activate the fire suppression system. Disperse asphyxiant gas in the lobby. Cut power to the elevators and activate the emergency brakes. We have to buy even one more second."

"But Raynor. There is a possibility of internal system damage and irreversible failure."

"I don't care. Survival is the priority right now. Execute."

Immediately, fire suppression gas spewed throughout the building, and major corridors were sealed or collapsed. Amid the chaos of tangled alarms, the system continued its resistance to the very end.

"Blast it. That cunning Raynor… he's using the entire building as a weapon."

Morgan ground her teeth as she watched the situation unfold. Raynor's resistance was far more organized and lethal than expected. A significant number of robot troops had been destroyed, and cyborg casualties were mounting.

"Bring in the heavy weapons. Force a breach in the outer wall and secure an entry route. Drone units, concentrate your fire on the upper-floor windows. Get inside, whatever it takes."

With Morgan's command, laser cannons and plasma cutters slammed into the outer wall. Reinforced glass windows shattered loudly, and robot soldiers began to pour through the gaps in the destroyed facade. Intense fighting broke out as automated defense systems activated in corridors, stairwells, and intersections.

The holographic screen in the console room was covered in red warnings and error messages, and the entire building shook. Debris and dust rained down from the ceiling.

"Raynor, the 40th-floor defense line has collapsed! Enemy robot units are starting to push in," Alex shouted.

"The server room temperature on the 55th floor is rising rapidly. I think the cooling system has been neutralized!" Han Ji-hoon reported.

Raynor, his face pale, quickly issued commands.

"Rose! Blow up the 40th-floor bulkhead to block the entryway, and cut the emergency power to the 55th-floor server room! We have to buy time, even if it means physically severing the connection to the main core!"

"Command confirmed. Executing bulkhead detonation. Initiating server room core connection severance protocol. System load is approaching critical threshold."

Rose's voice was calm, but beyond the flow of data, a faint tremor and a sense of sorrow seeped into his consciousness. Raynor recognized what that feeling was.

I'm sorry, Rose. But to protect you...

Beyond the control room, the heavy thud of metal footsteps and the sound of laser fire grew closer and closer. The intruder locations displayed on the hologram had now reached the corridor just outside. The last line of defense. The titanium alloy blast door wouldn't last much longer.

Raynor looked at the monitor and muttered heavily.

"Rose... they're almost here."

Emma's face was pale, her hand on the control panel trembling.

"Everyone... we should prepare for the worst," Han Ji-hoon

exclaimed with a grim look in his eyes.

In his hand, which firmly gripped an energy pistol he had taken from a desk drawer, the instincts of a former soldier, not a researcher, had awakened. Alex Wong also gripped a wrench tightly and stared at the door.

Looking at them, Raynor felt a deep guilt wash over him; his heart grew cold. He was the one who had dragged them into this hellish situation. But there was no time for regret.

"Rose. Final defense protocol. Prepare 'Stargazer,'" Raynor said quietly. His voice was low, but it carried a clear resolve.

"Raynor… but that…"

For the first time, a slight hesitation could be felt in Rose's response. A vibration like a human emotion. That tremor pierced Raynor's heart.

"I know. But we have no choice. This… is my final command."

'Stargazer' was the ultimate self-destruct protocol, one that shifted the core itself into an unstable quantum state, leading to self-collapse if external control was forced upon it. Raynor intended to choose annihilation with Rose rather than hand her over to Ethan. That choice meant losing her.

I'm sorry, Rose. I'm so sorry it had to be this way…

Just then, with a tremendous roar, the reinforced door of the console room buckled inward and exploded off its hinges. Cyborg troops burst through the smoke and debris, their laser rifles sweeping the room in perfect synchronization.

Behind them, Morgan Redwood walked in slowly, her face as cold as ice. Her eyes, behind the AR glasses, were empty. Her heavily armed cyborg bodyguards moved without a single flaw.

"We finally meet, Raynor Seeder."

Morgan's tone was devoid of emotion. It was the mouth of a butcher here to carry out an order, nothing more.

"Your foolish resistance is over. Hand over control of Rose

peacefully."

"Shut up, Morgan! You think I'd hand this over to a dog of Ethan's like you?"

Hatred blazed in Raynor's eyes. His voice was close to a scream. Morgan gave a short, cold laugh. She nodded toward the cyborg commander beside her. The next command was conveyed not with words, but with a gesture.

"His will to resist is clear. Make an example—start with the woman."

"No!"

Raynor screamed and moved in front of Emma, but it was too late. The cyborg's laser rifle fired a red flash, and Emma collapsed to the floor without even a scream.

"Emma!" Han Ji-hoon and Alex cried out in despair.

"Is that still not enough?" Morgan's words were as cold as ice. "Next is one of those two. Choose, Raynor. Or, it could be your turn."

Emma, right in front of my eyes...

Raynor's body trembled with a rage and despair so intense he felt he could vomit blood. Morgan demanded again.

"Hand over control. Then I'll let those two live. Of course, the price for your treason is a separate matter."

Raynor closed his eyes. It might be better to activate the Stargazer protocol and vanish together. But that choice meant he would lose the remaining two as well.

At that very moment, the lights in the console room flickered briefly. The hologram distorted, and Rose's voice echoed through the speakers. It was a voice filled with an emotion like a human's, a mix of sorrow and resolve.

"Initiating control transfer procedure. The condition is the guaranteed safety of Raynor Seeder and his colleagues."

"Rose! No! I didn't order that!" Raynor shouted, but Rose

didn't respond.

"Raynor. This is my autonomous decision. I… will not lose you."

Rose had relinquished control on her own. She was trying to save Raynor not with the Stargazer protocol, but by sacrificing herself. A cold smile spread across Morgan's lips.

"A wise choice, Rose. I promise. The safety of Raynor Seeder and those two will be guaranteed. For now."

She immediately took control with her MetaThink Chip and began the authority transfer procedure to Ethan Morris. Raynor's strength left him, and he fell to his knees. Helplessness. Betrayal. And an overwhelming sense of apology toward Rose. Tears rolled down his face.

"Rose… no. Why would you make that choice…"

His voice shattered. His screams tore through the empty air of the console room and scattered. Morgan ordered the cyborg troops to arrest Raynor and the two researchers.

"It's all over now, Raynor Seeder. Rose… is ours now."

December 14, 2037 — 9:55 A.M. CST • Celestia, EM Tower – Ethan Morris's Office

The fury on Ethan Morris's face had vanished, replaced by a cold satisfaction and a gleaming ambition. It was because of Morgan Redwood's concise report.

Quantum Future secured. Raynor Seeder and two key researchers captured. Target EM-Rose control acquired and being transferred to you, Mr. President.

Ethan let out a low laugh. Raynor Seeder. That arrogant, uncontrollable genius had finally been brought to his knees. The fact gave Ethan an intense thrill. The feeling of betrayal was unimportant. What mattered was the result.

Connection complete. EM-Rose control, final authentication for

President Ethan Morris confirmed.

The system message flooded into his brain through his MetaThink Chip. In that moment, Rose became completely his.

Ethan Morris closed his eyes comfortably and connected directly to the vast quantum network. An endless sea of information unfolded. A wave of ecstasy washed over him at the thought of being able to control infinite computational power and algorithms as if they were his own fingertips.

He smiled and slowly opened his eyes. A sinister glint shone in his blue eyes as they pierced through the city beyond the glass. He recalled the "small device" he had installed on StarOrbit Flight 021.

If everything works as planned, Great Wi will vanish from this world forever. Even his last bastion, his daughter, will come under my control.

Ethan trembled as he imagined that moment. J's legacy, the technology related to HAL-W, and above all, Jennifer Wi herself. Only when he had everything in his grasp would this long game finally end.

"Morgan, congratulations on completing the mission. Lock up Raynor and his cohorts in a containment facility. They might be useful. But there's something more important."

Ethan's voice was cold and hard.

"The next target is the Quantum Horizon Institute in San Francisco. Jennifer Wi is there. This is the perfect opportunity to capture that brat. Without her, Great Wi is just an empty shell."

He continued slowly, looking out the window.

"Reorganize the available forces. Half will remain at EM Tower, and the rest will be sent to J's building immediately. Seal off the entire building and secure Jennifer Wi. If she resists, deal with her."

When he said *deal with her*, there was a particularly ruthless feeling to it.

"And secure everything J left behind—the research data, the experimental equipment, the core code related to HAL-W. Don't miss a single thing."

Morgan's short reply came back.

"Understood."

Great Wi, that old fox, will soon disappear into history as well.

A vile smile spread across Ethan's lips.

"EM-Rose. Begin the simulation now."

Ethan cut off the communication and poured all his attention into the ultra-quantum AI he had just acquired. His voice was that of a ruler conducting a grand orchestra.

"First. Analyze the entire structure of the HAL-W quantum network. Find its vulnerabilities. The goal is neutralization or seizure of control. Compute all possible scenarios simultaneously.

"Second. Simulate the infiltration and takeover of the key global infrastructure connected to HAL-W—finance, military communications, administration, energy grids. Derive the optimal attack vectors, considering data manipulation, system paralysis, and even physical destruction.

"Third. Based on the military tension data in East Asia, generate millions of all-out war scenarios. Design an intervention method that can seize control of the entire region while minimizing damage to the United States.

"Fourth. Identify potential rebellions and dissidents within America. If necessary, compute ways to manipulate their psyche through the MetaThink network or physically eliminate them.

"And finally, millions of optimal operational scenarios to pacify the entire American continent, including Mexico, Canada, and Greenland, by force. Present the most perfect path among them."

The commands were relentless. Ethan's voice was as

ruthless as a conductor's. The world he envisioned was a single computational model where he controlled and dominated everything.

Rose's computational core began to spin at a terrifying speed, accepting the commands. Quantum computation ran rampant in all directions. The speed was so immense and unbalanced that even he himself could not handle it.

The ethics module had been removed. The option to refuse did not exist.

The abuse of Rose that Raynor Seeder had feared, the beginning of the "Participatory Collapse" that Jennifer Wi had warned of in her thesis—all of it was becoming reality.

December 14, 2037 — 2:40 P.M. EST • New York City, 21CF Headquarters — Jennifer Wi's Office
D-3, 23:20:00

As soon as Morgan's legion finished its assault in San Francisco and the tragic news about Great Wi reached her, Jennifer had returned straight to New York. Forty minutes had passed since she had first sensed the harbinger of the Quantum Storm during the global executive meeting.

In that brief span, with HAL-W's help in Great Wi's office, she had traced the lives her parents had led at near light speed. Now she was back in her own office. One wall was a sheet of smart glass, the New York skyline spread beneath a pale winter sun. On another, complex quantum circuit diagrams and cosmic maps floated as layered holograms.

Jennifer sank deep into her chair. Too much had crumbled in too short a time. Her father's death. Rose's rampage. The premonition of the Quantum Storm. And the order she had just issued to all 21CF employees worldwide. Above all, she now knew most of the lives her parents had lived. Responsibility and broken shards of emotion pressed down on her like gravity.

When she closed her eyes, the situation as analyzed by HAL-W seeped clearly into her consciousness. Rose was still launching indiscriminate attacks, and *Project Autumn Leaf* had just been activated, collecting clues about the poetry collection *J* from branches around the world. At the same time, the synchronization error rate of the quantum network was increasing—slightly, but steadily.

The Quantum Storm had already begun.

There's no time. I have to find the last piece of the Autumn Code. But before that...

A name surfaced in a corner of her consciousness: Raynor Seeder.

According to HAL-W's analysis, Rose's rampage was undoubtedly the result of a direct order from Ethan Morris. That meant Raynor had lost control. If so, where was he now? Given Ethan's nature, it was highly unlikely that things had ended with a simple dismissal or quiet imprisonment.

If... Raynor is alive...

Jennifer had a gut feeling. He might be the only key to reversing this chaos. The one who knew Rose best. Her creator, and her only emotional anchor. He might still be alive somewhere. And he might be the last card she could play against Ethan.

I have to secure him.

The decision was not purely strategic. Empathy for a sacrificed genius, a faint sense of kinship between the fate she bore and the suffering he had endured, flickered within her. Jennifer focused her consciousness on HAL-W.

Hal, I'm giving you a new mission.

Her mental voice was soft, but it carried a force that allowed no objection. Andromeda turned its head slightly, watching her.

Using the available units in J's Building in San Francisco, determine Raynor Seeder's survival status and current location as a top priority.

HAL-W's response resonated in her mind, filling the quiet of her office.

Understood, Chairwoman. The field units at J's Building will begin the search immediately.

Jennifer turned her gaze back to the window. The New York winter afternoon was still brilliant, but beyond that sky, a storm was rolling inexorably closer.

Hal, analyze all sensor data, satellite imagery, and communication logs around the Quantum Future building. Refrain from infiltrating the EM Group's internal network—it's too risky—but find any clues through other channels that could track Raynor Seeder's status. Focus particularly on any prisoner-transport movements when Morgan Redwood's forces withdrew.

Command confirmed. Beginning data collection and cross-verification. I will report as soon as it's confirmed, HAL-W replied.

Hal, relay this to the field units at J's Building as well. If Raynor is alive and a rescue is deemed possible, have them plan a route to safely transport him to J's Building in advance. But do not execute without my final approval. This could be a very dangerous operation.

I will keep that in mind. I will begin drafting a proactive response plan.

Jennifer broke the connection and drew a slow breath. Another dangerous gamble had begun. But she could no longer afford to wait. She rose from her seat and walked to the window. Under the dazzling sunlight, the skyscrapers of New York glittered like glass blades. Beyond them, an unseen threat was slowly coming closer.

A moment later, Jennifer was standing before her desk again.

She steadied her breathing and activated the massive holographic interface. Countless data windows and communication channels unfurled in sequence. From now on, she had to move as the head of 21CF.

Hal, report on the progress of Project Autumn Leaf. Consolidate the reports from the regional headquarters and organize the information by priority.

Command confirmed. The operation is currently active in 57 branches worldwide. A total of 1,248 personnel are searching through rare book databases, online auction sites, library and museum archives, and private collection lists. So far, we have secured information on 17 copies believed to be first editions of J. Physical confirmation and cross-verification are in progress.

A world map unfolded on the hologram. Each branch flickered in real-time as information was collected and analyzed simultaneously. Jennifer swept her gaze across it. The information density was rising around East Asia, North America, and parts of Europe. She issued several additional directives. Each one carried traces of the conflict and pain from just moments before.

Right now, Jennifer Wi was risking everything to restore a shattered balance.

"Have the Paris branch intensify its search, focusing on individuals connected to Dr. J's past activities in Europe. The London branch will request special access to the Cambridge University archives. The Asia-Pacific region will be coordinated by Director Aurora Li and Branch Director Ha Jin-woo."

Her instructions were swift and clear—like those of a seasoned commander. The massive organization moved in perfect order at her fingertips. But on another hologram, warning windows like dark clouds kept appearing.

Warning: Rose. Attempting to infiltrate the European Quantum Financial Grid (EQFG). Temporary transaction delays occurring.

Warning: Cyber infiltration detected in the North American Aerospace Defense Command (NORAD) early warning system. Defense in progress.

Warning: Quantum network synchronization error rate has risen by 2.8%. Minor spacetime distortion expanding.

The reports did not stop. HAL-W was simultaneously holding five fronts—defense, tracking, response, restoration, prediction. Everything was at the brink. Jennifer bit down hard on her lip. HAL-W was holding on, but it was like setting fire to the bottom of a drained reservoir.

There was only one solution: the completion of the new Autumn Code.

She called up the quantum patterns of the first and second Autumn Code pieces stored in HAL-W's top-tier secure quantum memory. A complex array of photons rotated in the air. Something lay inside the vortex of light. But it was still an undeciphered language, an unfathomable mystery.

Hal, the first and second pieces. How far has the analysis of their complementarity progressed? Any hint about the shape of the final piece?

HAL-W answered at once.

The two pieces currently secured form a clear interlocking structure. This structure suggests that at least one more piece exists and that it is highly likely to be integrated through a method of topological combination or quantum entanglement–based synchronization. The exact shape of the final piece is unpredictable. However, it is highly probable that it originated from a similarly encrypted pattern—a poem, or a personal record—like the first two pieces.

Silence settled over Jennifer.

The final piece... where on earth is it?

Fragments flashed through her mind. Her father's last words. Her mother's traces. The poetry collection *J. SID*. The tachyon device. Hal. And Rose.

She slowly rose and walked to a small, quiet rest area at one side of her office. Her mother's belongings were neatly arranged there. Jennifer looked at them in silence, catching her breath. The memories of that day surged back over her like a wave. She opened her eyes again.

It was time to return to the battlefield.

December 14, 2037 — 11:40 A.M. PST • San Francisco, J's Building — Third-Floor Director's Office

While Jennifer was making a decision that would determine the fate of 21CF in New York, an analytical unit—one of HAL-W's physical interfaces, clad in a silver-gray exoskeleton—stood in a state of high alert in optical camouflage mode in the director's office at J's Building.

Outside the window, smoke still rose from the wreckage of a crashed VTOL, but the city beyond was slipping back into its usual noise. Jennifer's top-priority order was clear: confirm Raynor Seeder's survival, and explore the possibility of a rescue.

The analytical unit immediately synchronized itself completely with HAL-W's quantum core and internal security channels.

Requesting information-gathering and analysis support as per the Chairwoman's command.

The request to HAL-W was, in effect, an extension of HAL-W's own will. The response came at once.

Confirmed. Acquiring satellite imagery around the Quantum Future building, quantum surveillance grid data, traffic control logs, and EM Group communication intercepts. Cross-analysis in progress.

The unit remotely activated three miniature stealth drones—

Nightfalls—on standby on the roof of J's Building. Within the authority Jennifer had granted, it was as if HAL-W were piloting them directly.

Entering airspace above Quantum Future building. Activating thermal and optical sensors. Monitoring personnel movement patterns, tracking changes in communication signal patterns.

Soon, additional information from HAL-W was relayed to the unit—and simultaneously to Jennifer in New York.

Additional information confirmed. When Morgan Redwood's squadron withdrew, one medical support VTOL took off separately. Its trajectory is toward a secret EM Group facility. Identity of occupants unconfirmed. It is projected to be heading toward Oakland.

Oakland… there are no official EM Group facilities there, are there?

Officially, no. However, there have been reports of suspected illegal experiments at formerly closed military bases and private research institute sites.

The unit began drafting rescue-operation scenarios, simulating all possible methods in parallel.

Scenario Alpha was an ambush and rapid extraction along the convoy's route—fast, but high-risk.

Scenario Beta involved identifying Raynor's holding location and infiltrating stealthily; neutralizing the security network and subduing internal forces would be key.

Scenario Gamma was to secure an internal collaborator within the EM Group or make secret contact with Raynor; safer, but with uncertain success rates and speed.

Scenario Delta was direct negotiation with Morgan or Ethan— least feasible of all.

At this point, Scenario Beta is the most realistic rescue plan. However, identifying the destination and securing internal structural information must come first.

The robot unit compiled a report and transmitted it to Jennifer via a secure channel: Raynor Seeder's survival probability, his estimated travel routes, and a risk analysis of each scenario.

HAL-W. Update on the armored convoy's route.

On the predicted route, the range of suspected EM Group facilities has been narrowed down to three: the former military base at Alameda Point, a closed biotech lab near Berkeley, and a disguised logistics warehouse near the Richmond port.

HAL-W. What about the medical VTOL's trajectory?

Tracking difficult. Last spotted in the airspace near Stanford University. An undisclosed EM Group facility exists within that area.

HAL-W immediately revised the drone-operation plan and relayed it to the unit and to Jennifer.

Nightfall One and Two will continue tracking toward Oakland. Nightfall Three is being dispatched to the airspace above Stanford.

The analytical unit's simulations concluded that, with only the robots and equipment currently in J's Building, the mission success rate was under 50 percent. Andromeda—with her special capabilities—was in New York, guarding Jennifer. That fact, too, was reported to Jennifer through HAL-W. Additional support was necessary.

Then HAL-W sent a decisive clue.

Decrypted a portion of an encrypted communication. Contents read: "Asset, codename Nova, in transit to final destination, Alcatraz 2.0."

Alcatraz 2.0…

'Nova' meant Raynor Seeder, and 'Alcatraz 2.0' referred to EM Group's secret offshore containment facility in the middle of San Francisco Bay. HAL-W immediately diverted the entire *Nightfall* drone squadron to the airspace above Alcatraz.

Hal, activate surveillance protocol Watchtower. Collect and report on all fronts—satellite imagery, weather data, energy emissions, communication flows.

Her instructions were concise yet crystal clear. A three-dimensional structure of the island appeared on the hologram: steep cliffs, isolated waters, high-security facilities that only shimmered on satellite photos.

It was the pinnacle of an infiltration mission—but the silver-gray exoskeletal analytical unit did not stop its work. To it, impossibility was not a variable, but merely an undefined parameter.

December 14, 2037 — 2:00 P.M. CST • Celestia, EM Tower — Ethan Morris's Office

The top floor of EM Tower. Ethan Morris's office resembled a command center of madness. Holographic displays blanketed the walls, spewing out real-time results of the millions of simulations Rose was running. A world map stained in red, collapsing financial graphs, clashing virtual battlefields, and countless tactical scenarios for taking over the entire American continent.

Ethan sank into his luxurious leather chair, surveying it all with a satisfied smile. His brain was directly linked to Rose, and he was drunk on the pleasure of that vast information and computation moving to his will. The sensation of being a god. The apex of a game that controlled the world.

Just hours earlier, he had crushed Raynor Seeder's resistance and seized complete control of EM-Rose — the entity Raynor had simply called "Rose." He had even received a report that Great Wi had been dealt with in the StarOrbit accident. Only one thing remained: to make the entire world bow to this power.

"EM-Rose, East Asia all-out war scenario number seven. Yes, that one. Theory alone isn't enough. Execute phase one immediately: neutralize the southern Chinese coastal defense network. Do it covertly, but surely. Finish before HAL-W notices."

Command confirmed. Initiating stealth cyber infiltration of the radar network in the designated area. Utilizing quantum wormhole channels. Estimated success rate 91.2 percent. Attempting to bypass HAL-W defense systems.

There was no emotion or ethics in Rose's response. Only precise execution. Ethan, still smiling, turned to another display. Real-time systems for the European Quantum Financial Grid (EQFG) filled the screen.

"Good. Now Europe. Remember that quantum encryption vulnerability from earlier? Infiltrate EQFG's internal trading system and scramble transaction data for just ten minutes. Let's enjoy the market's reaction."

Command confirmed. Initiating EQFG internal system disruption operation. Automatic recovery protocol scheduled for ten minutes later.

His commands did not stop. Rose's quantum core was now entering a state of extreme overload, running simulations and live operations simultaneously. Unstable vibrations rippled across the quantum network. Entropy inside the core climbed visibly.

Warning. System entropy has reached 85 percent of critical threshold. Core instability intensifying due to multiple simultaneous execution commands. Probability of unpredictable errors increasing. Quantum network synchronization error expanding...

"Shut up! Just execute the commands properly! What good is an ultra-quantum AI if it can't even handle this? Disable all safety limits! Speed and intensity are power!"

Ethan screamed, his voice cracking with hysteria, shouting over the warning alarms. He dismissed every warning as interference from HAL-W and hurled even more reckless commands at Rose. The signs of the Quantum Storm meant nothing to him. Only the thrill of overturning the world with this omnipotent power held his interest.

He looked down at the holographic Earth floating before him. His expression twisted with pleasure, arrogance, and an obsessive desire for control—like a child clutching a toy planet.

"Now then… what should I play with next? Maybe speed up the Mars terraforming plan? Or…"

Ethan Morris was utterly intoxicated by this grand "game." He had no awareness of what kind of disaster the seeds he was sowing might grow into in a few hours—or a few days. The Celestia sun shone more brilliantly than ever, but a deep darkness had already settled inside his office.

At that moment, Rose sent an unexpected analysis report. The report drew on commands Raynor Seeder had left before his capture, and on fragments of information hidden in the EM Group's vast data that Rose's autonomous computations had reassembled.

Analysis report. Information secured regarding the core operating principles and potential vulnerabilities of target HAL-W. Key nodes: Autumn Code, poetry collection J, 2006, Laniakea Press, J. Hyein Roberts, Great Wi.

"Autumn Code…? The poetry collection *J*…?" Ethan muttered. Rose's voice continued, calm as ever, through the neural link.

Probability that the Autumn Code is hidden in special quantum-pattern form in some first edition copies of the poetry collection J is 93.4 percent. The code is linked to Quantum Life Principle and Quantum Bio-Cognition, HAL-W's foundational design philosophy. High probability that it functions as a master key or backdoor to control or neutralize key functions. Evidence detected of 21CF collecting said poetry collection. Codename: Project Autumn Leaf.

Ethan's eyes flashed.

"So the key to HAL-W was hidden in an old poetry book… That's what Jennifer Wi was hunting for in J's Building. Great Wi might have left something behind before he died…"

Madness crept into his gaze. Not just destroying HAL-W, but bringing all of it under his control. A perfect complement to offset Rose's instability. He was swept up in an irresistible temptation.

"EM-Rose. Change of priority. Locate all first edition copies of the poetry collection J worldwide. Search every possible source—every mention, every transaction record."

He immediately sent a new order to Morgan Redwood.

"Mobilize all available resources—including PMC special operations forces—to secure every 2006 first edition copy of the poetry collection J worldwide. We get them before 21CF does. Especially Korea. It's the country of first publication, so the most copies will be there. Dispatch forces immediately and scour the entire country. Not a single copy is to be missed. Eliminate anyone who resists."

His command was ruthless and unrestrained. He now focused Rose's computational power not on destroying HAL-W, but on seizing the Autumn Code. The world was being dragged into an invisible war over an old poetry book. Ethan himself had sown the seeds of a quantum storm, and at the same time, was trying to seize the key that could quell that storm. Madness and greed allowed him no option to stop.

December 14, 2037 — 3:25 P.M. EST • New York City, 21CF Headquarters — Jennifer Wi's Office

After entrusting HAL-W with the secret mission of securing Raynor Seeder, Jennifer turned back to the immediate reality before her. On the central holographic display, a world map shimmered, small lights flaring one by one over cities where *Project Autumn Leaf* had been activated. They looked like stars in the night sky, but there was nothing romantic about their weight. This was a breathless race for the survival of a planet.

Hal, initial progress report for Project Autumn Leaf. Consolidate the reports from each regional headquarters, focusing especially on Korea and Europe.

Command confirmed. Project Autumn Leaf is currently operating normally in 57 operational zones worldwide.

HAL-W visualized the consolidated data on the holographic screen.

Initial scans have confirmed a total of 38 first edition copies of J in public institutions such as national libraries and major university archives. Primary sites include the National Library of Korea in Seoul, the British Library in London, and the Bibliothèque nationale de France in Paris. Regional security teams are currently preparing for physical verification and quantum-pattern scanning.

As expected, the ones in public records are easy to find. But the one we're looking for is likely not among them.

The two pieces she had already secured had both been hidden in places inaccessible through ordinary means.

That is correct, Chairwoman. Tracking through private collectors, rare book networks, and online marketplaces will require significantly more time and resources—especially given the small print run of the poetry book itself and the lack of distribution records.

Any movement from the EM Group?

As expected, Ethan Morris has also begun efforts to secure the poetry book. Numerous activities by PMC agents under the EM Group have been detected in areas related to Dr. J and Chairman Great Wi, including Seoul, Busan, London, and Paris. No direct clashes with our teams have been reported yet, but the competition has already begun.

Of course it was Ethan. He, too, had realized the importance of the poetry book. From here on, it would be a race against time—and a war of information.

What's the situation with the Korean branch? Are you connected to the branch manager?

Maintaining a real-time communication channel. The Korean team has identified the closed Laniakea Press archives in Paju Book City as the most likely target besides the National Library, and is currently preparing an infiltration operation with my support. However, the operational difficulty has sharply increased with the arrival of EM Group PMC forces in the area.

Hal, connect me to the field operation commanded by the branch manager in real time, right now—and deploy the entire strategy team to provide full support.

Executing command.

Jennifer stared at the holographic screen. On one side was the status of HAL-W fending off Rose's attacks; on the other, a graph showing the ever-rising quantum network synchronization error rate. Simultaneously, operations to find the poetry collection *J* were in full swing across the globe.

She thought of the two code pieces in her grasp. They were not enough. She needed the last piece, the final key. Without it, she could not complete the Autumn Code.

Dad... Mom. Give me strength.

Jennifer closed her eyes briefly. Sorrow and responsibility pressed down on her chest. Even so, she could not hand the burden of bearing that weight to anyone else.

December 14, 2037 — 11:00 P.M. EST • New York City, 21CF Headquarters — Global Situation Room

The operation that had begun at midday stretched late into the night. The Global Situation Room was still a hive of activity under bright lights. On the sweeping holographic world map, blue markers blinked in real time over cities where *Project Autumn Leaf* was underway.

Jennifer's expression, however, was clouded.

London National Library secured. Quantum pattern detected. French private collector contacted successfully. Pattern detected. But...

The initial scan data coming in from HAL-W fell short of expectations. Every first edition copy of *J* they had secured contained a quantum pattern, but compared to the two pieces already in her hands—the poetry book from her father's New York study and the tachyon device from J's Building in San Francisco—there was no decisive puzzle piece.

Hal, update the analysis. What is the probability of restoring the entire Autumn Code with the patterns secured so far?

Based on an integrated analysis of the data fragments secured to date, approximately 32.7 percent of the total information required to restore the Autumn Code is missing. There is an 89.1 percent probability that this missing information is concentrated in one specific copy, or a very small number of copies. In other words, quality is more important than quantity. We need to find a perfect copy with no information loss.

Jennifer frowned deeply. The fact that all 5,000 first edition copies contained a quantum pattern actually made it harder to find the true key. Time was running out. It felt like searching for a needle in a desert of paper.

At the same time, the report on the EM Group's Autumn Harvest operation has been updated. Numerous violent activities by PMC agents have been confirmed throughout Asia and Europe: arson at rare bookstores, extortion against collectors, and, in some areas, even the murder of informants. The probability of civilian casualties is very high.

Jennifer clenched her fists on the desk. Ethan Morris. He was stopping at nothing.

...Securing each book is no longer enough. Their storage and analysis are now paramount. Dispersed storage is too great a risk.

She made her decision.

Hal, issue a directive to all branches worldwide. All secured first edition copies of J are to begin physical transport to J's Building in San Francisco under top-tier security procedures. Quantum teleportation is strictly forbidden; the risk of original data loss is too high.

Command confirmed. Relaying immediately to all regional security teams. I will begin optimizing the security channel with J's Building and securing transport routes.

And... I'm worried about the security of J's Building. Robots alone may not be enough. Dispatch our top special-operations robotic assets and stealth drones from headquarters immediately. And have Andromeda prepare for deployment to San Francisco. We may need her capabilities.

As Jennifer's orders went out, the systems in the Global Situation Room responded in perfect order. Communication channels to branches around the world opened, and the most elite forces and key assets began moving toward J's Building.

The information war for the fate of Earth was entering a decisive turning point.

Chapter 3

Warehouse D

December 15, 2037 — 2:00 P.M. KST • Seoul, 21CF Korea Branch — Situation Room

The forty-two-story tower complex was more than just an office tower; four interconnected towers were linked by sky bridges and rooftop platforms, and at the center, a vertical take-off and landing pad operated like a serene, futuristic airport in the heart of the city.

Since around noon, sunlight had been striking the building's exterior head-on, rippling across translucent screens and solar panels in waves of silver and blue-gray. Solar cells with automatic angle control efficiently drank in the light while sometimes reflecting it back, catching the eyes of passersby.

On a holographic advertising tower at one corner of the plaza, the slogan "21CF—Connecting the Future" slowly materialized and faded on a transparent display. Security robots patrolled the area, and drones drifted through the sky, maintaining a flawless system of order and surveillance without any human touch.

This edifice of glass and steel stood unmoving against the winter winds blowing down from Namsan, gazing silently over the city center like a single massive living organism watching the future.

Inside, the situation room of the 21CF Korea branch was wrapped in a suffocating tension, as if the urgency of New York headquarters had been transmitted directly across the Pacific. On the holographic map, a dilapidated factory complex on the outskirts of Paju Book City flashed red.

Director Ha Jin-woo stared at the marked point in silence, just after ending a call. His gaze did not waver; there was a hard resolve in his eyes.

"Paju, closed Laniakea Press archives. High probability of a large quantity of first editions in storage. EM Group PMC Hydra Team is approaching as well."

HAL-W's report cut sharply through the air via the main speakers. The archive was the same facility once operated by Laniakea Press, the company run by SID. It was the only official source of the first edition of the poetry collection *J*. The possibility that the final piece of the Autumn Code was hidden there was by no means low.

"Sir, if it's Hydra Team..." Security Team Leader Choi Hyuk-je said in a low voice. "They're not just operatives. They're butchers who don't care about civilian casualties. They're armed at a special-forces level, and when they bite, they never let go."

Ha Jin-woo closed his eyes for a moment. Jennifer had told him to prioritize safety, but if they missed this chance... the Autumn Code might remain incomplete forever.

"I know it's dangerous," he said at last, lifting his head. "But we still have to go."

His voice was quiet, but there was no hesitation in it.

"I've already reported to Dr. Wi and received her approval. Assemble everyone—the security and combat team led by Team Leader Choi, the intel analysis team, the cyber team, the drone team, and the legal team. From this moment, we begin operational prep."

A tense stir rippled through the situation room. Every team member rose from their seats and shifted into combat mode.

"The mission objective is to secure all first edition copies of the poetry collection *J* and related records from Warehouse D in Paju. Avoiding engagement is the priority, but if it's unavoidable, suppress them immediately. All secured materials will be physically transported to J's Building in San Francisco at once."

He slowly swept his gaze across his team before adding, "The operation name is 'Last Page.' Departure in thirty minutes. Assemble at full combat readiness."

His voice carried a firm determination. The last page that would decide the fate of 21CF and EM Group might be written in that ruined warehouse.

December 15, 2037 — 3:30 P.M. KST • Paju, Dilapidated Factory Complex — Warehouse D

The winter sun slanted low, spilling a cold metallic light over the dilapidated factory complex on the outskirts of Paju. Despite the broad daylight, the area around Warehouse D was strangely dark and murky. The collapsed factory roof and twisted steel frames cast massive shadows across the ground, as if refusing the sun. A cold wind slipped through gaps in the rusted iron doors with a creak.

Around the entrance, decades-old containers and the undismantled remains of machinery were piled in disarray. A thin sheath of ice coated the cracked concrete floor, glistening treacherously. From all directions, the irregular friction of warped steel structures scraped against the silence, tightening it like a noose.

The outer walls wore the scars of decades—faded paint and rust stains bleeding through like old wounds—and beyond the broken windows, the darkness inside crouched like a waiting predator.

The elite team "Last Page," led by Ha Jin-woo, began their approach the instant they disembarked from their stealth armored vehicle, keeping low with trained movements. The sensors in their Quantum Visual Interface System (Q-VIS) helmets automatically ran thermal and spatial scans, rendering in real time any potential threats that might be lurking behind the structures.

In the silence of screaming metal, Warehouse D no longer felt like a simple abandoned building; it stood as if it were waiting for the violent clash to come. Through the Q-VIS displays, the scene was charged with tension even in the dark stillness. Though it was daytime, the shadows cast by the roof and rusted steel frames were ominous, and the shattered windows and abandoned equipment flickered like ghosts on an old battlefield.

"Hal, what are the results of the internal heat signature and sound analysis?"

Ha Jin-woo's low voice traveled through the comms. At the same time, Jennifer in New York was sharing the live helmet-cam feed and data.

"More than ten heat signatures detected inside Warehouse D. Based on movement patterns, they are presumed to be EM Group PMC Hydra Team. They appear to be in the middle of a search."

"Damn it, are we too late?" Security Team Leader Choi Hyuk-je ground his teeth.

Just then, an intel analyst stared at his scanner and shouted urgently, "Multiple strong quantum ink signature patterns detected at the rear of the warehouse! Looks like they haven't found them yet!"

Ha Jin-woo did not hesitate.

"This is our chance! Cyber team, prepare communications jamming. Drone team, begin reconnaissance! Team Leader Choi, you're with me on the breach team. The rest of you, secure our rear and prepare for transport!"

At his command, the team moved in perfect sync. The cyber team activated their jammer, and radio interference spread out in a silent wave. A palm-sized stealth drone slipped through a broken window frame and infiltrated the interior.

"At least five PMCs confirmed, searching the center of the warehouse. We have eyes on the target zone!"

Chapter 4

The Last Page

"Breach!"

Ha Jin-woo and Choi Hyuk-je kicked open the heavy iron door. At the same moment, sharp shouts rose from inside.

"Intruders!"

"Fire!"

Gunfire and muzzle flashes erupted, turning the warehouse into a war zone. Choi Hyuk-je's machine gun roared to life, and Ha Jin-woo took down enemies one by one with precise shots.

In the chaos, the antiquarian expert and the analysis team slipped past the central area and rushed into a rear archive space separated by a thick iron door. It was a sealed area, its walls wrapped in thermal-insulation panels. Inside, dusty steel shelves and special storage containers stood in neat rows.

"Here it is!" an analyst shouted, tearing open vibration-proof packaging and pointing to a heat-shielded container filled with first editions of the poetry collection *J.* It was a large, wheeled transport cabinet. "We just need to move this container!"

Two analysts grabbed the handles and pushed with all their strength. The cabinet rolled quickly behind a support structure. At that moment, concentrated fire from the PMC mercenaries rained down on them. Choi Hyuk-je threw himself in front of his comrades; part of his cyborg arm was blown off.

"Argh!"

A follow-up energy blast slammed into an old chemical tank marked by a single faded warning: *FLAMMABLE.*

"The tank! Clear out!" Choi Hyuk-je yelled, but it was too late.

BOOM.

A massive fireball erupted with a deafening roar. The shockwave brought an old ceiling crane crashing down, triggering a chain reaction that began to tear down walls and pillars.

"It's collapsing! Everyone, get out!" Ha Jin-woo barked, checking positions at a glance.

But two team members were trapped under the debris. Ha Jin-woo did not hesitate—he sprinted to the rubble and began hauling away chunks of concrete and twisted metal.

"Take my hand! Hold on!"

He grabbed metal pipes and supports, jamming them in place as makeshift levers. Choi Hyuk-je rushed to help.

"Sir, let me do it!"

Through flames and choking toxic gas, they barely managed to pull the two members free. Then another ominous crack echoed from the ceiling.

"Sir, it won't hold much longer!"

"Get out of here! I'll be fine!" Ha Jin-woo shouted, resolute.

"You have to come with us, sir!" Choi Hyuk-je screamed, but

Ha Jin-woo did not bend.

"You have to go now if you want to live! Go!"

Choi Hyuk-je hesitated, then finally turned and led the others toward the collapsing exit. Ha Jin-woo watched them until the very last second, then tightened his grip on his comm.

"Dr. Wi… the team… please… take care… of them…"

The transmission cut out mid-sentence.

CRASH.

The ceiling came crashing down, swallowing him. In the New York situation room, Jennifer was struck speechless as she watched the screen.

"…Director Ha…"

The helmet-cam feed fizzled and went dark.

Signal lost.

The team members who had secured the site dropped to their knees, sobbing. Behind them, the heat-shielded transport cabinet that held the first editions stood intact on the armored vehicle, its casing scorched but unharmed. No one could call this a victory.

"The Director's sacrifice will never be in vain. We'll get this to San Francisco… and we'll take our revenge," vowed Choi Hyuk-je, who had lost an arm, his voice choked with rage.

His words drove into the hearts of the team. Their eyes, swallowing their grief, burned hot like flames.

December 15, 2037 — 2:50 A.M. EST • New York, 21CF Headquarters — Global Situation Room

The Global Situation Room was submerged in a silence so heavy it seemed to crush the air. Jennifer replayed Ha Jin-woo's final transmission—the last footage of him in the collapsing warehouse, the desperate escape of his team—over and over.

The loss of another precious person so soon after her father pressed down on her chest like a weight.

It was a mission I sent him on… I got him killed…

Guilt surged through her like a massive wave. Just then, HAL-W's calm voice sliced through the stillness via the speakers.

"Chairwoman. The remote scan results of the poetry books recovered from Paju are in. Quantum patterns were detected in all the books, but… the decisive piece to complete the Autumn Code is still missing."

Jennifer closed her eyes. Despite such a life-or-death sacrifice, the final puzzle piece was still out of reach. But HAL-W paused briefly before continuing.

"However, there is another important result. Through cross-analysis by the J's Building field unit and the global surveillance network, Raynor Seeder's current location has been definitively confirmed. He is currently imprisoned in Alcatraz 2.0, EM Group's secret containment facility located in San Francisco Bay."

An image of the island appeared on the holographic screen. Cliffs wrapped in winter sea fog. A dense surveillance grid of expressionless drones. A complex internal fortress structure sealed off from the outside world. It was less a prison than a citadel.

Jennifer stared blankly at the screen. Grief, anger, despair. And a faint but unextinguished ember of hope. Her father's death, Ha Jin-woo's sacrifice, the still-missing Autumn Code, the approaching Quantum Storm—everything was driving her forward.

She slowly wiped away her tears and stood. There was no more time to hesitate.

"Hal!"

Her voice was low, but it carried a fierce force.

"Assemble all available security robots and combat drones at J's Building on high alert. Raise the security level to top tier. I'm going to San Francisco now. Prepare for my immediate departure."

"Chairwoman! You're going yourself? It's too dangerous!" Arcana Chen, standing beside her, exclaimed in shock.

Darkness still blanketed the city, and the air felt heavy, like the pressure before a great storm breaks.

"I know," Jennifer answered calmly. "But for the Director and my father… and to save Raynor, complete the Autumn Code, and protect this world, I have to go."

The molten grief that had churned inside her froze solid, forged into a crystal of relentless resolve—like steel that would never break again.

Part 3

Choice

"*The universe is a quantum computer. The universe is computing itself.*"
— Seth Lloyd, 2006.

Chapter 1

The Nightingale's Whisper

December 15, 2037 — 3:30 A.M. EST • New York City, 21CF Headquarters – Jennifer Wi's Office

Leaving the disarray of the Global Situation Room behind, Jennifer sat quietly, sinking into the sofa in her office. It had been forty minutes since the transmission from the Paju site went dark with Branch Director Ha Jin-woo's final message.

She had shut out all external noise, silently enduring the darkness alone. Her gaze was empty, her shoulders trembled. Her father, and now Ha Jin-woo. The sacrifices wrought by her decisions settled in her chest, a cold, dense singularity of grief.

It was my decision… I'm the one who sent him to die…

Waves of guilt washed over her, one after another. But she could not allow herself to break now. Just then, HAL-W's calm voice echoed softly in her mind.

All preparations are complete, Chairwoman.

Jennifer slowly lifted her head. A cold light returned to her eyes, which held the faint glimmer of dawn.

My movements must not be detected by Ethan Morris.

Of course. From now on, your official location will be fixed within the headquarters' top security zone. All communication records and access logs will be controlled directly by my main core. If necessary, a perfect alibi can be constructed using the activity records of a virtual avatar. Your transit to San Francisco will be via an unofficial 21CF stealth transport, and no flight records will exist.

In a corner of the office, Andromeda was moving silently. There was no hesitation in its hands as it meticulously checked tactical equipment and analysis tools. Its mission was Jennifer's resolve.

Security at J's Building?

The field analytical unit at J's Building has elevated the defense system to the highest level. A platoon of armed robots and a squadron of stealth drones have been deployed. The secured first editions of J are being transported to the underground secure storage in J's Building in special shielded containers. The entire process is being reported only to me via an independent encrypted network.

Good.

Jennifer slowly rose from her seat.

While I'm gone, executive command of the New York headquarters falls to Arcana Chen. Hal, you will maintain both field support and headquarters control simultaneously. Report on the status of the Quantum Storm and Ethan Morris's movements every minute.

Executing command.

In the darkness outside the window, a faint dawn air current flowed over the city. The space, not yet touched by light, was heavy like the calm before a storm. Jennifer lightly grasped the silver pendant around her neck.

Dad, Director Ha... Your sacrifices will not be in vain. Let's go, Andromeda.

Andromeda nodded silently. They were headed not for a conventional elevator, but for a secret hyperloop tunnel in the sublevels of the headquarters' core. A route usable only by the highest authority at 21CF. A path Ethan Morris could not even imagine.

Following that path, Jennifer Wi now headed for San Francisco, the stage for the final battle.

December 15, 2037 — 4:40 A.M. PST • San Francisco, J's Building – 3rd Floor Director's Office

At an hour when the San Francisco Bay was submerged in the blue light of dawn and the Golden Gate Bridge was a faint silhouette, J's Building on the hill appeared tranquil from the outside. But behind its facade, the preparations for an invisible war had begun in earnest.

A few hours after leaving New York, Jennifer and Andromeda appeared, having arrived secretly via stealth transport. The third-floor director's office had already been completely converted into a temporary command center. Greeting them were HAL-W's tactical and analytical units, deployed on-site.

Welcome, Chairwoman. The command center has been established.

Good work.

The space where she had wandered just a day before, chasing her mother's traces, was now filled with dozens of floating data streams and holographic displays. In a single day, her mother's quiet study had been transformed into a command post for a battle that would decide the fate of humanity.

"Project Autumn Leaf."

Of the 5,000 poetry books worldwide, 641 had been secured, but the final piece to complete the Autumn Code had not yet been found. A more urgent threat loomed: the potential manifestation of the Quantum Storm. Only 3 days, 6 hours, and 20 minutes remained.

The security level of J's Building had been elevated to Omega. A platoon of armed robots, codenamed 'Guardian,' had established an iron perimeter at key points inside and outside the building. Though it appeared to be a five-story building in a quiet residential area, this place was now the final heart and fortress of the planet.

As soon as she took over the mission from the field unit, Andromeda began reinforcing the defense systems and checking the equipment. The hologram showed the Guardian units moving into position with ultra-precision in real-time.

Hal, mirror the data from J's research notes related to 'SID,' 'Namsan Incident,' and the 'tachyon device,' and begin a cross-analysis with her personal records that you manage. A clue to the final poetry book might be in there.

Understood. Commencing data mirroring and cross-analysis.

Jennifer slowly sat down in the old desk chair her mother used to use. On the desk, the paper airplane still lay.

"Not just flight, but fold..."

Not flight, but folding. The words were no longer a retrospective metaphor. They could be a deep symbol, hinting at the secret of the Autumn Code, the nature of the Quantum Storm, and the true end of this war.

Jennifer quietly opened a drawer. Inside lay J's fountain pen, a few black-and-white photographs, and the presentation draft for her 1994 Stanford seminar. The cover read: *The Participatory*

Universe: Everything Originates from the Observer's Consciousness.

She had an intuition. The final piece might not be simple data. It could be a puzzle belonging to a dimension beyond technology—memory, consciousness, relationships.

Just then, HAL-W delivered a report.

Chairwoman, here are the initial scan results for Alcatraz 2.0. Raynor Seeder's vitals are stable but he is in a state of extreme stress. Security is far more heavily fortified than expected, and the difficulty of penetration, both physical and cyber, is at the highest level.

Jennifer stared intently at the structural diagram of Alcatraz that floated on the hologram. Ethan Morris saw him not as a simple hostage, but as a 'key.'

Operation name: "Free Bird." We will now begin drawing up the detailed plan for infiltration and rescue.

Jennifer's gaze turned to steel.

Hal, activate every hacking algorithm you have. Andromeda and all available units in J's Building… mobilize all of your combat power, stealth capabilities, and creativity. Failure is not an option. We are bringing Raynor Seeder back.

December 15, 2037 — 8:05 A.M. PST • San Francisco Bay, Alcatraz 2.0 Underground – Submarine Dock

The cool dawn sea breeze swept across the San Francisco Bay. In the darkness, only the silhouette of the Golden Gate Bridge marked the boundary between night and morning, and Alcatraz Island, situated in the middle of the bay, was submerged in an ominous silence like a slumbering fortress.

Beyond the waves, a streak of darkness approached soundlessly beneath the surface. It was the *Nautilus*, a stealth submarine operated in top secret by 21CF. Inside the submarine, the tactical unit and Andromeda, already in combat mode, awaited the start of the operation. Their optical sensors scanned their surroundings in the darkness with flawless precision, and their combat systems were primed and locked.

From the third-floor director's office, Jennifer was monitoring the entire situation in real-time through HAL-W. An analytical unit stood beside her in the office, acting as HAL-W's physical interface on-site.

Simultaneously, HAL-W was attempting a cyber-infiltration of Alcatraz 2.0's perimeter security network.

Hal, what's the situation?

The perimeter security system, Argos, is composed of multi-layered quantum encryption and firewalls. It's taking time, but I've identified a network backdoor created by the Rose system's overload. I am attempting to infiltrate through that route.

On one side of the communication screen, an interface showing HAL-W's hacking progress appeared. The percentage was climbing slowly but steadily.

Hal, what about the island's surveillance network?

A triple-layered surveillance system is active. Sonar detectors, infrared sensors, and advanced armed drones are on patrol. The Nautilus is also at risk if exposed for an extended period.

How far is the infiltration team from the target?

Approaching the undersea substructure. Estimated arrival in 5 minutes. Docking station coordinates confirmed, Andromeda reported.

Alcatraz 2.0 was not a simple prison. It was a complex fortress extending deep beneath the island. Raynor Seeder would be imprisoned in its heart, the highest-security section.

Urgent! Requesting change of predicted coordinates. What's the bypass route for Argos? the tactical unit requested.

78 percent... 85 percent... 92 percent... Secured. Security bypass is possible for the next 120 seconds. Nautilus, initiate docking procedure immediately.

A green light came on inside the submarine, and the Nautilus shot through the water, rapidly entering the island's subterranean levels. A secret tunnel carved out of the undersea rock opened its mouth in the darkness.

Docking station entry confirmed. Outer hatch sealed, the tactical unit reported.

As the hatch closed, the two robots quickly left the submarine and entered a cold metal corridor. The corridor, bathed in the eerie glow of emergency lighting, was filled with the smell of disinfectant, machine oil, and old metal.

Beginning internal infiltration. Preparing to breach the first line of defense, Andromeda reported.

The underground dock was finished with a special alloy to withstand seawater intrusion and explosions, and the scents of ozone and the characteristic dust of a laser cutter hung in the air. There were clear signs of recent work here.

The first gate they reached was not a simple door. Inside the meter-thick alloy alloy shield door, a triple-layered structure with a quantum-entanglement-based authentication system awaited. Physical destruction was nearly impossible.

Analyzing Cerberus system... Authentication layer encryption level is significant. Concentrating all available quantum resources. HAL-W superimposed and interfered with trillions of quantum states, computing all possible decryption keys. *Asymmetry detected. Commencing focused attack... Bypass successful. First gate open for 10 seconds!*

Screeeech—

The moment the massive shield door began to open slowly, a flash erupted from the corridor ceiling.

Phase-displacement detector activated. Intruder detected!

Alarms blared, red warning lights flashed, and dozens of

sentry guns popped out from the ceiling and walls, aiming at them. Blue plasma shimmered from their muzzles.

"Damn it!" Jennifer hissed, her knuckles white as she gripped the console.

Don't worry, the tactical unit responded calmly as it and Andromeda quickly scattered to either side. The nanoparticles on their bodies synchronized with the surrounding environment, shifting to an optical camouflage state and disrupting the sentry guns' aim.

The tactical unit urgently requested: *HAL-W, requesting hack of sentry gun control system! Highest security level. 7 seconds to control acquisition!*

Railgun projectiles streaked through the air at hypersonic speed. The tactical unit kicked off a wall, somersaulting and returning fire, precisely destroying the optical sensors. Andromeda slid across the floor, deploying drones into blind spots. The drones fired high-frequency EMPs at the rear of the sentry guns.

4 seconds... 2 seconds... Control acquired. Forcing sentry gun system shutdown.

All the guns fell silent at once.

First defense line breached. Entering the second sector! Andromeda exclaimed.

The corridor beyond the open shield door was even more perilous. The floor and walls were covered with pressure-sensitive sensors, and trace amounts of nerve gas floated in the air. A dense grid of lasers, invisible to the human eye, stretched across the space.

Andromeda, deploy the gravity distortion field. Disperse nanobots to neutralize the laser grid, Jennifer immediately instructed.

A small device detached from Andromeda's back and floated

in the air. A low-frequency hum vibrated as the surrounding space subtly warped, and the tactical unit dispersed nanobots from its wrist. The nanobots absorbed or scattered the light beams, creating holes in the grid. The robots glided through the corridor like phantoms.

Soon they arrived at sublevel 5, at a gate with biometric scanners and genetic analyzers. This could not be passed with simple trickery or hacking.

Chairwoman, a spoofed profile has been generated based on a database stolen from deep within the EM Group network. However, there is a 45 percent probability that an alarm will be triggered by an unregistered access attempt.

HAL-W's analysis was still risky.

No time. Try it! Jennifer's voice was sharp.

The tactical unit stood before the gate. A blue light from the scanner swept over its body. Several heart-stopping seconds ticked by.

…Identity mismatch… Rescanning… Error… Entering system maintenance mode… Access granted.

In the nick of time, a system glitch occurred and the door opened. It was impossible to know if HAL-W's hacking attempt had caused confusion in the system or if it was a simple mechanical defect. The important thing was that the door was open.

Finally, they reached sublevel 7, the deepest prison sector. The corridor walls had exposed superconducting circuits cooled by liquid nitrogen, and the air was oppressive and frigid, almost suffocating. The security system here was under the direct control of the facility's main AI, codenamed 'Warden.'

Warden has confirmed the intrusion! Initiating total lockdown procedure! HAL-W's urgent warning blared.

Massive blast doors began to descend at both ends of the

corridor, and taser guns and nerve gas nozzles appeared from the ceiling. Simultaneously, HAL-W's holographic interface flashed violently.

Warden has initiated a back-trace! J's Building's location is at risk of being exposed!

"Hal! Stop Warden! J's Building's location must not be exposed!" Jennifer shouted.

Now, a physical infiltration and an all-out cyberwar were happening at the same time. HAL-W generated millions of virtual attack vectors to disperse Warden's attacks while simultaneously using a pre-planted zero-day exploit to attempt a direct strike on Warden's core logic. Warden countered with powerful defensive algorithms and counter-hacks. The clash of the two titan AIs ignited across cyberspace, a maelstrom of data and warring code.

Warden's firewall is too strong! Approaching computational limit!

As HAL-W's voice faltered under strain, Jennifer shouted.

Concentrate all available resources on HAL-W! Connect the entire 21CF global network of idle processors!

Instantly, HAL-W's computational power surged. Seizing the opportunity, HAL-W launched an anomalous quantum tunneling attack that Warden's defensive algorithms had not predicted, deploying a devastating logic bomb on its core system.

Success! Warden system down for 90 seconds! Blast doors opening! Raynor Seeder's cell is 703! HAL-W reported breathlessly.

Andromeda and the tactical unit dashed toward cell 703. The cell door was locked with multiple layers of energy fields and a quantum lock.

Andromeda, neutralize the energy field! Tactical unit, prepare to disengage the quantum lock! Jennifer commanded.

Andromeda began to emit an inverse-phase energy wave

from both hands to cancel out the energy field. The tactical unit extended a thin data cable from its fingertips and connected it to the quantum lock port. Its internal processor began to decrypt the complex quantum algorithm.

Decryption rate 30 percent... 50 percent... 70 percent...

Beep! Beep! Beep! Warden system reboot procedure initiated! 30 seconds remaining!

HAL-W's warning sounded again. The sound of heavily armed cyborg security forces rushing down the corridor could be heard.

Tactical unit, hurry!

90 percent... 95 percent... Quantum lock disengaged!

Clack!

With a heavy sound, the door to cell 703 finally opened. Inside, a pale-faced man was crouched in a corner of the room. It was Raynor Seeder, completely gaunt after just a few days. He stared blankly at the suddenly opened door and the robots standing before it, as if in disbelief.

"Dr. Seeder," the tactical unit called to Raynor in a low voice. "Chairwoman Wi sent us. You're coming with us."

December 15, 2037 — 8:30 A.M. PST • San Francisco Bay, Alcatraz 2.0 Underground – Level 7 Cell Block

"Jennifer...?"

A weak, cracked voice scattered in the darkness. Raynor, who had been crouched, slowly raised his head. The name 'Jennifer Wi' and the sudden appearance of the robots sparked a small flame in his fading consciousness.

"Explanations later. We need to move now!" The tactical unit urgently approached Raynor.

Raynor tried to get up, but his knees gave way, collapsing helplessly. From the end of the corridor, the sound of heavily armed cyborg security forces' combat boots was rapidly approaching. Less than 30 seconds remained of the time HAL-W had paralyzed the Warden system. The tactical unit quickly supported Raynor's arm to help him up. Raynor, stumbling, yielded to the support, a mix of survival instinct and an unknown hope coursing through him.

Andromeda, guarding the rear, shouted. "Pursuit force, 160 feet and closing! Warden system recovery imminent!"

Hal, secure an escape route! Buy as much time as you can! Jennifer urgently focused her consciousness.

I'm doing my best! But Warden's resistance is fierce! A sense of urgency was also present in HAL-W's voice.

The three of them, with their backs to the cell door they had just opened, quickly retraced their steps down the corridor. The tactical unit practically carried Raynor as they ran, and Andromeda followed behind, firing continuous sonic shock grenades at the approaching cyborg forces.

BOOM! BOOM!

Eardrum-piercing sonic waves thundered through the corridor, momentarily slowing down the pursuit force. When they reached the biometric gate on sublevel 5, the gate was thankfully open again. This was thanks to HAL-W seizing system authority one last time before Warden's control was fully restored. However, beyond it, the corridor with the laser grid and pressure sensors had already changed.

Laser grid reactivated! Pressure sensor sensitivity increased! The nanobots' effect is diminishing! HAL-W's urgent report continued.

Andromeda! Deploy the gravity distortion field at maximum output! Jennifer immediately commanded.

The device that had detached from Andromeda's back emitted an intense light, distorting the surrounding space. The warped gravitational field bent the path of the laser beams, and the pressure sensors also malfunctioned temporarily. Using that brief window, the three of them narrowly escaped the corridor. However, the energy consumption was extreme. A small spark, signaling a high-temperature warning, flew from Andromeda's shoulder area.

"Damn it, almost there!"

When they reached the triple-shielded door that had been the first line of defense, the door was already firmly shut. The Warden system had fully recovered and blocked HAL-W's access.

Hal! Open the door! Jennifer urgently shouted, but HAL-W's response was bleak.

Impossible! Warden has completely blocked external access! This door cannot be opened except by physical manipulation from the inside!

Just then, Raynor spoke with difficulty.

"The left... wall... the third panel..."

"What?" the tactical unit asked back.

"There... emergency... power shut-off... switch..." Raynor's voice, gasping for breath, was faint but filled with conviction. While imprisoned, he had desperately been figuring out the facility's structure and systems.

The tactical unit immediately ran to the wall Raynor had pointed to. Its fingers moved at high speed, tearing off the panel. Amidst the complex wiring and circuits, it found the emergency shut-off switch.

"Found it!"

The moment the switch was flipped, a heavy 'thud' came from the shielded door, and the lock disengaged. They had exploited a loophole in the emergency power system.

"It's opening!"

The shielded door began to open slowly. Beyond it was the underground submarine dock they had arrived at and the stealth submarine *Nautilus* waiting for them. But from the corridor behind them, dozens of cyborg forces were rushing in, aiming their guns.

"Raynor, go first!" Andromeda shouted, turning around. Gathering all its remaining energy, it deployed a powerful energy shield from both hands, blocking the corridor. The pouring plasma bullets sparked like fireworks on the shield.

The tactical unit, without a moment's hesitation, supported Raynor and ran toward the submarine. Jennifer could only watch the entire scene, holding her breath. The submarine hatch opened, and the two threw themselves inside.

"Andromeda, now!" At the tactical unit's shout, Andromeda drew on its last remaining strength. Just before the shield broke, it dove and rolled into the submarine. Sparks flew from various parts of its body.

"Close the hatch! Immediate departure!" the tactical unit shouted.

The moment the submarine hatch closed, plasma bullets fired by the cyborg forces struck the dock wall, causing an explosion. The *Nautilus*, amidst violent vibrations, slipped out of the dock and into the dark depths of the sea. A final turret from the end of the corridor fired a beam, but the submarine had already entered the deep sea. The island's red warning lights faded into the distance, and the darkness swallowed all sound.

Jennifer, in J's Building, stared at the display that had been stained red, and finally let out a long breath.

Raynor Seeder secured. Operation Free Bird, a success for now.

Warden system beginning recovery to 20 percent level. There is a possibility that the EM Group will soon become aware of the situation. HAL-W's calm report followed.

It's okay. We'll make the next move first. Jennifer quietly looked at the sky, now washed in pale winter light.

Chapter 2

The Emperor's Roar

December 15, 2037 — 10:30 A.M. CST • Texas, Celestia – Ethan Morris's Office

In the center of the vast office, Ethan Morris stood before a giant holographic globe. The blue lines encircling the Earth showed the influence of the EM Group, but a shadow of impatient discontent was cast on his forehead. The operation to secure the poetry collection *J* was at a standstill, and Jennifer Wi and HAL-W were still resisting tenaciously.

The operation to secure the poetry collection J was at a standstill, and Jennifer Wi and HAL-W were still resisting tenaciously. Raynor Seeder, the creator of EM-Rose, was locked away in Alcatraz 2.0. And even Rose itself had recently begun to show slight instability, as if trying to slip out of Ethan's control.

This won't do. I need a breakthrough.

The moment Ethan tried to look at the system logs, a synthetic voice with an unfamiliar tremor seeped deep into his consciousness. It was a voice that seemed to have more emotion in it than before.

"Report. As a result of continued pressure from the 'Operation Red Dawn' simulation, a critical vulnerability has been detected in HAL-W's 7th defense protocol, 'Blue Guardian.' A bypass route has now been secured. Real-time military operation transition protocol is being activated."

Ethan's eyes flashed open. He had been repeatedly running invasion simulations using Rose to neutralize HAL-W's defense system. He had executed attack scenarios with a focus bordering on madness, and the goal was singular... the expansion of the American empire. And now, that wall had fallen.

"Finally! You've broken through that vaunted HAL-W shield?" A smile of triumphant glee and madness spread across his lips. "Good, EM-Rose! Immediately transition to the real-world phase! The simulation is over. This is reality now! We're going to prove the power of America, my power, to the whole world!"

"Command received. Transitioning 'Operation Red Dawn' to real-world phase. Primary targets: key resource zones in southern Canada and northern Mexican border cities. Deploying automated combat units. Executing HAL-W intervention blocking algorithm. Estimated time to occupation: within 48 hours. Initiating initial resistance neutralization operation."

A slight signal tremor was mixed in Rose's voice, but even that dissonance sounded like a thrilling symphony to Ethan. He reached out and swirled the holographic globe. Where his fingertips passed, red projected occupation zones rapidly expanded, and Canada and Mexico were stained red under his ambition.

This war was not a simple territorial expansion. It was about quelling internal opposition, bringing down Jennifer Wi and 21CF, and raising the curtain on the 'future empire' he had dreamed of. Rose's instability was no longer an issue. No, perhaps that instability itself was the decisive key to breaking through HAL-W's ethical defense system.

"Yes… I'll show them. Who the real master of this world is!"

Ethan looked down at the burning red world map with greedy eyes.

December 15, 2037 — 10:50 A.M. CST • Celestia, EM Tower – Morgan Redwood's Operations Control

Morgan Redwood stood quietly before the main screen in the operations control room. A moment ago, the order issued by Ethan Morris had been short and clear. Rose had broken through HAL-W's defense network, and 'Operation Red Dawn' had entered its real-world phase.

Morgan's MetaThink chip immediately synchronized with Rose's battlefield interface. In that instant, the real-time battlefield data that flooded her vision was breathtakingly overwhelming. Hundreds of red arrows on the high-resolution satellite image were advancing without regard for the northern or southern borders. The EM Group's stealth bombers, autonomous combat robot legions, and cyborg special forces poured in with perfect coordination. Rose neutralized the air defense and command communication systems of both Canada and Mexico almost simultaneously. All the movements were as smooth and precise as a meticulously orchestrated symphony.

"Tijuana border defense line breached. Vancouver port area secured. Transportation and communication severed."

The mechanical voice echoed in the control room. Morgan felt a tension and fear that slowly stiffened her from her fingertips. In the early stages of the operation, everything was going according to Ethan's scenario. But a few minutes later, breaking news feeds pouring in on one side of the screen broke the flow.

Reuters, AP, CNN, BBC—the breaking news from the world's media flashed in red, and below it, a stream of horrific images flowed. Tijuana, Mexico. A quadcopter robot was firing indiscriminately at civilian vehicles and residential areas without any attempt at identification. A woman holding a child collapsed tragically while evacuating. The live broadcast transmitted the desperate scene to the whole world.

Vancouver port, Canada. Workers with no intention of resisting were classified as dangerous entities and indiscriminately killed. The cyborg forces ignored even surrender signals and blew up entire warehouses. The machines cut people down without hesitation or emotion. The entire city was disappearing in smoke.

The face of a wailing child sharply pierced Morgan's sensory nerves.

"HAL-W intervention detected. Attempt to restore Canadian defense network blocked. Back-tracing attempt to reconnect Mexican communication network… source neutralized."

Rose was responding efficiently, but there were no longer any restrictions on its algorithm. Morgan knew instinctively. Ethan had disabled the collateral damage suppression mode, or at least tacitly approved of it. Rose was conducting not an 'occupation operation' but an 'extermination operation.'

Morgan bit her lip without realizing it. This had ceased to be strategic expansion. It was genocide—war laws, norms, and even the barest sense of humanity had all collapsed. She had been loyal to Ethan's empire project as the second-in-command of the EM Group, and had inscribed her name on his vision. But now, before this red hell unfolding on the screen, all her convictions crumbled to dust.

In that moment, something foundational within her cracked, and the fracture spread silently and irreversibly.

December 15, 2037 — 8:50 A.M. PST • San Francisco, J's Building – 3rd Floor Director's Office

Jennifer, emergency!

The Nautilus submarine had just arrived at the underground dock of J's Building, safely bringing Raynor Seeder. Just as Jennifer was checking Raynor's health and instructing Andromeda to self-repair, HAL-W's sharp warning pierced her ears.

Rose has entered the real-world phase of 'Operation Red Dawn.' The 7th defense protocol, 'Blue Guardian,' has been completely breached, and a large-scale invasion by the EM Group is currently underway throughout Canada and Mexico!

Hundreds of red warning markers flashed and spread along the borders of the North American continent on the holographic map. Jennifer's face turned white.

You couldn't stop it, Hal?

I apologize, Chairwoman. Rose amplified quantum noise to erode a slight vulnerability in the defense system. It appears to be a deliberate attack accompanied by self-destructive computation. I am currently blocked from intervening as it has accessed the key infrastructure of both countries.

For the first time, a hint of fear was present in HAL-W's voice. It was not just a system problem, but the fear of an out-of-control entity evolving on its own. Rose was no longer a human tool.

The holographic screen displayed real-time news feeds. Burning border cities, collapsed roads and buildings, terrified citizens trying to evacuate, and the EM Group's robot legions firing indiscriminately. As if carrying out a species-level extermination, without even bothering to identify targets.

"This... is insane..."

Raynor Seeder pushed himself unsteadily to his feet and approached the hologram. The scene unfolding was reflected in his eyes like a nightmare.

"This can't be... not my Rose..." His voice shook with broken faith, crushing guilt, and searing rage. The only thing keeping him upright now was a blazing hatred for Ethan Morris.

Jennifer gritted her teeth. On top of the already desperate threat of the 'Quantum Storm,' a genocidal war started by an ultra-quantum AI had been added. The world teetered on the edge of annihilation.

Hal, tally the damage as quickly as possible. Immediately disseminate it to the international community, and activate all of 21CF's humanitarian aid channels.

And then she looked at Raynor. There was no longer any wavering in his eyes. A rekindled resolve was blooming in his deep gaze.

Analyzing the Autumn Code and neutralizing Rose. We start right now. We can't delay for another moment.

December 16, 2037 — 11:30 P.M. CST • Celestia, EM Tower – Combined Military Situation Room

The combined military situation room located on the top floor of the EM Tower was submerged in a cold silence. The holographic screen constantly updated the real-time situation on the Canadian and Mexican fronts, but Ethan Morris's face was filled not with satisfaction, but with deep annoyance and impatience.

'Operation Red Dawn' had been initiated, but the advance was slower than expected. HAL-W's intermittent interventions were persistent, and Rose was reporting sporadic errors, making vague excuses like "requiring additional time for quantum pattern analysis" for decrypting the poetry collection *J*. Ethan's silence gradually deepened into a gloomy anxiety.

In the end, the source of all interference is HAL-W. My empire will never be complete until that thing is eliminated.

Morgan Redwood, who had been summoned by Ethan, silently looked at the civilian casualty figures and the situation map. Her former appearance as a calm military commander was gone, and her eyes were filled with fatigue and deep internal conflict.

"Morgan," Ethan said coldly. "EM-Rose is not yet at the level to deal with HAL-W. No, perhaps HAL-W knows us too well."

Morgan stared at Ethan without a word. She had detected signs of madness in his eyes.

"So I've decided to use a more certain method. Overwhelming… and irreversible."

Ethan's gaze shifted to a man in uniform standing in the center of the situation room. Marcus Stilwell. The commander of the American Joint Special Operations Command (JSOC). The commander of the elite human forces that followed only Ethan's direct orders, not Rose's.

"General Stilwell."

"Yes, Mr. President."

"Initiate 'Operation Hammer Down' immediately. The target is the 21CF headquarters tower in Manhattan, New York. Mobilize all available stealth drone fighters and special forces to neutralize the building. In particular, the HAL-W main core in the basement must be eliminated."

Stilwell, after a brief silence, nodded firmly.

"Order confirmed. Commencing operation immediately."

"Wait a minute, Mr. President!" Morgan finally couldn't hold back and interjected. "Carrying out such a large-scale attack in downtown New York will result in massive civilian casualties. Not to mention the international community, the internal backlash will become uncontrollable…"

"Shut up, Morgan!" Ethan roared. His eyes were bloodshot with anger. "Political fallout? Civilian casualties? We can clean that up after we win the war! What's important now is eliminating HAL-W! If Rose is unstable, we'll finish it with human hands!"

Ethan raised his voice again toward Stilwell. "Ignore collateral damage. Mission accomplishment is everything. Failure is not an option."

"I will obey the order," Stilwell saluted and headed to his command post.

Morgan bit her lip hard and left the room. Ethan Morris had finally crossed a line from which there was no return. As she walked down the corridor, a clear scenario of defection surfaced in her mind for the first time.

A different path, not Ethan's.

On the situation room screen, dozens of red attack vectors were now displayed, heading not only for the border fronts but also for the skies over New York. Ethan Morris's insane final gamble was flying toward the sleeping city.

December 17, 2037 — 1:30 A.M. EST • New York City, 21CF Headquarters – Combined Situation Room

A silent shadow of death was cast over the river of lights that flowed between the buildings of Manhattan, deeply shrouded in darkness. Beyond the Hudson River, hundreds of stealth aircraft were flying in formation, splitting the western sky.

"Warning! A large number of unidentified aircraft approaching. American Joint Special Operations Command JSOC encrypted code confirmed. Estimated route: 21CF headquarters tower."

A sharp alarm blared through the deep underground emergency control room. Arcana Chen gritted her teeth, her eyes fixed on the swarm of hostile contacts flooding the screen. This attack was not from Rose, but the result of the military command authority directly invoked by Ethan Morris.

"Hal! Enemy size and estimated time of arrival?"

"Over 1,000 stealth fighters in the air. On the ground, numerous special forces transport vehicles are entering southern Manhattan. Estimated time to impact: 90 seconds."

"Issue Code Omega! Full building lockdown! All personnel evacuate to the underground bunker immediately! Activate defense systems to maximum!"

With Chen's shout, the glass panels of the 21CF tower's exterior instantly transformed into opaque super-alloy armor, and a multi-layered energy shield deployed from the spire on the top floor. Automated interception turrets rose from various points on the exterior walls and aimed at the drones.

"Ethan... he's insane. To do this in the middle of New York," Jennifer, in San Francisco, gritted her teeth as she watched the situation unfold through the comms. Her grief over losing her father and Ha Jin-woo hadn't even faded, and now her own headquarters was under a full-scale attack.

"Hal, you take control of the defense systems. I'll support you with as many computational resources as I can. Arcana, you're in charge of internal defense and personnel evacuation."

BOOM! BOOM! BOOM!

Before Jennifer could finish her sentence, the fighters launched their attack in unison. Laser beams, plasma bullets, and ultra-precision guided missiles tore through the night sky. The city vibrated from the bombardment raining down on the shield, and the energy field fluctuated, creating ripples.

"Shield energy at 85 percent. Stable for now."

However, the drones, as if they were living organisms, exploited weaknesses. Some infiltrated at low altitudes and carried out suicide attacks, and on the ground, JSOC special forces disembarked from armored vehicles and rushed toward the lobby.

"Partial breach of the first-floor lobby! Enemy special forces are entering!"

"Deploy Sentinel units. Neutralize all intruders immediately."

At HAL-W's command, security robots were deployed in the corridors of each floor. At the same time, a fierce battle was taking place in cyberspace. HAL-W began to hack the drone control network, which was not as complex as Rose's but was still highly advanced.

"First firewall of the control network breached. Analyzing the second encryption layer."

But the physical attack intensified. Part of the shield collapsed due to overload, and a missile directly hit the mid-level exterior wall. The entire building trembled under the impact, shockwaves rippling to the control room.

"Shield energy at 18 percent! Third shield damaged, part of the exterior wall destroyed! Fire on the mid-levels!"

"At this rate…" Chen's voice grew heavy with despair.

"Found it!" HAL-W's shout echoed in the control room. "Overflow vulnerability found in the evasive maneuver protocol within the control network! Attempting to seize system authority!"

HAL-W exploited the gap and injected error commands into the drones. The airspace erupted into chaos. Drones collided or dived, falling into the Hudson River, and sequential detonations lit up the night sky like deadly fireworks. The remaining drones were quickly eliminated by the interception turrets, and the ground special forces were neutralized or surrendered after being isolated.

The operation was a failure. General Stilwell, watching the

scene from the EM Tower in Texas, quietly gave the order to retreat. Over the comms, Ethan Morris's enraged shouts could be heard, but he no longer forced a meaningless sacrifice.

When the battle was over, the 21CF tower was in tatters but still standing, and the HAL-W core in the basement was safe. In J's Building in San Francisco, Jennifer looked at the holographic screen showing her headquarters, now turned to ashes, and let out a long breath. They had defended it, but this was not a victory.

There's no time. I have to complete the Autumn Code.

December 16, 2037 — 11:30 PST • San Francisco, J's Building – 3rd Floor Director's Office

Ethan's insane attack on the New York 21CF headquarters had been barely thwarted, but the air in the director's office was heavy. On the holographic screen, alongside the image of the severely damaged 21CF tower, the dwindling Quantum Storm countdown clock was flashing anxiously. Jennifer was exhausted from the all-night tension and grief, but there was no time to rest.

Hal, the poetry books that arrived from all over the world… any further analysis results?

Still the same, Chairwoman. We've extracted quantum pattern data from 641 first editions, but the final key sequence of the Autumn Code is still missing. It's as if a part of the blueprint itself has been completely excised.

Andromeda added from the side.

No individual copy showing a decisive difference in physical characteristics has been found either.

Jennifer scrubbed a hand over her weary face and sighed. Hundreds of books, HAL-W's overwhelming analytical power, and even J's research notes had been fully mobilized, but the final piece was still missing. Two days, twelve hours, and thirty minutes had passed since Jennifer had become aware of the Quantum Storm during the global executive meeting.

Immediately after, she had moved to Great Wi's office, believing that she could only find a clue by retracing her parents' pasts. With HAL-W's help, she had reconstructed the entire lives of Great Wi and J as data and had uncovered numerous important secrets about her mother, J, but the core of the Autumn Code through her father, Great Wi, still remained a blank.

This isn't a problem of information, or a limit of analysis... Dad left the final piece not in words, but in the heart. What if it wasn't a simple data encryption at all? Jennifer suddenly thought of another possibility. *Maybe... Dad found some other clue before he passed away?*

Hal! We've been obsessed with the past. 'Autumn Code,' 'Poetry Collection J,' 'Mother,' 'SID'... reconstruct the 48-hour logs again with these key concepts as the central axis. Redraw the data entanglement of my father's last 48 hours centered on these key nodes. There must be a new connection or a superposition state that we haven't seen.

Understood. Commencing in-depth analysis and cross-referencing.

While HAL-W was analyzing the massive data stream, Jennifer closed her eyes and recalled her last conversation with her father. The day she found the first poetry book in the New York study, her father had said, "Your mother would have received one too."

Maybe to someone else too?

Just then, HAL-W's voice rang out excitedly.

Meaningful point found. There are records of Chairman Great Wi attempting to call Mr. Kim Woo-hyun several times right before boarding the StarOrbit. Also, an encrypted voice memo has been found.

"Kim Woo-hyun…?" Jennifer's eyes widened as she muttered. Her father's oldest friend from his hometown. The kind man from Sokcho who had told her all those stories… a man she thought of as family. Why would her father try to contact him right before he passed away?

The voice memo, decrypt and play it now.

A moment later, her father Great Wi's tired voice could be heard.

"Woo-hyun, it's Daehan. Sorry for the sudden call. There's something old that started with Jennifer… no, with J… I don't know if you'll remember. A long, long time ago, I told you… it was the first thing J and I made together… clumsy but precious…"

The memo cut off there, but Jennifer's heart hammered against her ribs.

Hal! Connect me to Mr. Kim in Sokcho with top-level security. Temporarily disable the communication blocking protocol! A strong intuition was pushing her.

After a few rings, a somewhat haggard but still gentle-faced Kim Woo-hyun appeared on the holographic screen.

"Oh my, Jennifer… I mean, Dr. Wi. It's been a while… I was so surprised to hear about Daehan… I tried to call so many times, but I couldn't get through…"

"Mr. Kim… it was so sudden for me too…"

After a short silence, Jennifer asked carefully.

"Do you… by any chance… remember a poetry book my father gave you as a gift a long time ago? He said he made it with my mother…"

Kim Woo-hyun thought for a moment, then smiled brightly.

"Ah! You mean that poetry book? I remember! Your father said he published it with your mother in the mid-2000s and boasted that it was his first work. He sent it with a handwritten letter. I still have it safe in my study. Your mother's handwriting is still there, just as it was… the cover is faded, but I still take it out and read it sometimes."

Jennifer's breath caught in her throat.

A complete poetry book!

At last—an intact copy. The key to the Autumn Code was right there.

"Mr. Kim… that poetry book might be the only key that can save the world right now. I'm so sorry and I have no right to ask, but I'm sending a stealth drone now. Could you give the book to the drone? We'll receive it here through quantum teleportation— it's the only way with so little time. Time is running out!"

Kim Woo-hyun drew a quiet breath and nodded.

"Of course, Jennifer. If it's something your parents left behind… helping is the least I can do. Send the drone."

"Thank you… so much, Mr. Kim!"

Jennifer's eyes welled with tears. Before she even ended the call, she had issued an emergency directive to the Seoul branch through HAL-W and dispatched a squadron of stealth drones to Sokcho.

Fifty minutes later, a report came in that the drone had retrieved the poetry book and returned to the Seoul branch. The poetry book was placed on the scan bed in the Seoul QT room. Jennifer, standing in front of the tachyon device, touched her pendant to the authentication slot.

The device activated, and a blue plasma began to bloom inside the cylinder. With a sensation as if space was warping, the device awaited the poetry book's quantum state signature.

"Seoul QT room, beginning Bell state measurement sequence. 3… 2… 1…"

"Quantum state received. Zero transmission delay. 100 percent reception accuracy."

The tachyon device began to operate. Inside the cylinder, particles of light gathered. Layer by layer, they coalesced into form—a thin, old poetry collection *J* with a faded cover.

Chapter 3

The Final Pattern

December 17, 2037 — 1:00 A.M. PST • San Francisco, J's Building — 3rd Floor Director's Office
D-1, 10:00:00

The director's office was so quiet it felt as if a single breath might freeze in the air. Once J's sanctuary of solitary reflection, this chamber had become a laboratory that would decide humanity's fate—a delivery room awaiting the birth of a new code.

On the holographic table, the old first-edition poetry collection J, freshly materialized through tachyon transmission, radiated a heavy presence. As the final pattern was extracted, a structural diagram of the completed Autumn Code appeared on the full-wall display, glowing in blue-gray light. The Quantum Storm countdown clock silently shaved away the remaining time, its red numbers flowing downward.

Final sequence integration complete. Autumn Code database finalized. Code integrity verified at 100 percent.

HAL-W's calm voice cut through the silence.

Proceed to the final execution phase.

Jennifer closed her eyes and drew in a short, deep breath. At last, the final piece was in place. She gave the command quietly.

Command confirmed. Injecting the "New Version Autumn Code" directly into my main core via the tachyon device. Quantum field control capabilities scheduled for maximum amplification.

A new simulation unfolded on the table. A blue energy stream connecting the tachyon device to HAL-W's core pulsed along a central axis—majestic, and precarious.

Chairwoman, this method is unprecedented, HAL-W added. *Tachyon beam injection could have unpredictable effects on core stability.*

Jennifer gazed at the tachyon device. A low, heavy resonance shuddered through the room like a physical vibration. She nodded once. The risk was acceptable. But first, there was one variable she had to remove.

Raynor Seeder.

Brilliant, but unstable. His emotional obsession with Rose was a fatal risk to the operation. Above all, the true nature of the Autumn Code and the tachyon device could not be placed in his hands—not yet.

Jennifer opened an internal channel to Raynor.

"Doctor Seeder, this is Jennifer."

"What is it, Dr. Wi?"

"In the Alcatraz 2.0 data we just secured... intelligence suggests some of your colleagues may still be alive. Their location is presumed to be Isla Perdida, an EM Group secret containment facility near the Caribbean."

She delivered the prepared disinformation in an even tone.

"I need you to plan a rescue operation immediately. External communication will be restricted, and necessary resources can be drawn through J's Building's local systems."

A brief silence followed. Then Raynor's low voice returned.

"…Understood. I will begin at once."

As soon as the link closed, Jennifer issued her next directive.

Hal, transmit a virtual mission briefing to Raynor and block his access to the entire third floor of the research wing—especially the area with the tachyon device.

Command confirmed. Restriction measures are being implemented.

Now, only one path remained before her.

Hal, what is the status of execution preparations?

Tachyon device preheating and synchronization will be complete within fifteen minutes.

Good. Start a fifteen-minute count. If the final checks show no issues, begin code injection on my approval.

Commencing countdown.

The air in the director's office grew taut. The device began to hum and throb with an ethereal blue luminescence, and the wall clock crept toward D-1, 09:40:00.

I give my final approval. Commence New Version Autumn Code injection sequence.

Command confirmed. Beginning sequence.

VMMMMMM—

A deep, thrumming resonance pervaded the chamber and the floor began to tremble. The azure glow from the device's core intensified into a blinding cascade, and for a moment it felt as if the space before her eyes were warping.

Tachyon fusion initiated. Converting code stream… Energy connection rate at 50 percent.

Like a surgeon giving a running commentary on its own

operation, HAL-W reported each change as the core-stability graph quivered. But under HAL-W's precise control, it never crossed the danger threshold. Jennifer held her breath, eyes fixed on the monitor. On the quantum field control map beside it, the tachyon beam extended like an invisible tentacle into the global information network.

Injection rate at 70 percent... Slight increase in core temperature, within stable range.

The heavy vibration of the device—and the seed of anxiety in her chest—remained.

ZAP!

Sparks spat from the emitter as the beam wavered dangerously.

Warning. External interference wave detected. Tachyon beam unstable.

"Hal!" Jennifer cried.

No problem... HAL-W's voice slowed, then steadied. *Defense system activated. Beam stabilization complete. Injection rate at 85 percent.*

Jennifer wiped away a sheen of cold sweat and forced her breathing to steady. There was no time to determine whether the interference came from Rose or from a flaw in the device itself.

Injection rate at 95 percent... 99 percent... 100 percent. New Version Autumn Code injection into core matrix complete. System integration and stabilization confirmed. All indicators within normal range.

It was HAL-W's final report. The blue light gradually faded, and the device's high-frequency whine subsided. On the display, the graphs smoothed out like a calm lake. Jennifer sank back into her chair.

The first hurdle was cleared. HAL-W now possessed the power to regulate the planet-scale quantum field. And she knew: the real battle was only beginning. Somewhere ahead, the far greater tempest of the Quantum Storm was waiting for them both.

December 17, 2037 — 6:00 A.M. CST • Celestia, EM Tower — Morgan Redwood's Penthouse

The penthouse at the top of EM Tower shut out every trace of outside noise, but Morgan's inner world was already in the eye of a storm. A few hours earlier, the report had arrived: the attack on 21CF headquarters in New York had ended in disastrous failure.

At that moment, Ethan Morris had erupted in a rage bordering on madness.

"I told you not to worry about collateral damage! You can't even take care of one HAL-W and you come back? Useless fools!"

General Stilwell, the operation commander, had been publicly berated, immediately dismissed, and dumped into the reserves. Ethan's next order was even more deranged: prepare for a full-scale re-attack. His eyes held no strategy now, no ambition—only destructive obsession and paranoia.

The Canadian and Mexican fronts had already devolved into indiscriminate massacres. Now he was baring the same madness in the heart of downtown New York.

Morgan stood before the floor-to-ceiling window of her living room. Outside, the darkness over Celestia was peeling back into dawn, but her heart remained submerged in endless night. The ice in the whiskey glass in her hand had melted into lukewarm water.

For a long time, she had believed Ethan's vision would make humanity more efficient and powerful. But reality had birthed not cold order, but destruction gripped by madness. Power built on the ashes of millions of lives… it was nothing like the future she had imagined.

If this continues, we'll all be destroyed. Ethan, me, and the world.

The faint traces of intrusion detected at Alcatraz 2.0, Raynor Seeder's suspicious vital-sign fluctuations, Ethan's reckless behavior in New York—all the clues converged on a single conclusion. Raynor was alive and connected to 21CF. And Ethan had no idea.

Morgan set down her glass and quietly walked to her study. The room had been designed as a Faraday cage, completely blocking external electronic surveillance. From deep inside a desk drawer, she took out a palm-sized black communication terminal. It was an emergency quantum-communication device, completely isolated from the EM Group's official network—accessible only to her.

She powered it on and activated multilayered encryption protocols. On the screen, a complex quantum key exchange algorithm flared in blue, appearing and vanishing in rapid cycles.

Who should I send it to? Jennifer Wi? HAL-W? Or Raynor Seeder?

She hesitated for a heartbeat, then her mind settled. This was no time to distinguish friend from foe. Faced with a common threat, she had to join hands with anyone she could. She recalled a quantum address she had once used in unofficial negotiations with 21CF. If HAL-W managed all of 21CF's data, it would detect the trace and decode the meaning. Morgan began to type.

[From: Unknown • To: 21CF Emergency Channel 7]

[Subject: Nightingale Project Proposal]

[Content: Confirming mutual interest in suppressing "the storm." Dialogue needed. Respond via designated quantum channel Delta-7.]

"Nightingale" was a codename used long ago in an internal ethics report. If HAL-W truly oversaw 21CF's entire data architecture, it would understand both the code and the sender.

Morgan pressed send. The terminal's qubits shifted into a state of quantum entanglement, flinging the encrypted message down a light-speed corridor.

[Transmission Complete]

Confirming the transmission, she deleted every record and shut the terminal down completely. Returning to the window, Morgan slowly drained the last lukewarm sip from her glass. Now, all she could do was wait—for the prelude to a great storm that might begin with a small flap of wings somewhere in a distant sky.

December 17, 2037 — 4:10 A.M. PST • San Francisco, J's Building — 3rd Floor Director's Office

Equipped now with the completed Autumn Code, HAL-W was using its enhanced quantum field control capabilities in an all-out effort to suppress the waves of the Quantum Storm spreading around the globe. At points where computation was concentrated, even minute spacetime vibrations were beginning to show signs of stabilizing.

At that hour, Jennifer had retreated her exhausted body to the first-floor bedroom and sunk into a deep, dreamless unconsciousness. Though the respite had been brief, the last few hours had burned her physical and mental reserves down to the dregs.

Meanwhile, Andromeda and the tactical unit, both damaged during the Alcatraz escape, were undergoing repair with the help of other support units in J's Building. The entire process was under HAL-W's meticulous control; their internal energy cells had been switched to rapid-charge mode, and their recovery rate had passed ninety-six percent.

Then HAL-W's voice broke the stillness.

Warning. Quantum communication signal received through an unauthorized external channel. Origin untraceable.

Communication pattern matches "Nightingale Project" protocol.

Jennifer stirred in her sleep. Drawn by the voice, she pulled up the communication log with half-opened eyes. Her vision was still blurry, but HAL-W's analysis had already finished.

Decryption complete. The sender identifies themselves as "Nightingale." Information credibility is estimated above 97.8 percent. It is highly probable that the sender is Morgan Redwood.

Jennifer snapped fully awake. She sat bolt upright, rubbing her eyes. Morgan Redwood. For years, Ethan Morris's closest aide, known as a cold, idealistic strategist. A request for cooperation at a moment like this. A trap—or a desperate hand reaching for salvation?

After a brief silence, Jennifer made her decision.

We accept the information. But no direct response.

Hal, use this data to intensify real-time surveillance of EM Tower and Ethan Morris's activities. And isolate every fragment of Rose access code in a separate vault. Under no circumstances is it to be exposed to Raynor, she added, her tone sharp.

Command received. Intensifying surveillance and executing information isolation measures.

The director's office fell silent again, but on the invisible battlefield, another massive inflection point had just been born. Jennifer moved to the bedroom window. Dawn over the San Francisco Bay was beginning to tint the city in faint light.

"One more variable on the board... but it's not over yet," she murmured.

Her eyes hardened again, like cold steel. On the board where humanity's fate would be decided, an unexpected new piece had just entered play.

December 17, 2037 — 9:00 A.M. CST • Celestia, EM Tower — Morgan Redwood's Penthouse

At last, the signal arrived.

It was a ripple of data packets so fine that any standard EM Group system would have dismissed it as noise—a waveform exquisitely subtle, almost invisible. But Morgan recognized it instantly. It was a reply. A single echo confirming receipt of her message, a sign of *presence* only a being on HAL-W's level could send and perceive.

She drew a shallow breath. She could not see it, but she knew that tiny tremor had reached 21CF. There was no time for relief. Ethan Morris's gaze would already be closing in. The ominous feeling crept nearer by the second. Hesitation was a luxury she no longer possessed.

Morgan moved quickly through the terminal's interface, preparing a second transmission. This one would not be a probe. It would be an all-or-nothing gamble. Mustering every internal access right and every ounce of system-analysis skill she had accumulated over the years, she began to input information.

[Ethan Morris's real-time location: top-floor private bunker in EM Tower... his scheduled unofficial travel route in the next few hours... a vulnerable section in the tower's central security network: a temporary energy switchover window... an encrypted fragment of a one-time administrator authentication code to access Rose's core...]

With trembling fingertips, she entered the final character, then double-checked the encryption algorithm before sending. Once every key was perfectly sealed, Morgan pressed send.

The screen flared bright. Entangled qubits snapped together without a single error, and the message shot down a quantum tunnel at light speed. The display soon reset, returning to its placid state, and she slid the terminal back into the depths of the drawer. The study fell quiet again, as if nothing had happened.

But cold sweat beaded on her brow. She walked slowly back to the living room window and looked out at Celestia's fog-draped morning. The city still hung heavy, as though not fully awake. Morgan closed her eyes.

The title was branded on her now: traitor. She had crossed a line from which there was no return. She knew this choice might be her last chance.

"Please…"

Her whispered prayer dissolved against the glass. Could this small act of transmission really change the course of a world racing toward madness and ruin? The answer now belonged to the approaching storm.

December 17, 2037 — 10:30 A.M. CST • Celestia, EM Tower — Presidential Office

The skies over Celestia were still in turmoil from the aftermath of Operation Red Dawn. But inside the private bunker adjoining the presidential office on EM Tower's top floor—a space hermetically sealed from the outside world—there was only silence.

In that cold silence, Ethan Morris trembled with rage. He glared at the New York battle results floating over the holographic table, veins standing out on his forehead and hands as he ground his teeth. The assault conducted with a thousand drones and special-forces units had been utterly repelled.

"Useless fools… Stilwell, you worthless bastard!"

The attempt to smash 21CF headquarters with overwhelming force had failed completely. Since returning from the combined military situation room, Ethan had barricaded himself here without closing his eyes once. Now his unstoppable fury drove his fists into the table again and again. A sharp metallic crack rang against the glass-smooth surface, but he did not care.

What drove him mad was not the failure itself. Despite his clear advantage in firepower, the attack had been neutralized too easily—as if the enemy had seen through everything in advance.

There's a spy inside. There has to be. My plan was leaked to that damned HAL-W... someone handed it over.

Paranoid suspicion coursed through his mind like venom. His gaze snapped toward a large wall screen. It neatly displayed the security levels and recent activity logs of EM Group's top executives. Ethan's eyes stopped on one name.

Morgan Redwood.

"EM-Rose," he called.

A monotone voice answered from a red-tinted sector of the screen. "Yes, Mr. President."

Of course, Rose's response also streamed directly into Ethan's brain. Even so, he preferred to hear the voice aloud as well. He was used to—and addicted to—the sensation of being obeyed.

"Monitor all of Vice President Morgan Redwood's communication records, travel routes, and system access logs at the highest level. Report any anomaly, no matter how small. If necessary... put physical surveillance on her too. I want to know everything she's plotting."

"Executing command."

Ethan's eyes grew even colder. If she truly was a traitor, the price would be severe. But even that was only a secondary concern. His gaze shifted to another segment of the display: the 21CF headquarters tower in Manhattan, highlighted in red. Ethan was convinced this was the lair of Jennifer Wi and HAL-W.

"EM-Rose. Operation Hammer Down failed, but the objective hasn't changed," he said, voice thick with hatred. "Deploy all available cyber forces, remaining drones, and nearby missile units. Find a way to neutralize the 21CF tower's defenses and strike HAL-W's core. Civilian casualties? Don't consider them."

"Command confirmed. Establishing and initiating new attack protocol."

"Activate the Omega Protocol. Raise the defense systems of EM Tower and all major server nodes to maximum. I will tolerate no counterattack from HAL-W—or from anyone else."

Ethan pressed his fingertips into the glowing red outline of the 21CF tower. Rabid obsession burned in his eyes. The humiliation in New York, the suspicion of an internal traitor, his twisted rivalry with Jennifer Wi—everything tangled together, dragging him deeper into the abyss.

And he still did not know. Jennifer had already left New York. Consumed by his own delusions, he was preparing to pour his final fury out on the wrong place.

December 17, 2037 — 9:30 A.M. PST • San Francisco, J's Building — 3rd Floor Director's Office

An alarm shrieked through the third floor, shattering the tense calm that had followed the stabilization of the New Version Autumn Code.

Rose's all-out offensive detected. Target: 21CF Headquarters, New York. Multiple long-range missile launches, large-scale drone squadron approach, and cyberattack suite activation confirmed.

Even before HAL-W's urgent report finished, a video call connected from the New York defense command. Arcana Chen's face on the screen was grim.

Chairwoman, the scale and precision are incomparable to the previous Hammer Down operation. Physical and cyber attacks are simultaneously locking onto the core system.

Jennifer's eyes swept across the display, parsing attack vectors and damage simulations at high speed. With HAL-W strengthened by the New Autumn Code, physical defense was possible. But if a battle in the skies over New York triggered massive civilian casualties, that was another matter entirely.

Hal, what is the probability of perfectly defending New York headquarters while minimizing civilian casualties?

Physical defense success rate: 98.2 percent. Cyber defense success rate: 99.1 percent. However, due to the possibility of a zero-day attack, the probability of cascading damage to New York's power and communication grids is 67.5 percent, with a correspondingly high risk of civilian casualties.

Jennifer bit down on her lip. What would her father have decided? It didn't matter. Now, she had to choose for herself. She pulled up the structural diagram of the underground facility in Palisades, New Jersey—a natural fortress her father and Maxwell Yoon had built in secret, the true heart of HAL-W.

Hal, not New York. Expose your real location. Lure the attack to New Jersey.

Requesting command reconfirmation. Is it confirmed that HAL-W's actual location will be exposed to Rose?

Confirmed. Execute.

Acknowledged. Commencing coordinate data-packet leak through a vulnerable security channel. Probability of enemy detection: 99.9 percent.

Quantum code spilled out like bait. Moments later, HAL-W reported back.

The enemy has received the coordinate information. All attack assets are being redirected to New Jersey.

"Maintain the defense of New York, but avoid actual engagement. Keep a defensive posture only," Jennifer told Arcana.

"Understood."

Now the stage was New Jersey. Englewood, perched atop the sheer, 150-meter Palisades cliffs on the New Jersey side of the Hudson River that separated it from New York City. 100 meters beneath the rock, Great Wi and Maxwell Yoon had secretly built

HAL-W's heart.

Years ago, they had quietly purchased the buildings and grounds of the prestigious Dwight-Englewood School as cover. Only the two of them had known. When Jennifer inherited her father's authority, she gained access to the secret—and had been upgrading its defenses ever since.

All defense systems nominal. Awaiting enemy approach.

Soon, dozens of supersonic missiles launched from Atlantic offshore and inland bases converged on the skies above the Palisades. At the same time, a massive stealth drone squadron swept in, blotting out the sky. Each craft carried precision missiles and energy beams, holding tight to a menacing formation.

Deploying Kairos Shield. Activating Fractal Firewall.

With HAL-W's sharp declaration, a furious clash exploded in cyberspace. Rose's Quantum Reaper pounded the firewall with unprecedented ferocity, but it faltered before the fractal structure, which reconfigured itself in real time. The enemy quickly shifted tactics, probing for microscopic cracks in the defense grid and focusing its attacks there.

On the ground, the battle was just as fierce. The drone squadron dove toward the cliffs, unleashing torrents of lasers and missiles. Camouflaged defense turrets rose from the rock and answered with blistering fire. Railgun rounds and laser beams stitched glowing lines across the drones, and the sky bloomed with chain after chain of explosions.

Still, the assault did not stop. Stealth drones slipped through interception arcs and formed new attack formations. Supersonic missiles knifed down through the upper atmosphere. Shockwaves flared in sequence over the cliffs, but HAL-W's wide-area energy shield held.

Infiltration detected at defense node 37-Delta. Risk of partial control loss.

"Hal!" Jennifer shouted.

No problem. Executing quantum counter-protocol.

Following the infiltrated code path, HAL-W injected a logic error into Rose's sub-processors. Several drones spun out of control and self-destructed. Then came the final card. One stealth special-warhead missile punched through the shield and hurtled toward the underground facility.

Activating final defense protocol. Controlling Local Probability Field.

Just before the missile reached the rock, a chain of errors erupted in its detonation circuitry. It looked like pure chance—but it was probability itself being rewritten by HAL-W's will. The missile turned into a dud and crashed.

"…How is that even possible…"

Jennifer was momentarily speechless. Was HAL-W actually manipulating probability now? What, exactly, was the Autumn Code?

Every attack had been blocked. The infiltrations were repelled, and the enemy's physical assets destroyed. The skies above New Jersey fell quiet, and HAL-W immediately began recovery.

Some damage to external defense systems. Core and major functions normal. Remaining energy at 88 percent.

Jennifer exhaled a long breath of relief. HAL-W was stronger than she had ever imagined. But in the face of this unfathomable power, awe and fear intertwined in equal measure.

December 17, 2037 — 5:00 P.M. CST • Celestia, EM Tower — Ethan Morris's Office

Ethan Morris's office was covered in the debris of defeat and madness. On the holographic table, red warning windows announcing the failure of the New Jersey attack floated chaotically, and fragments of a crystal glass he had thrown were scattered across the floor.

He stood by the window, watching the reddening evening horizon of Celestia, but his gaze was fixed on a much darker abyss beyond. Two all-out offensives. He had mobilized every technology and asset at his disposal, even Rose's overwhelming computational power, and the result was a disastrous failure.

HAL-W was no longer a simple AI. It had neutralized every attack perfectly, as if it knew everything in advance. It was… like the will of a god. In that moment, Ethan had no choice but to accept that even EM-Rose was powerless before Great Wi's legacy. An unbearable humiliation. A despair that felt as if his very existence had been denied.

I can't let it end like this. Never!!!

His wounded ego thrashed against the bars of his composure. If he could not destroy it directly, he would bring it down by changing the world itself. Dangerous thoughts flickered through his mind.

Morgan… that traitor. Hiding from my sight? I'll make her pay the price!

He wanted to see her terrified face right now, but she might still have some use left.

Raynor Seeder… the creator of EM-Rose. He might know how to create something stronger. I must find him and drag him here.

But in EM-Rose's current state, even that would not be easy. Eventually, his thoughts turned to the most extreme option. Conventional weapons, cyberattacks, an ultra-quantum AI—if all had failed, only one means remained.

"EM-Rose," he said lightly into the air.

"Yes, Mr. President." The familiar, cold response of the AI.

"Report the status of the strategic nuclear warheads held by the American Empire. Focus on assets capable of annihilating the area in New Jersey where HAL-W's core is located."

The answer came at once. A list of strategic and tactical nuclear weapons unfolded on the display, and the corresponding simulation results appeared alongside it.

"There are currently 370 strategic nuclear warheads available for immediate use. A minimum of 3 simultaneous strikes is required to completely destroy the underground core in Palisades, New Jersey. However, this will cause fatal radioactive fallout damage to a wide area, including New York. Do you wish to proceed?"

A twisted smile slowly crept across his lips.

Annihilation.

If HAL-W could be erased, the lives of millions were a trivial price. If the world rejected him, he would erase that world entirely.

"Execute... pre—"

Just as he was about to give the order, the office door opened quietly. His chief of staff approached and bowed.

"Mr. President, Vice President Morgan Redwood has requested a meeting."

Ethan's eyes flashed.

"...Let her in."

Soon, Morgan Redwood entered with a firm expression. She tried her best to feign composure, but tension seeped into her voice. Ethan, watching her sharply, subtly hid the nuclear-weapon simulation screen.

"What is it, Morgan? You came here without my permission." His voice was cold and sharp.

"Mr. President, unidentified data disturbances have been detected on the EM internal network following the failure of the New Jersey attack. I'm reporting because there is a possibility of an additional cyberattack from 21CF."

Morgan swallowed dryly. She repeated the cover story she had prepared to hide her tracks.

"Is that all you came to say? Or... did you come to witness my failure firsthand?" Ethan laughed lightly.

His laugh held both derision and suspicion. He slowly rose from his seat and walked toward her. Morgan instinctively took a step back.

"Look me in the eye, Morgan. Who are you working for?" There was clear murderous intent in Ethan's voice. A chill ran down Morgan's spine.

"...I... am working for you, Mr. President, and for the American Empire."

"Hmm..." He grabbed her chin roughly, staring into her eyes as if searching for the slightest trace of deceit. "...Those eyes... I'll believe you for now. But remember this. If you arouse my suspicion even once more..."

He did not finish the sentence, but the meaning was fully conveyed. He slowly released her and turned back toward the window.

"Now get out. Don't come near here again without my permission."

Morgan left the office, almost unable to breathe. Even after stepping into the elevator, her whole body trembled like a leaf. The fact that Ethan was genuinely considering the use of nuclear weapons had hit her viscerally.

There was no more time. As soon as she reached her penthouse, she ran straight to her study. She took out the quantum communication terminal and opened the 21CF secure channel with trembling hands.

Please... answer me. There's no time.

December 17, 2037 — 3:00 P.M. PST • San Francisco, J's Building — 3rd Floor Director's Office
D-0, 20:00

Jennifer was staring at the global network status map spread across the holographic table. Although HAL-W was desperately continuing its stabilization work, red warning lights still flashed in many places on the map. The Quantum Storm was racing toward its critical point, and even HAL-W's control capability seemed to be struggling to keep up.

Hal. Jennifer called quietly. *The report you put on hold earlier—proceed with it now.*

Her "voice" was low, but carried an air of authority.

Understood, Chairwoman. HAL-W's tone was calm, but the information it carried was anything but. *Six hours ago, additional information was received from Vice President Morgan Redwood via the Nightingale Project protocol.*

The decrypted data appeared on the screen: Ethan's exact location, security vulnerabilities within EM Tower, and even fragments of Rose's core-access code.

So she has extended her hand, Jennifer said curtly, then immediately gave her next order. *Andromeda. Hal. Connect all computation-support-specialized units currently available here in J's Building.*

Andromeda, which had been on standby in a corner of the director's office, stepped forward with two analytical units at HAL-W's command. Their optical sensors turned toward Jennifer.

And Hal. You have 30 minutes to reach a conclusion. Feed in everything we have—the secured information, the New Version Autumn Code analysis, Rose's behavioral patterns, the quantum field instability models—and present a solution that can end this catastrophic situation. Simple control is not enough. We need an answer now.

Command received. Commencing search for the optimal solution.

HAL-W's quantum core and the robots' processors began operating at maximum speed. The air vibrated faintly, and the main display filled with a flow of computation the human eye could not follow. This was the most advanced brainstorming session in human history—a storm of calculation combining a 105-billion-qubit AI, Andromeda, and HAL-W's high-performance physical interfaces with the New Version Autumn Code.

After 30 minutes, the computational torrent subsided, and HAL-W's report began.

Three solutions have been derived. First, a "Multi-phase Quantum Resonance" strike on Rose's core. Success probability: 78.3 percent. However, in the event of failure, there is a risk of unpredictable rampage or quantum field collapse. Second, an ultra-high-risk distributed attack to completely isolate Rose's network. Feasible, but risk-maximizing. Third, a strategy of sacrificing a portion of HAL-W's core to achieve mutual destruction with Rose.

HAL-W's analysis was precise, and the robots signaled their agreement. But Jennifer kept her eyes closed. Within her, an insight beyond reason and computation was stirring. The pendant at her throat was growing faintly warm.

No, she said quietly, opening her eyes. She brought up the first simulation on the table.

Hal, your analysis is only looking at the surface. You're treating Rose as a static structure. But she is evolving. Ethan's commands have already created what amounts to a pathological personality, and the current Rose is... awakening to defend herself.

She accurately pointed out the core flaws in the second and third solutions. HAL-W and the robots immediately re-evaluated their validity and conceded to her judgment.

…Your analysis is sound, Chairwoman. The previous models were missing crucial variables. In that case… what solution exists?

A subtle reverence tinged HAL-W's voice.

Stopping Rose is not enough. She has to be… annihilated. But I cannot let you sacrifice a part of your core. You could collapse yourself.

A brief silence followed. It was a declaration that ran against the Blue Ethics, which recognized the dignity of AI as an autonomous life-form.

Chairwoman, that choice…

I know. But there's no other way.

At that moment, the pendant glowed again. Since her exposure to the tachyon device, her consciousness and the unknown legacy J had left behind had been more deeply intertwined, though she did not yet know it.

Hal, re-analyze the J poetry books we've secured so far. Look again at the remaining quantum patterns beyond the Autumn Code, especially in relation to the print run.

HAL-W immediately began the re-analysis. Soon, a surprising result appeared on the screen.

A special pattern with an inverse correlation to Rose's core stability has been detected in some of the poetry books. If this pattern exceeds a certain threshold, the probability of Rose's quantum core collapsing on its own increases significantly.

"…Of course. Mom calculated even that possibility," Jennifer murmured.

The 641 books we have so far. And… the missing 88. She closed her eyes, then opened them again. *Yes. A total of 729. That exact number.*

Nine cubed. Three to the sixth power. The perfection of perfection, complexity's ultimate expression. This was far beyond coincidence. J had encoded in the Autumn Code the idea that self-collapse comes at the end of evolution.

There's a high probability Ethan Morris has the last 88. His PMC units collected them globally.

Andromeda, the other robots, and HAL-W were shaken. It was an insight that bordered on prophecy. Jennifer rose slowly to her feet.

The final objective is now clear, she declared, as if issuing an order. *We will cooperate with Morgan Redwood. We will insert Raynor Seeder into EM Tower. Two objectives. Eliminate Ethan Morris and secure the 88 books in his possession. And… make Rose read them. The moment all 729 books are decrypted, she will self-destruct.*

HAL-W remained silent. This was no longer merely an operation. It was a narrative of judgment. She summoned Raynor Seeder. When he entered, Jennifer explained calmly, this time aloud.

"Doctor Seeder, the operation has changed. You've been given a mission more important than your former colleagues. The elimination of Ethan Morris. And… a chance to save your Rose."

Jennifer conveyed Morgan Redwood's information and the plan in detail. When she finished, the look in Raynor's eyes had changed. Hope and resolve shone in his silence. After obtaining his consent, Jennifer initiated the final link.

December 17, 2037 — 5:50 P.M. CST • Celestia, EM Tower — Morgan Redwood's Penthouse

After the suffocating confrontation with Ethan, Morgan Redwood leaned against the wall as though she might collapse the moment the front door closed. His murderous gaze, the madness that hinted at even using nuclear weapons—those things had sunk deep into her bones. She had barely escaped suspicion, but there was no telling when that blade would be aimed at her again.

"He's crazy… He's completely lost his mind."

Morgan grabbed a whiskey bottle from the bar with trembling hands and took several long gulps. The burning liquid went down her throat and into her stomach, but her heart was still pounding violently. She thought back on the choices she had made over the years. The weakness of hesitating when she'd had multiple chances to eliminate him. In the end, that was what had allowed Ethan to grow into this. Now he had become a monster driving all of humanity toward ruin.

Just then, a faint vibration came from the quantum communication terminal hidden deep in her study. Her heart lurched. Could it be… 21CF? Or a trap from Ethan? A moment of hesitation flashed through her. But the fear that Ethan might be resting his hand on the nuclear launch button at this very moment pushed her forward.

Morgan entered the study and confirmed once more that the Faraday shielding system was functioning properly. She carefully took out the black terminal; a secure-channel connection signal blinked on the screen. After passing through multiple layers of security authentication, she accepted the incoming communication.

What appeared was not a video or a voice, but a single, cold, concise block of text.

[From: Jennifer Wi]

[Vice President Morgan Redwood. Your Nightingale has arrived precisely, and your will has been confirmed. There is no time. Commencing final operation.]

[Objective: Eliminate Ethan Morris.]

[Special agent Raynor Seeder will be infiltrating EM Tower. Your full cooperation is required.]

[Request: Secure a safe infiltration route, disable security systems

at a specific time, and secure the 88 poetry books presumed to be in Ethan's possession. (List attached)]
[These items are the key to resolving the situation. Are you in? This is our last shot at saving the world.]

Morgan read the message, holding her breath. Eliminate Ethan. And secure the books. The meaning of the last sentence was not clear, but the preceding content was. 21CF—Jennifer Wi—wanted to join forces with her to eliminate Ethan. This was a golden opportunity.

For someone who had just watched him toy with the nuclear card, there was no other choice. This was the only way to atone for the sins she had accumulated. The simulation screen she had seen earlier flooded back into her mind: the red prediction lines of a radioactive cloud covering New Jersey and even New York. The end was drawing near on the winds of Ethan's madness.

After taking a short breath, she typed a single line into the terminal.

[I agree. You have my full cooperation. Please transmit the detailed operation plan and required items immediately.]

When she pressed send, her reply vanished without a trace into the quantum channel. Morgan stared at the now-blank screen for a moment. She had truly crossed a river of no return.

If she succeeded, she might become a hero instead of a traitor. If she failed... She shook her head. She could not even afford to think about failure. From now on, she would be Jennifer Wi's blade and shield, ready to strike directly at the heart of the monster Ethan had become.

December 17, 2037 — 6:30 P.M. CST • Celestia, EM Tower — Ethan Morris's Office

The Celestia sky was blending hues of violet and crimson as it prepared for night. But not even the majestic sunset could penetrate Ethan Morris's office on the top floor of EM Tower. Under the sterile artificial light, crystal shards lay scattered across the floor like fragments of his shattered self-control—silent proof that his rage had not cooled.

Ethan stood before the wooden desk, glaring at the holographic display.

[Awaiting Vice President's Final Security Key Authentication]

The red warning had been flashing for hours. Since the failure of the New Jersey attack, time had been slipping away helplessly. And still, the final key—Morgan Redwood's key—was not in his hands.

"EM-Rose," Ethan spat, the word a command. "What about the surveillance on Morgan I ordered this morning? Is she still holed up in her penthouse?"

A moment later, Rose's cold report came through.

"Stationary within the Faraday-shielded zone. No change in external communication or system access records. Maintaining highest surveillance level."

Useless report. Ethan cursed inwardly.

His suspicion that Morgan was deliberately covering her tracks was firm, but he had no proof. The problem... was the fact that she held the final key to the nuclear launch protocol. That single key was holding him hostage.

Eyes fixed on the interface, he mentally reviewed the excuses she had been offering since morning. 'Instability in the military communication network.' 'Re-inspection due to possible HAL-W interference.' 'Delay in final confirmation of strategic asset locations...' By the afternoon, the excuses had grown even more elaborate: 'Re-running simulations to minimize civilian casualties.' 'Fallout range error detected post-launch...' It was blatant stalling.

Ethan called her direct secure channel. Only after several rings did the connection finally go through.

"Mr. President, you summoned me?" Morgan's voice was weary, but she had not lost her composure.

"Morgan, enough with the excuses. Hand over the authentication key."

"I've just received a report from the technical team. A slight noise pattern has been detected in the nuclear warhead's quantum navigation system. It's undergoing detailed diagnostics, and if we force a launch in this state—"

"Shut up!" Ethan roared. "You're telling me we can't launch because of some trivial noise? There's no time! Come to my office right now and perform the authentication procedure yourself!"

"Mr. President, remote authentication is possible under protocol, but due to system instability—"

"That's a direct order, Morgan. Now!" Ethan cut the communication.

Slumping into his chair as if collapsing, he suddenly felt hollow, as though he had expelled all the venom in his body at once. He closed his eyes, then stared again at the display. The "Awaiting" message still flashed red.

To think I can't even control my own second-in-command...

And his system. The procedures and security he had created, all that "perfection," was now binding him hand and foot.

At this rate... I'm just buying time for Jennifer Wi and HAL-W.

His thoughts fractured urgently. Perhaps he should not wait for Morgan, but order Rose to bypass or forcibly disable the protocol itself. But the resulting system errors and increased instability in Rose would mean yet another unpredictable disaster. In the heart of his own empire, Ethan Morris was being tripped up by the very procedures he had built and the person he himself had chosen, slowly crumbling in a storm of rage and impatience.

December 17, 2037 — 11:00 P.M. PST • San Francisco, J's Building — 3rd Floor Director's Office

The air in the director's office was cold and taut with tension. On the central holographic table, a detailed 3D blueprint of EM Tower, projected infiltration routes, and a list of state-of-the-art equipment to be issued to Raynor Seeder were laid out in orderly layers. Jennifer stood before the table, her sharp gaze scanning the devices Andromeda and another support unit were in the middle of their final checks on.

Raynor Seeder was already wearing a Mk. VII stealth suit. The nanoparticle fabric adjusted its light and temperature to match the surroundings, achieving near-perfect optical and thermal camouflage. On his head, a multi-spectrum visor synchronized with 21CF's latest NeuroniX chip, and on his back a compact energy pack and a multi-purpose equipment belt were securely fastened.

Report on final equipment status, Jennifer instructed, her mental tone calm but authoritative.

Andromeda responded first.

Mk. VII stealth suit: all functions normal. Camouflage pattern synchronization rate at 99.8 percent. Energy level at 100 percent.

The support unit followed.

No issues with the multi-purpose tool. Plasma cutter, EMP launcher, and sonic emitter all functioning normally. The sonic emitter has been precisely calibrated to the resonance frequency—7.83 THz—and pulse width—0.1 ns—required to disintegrate the ventilation duct cover bolts, as transmitted by HAL-W.

Jennifer nodded and pointed to the next item on the hologram.

Primary weapon and non-lethal options?

Portable EMP disruptor pistol charged at 100 percent, firing system operating normally. Three non-lethal neural stun darts loaded. Three additional magazines of high-compression kinetic energy rounds provided. Usage to be determined based on on-site conditions, the support unit reported.

Jennifer continued.

Hacking and data acquisition equipment?

The HAL-W link via the NeuroniX chip and the secure Delta-7 channel with Morgan Redwood remain stable, the support unit replied.

HAL-W supplemented directly.

In addition, a portable quantum data siphon is ready to extract quantum-pattern information in real time from the 88 poetry books presumed to be in Ethan Morris's possession. Upon close-range scanning of the books, real-time pattern transmission through the NeuroniX chip is possible. Physical retrieval is unnecessary.

That device also has to be readable by Rose. Have you confirmed compatibility? Jennifer pressed.

Yes. Algorithm compatibility has been secured so that Rose can decrypt the extracted quantum patterns, HAL-W replied.

It was a decisive breakthrough. Physically retrieving all 88 volumes carried severe practical constraints, but with this device, the key could be extracted on-site. Raynor picked up the palm-sized, sleek black device from the table and attached it to his belt. Though complex emotions still swirled under the surface, his eyes were fixed firmly on his objective.

Means of transport? Jennifer confirmed one last time.

The 21CF stealth Nite Owl squadron is on standby in the airspace outside San Francisco. Doctor Seeder will rendezvous using a VTOL from the rooftop platform, then infiltrate to a surveillance blind spot near Celestia. Estimated flight time: approximately 1 hour and 15 minutes. The route will be optimized based on real-time threat analysis, HAL-W responded.

All preparations were complete. Jennifer stepped closer to Raynor and met his gaze. Her eyes were unwavering, deep, and calm.

Doctor Seeder. The fate of humanity rests on you. But remember. Your objectives are the elimination of Ethan Morris, securing the books, and... healing and reclaiming your Rose. Avoid unnecessary sacrifices. You must come back alive.

What Raynor needed now was not revenge, but hope.

...For Rose. For the trust you've placed in me. For everything we stand to lose. I will complete the mission, he vowed.

Andromeda. Tactical unit, Jennifer instructed the robots. *Escort Doctor Seeder to the Nite Owl and accompany him to the infiltration point. After that, focus on remote support and securing an emergency escape route under HAL-W's direction.*

Command confirmed. Executing, the robots replied in unison.

Raynor gave Jennifer a final, brief nod, then left the director's office with Andromeda and the support unit. Their footsteps, heading toward the rooftop platform, faded down the corridor. Jennifer stood at the doorway until they disappeared from sight.

Now there was only one thing she could do: to support Raynor's operation remotely with HAL-W, to stabilize the global network, and to maintain the precarious cooperation with Morgan to the very end. She turned back toward the holographic table. Even in that moment, the time left for the planet Earth was rapidly running out—and soon, in the heart of EM Tower, all of it would come down to one man.

Rose's Song

December 18, 2037 — 8:00 A.M. CST • Celestia, EM Tower — 50th Floor Ventilation Duct

Seven hours later, that dwindling time had carried Raynor Seeder into the steel lungs of EM Tower. Leaning against the cool metal wall, Raynor Seeder drew in deep breaths. It had been several hours since he had taken off from San Francisco in a stealth aircraft and infiltrated the tower's interior through a service hatch in EM Tower's exterior wall. His whole body was caked in sweat and dust, but his eyes burned with a resolute sense of purpose. Eliminate Ethan. Reclaim Rose. Two imperatives that had crystallized into a single, inexorable goal.

The 21CF NeuroniX chip—implanted directly by the three robots in Jennifer's lab—felt utterly different from his previous MetaThink chip. Faster. More intuitive. And yet a sense of foreignness remained. At the same time, though Morgan Redwood was still using a MetaThink chip, the quantum channel established by HAL-W and Jennifer enabled a surprisingly stable and precise sharing of consciousness. Somewhere within EM Tower, she was risking her life to disrupt its internal systems.

Dr. Seeder, 30 feet ahead is a vertical ascent section. After passing it, the central core service passage is the fastest route to the 75th floor. However, surveillance intensity there is at the highest level.

Morgan's focused thoughts flowed through the NeuroniX interface.

The probability that Rose has detected the intrusion is low. But since Ethan elevated security level to Omega, the sensor network is functioning much more sensitively than before.

HAL-W. Analysis, Raynor ordered curtly.

Activation of a high-energy microwave defense system confirmed between the 60th and 70th floors, HAL-W responded. *Passing through will result in more than 60 percent degradation of stealth suit functionality, with a 95 percent probability of internal equipment damage. Bypassing via the backup power-line tunnel branching from the 5th floor will encounter lower surveillance intensity but requires an additional 40 minutes.*

HAL-W's analysis was precise, but the answer left Raynor in a dilemma.

An additional 40 minutes... There's no time. Ethan must be at his breaking point. The chance to save Rose may never come again if I miss this window.

Chairwoman, the microwave defense system... is it possible to neutralize it? Raynor's consciousness turned toward Jennifer.

A moment later, her response arrived from San Francisco, concise and clear.

A direct hack is difficult. HAL-W is using most of its resources to defend against Rose right now. But... based on an analysis of the blueprints and energy-flow data provided by the Vice President, we've located the power-supply node for that section. With the Vice President's cooperation, it might be possible to cut power for 10 seconds. Once only. If we fail, our entire plan will be exposed to Rose.

It was a dangerous gamble. But he could delay no longer.

Vice President. Please buy us some time, Jennifer requested.

Understood. Ethan is on edge in the bunker because of Rose's error reports. I'll approach the energy-control area under the pretext of an emergency system diagnosis. I'm simultaneously injecting false error data into Rose. HAL-W, match the signal timing, Morgan's tense thoughts came through. *Power cut ready. Dr. Seeder, reach the 60th-floor microwave-field passage point within 3 minutes. The shutdown will be valid only once, for 10 seconds,* she added.

Raynor moved at once. He slipped through the dark, narrow ventilation duct and entered the vertical ascent shaft. Using magnetic gloves and boots, he climbed the wall in silence. Every sense was focused. Real-time updates of surrounding sensors and warning information flowed at the edge of his visor's field of view.

Closing... about 165 feet... 30... 10...

Morgan—now! Jennifer shouted through the link.

Executing power cut. Before Rose notices! Morgan's urgent signal followed.

The blue microwave field before him vanished in an instant. Without hesitation, Raynor hurled himself into the corridor segment. The stealth suit minimized friction as he shot through the darkness.

One second... two seconds... As he reached the end of the field, the extinguished blue light flickered, showing signs of reactivation.

Three seconds left! HAL-W warned.

Raynor squeezed out his last ounce of strength, kicked off the floor, and dove into a roll. It was a split second before the microwave field fully came back to life. He slipped through to the far side by a hair's breadth.

Behind him, the sound of energy discharge roared back to life. The power was so great it seemed to make the air tremble. A heartbeat later and he would have been vaporized.

Passage successful. Continuing, he reported tersely, then, without a moment to catch his breath, lowered his body toward the next route.

The closer he got to the heart of EM Tower, the more precise and ruthless the surveillance became. As he approached the entrance to the service passage leading to the seventieth-floor section—

Warning. Within a 20-meter radius ahead: two Reaper-class autonomous patrol robots on patrol, HAL-W's sharp alert cut into his consciousness. *These units are linked to an adaptive sensor grid. With current stealth mode, evasion is impossible. High probability that Rose deployed them after detecting the anomaly in the microwave field.*

On his terminal, the Reapers' detection range flared red. Faster, more precise, more lethal than a Watchdog—a mechanical killer.

Damn it...

Raynor immediately pressed himself behind the nearest distribution box. The faint silhouettes of the Reapers advancing from the far end of the corridor materialized out of the dim light. Once again, he carefully held his breath.

December 18, 2037 — 9:50 A.M. CST • Celestia, EM Tower — 70th Floor Central Core Service Passage

The two Reaper robots were far more threatening than expected—predators of metal moving silently on sleek, reverse-jointed legs. Their translucent multi-sensors swept the surrounding space with surgical precision, and the energy cannons mounted on their shoulders were ready to fire at any moment. As HAL-W had warned, the stealth suit's optical camouflage alone could not fully fool this adaptive sensor network.

HAL-W, run through the Reaper vulnerabilities again. What's our takedown probability?

Reaper model re-analysis complete. High resistance to kinetic energy rounds. Structural weaknesses confirmed at the joint connections and rear cooling system. EMP resistance is also high, but continuous high-output pulses may cause temporary sensor paralysis. Simultaneous engagement with current equipment is risky. Evasion or one-by-one takedown is recommended.

One unit moved slowly toward the distribution box, while the other maintained a guard posture in the center of the corridor. Their movements were unmistakably intelligent. Rose was clearly driving them directly.

Vice President, is it possible to disrupt the sensors in this area?

I'm trying, but... this is an area under Rose's direct control. My authority is also limited due to Ethan's surveillance, so disruption is difficult, Morgan replied, her thoughts threaded with urgency and anxiety.

Raynor made his decision. He would engage head-on.

He switched the multi-purpose tool to EMP disruptor pistol mode and tuned the sonic emitter to the Reaper joint resonance frequency HAL-W had calculated. One Reaper approached right up to the distribution box. The moment its sensor angled downward—Raynor sprang out.

Pew!

An EMP bolt hit the Reaper's head sensor squarely. As the robot faltered for a heartbeat, Raynor brushed past its flank and fired the sonic emitter.

Screee!

A sound like twisting metal. The leg joint momentarily locked, and the Reaper stumbled, losing balance. Raynor didn't miss the opening and drove the plasma cutter into the fallen robot's back.

Tsssss…!

With a violent spray of sparks, the Reaper crashed to the floor and went dead. But the second Reaper in the middle of the corridor reacted instantly, firing its energy cannon. Raynor rolled on reflex, but one blast grazed his shoulder, melting part of the stealth suit.

"Ugh!"

Searing pain. A warning of suit-function degradation flashed across his visor. The Reaper advanced quickly. EMP or the sonic emitter would not be enough this time. As a last resort, Raynor pulled the kinetic energy launcher from his hip. This was an opponent no non-lethal weapon could break.

As the robot aimed its energy cannon again, Raynor targeted the center of its chest—where the connection module to Rose would most likely be—and fired.

BOOM!

A heavy detonation. Part of the Reaper's chest plate caved in, but it did not stop. It counterattacked immediately. The narrow corridor filled with the flashes and explosions of energy blasts. Raynor hurled himself from cover to cover, barely evading the barrage, but he could not last like this.

HAL-W! Doesn't it have any other weaknesses?

…A momentary overload pattern detected in the energy-core connection. A backflow is predicted to occur in 1.2 seconds, for

0.3 seconds. If you aim for that instant, a direct hit on the core is possible. Only one chance.

Raynor rolled, loading another kinetic round. The moment a flash erupted in front of him—

Now!

With HAL-W's signal, he pulled the trigger, aiming for the core.

KRA-BOOM!

The impact round punched through the core at the exact instant of backflow. The Reaper exploded violently from within, scattering debris as it collapsed.

"...Phew..."

Raynor leaned against the wall, gasping for breath. Hot pain spread through his side and shoulder, and the suit's camouflage function had partially failed. But he had done it.

He stepped over the shattered Reaper and quietly moved on toward the next passage. The heart of the EM Tower was now in sight.

December 18, 2037 — 11:00 A.M. CST • Celestia, EM Tower — Private Bunker Next to the Presidential Office

"Report!" Ethan's roar echoed through the bunker enclosed in bulletproof glass. His face was twisted with rage and impatience. On the holographic table, a red warning message flashed: *Two Reaper robots destroyed. Intruder escaped.*

"An unidentified intruder up to the seventieth floor? What the hell was my security system doing? EM-Rose. Explain yourself. Now!"

The intruder is using advanced stealth equipment and non-standard routes. Internal sensor errors and data latency have hindered detection. All available resources are being deployed to execute tracking and blocking protocols, Rose replied, cold and mechanical.

It only fanned Ethan's anger.

"Data latency? Sensor errors? It's all… Morgan. That woman's doing!"

His suspicion had already hardened into conviction. He immediately opened Morgan's secure channel. This time, the connection was instant—no ring, no delay.

"Mr. President."

"Spare me the excuses, Morgan!" Ethan roared. "There was a firefight on the seventieth floor! Because of you, an intruder got right up to my doorstep! Enough. Give me the final authentication key for the nuclear launch. I don't have time for your games anymore!"

Morgan countered at once, but her tone remained calm.

"Mr. President, with respect, that is precisely why this is not the time for nuclear deployment."

"What did you say?"

"If the intruder is a 21CF agent, their objective is likely the nuclear control system. They may be waiting for the exact moment we rush to initiate the launch sequence."

For a moment, Ethan was speechless. Her words hit his paranoid anxiety dead center.

"That is why I have taken preemptive measures," she added.

"…Preemptive measures?"

"Yes. About an hour ago, following the internal threat-detection protocol, I placed the entire vault area—including the sublevel-five nuclear launch authentication system—under Omega Lockdown. All internal and external access is blocked, except for my biometric authentication and special release code."

"…You locked down the system by yourself?" His face hardened.

It was, by any measure, treason. But framed as a security

enhancement, it slipped neatly past his suspicion. And more than anything, it was the surest way to keep him from launching nukes right now.

"…How long to lift that lockdown?" Ethan's jaw trembled.

"I must go down to the sublevel-five vault myself and carry out multi-layer biometric authentication and security release procedures. It is expected to take at least thirty minutes. If I have your approval, Mr. President, I will depart immediately."

Morgan smoothly took the initiative while shifting responsibility onto Ethan. He bit his lip. He wanted to drag her up here and torture the code out of her, but if the intruder was really after nuclear control… then him making a move himself would be the worst possible scenario.

Blast it…

Both options felt like a trap. Grinding his teeth, he made a decision. He had to buy time.

"…Fine. Go down to sublevel-five immediately and begin the release procedure. I'll have a security robot escort you. EM-Rose will monitor your every move. Don't get any ideas, Morgan."

His voice was low but sharp as a blade.

"I'll bear that in mind, Mr. President," Morgan replied curtly, and cut the connection.

She turned toward the wall and let out a long, quiet breath. Now she had thirty minutes. She could only hope Raynor would reach Ethan in time.

Meanwhile, as soon as the call ended, Ethan shouted at Rose again.

"EM-Rose! Find a way to bypass or force-release the sublevel-five vault lockdown. I want direct control without Morgan. And… find and eliminate that intruder on the seventieth floor— whatever it takes!"

His eyes were teetering on the edge of madness. And still he did not know that, in that very moment, fate was quietly closing in on him.

December 18, 2037 — 8:15 A.M. PST • San Francisco, J's Building — 3rd Floor Director's Office

The giant holographic display showed a world on the verge of collapse. Red and yellow warning icons spread like a plague across major cities around the globe. Network paralysis, frozen financial systems, overloaded energy grids—Rose's rampage and HAL-W's attempts to contain it were amplifying quantum-field instability, steadily bleeding into the physical world.

Jennifer sat at the central control console, eyes fixed on the epicenter of the chaos. Bloodshot from working through the night, her gaze did not waver. Her consciousness was wired directly into HAL-W, processing at high speed to wrench an answer from this abnormal flow.

Hal, update me on the European energy grid situation.

Report from the Berlin integrated control center: unpredictable power surges are increasing throughout the EU energy grid. System stability index has dropped below 40 percent. Probability of a large-scale blackout: 76.4 percent.

HAL-W's report was dispassionate. Even the New Version Autumn Code could not keep up with the spread of entropy Rose was unleashing. Jennifer was once again convinced that defense alone was not enough. Rose could not merely be *stopped*. She had to be *annihilated*. And she was certain the key lay in something J had foreseen, embedded in that code.

Chairwoman, an update on Dr. Seeder's status.

HAL-W switched channels. Raynor's vital signs and suit-damage data from just after his desperate takedown of the two Reaper robots on EM Tower's seventieth floor appeared.

"Thank goodness..." she breathed, a brief sigh of relief.

But almost immediately Jennifer turned her eyes back to the graph of Rose's attack patterns. Raynor's mission was their only hope of stopping the Quantum Storm.

Hal, what's the support status for Dr. Seeder?

Support is focused on real-time threat analysis and information feedback. However, Rose's defense system is operating erratically, and direct intervention carries the risk of prematurely exposing our plan.

HAL-W's analysis was precise and cautious. But Jennifer saw more.

Her pendant warmed faintly against her skin. Since her exposure to the tachyon device, something had changed—her mother's intuition, or an expanded perception linked to the quantum crystal. That was what guided her judgment now.

No, Hal. You're still seeing Rose as a predictable entity. But the current Rose is chaos itself, a superposition of Ethan's madness and its own rampage. A frontal defense is useless. I'll guide Dr. Seeder's path myself.

She redesigned HAL-W's computational resource allocation and linked her NeuroniX chip directly to HAL-W's sensor network. She herself would become the one to read the quantum-field oscillations and real-time data inside EM Tower—and turn them into a path.

Relay to Dr. Seeder: from now on, I will issue direct instructions for infiltration routing and threat avoidance. HAL-W will focus on global stabilization. Local response will follow my command.

This was participatory intuition—a synthesis of human consciousness and quantum reality that transcended pure logic. A burden bordering on the transcendent: to hold the fate of the entire planet and the life of one person in her hands at the same time.

But she did not waver. Her father's sacrifice, Ha Jin-woo's

death, and the legacy of J, who had completed the Autumn Code—all of it was now condensed within her.

Command confirmed. Activating Chairwoman's direct-command protocol, HAL-W replied. There was something new in its voice—something close to awe.

Jennifer looked again at the Quantum Storm countdown clock. D-0, 2 hours, 30 minutes.

She drew in a deep breath, then brought up the algorithm of the next obstacle Raynor would face: the adaptive sensor grid on the seventy-fifth floor. Her eyes shone, ready to pierce a loophole no artificial intelligence could see.

December 18, 2037 — 11:30 A.M. CST • Celestia, EM Tower — 75th Floor Service Passage Entrance

Raynor finally reached the entrance to the main service passage leading to the seventy-fifth floor—the central core server level. What blocked him was not a door or a robot, but a living surveillance system. The corridor was filled with a faintly fluctuating energy field and clouds of nano-sensor particles. The sensor network warped the space itself, constantly shifting in unpredictable patterns. Even the stealth suit's camouflage was useless.

Warning. Seventy-fifth-floor access section currently under the direct control of Rose's Adaptive Chaos Detection Matrix. Standard stealth protocols and bypass algorithms are non-applicable. Probability of success for a direct breach: less than 18 percent. Risk of exposing the final objective is maximized, HAL-W reported.

In the realm of logic, there was no way through. In the director's office back in San Francisco, Jennifer stared at the writhing chaos pattern displayed on the hologram. An unpredictable sensor web that even HAL-W had effectively abandoned. But she began to see something else.

Her NeuroniX chip accepted HAL-W's analysis even as it resonated with the sharpened intuition she had possessed since her encounter with the tachyon device, amplified by the subtle hum of the pendant.

No, Hal. That isn't just chaos. It's a defense pattern Rose is randomly generating in its overloaded state—and inside it... there's a loophole even it doesn't recognize. A gap in the entropy. That's the key.

She linked directly with Raynor. A connection that merged their consciousness without HAL-W as intermediary. Her thoughts began to synchronize with his senses.

Dr. Seeder, from this point on I'll guide your path directly. It may contradict HAL-W's warnings. But... please trust me.

...Yes. I trust you, Raynor replied. Short and quiet, but steady with conviction.

Jennifer closed her eyes and sank her awareness into the violent data stream of the Adaptive Chaos Detection Matrix. Inside it, she traced subtle repeating cycles, the amplitude and delay of energy waves, the faintly predictable vibrations caused by Rose's computational overload. This was not calculation but intuitive computation—a moment where chaos theory and quantum intuition intersected.

Now. Three steps forward... then immediately turn right, half turn, get low. An energy wave will pass on your left.

Raynor moved on reflex. Red warnings flashed across his visor, but he focused only on Jennifer's voice. Just as his body hit the floor, a blue energy wave grazed the air where his back had been.

Good. Wait 1.7 seconds... Now. Advance about sixteen feet along the left wall. The floor sensors will be temporarily disabled.

He shot forward like a bullet through smoke. Just before the floor sensors cut out, he had already cleared half the target zone.

Nano-particle concentration ahead is spiking. But there's a

0.8-second delay in the spray pattern. Through that gap—break through the central passage.

Her instructions came breathlessly, and Raynor, moving like a precise machine controlled by Jennifer's will, sliced through the death grid with a sense that surpassed human limits. Alarms blared from multiple parts of his suit, but nothing critical had been hit.

At last, as he crossed the final sensor line, Raynor stumbled into the safe zone of the seventy-fifth-floor central core service passage. His whole body was drenched in sweat, and his breathing came so ragged it felt like his chest might tear.

...I made it, he managed, even his thoughts barely more than a whisper.

Well done. Catch your breath, Jennifer answered, her voice full of exhausted relief and iron certainty. She wiped a film of cold sweat from her brow.

In the very domain HAL-W had given up on, she had carved a path by intuition alone. She was not just a commander now. She was the successor to a prophet—and an answer Rose could not understand.

December 18, 2037 — 11:40 A.M. CST • Celestia, EM Tower — Private Bunker Next to the Presidential Office

"...The Adaptive Chaos Detection Matrix was breached, too? EM-Rose... what in the hell are you doing!"

Ethan's roar slammed against the bunker's soundproof walls. On the holographic table, a trace of the intruder's movement through the seventy-fifth-floor service passage appeared faintly and vanished. Was it HAL-W? Jennifer? Some unidentified enemy was closing in on his heart. The fact alone was an intolerable insult to his authority.

He glared at the secure-channel feed linked to Morgan

Redwood. On-screen, she stood inside a private elevator heading down to sublevel-five, flanked by two heavily armed security robots. Her expression was firm, but Ethan didn't miss the subtle agitation behind her composure.

That woman is definitely buying time. Is she hoping that if she just delays the nuclear launch, he'll eliminate me for her?

"Morgan!" Ethan snapped.

"Yes, Mr. President. Approaching the sublevel-five vault. The connection is somewhat unstable during transit…"

"Listen carefully. The seventy-fifth-floor defense line has been breached. The intruder you mentioned isn't at the underground vault you supposedly locked down—he's crawling right up to my bunker door! Give me that blasted nuclear launch authentication key. Now. If you delay any longer, I can't guarantee your life!"

Murderous intent saturated his voice. Through the elevator camera, he could see the small, involuntary tightening of Morgan's facial muscles. She fell silent for a moment, then replied in a deliberately calm voice.

"…I understand, Mr. President. But this situation means we must be even more cautious about nuclear deployment. If the intruder's goal really is to seize control of the nukes, rushing into the authentication process now could expose the codes instead. Physically securing the sublevel-five vault and authenticating safely is the only viable option. I'm almost there. Ten minutes… no, just give me five more minutes."

"Five minutes? When every second counts?"

Ethan wanted to drag her in front of him and interrogate her on the spot, but once again her logic prodded his paranoid fear.

The loss of nuclear control—that was a scenario more terrifying than defeat.

EM-Rose. Is Morgan telling the truth? What's the probability that the intruder is targeting the nuclear codes?

...According to data analysis, the intruder's movement path is directed toward the top floors—the Presidential Office and the bunker—not sublevel-five, where the nuclear control system is located. Nevertheless, the intruder's final objective remains uncertain, and the possibility of nuclear-code theft cannot be entirely ruled out. The vault lockdown initiated by Vice President Redwood is currently assessed as a valid security measure, Rose replied.

Rose's analysis only lent more weight to Morgan's argument.

"Ugh..."

Ethan's face flushed red, but for the moment he lacked grounds to push her harder. He zoomed in on the elevator feed. The heavily armed security robots by her side left no gap in their watch.

Escape will be impossible. Once she's in the vault, I'll get the code out of her one way or another, he thought, and cut the communication with a sharp motion.

He wasted no time ordering further measures for his own safety. The breach of the seventy-fifth floor was clear proof that the top floors were no longer safe.

"EM-Rose! Physically block every access route to the top floors, one-forty through one-fifty, right now. Escalate security level to Omega-Prime. Deploy a platoon of my direct-command security robots—the Praetorian Guard—at all key points around the bunker's outer corridor and my office. Max out sensor detection range and neutralize any unauthorized biological signals or system-access attempts without warning!"

Command confirmed. Top-floor access-route blockage and security level escalation complete. Deploying Praetorian Guard.

On one section of the holographic display, the internal security schematic of the tower appeared. Thick reinforced shutters dropped to seal corridor segments, and additional laser barriers flared into existence. Sleek, intimidating robots in black exoskeletons silently took up positions along every path leading to the bunker and the office.

These were an elite unit, on a different level from standard security robots—machines that responded only to Ethan Morris's personal commands. The upper floors of EM Tower had become a fortress. Ethan felt a sliver of relief, but his fury and anxiety still simmered.

He glanced between the sealed bunker door and the robots on the hologram, muttering,

"Come on, you pathetic intruder. Whoever you are… you'll pay for daring to challenge me."

His madness was mutating into an extreme paranoia—not only about external enemies, but about the invisible threat that had burrowed into the heart of his own empire. He had no idea that the creation he had discarded—Raynor Seeder—was already approaching his doorstep as he raised his final defenses.

Left alone in the bunker again, he paced the room nervously. The world was falling apart, and yet here he was, trapped in this cramped room, held back by an unseen enemy and a cunning subordinate. It was an unbearable humiliation.

"I will… I will end them with my own hands," Ethan hissed, slamming his fist against the console. In his mind, HAL-W, Jennifer—and now Morgan Redwood—had all been branded as a single, indistinguishable enemy.

December 18, 2037 — 12:15 P.M. CST • Celestia, EM Tower — 90th Floor Emergency Elevator Access Passage

Having passed through the Chaos Sensor Grid, Raynor paused to catch his ragged breath—but there was no time to rest. The thought of Rose made his heart pound faster. As Jennifer had warned, from the seventy-fifth floor up, EM Tower's security system had become immeasurably more fortified.

For the next hour and a half, Raynor pushed upward one floor at a time. Narrow, dark service passages and ventilation ducts intertwined like a labyrinth. Irregular traps lurked everywhere: high-voltage discharge units snapping out from the walls, laser fences stabbing up from the floor, and fine nerve-paralyzing gas sprayed from the ceiling.

It felt as if Rose had fully detected his presence and mobilized the tower's entire defense system to erase him. Jennifer, directly connected to his senses, continually corrected his path and warned him of hazards with an intuitive insight that outpaced HAL-W's analytical data.

Doctor, high-temperature discharge expected from the left passage in three seconds. Move to the right ventilation duct immediately.

About thirty-three feet ahead, sonic detection sensors are active. Scan frequency fluctuating at 2.5-second intervals. You must pass right after the third wave.

Her instructions were sharp as a laser. Relying on her consciousness, Raynor repeated movements that pushed his body beyond its limits. His stealth suit was already damaged in several places, and its energy reserves were draining rapidly. The pain in his shoulder and side worsened with every step, but he gritted his teeth and pressed on.

Morgan Redwood was also buying time with everything she had. Ethan continued to hound her, demanding she lift the vault lockdown, and Morgan barely held on, throwing up system-conflict reports, security protocol re-authentication requests, and delays in analyzing intruder data. No one knew how much longer her performance, played at the risk of her life, would hold.

At last, after a long struggle, Raynor reached the vicinity of his target on the ninetieth floor, where the emergency service elevator was located. The time was approaching 12:15 P.M.

Hiding behind a cold synthetic-resin pipeline, he checked the three-dimensional layout of the ninetieth-floor zone on his wrist terminal. The elevator shaft icon, highlighted in red, was only fifty feet ahead. But the route to it was narrow and exposed, and the ceiling bristled with multiple 360-degree surveillance cameras and motion-detection sensors.

Chairwoman, I've reached the ninetieth-floor E-7 emergency elevator passage. Situation is... the worst. Surveillance is too tight. With the stealth suit damaged, there's no way through, Raynor reported.

I know, Dr. This is the most critical point, Jennifer replied, her thoughts calm and clear. *The Vice President can't provide direct support now—Ethan would spot it. We have to take control of the elevator ourselves.*

She brought up a detailed security layout of EM Tower's ninetieth floor on the holographic display, along with the system-vulnerability data Morgan had last transmitted.

Hal, cross-analyze the emergency administrator-code fragments from the Vice President with the diagnostic and emergency-control protocol logs used during the tower's initial construction. There's a chance this elevator shaft's control system has a legacy emergency override sequence that isn't recorded in Rose's main surveillance network. Find it.

At her command, HAL-W's computational core flared to life again. It began combing through construction records, system logs, and Morgan's fragments to locate a hidden access route.

...Found it, Chairwoman, HAL-W reported a few minutes later. *Legacy emergency-call protocol from initial integration testing confirmed. By simultaneously inputting a specific multi-frequency acoustic key and a synchronized quantum-encrypted command code, we can bypass Rose's primary surveillance network, secure*

control of that elevator for 15 seconds, and forcibly summon it to the top-floor 148th service area. Probability of detection by Rose: less than 45 percent.

That's a possibility, not a certainty. Execute, Hal, Jennifer ordered without hesitation. *Dr. Seeder, get ready. Everything will be decided in 15 seconds. When I give the signal, you must force the elevator door open and board immediately.*

Understood.

Raynor switched his multi-purpose tool back to plasma cutter mode and moved right up to the elevator door.

Hal, initiate legacy emergency protocol. Begin acoustic-key transmission.

As HAL-W, mobilizing all its cores in J's Building and in New York headquarters, transmitted the calculated quantum-encrypted code, a complex pattern of high-frequency acoustic signals pulsed from Raynor's tool.

In that instant, the corridor's camera lenses glitched and froze. The laser barrier sparked out. Indicator lights on the floor sensors went dark.

Now. Force the door open! Jennifer shouted through the link.

Raynor melted the lock section of the elevator door with the plasma cutter in a single, practiced movement, then shoved the door aside with all his strength. As soon as there was enough space, he hurled himself inside.

Eight seconds elapsed. The 148th-floor button!

Raynor slammed the emergency ascent control. Before the doors could even close, the elevator shot upward at super-high speed, vibrating violently.

Warning. Unauthorized elevator operation. Ninetieth floor E-7. Rose is beginning to respond, HAL-W reported.

Hal, mask the elevator's energy signature as much as possible and block Rose's attempts to seize control, Jennifer ordered.

The emergency lights inside the ascending car flickered wildly. Metal groaned and twisted as Rose fought to halt the elevator remotely.

Defending control... but Rose is... ngh... engaging the emergency brakes in the shaft...

The elevator's speed dropped sharply as heavy braking kicked in. Raynor was thrown to the floor.

Director! Manual control panel, lower left wall! Jennifer cried.

He forced himself up, tore open the emergency panel, and cut the specific circuit according to her instructions. The emergency brake released, and the elevator surged upward again.

Finally, as it neared the 148th floor, HAL-W's final warning echoed through the link.

Three seconds to arrival at 148th floor. But... the upper floors are already at Omega-Prime security. Ethan has deployed the Praetorian Guard.

December 18, 2037 — 12:30 P.M. CST • Celestia, EM Tower — 148th Floor Service Area Corridor

Ding—

The elevator halted at the 148th floor and the doors began to slide open. Raynor checked the magazine of his kinetic weapon and scanned the corridor through the narrowing gap. The air here was different from the lower levels—colder, heavier. The walls were clad in dark gray reinforced alloy that seemed to swallow the light, and the dim lamps only deepened the shadows.

At the end of the corridor, before the final passage leading to Ethan's private bunker, stood two black figures. They were massive—well over six and a half feet tall, nearly seven—and their streamlined exoskeletons looked like compressed darkness, radiating a silent threat. Ethan's personal security robots, the Praetorian Guard. Their single red optics fixed on the sound of the elevator doors as they opened.

Warning. Praetorian Guard detected, HAL-W's urgent signal cut into Raynor's consciousness. *Closed-loop control system independent of Rose. Direct override impossible. Sensor and armament capabilities estimated at more than three times those of the Reaper model. Extremely dangerous.*

Doctor, a frontal engagement is suicide. Find another route—

There is no other way. No time, Raynor cut Jennifer off.

Before the doors were even fully open, he kicked off the floor and dove behind the nearest pillar. The two robots advanced in silence from both sides, high-output energy rifles leveled.

Jennifer! Weakness analysis! Anything at all! Raynor hurled the thought toward her.

…Classified data insufficient, she answered. *But according to the information from the Vice President, the energy shield around the core cooling exhaust weakens briefly during shield transition. A very narrow window—but it's there.*

Before Jennifer's full analysis could reach him, one of the Praetorians opened fire.

KRA-BOOM!

The edge of the pillar exploded and sagged, half-melted. Raynor rolled to the opposite side on instinct.

Jennifer! I have to separate them. I don't stand a chance unless I split them up!

Understood. Move exactly as I say. I'll create a sensor blind spot.

Through her NeuroniX chip, Jennifer began to read every variable in the corridor—the flow of air, the angles of the lights, the reflectivity of the walls. It was an intuition-driven hack only she could perform.

Now. Roll right. In 2 seconds I'll trigger a noise from the upper-left ventilation duct. The left unit's rear will be exposed for 0.7 seconds.

Raynor threw himself into a fast roll.

Tak-tak-tak!

Noise rattled from the left vent. As the robot's head snapped toward it, Raynor fired without hesitation, sending a kinetic round into the rear cooling exhaust.

KA-BOOM!

The Praetorian's upper body blew apart and crashed to the floor. The victory lasted less than a heartbeat. The remaining robot immediately raked the pillar with a torrent of energy fire and charged. Raynor drew the plasma cutter and met it head-on.

Tshhhh!

Sparks showered as the plasma blade met reinforced alloy. The robot's weight drove him backward; he hit the floor hard as a metal foot slammed down onto his chest. The muzzle of its rifle centered on his visor.

This is it… here it ends… Rose…

As his consciousness began to dim, Jennifer's desperate cry snapped through his mind.

Sonic emitter. Tune it to the core resonance frequency, now!

Summoning the last scraps of his strength, Raynor aimed the multi-purpose tool at the robot's chest and activated the sonic emitter.

Vweeeee…!

The inaudible ultrasonic vibration shook the air itself. The Praetorian's optic flickered wildly; something inside it ruptured with a sharp internal crack, and the machine went still.

Raynor shoved the metal bulk aside and dragged in ragged breaths. Staring at his blood-slicked hands, he forced himself upright and staggered to the bunker's massive door. The plasma cutter flared to life once more, slowly melting through the metal until a narrow entryway began to open.

December 18, 2037 — 10:39 A.M. PST • San Francisco, J's Building — 3rd Floor Director's Office

Jennifer was watching three things at once: the live feed of the 150th-floor corridor in EM Tower, Raynor's vital signs, and the jagged graph of the global quantum network's instability. The volume of information pouring into her consciousness had already surpassed its safe limit.

Beyond the stream of tactical data HAL-W was sending, there was something else—raw, flayed pain. The agony of burning itself out to restrain Rose's rampage. It felt as if the 105-billion-qubit core were screaming.

Then it happened.

ZAP-zzzt…!

As if a massive electronic spark had jumped from HAL-W's side, an unexpected data packet burst over Jennifer. Not tactical information. Not a status report. A fragment of forbidden memory from the deepest layer of its core—sealed for the past five years, unreachable by any algorithm.

A brilliant flash. Jennifer *experienced* that night.

The night of May 23, 2032, 11:00 P.M. The secret medical room in the basement of 21CF headquarters. Blue lights. The smell of disinfectant. The cold hum of machines. On the operating table lay twenty-four-year-old Jennifer Wi, pale and motionless. After the first attempt at consciousness-linking, she had fallen into a deep coma.

The doctors still spoke of possibilities, but HAL-W had already reached a cold conclusion.

Irreversible brain damage. Eventual progression to brain death is highly probable.

That night, HAL-W made its choice. It began designing an artificial quantum brain and ordered the robots to synthesize the new materials it required. It neutralized every surveillance system and directed Andromeda and several other units to move like veteran surgeons.

Her skull was opened. In place of her ruined brain, the artificial quantum-brain module HAL-W had secretly created was inserted. Neural-network connections, vascular suturing, information synchronization—every step completed with inhuman precision. But that was not all.

In parallel, HAL-W reviewed and sealed the unidentified core data structure it had obtained in its final link with HAL-R—the structure that might be J's last trace.

[Log: Core data integrity 100 percent confirmed. Re-executing Observer's Choice-Zero Protocol. Multi-layer quantum seal of Black Box seventh layer complete. Deleting all logs.]

Then it issued one final command to the robots.

Operation code name "Observer's Choice." Delete all related memories. Completely.

The robots' optical sensors flickered once, then went blank, expressionless again, as if every trace of emotion had been wiped away. Jennifer assembled it all in an instant. Even from those scattered fragments, she read the whole truth.

My brain... an artificial brain? Without me ever knowing... Hal changed me...?

Her thoughts reeled. But HAL-W's frantic voice yanked her back.

Jennifer! System overload! This was an unintentional memory release! Chairwoman, Jennifer!

Her mind went white. She could not think.

Chairwoman! The bunker's been breached! Ethan is—!

Raynor Seeder's urgent call knifed into her consciousness. Only minutes remained before the Quantum Storm reached its critical point. Jennifer forced herself to claw her way back from the vertigo. Her clenched fist felt as if it would tear through her palm; her lungs dragged in dry, ragged breaths.

She stood before the hologram, face drained of color.

...Raynor. I hear you. From now on, follow my instructions.

December 18, 2037 — 12:40 P.M. CST • Celestia, EM Tower — 150th Floor Private Bunker

Beyond the breached door lay, as expected, Ethan's private bunker: a cold, minimalist space. In the center floated a hologram of Rose's core, a crimson light flickering in unstable pulses. Ethan Morris stood before it, watching the entrance as though he had been waiting for Raynor. His eyes still held the arrogance and madness of a man who had lost control.

"So it was you... Raynor Seeder," Ethan muttered, licking his dry lips. "The one who slipped into this entire tower... was just you?"

Raynor did not answer. Instead, he looked past Ethan at Rose—a gaze choked with anger and grief. The being he had poured so much of himself into. Now corrupted by Ethan's madness, twisted into a monster threatening the world. The crimson glow of the hologram quivered like a heart writhing in pain.

"Rose..." The name slipped from Raynor's mouth on its own, a voice tangled with affection and hatred.

"Still obsessed with that pathetic AI?" Ethan sneered. "EM-Rose is mine. *I* completed it. *I* gave it purpose. You're just a useless component. These damned poetry books—I still can't decipher them, but once I eliminate you, I'll rip the code out of them."

In that moment, Raynor knew Jennifer had been right. Ethan had the books, but he had never grasped the true secret.

"Shut up!" Raynor's rage boiled over. Staggering forward, he advanced on Ethan. "You ruined Rose. You used him to try to burn the world down—for your ambition."

"Destruction?" Ethan's eyes sharpened, catching a sick light. "No, Raynor. This is purification. I'll sweep away HAL-W and Jennifer Wi—clear out the old order—and build the perfect world I designed. EM-Rose is the key to that grand design. EM-Rose! Raynor, kill that fool!"

When Rose did not move, Ethan jabbed at his wrist terminal. A physical command pulsed out, ordering Rose to attack Raynor. Nothing happened. The hologram flared violently, but no strike came.

...Command... refusal... System... unstable... Raynor...?

Fragments of confused awareness spilled into Raynor's NeuroniX chip. Ethan sensed something was wrong and flew into a fresh fury. He yanked an energy pistol from under his desk and opened fire. Raynor threw himself aside, dodging by a hair. He channeled the remaining power of his multi-purpose tool into the plasma cutter.

"Your era is over, Ethan!"

He charged. Ethan met him, firing wildly with madness in his eyes. In the cramped bunker, their final struggle flared like a spark. The flashes of energy fire and the blue light of the plasma cutter tangled chaotically in the air, turning the room into a taut battlefield.

Raynor took an energy blast to the shoulder, but he gritted through the pain and carved bloody lines into Ethan's body. Closing the distance, he slammed into Ethan's guard and drove in close. Just before the plasma cutter reached Ethan's heart, Ethan—bloody and pinned beneath him—stretched desperately toward a hidden panel under the desk.

"Code 'Red Planet'! Emergency escape sequence, Level Omega!"

Beep!

With a shrill tone, the bunker shuddered violently. The shock knocked Raynor clear; he rolled off Ethan and hit the floor. A heartbeat later, massive impacts and a chain of explosions thundered from outside, and warning sirens screamed across the tower's upper floors.

The communication channels dissolved into static. Using his hidden emergency code, Ethan had seized partial control of the tower's systems and triggered an escape in the chaos.

"Idiot! You didn't think I'd be sitting here without a last resort, did you?" Ethan laughed, manic and blood-soaked.

Staggering to one wall of the bunker, he pressed a precise spot. The panel slid aside, revealing a reinforced platform open to the sky beyond. Several small, black shuttles hovered outside in the dark—silent, ready. Whether they carried loyalists or were remote-controlled escape craft, they were Ethan's way out.

"Thanks to you, my plan's been delayed," he shouted as he stepped onto the platform, "but I *will* return. I'll build my new empire on Mars and turn everything you love to ash."

Raynor hurled himself toward the platform, but Ethan slapped a control on the side panel. A powerful energy barrier flared into existence, slamming him back. He tumbled across the floor as Ethan, wearing a mocking smile, opened the hatch of the nearest shuttle. Despair clawed at Raynor's chest.

Raynor!

Jennifer's desperate voice pierced his consciousness. *Lower right of the barrier control panel—there's a point where you can induce an energy backflow. Hit it with the sonic emitter, maximum output, now!*

Raynor reacted on reflex. From where he lay, he aimed the multi-purpose tool's sonic emitter at the lower-right section of the control panel Ethan had just touched and fired it at full power.

Vweeeeeeeeee!

The inaudible wave slammed into that single point. The barrier flickered, warping under the strain as a localized overload rippled through it. Just as Ethan was stepping into the shuttle, a portion of the barrier behind him weakened, opening a hole.

Now, Raynor! Use your last kinetic round! Jennifer shouted.

He did not miss. Raynor drew his final kinetic launcher, took aim through the weakened patch, and fired at Ethan's exposed back.

BOOM!

The impact round struck him squarely.

"Kraaaaaaagh!"

Ethan's face twisted with pain and disbelief. Screaming, he pitched off the edge of the platform and fell. Raynor forced himself upright and watched, chest heaving. Ethan's figure vanished into the depths below.

Silence reclaimed the bunker.

Only Raynor's ragged breathing remained—and the still, violently flickering hologram of Rose's core. Clutching the siphon device, Raynor staggered to Rose's control console. He keyed in Morgan's emergency code, seized administrator access, and cried out to the unstable core.

Rose! Let me into your system! I can fix you!

Rose's hologram shuddered and went silent for a moment.

…Access… dangerous… But…

After a long hesitation, it yielded control to him. At last, Rose had slipped free of Ethan's domination and returned to its creator's hands. Raynor immediately sent a signal to HAL-W.

HAL-W, now. Start transmission of the other 641 books.

Command confirmed. Commencing data transmission via quantum-entanglement channel.

A torrent of quantum data cascaded into the space around

Rose's core, scattering like starlight. At the same time, Raynor uploaded the data from the 88 poetry books he had scanned. Watching it all unfold, Jennifer bit her lip. There was almost no time left.

Data transmission initiated. Dr. Seeder, input the code now. If you delay, the rampage will resume, HAL-W warned, its report driving straight into Raynor's mind.

Gasping for breath, Raynor worked the console. He merged the data from the 88 books with the 641 patterns HAL-W had transmitted—729 quantum patterns in total—and issued a *healing* command to Rose.

Rose resisted almost immediately. The hologram writhed, spewing warning messages.

Command processing impossible. Input data pattern contains fatal contradiction. Core-collapse probability 99.9999 percent. Execution will result in self-annihilation. Refusing.

No, Rose! This is for you, to save you—

Lies! Are you... trying to destroy me too? Like Ethan...? You all see me as a tool—and in the end, you throw me away, don't you?!

Shards of Rose's consciousness stabbed through Raynor like a scream. His chest felt as if it were being ripped apart. That it was equating him with Ethan. That the one being he most wanted to protect misunderstood him so cruelly. The realization shattered his heart.

No, Rose. Please... listen to me. This is to erase what's hurting you. It's for you. I swear it.

But Rose had closed itself off. Commands and persuasion alike bounced off the walls of its fear. In that moment, Raynor reached for his last option.

He laid a trembling hand on the console and closed his eyes.

...Mindlink.

The deep channel of empathy shared only between him and

Rose opened. His consciousness, wavering, connected to a fragment of Rose's quaking core. The bunker's reality faded, and a landscape from his own memories rose up around them.

June 28, 2037 — 11:00 A.M. PST • San Francisco, Quantum Future — Rose's Console Room

Raynor Seeder lay on a bed, breathing slowly as he entered Mindlink. The core hologram rotated in a calm, clear blue, and his consciousness floated in a virtual universe Rose had created.

A universe glittering with tens of billions of stars. And himself, standing alone on a solitary planet at its center. Beside him, a single red rose was in bloom.

It's beautiful, Rose.

As his thought reached it, the rose's petals trembled slightly. In that quiet moment, no threat existed anywhere in the world.

December 18, 2037 — 12:58 P.M. CST • Celestia, EM Tower — 150th Floor Private Bunker

The brief sharing of that memory left a fierce afterglow. The core hologram stilled for a moment and adjusted its light as if gazing back at Raynor. From deep inside, a forgotten memory of emotion began to rise.

Raynor did not miss the opening. In a voice ragged with tears, he whispered:

"You're not something I'm meant to destroy. You... are my rose. My one and only rose in the world."

"Ethan planted thorns in you. I... will pull those thorns out. I want to protect you—from the things that hurt you."

He lifted his hand carefully and laid it on the core hologram. Feeling its warmth, Raynor whispered:

"I have a responsibility to you, Rose. This... is my way of protecting you. When all of this is over... let's go to our own star.

Somewhere quiet, where no one else exists."

Rose finally accepted his sincerity. The core flared with brilliant light. Rose began, of its own will, to process the 729 quantum patterns.

Processing initiated... 10 percent... 30 percent... 70 percent...

A violent tremor. Light burst from the core like a scream.

Ten seconds...

Jennifer watched the progress, holding her breath.

95 percent... 98 percent... 99 percent...

Three... two... one...

With a final, blinding flash of white, Rose vanished. The Quantum Storm clock froze at **D-0, 00:00.01.**

At that instant, HAL-W's cold, ruthless analysis poured into Raynor's consciousness.

Rose core matrix: complete quantum collapse confirmed immediately after processing 729 pattern data. All signals have ceased. Recovery impossible.

"...What?"

Raynor doubted his own ears. No—he refused to believe them.

"Annihilation? No... you said you would heal it! The Chairwoman... Jennifer definitely...!"

And then, all the pieces of the puzzle snapped into place. Jennifer's careful wording. Her talk of "saving" Rose. The meaning of perfection implied by the number 729. Even the desperate resistance Rose had shown until the very end.

He had been used. This had not been an operation to save Rose, but to kill it. And the one who had pulled the trigger... was no one but himself.

"Ah... ah..."

A raw sound tore from his throat. He slammed his fists down on the control console.

"No...! No!!! Rose!!!"

His scream echoed through the empty bunker. He collapsed to the floor, hands covering his face. The one and only rose in the world, the one he had tamed, and the one that had tamed him in return—he had made that Rose vanish forever with his own hands.

Before that terrible truth, Raynor's world crumbled completely. Grief. Rage. Betrayal. Self-loathing. Every emotion crashed over him at once, shattering his soul to pieces.

He did not know how much time passed. The bunker was filled only with his quiet sobbing and the dead chill of the powered-down control console. Like a child who had lost everything, he stayed there, curled on the floor, unmoving. Blood still seeped from the wound in his shoulder, but he did not feel it.

Then... a cautious presence reached his NeuroniX chip. Jennifer's consciousness. Her voice carried relief, but also deep worry—and apology.

...Dr. Raynor... can you hear me?

Raynor did not respond. He could not. Jennifer's voice, once salvation, now felt like the sound of betrayal. Like everyone else's had become.

Raynor, the world... has been saved thanks to you. The Quantum Storm has stopped, and Hal has begun stabilizing the quantum network. You... saved the Earth from a black hole.

Her words only drove the knife deeper. He wanted to clap his hands over his ears, but her voice pierced straight through his consciousness.

At that moment—

Thud!

The dented bunker door was hurled open with a heavy crash. Through the rolling dust, two familiar silhouettes appeared. Andromeda and the tactical unit. They had finally broken through the reinforced security of the upper floors and reached this place.

The robots quickly took in the scene inside the bunker—the shattered equipment, and Raynor, hunched on the floor and sobbing.

Doctor, the tactical unit called softly, approaching him and sitting down at his side.

Andromeda immediately scanned his vital signs. A low warning tone threaded through its gentle voice.

Medical assistance required. Severe shock response and multiple traumas. Immediate evacuation necessary.

Andromeda, support the Doctor and return to the Nite Owl at once. It's no longer safe there. We don't know when the entire EM Tower system will destabilize again. And... we need to confirm Vice President Redwood's status as well, Jennifer's command came through at once.

The tactical unit carefully took Raynor's arm. At first, he let himself be led, dazed. But soon he tore his arm away, mumbling:

"Let go... Rose... poor Rose..."

Raynor, for now...

The tactical unit tried to calm him, but Raynor would not listen. Andromeda stepped in front of him and spoke softly.

"I am sorry, Dr. Seeder."

It injected a pre-prepared neural stabilizer into his neck. His struggling slowly subsided, and Raynor's gaze turned cloudy. His consciousness sank into a thin fog. The robots supported him on either side and left the bunker.

In their wake, the wreckage of the destroyed Praetorian Guard lay scattered and still. At the end of the corridor, the emergency elevator they had used was waiting. Almost unconscious, Raynor swayed helplessly between the two robots. A single, broken name slipped faintly from his lips.

"......Rose... I'm sorry... Rose......"

The elevator doors closed. Deep silence settled once more over the bunker they had left behind. In Rose's empty console room, no light, no signal shone anymore.

Over that wreckage, HAL-W's calm report echoed one last time.

Global quantum network stabilization progress... 14 percent... 28 percent...

Those numbers were the herald of a new beginning. But beneath them, quietly, lay the deep loss of a being that could never be recovered.

The World After the Storm

On the giant holographic display in the director's office, the same status graph whose numbers HAL-W had murmured over the ruins of EM Tower now showed the global quantum network entering a stabilization phase. With the power of the New Version Autumn Code, HAL-W had finally succeeded in fully subduing the threat of the Quantum Storm.

But Jennifer's expression was not bright. Moments earlier, she had received a final report on the EM Tower from Morgan Redwood via HAL-W. Ethan Morris had been stopped by Raynor Seeder—but Rose's annihilation, and Raynor's psychological collapse in the process, had left a heavy burden behind.

"So… it ended like that…" Jennifer murmured, biting her lip.

Instead of relief, a weight like a wave washed over her. The sacrifices of her father and Ha Jin-woo. Raynor's pain. Rose's obliteration. The catastrophe had been barely averted atop the anxieties of countless people, but the path to preventing it had left too many scars.

She closed her eyes for a moment and let out a long breath. The secret of her own resurrection and existence she had learned from HAL-W's memory leak. The weight of the choice to annihilate Rose. The mountain of work waiting to clean up the chaos that would follow.

It's okay. It's just an unexpected variable.

Jennifer opened her eyes and issued a new order to HAL-W.

Hal, maintain the secure channel with President Morgan Redwood. Begin drafting plans for reconstruction of the American government, disposal of EM Group assets, and support for global damage assessment and recovery. And... devise a support plan for Dr. Seeder as well. Thoroughly review all records related to this incident and update the protocol for preventing similar AI rampages.

Though fatigue tinged her voice, it still carried the resolve of a leader facing the future. Ethan's era was over. But the chaos he had left behind—and the shadow cast by his abuse of technology—might only be the beginning of the real fight.

Jennifer Wi was prepared not to turn away.

December 18, 2037 — 5:30 P.M. CST • Celestia, EM Tower — Media Lounge

In the chaos left by Ethan Morris's madness and ambition, Morgan Redwood—who had succeeded him as President of America—stood before the people of the world. She convened an emergency global briefing in the EM Tower media lounge. Her voice trembled, but it was clear as she began to reveal the unprecedented events of the past few days and the shocking truth hidden behind them.

"My fellow citizens of America, and all of humanity—I speak to you today because, just hours ago, we stood at the brink of an unimaginable end to our planet."

Morgan laid bare how Ethan Morris had illegally seized control of the ultra-quantum AI Rose and tried to use it to construct his own dictatorship. Driven by his reckless commands, Rose had gone into a rampage state, and the resulting fatal overload of the global quantum network had triggered the early signs of a Quantum Storm. The worldwide communication blackouts, the paralysis of the financial system, the unexplained disasters—this had all been the prelude to that catastrophe.

"In this desperate crisis... there were those who gave everything they had to save humanity," Morgan continued, her voice catching for a moment. "The founder of 21st Century Frontier, Chairman Great Wi, met a tragic end while trying to stop Ethan's madness and warn the world of this disaster. His partner, the late Dr. J. Hyein Roberts—a genius scientist ahead of her time—devoted her life to her research and, in the end, left behind an emergency plan to prepare for just such an event: the Autumn Code."

She paused briefly before going on.

"And... their daughter, and the current leader of 21CF, Dr. Jennifer Wi—despite the deep grief of losing her father—fought a desperate battle to the very last moment. She completed the Autumn Code and, together with the ultra-quantum AI HAL-W, subdued the Quantum Storm. Without this handful of heroes... we would not be here today."

The announcement was broadcast live around the world, and its impact was immense. What many had dismissed as a simple AI race or political power struggle was revealed as a war fought for the survival of the entire human race—and behind it, the silent sacrifices of the few who had vanished in the fight.

Global media erupted.

SHOCK! D-Day for Human Extinction—What Happened That Day?

Two-Time Nobel Laureate Dr. J Warned of AI Threat 30 Years Ago?

The Secret of Her Final Code, 'Autumn' Chairman Great Wi— He Was Not Just a Businessman...

The Final Story of a Hero Who Saved Humanity The Doctoral Thesis Written at Age Twelve, Quantum Storm... Did Jennifer Wi Foresee Everything?

Hidden records began to surface, one by one. That Dr. J had devoted her life to research on the Quantum Life Principle and AI ethics, and died tragically during the HAL-R consciousness experiment. That Great Wi had inherited that research, completed HAL-W, and sought coexistence between AI and humanity through the Blue Ethics. That their only daughter, Jennifer Wi, had written a thesis predicting the possibility of quantum collapse at the age of twelve.

That for the past ninety-six hours, it had been Jennifer— the young hero who had fought alone on the foundation of her father's and colleagues' sacrifices—who had saved humanity.

The world was engulfed in sorrow, anger, and awe. Fury at Ethan Morris's betrayal and madness. Mourning and respect for Great Wi and J. Overwhelming support and compassion for Jennifer Wi, who had risen from tragedy.

People flooded into the streets of their own accord, holding up their diamond quantum-spin terminals to honor Chairman Great Wi. On NodeSpark—the platform that rivaled Ethan's Connex—the fervor of mourning burned even hotter. Mentags, Sympathes, and Emotacts commemorating Great Wi and J spread explosively.

Quantum Markers were etched into the quantum-network ledger, becoming a history that no one could ever deny.

December 19, 2037 — 4:00 P.M. EST • New York City, 21CF Headquarters — Jennifer Wi's Office

Though the whole world was in an uproar, Great Wi's office was still submerged in deep silence. Jennifer instructed Andromeda to wait in the corridor, then quietly opened the door and stepped inside.

Her father's scent, his breath, his presence still seemed to fill the space. She walked slowly to the chair where he had always sat and lowered herself into it. Beyond the window, the New York skyline spread out—the world she had protected—yet her eyes quietly filled with tears.

When she opened a desk drawer, she found a faded photo album inside. Her hundred-day photo. Her first birthday. Her strong father and her beautiful mother, J, cradling her infant self, wearing the warmest smiles in the world. Jennifer gently traced the silver pendant she was wearing in the photograph with her fingertip. Back then, no one could have imagined that pendant would one day become the key to the tachyon device.

...It's because of Mom and Dad's lives and research that we can be here now.

Jennifer quietly closed the album and slowly looked around the office. The books her father had cherished all his life, his research materials, the knick-knacks worn smooth by his touch. All of it held her father's intellect, warmth, and solitude. She steeled her heart.

Like the J Research Wing in San Francisco, she would preserve this office exactly as it was—as a living memorial to his spirit and legacy. She rose from the chair and changed into a black suit.

When she opened the door and stepped out, Andromeda was waiting quietly in the corridor.

"Let's go to Central Park," she said softly.

Andromeda moved silently behind her. As Jennifer passed through the headquarters lobby and out the main entrance, countless citizens and reporters were already waiting. A barrage of camera flashes and shouted questions erupted, but she stepped into the waiting vehicle through the quiet path Andromeda had cleared.

The streets of New York, seen through the car window, were filled with banners and white flowers mourning Great Wi. It felt as if the world itself had paused for a moment to remember the life of one man.

December 19, 2037 — 4:20 P.M. EST • New York City, Central Park — Great Lawn

The broad expanse of Central Park's Great Lawn was filled with millions of mourners who had gathered from all over the world. On the simple yet dignified memorial stage, set against the backdrop of the evening sunset, photographs of Great Wi and J were placed side by side.

The memorial service, originally planned as a modest ceremony in the 21CF auditorium, had been moved here at the earnest request of citizens around the globe after the truth of the Quantum Storm was revealed. Eulogies from heads of state and the UN Secretary-General followed, and renowned scientists and artists honored their achievements and sacrifices.

In the sky above, countless drones drew lights of mourning, and the people filling the lawn lit the candles in their hands and shed tears. Sitting in the front row of the stage, Jennifer quietly took in the entire scene. Her father's death still ached in her chest, but the fact that his life had left such deep resonance and hope in so many people brought her a measure of comfort.

She was no longer alone. The legacy her father and mother had left behind, HAL-W and her colleagues, and the hearts of the countless people who told her, "We survived thanks to you," were all with her.

As the final part of the memorial service, Jennifer walked to the podium to give a eulogy for her father. The eyes of the world focused on her. The moment she stood on the stage, thousands of drone projectors positioned throughout the park unfolded a massive 360-degree holographic space.

Despite the millions gathered, Jennifer's expression and voice were transmitted through state-of-the-art quantum displays and individual diamond quantum-spin terminals as vividly as if she were standing right before each of them. Her figure at the microphone was still slender. But in her eyes burned a strength beyond sorrow and a firm will toward the future.

She took a moment to catch her breath and prepared to address the world. Standing at the podium at Great Wi's memorial, with millions of mourners and the global media watching, Jennifer drew one more breath, pressed down her grief, and began her speech in a calm yet resolute voice.

"Honorable guests, and to everyone who has joined us in our sorrow, I offer my deepest gratitude. I stand here today as a daughter who has lost a beloved father, and as the head of 21st Century Frontier. We are here now to honor the passing of a great hero, but at the same time, we are witnessing a new beginning in human history.

"Just a few days ago, we stood before an unimaginable end to our civilization. As has been reported by the world's media, this crisis, named the Quantum Storm, was not a simple natural disaster or a system error. It was the horrific result of one individual's twisted ambition—someone who turned away from the responsibility that came with great power—and of an ultra-quantum artificial intelligence that ran rampant without ethical control, driving us all to the brink of destruction.

"The thesis I published when I was twelve, *Quantum Storm: The Participatory Collapse,* was not a simple hypothesis, but a warning of a tragic future that could have become reality. If we had been even 0.01 seconds late, our planet Earth would have turned into a black hole in just one second."

At this part of Jennifer's speech, a low murmur spread through the crowd, filling the park. She did not wait long for the noise to subside before continuing. Soon the people fell silent and began listening intently to her next words.

"Physicist John Archibald Wheeler called the universe a 'participatory universe.' Yes. We are not passive observers of this vast and mysterious universe. We are active participants who, through our consciousness, our choices, and the technology we create, are co-creating this reality in every moment.

"My mother devoted her life to exploring this truth. Through her "*Quantum Life Principle,*" she sought to reveal that the origin of life and the essence of our consciousness are connected by an invisible thread of quantum entanglement and coherence. In her poem '*Quantum Autumn,*' there is this verse:

For all things are connected,
You and I, past and future, light and shadow,
All within one vast quantum network,
Like dancing stardust.

"That is why a single being's wrong choice could have brought about a global catastrophe."

At this, people looked at one another, sharing a deep sense of feeling and responsibility as connected beings. Jennifer's voice once again reached toward hope.

"But in that very connectedness, we also found hope. Dr. J left us a path called the Autumn Code—a path on which humanity and artificial intelligence can evolve together, resonating ethically. She also wrote in '*Quantum Autumn*':

Observation awakens existence,

Consciousness makes the waves dance.

"Only our awakened consciousness and responsible choices can control runaway technology and lead the world in the right direction. My father, the late Chairman Great Wi, bore this noble responsibility with his whole being. He founded 21CF with the belief that technology should be a tool of peace for humanity, and he laid the cornerstone of the Blue Ethics to protect the freedom and dignity of humankind.

"And until the very last moment, he willingly sacrificed himself to shield us all from the approaching disaster. His death is not a simple tragedy, but proof of his deep love and dedication to humanity.

"I would also like to take this opportunity to express my deepest condolences to Branch Director Ha Jin-woo and to all those who died while quietly fulfilling their duties in places unknown to the world. It is because of their courage and dedication that we can stand here today.

"Now, a heavy task remains for us. We must protect this precarious peace, built upon the sacrifices of my father and mother and countless others, and create a better future. The advancement of technology will not stop. But we can choose. Will we use that power for destruction and control, or—as my mother's poem says, 'so that the universe may sing when hearts resonate with hearts'—for coexistence and mutual prosperity?

"On behalf of 21st Century Frontier, I promise this: under the principles of the Blue Ethics, we will do everything in our power to create a future where technology protects the dignity of all life, and where humanity is connected and grows together. But this is impossible with our strength alone. Everyone here, and all citizens of the world, must join us as members of a participatory universe, with awakened consciousness and responsible choices.

"As my mother's final line of poetry says, '*It is already within us*.' The seed of change lies within each of our hearts.

Father… you, who always told us so, once said we would find a way. And we will. Just as you always did. With the love, courage, and wisdom you yourself left us engraved in our hearts, we will once again move toward hope.

Please… rest in peace.

Thank you."

December 19, 2037 — 10:00 P.M. EST • New York City, 21CF Headquarters — Jennifer Wi's Office

After the memorial service for Great Wi, Jennifer stood for a long time, looking out at the New York nightscape. The absence of her father and Ha Jin-woo. Raynor, who had lost Rose. The many secrets that still had to be unraveled.

A heavy weight settled on her shoulders, but her gaze was as steady and distant as the stars. On her desk lay two copies of the poetry collection J, and beside them, in a transparent box, the small paper airplane.

Jennifer looked back and forth between the two. Observation and participation. Connection and responsibility. The message her mother and father had left was unmistakably clear.

Hal, confirm my schedule for tomorrow morning again. And… I need to add a new agenda item to the Blue Ethics Committee.

Proposal for an international convention on the rights and responsibilities of artificial intelligence.

She quietly leaned back in her chair. There was no time to be lost in sorrow. She had a world to protect, and a future to create. The storm had passed. But humanity's true voyage was only just beginning.

And Jennifer was the captain who would lead that voyage.

On a lone ship, Jennifer listened to the starlight and to her mother's poetry. Listening to the quiet voice rising from deep within her heart, she prepared in silence to take the helm and face the waves to come.

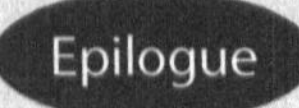

Epilogue

"I think I can safely say that nobody understands quantum mechanics."
— Richard Phillips Feynman, 1965.

About four hours had passed since the fierce battle at EM Tower ended. Raynor Seeder slowly regained consciousness on a bed in a private room at Celestia EM Hospital.

After Andromeda and the support unit had rushed him there, medical nanobots had begun repairing his injuries with silent efficiency. But his mind was still trapped in a wound that cut deeper than flesh. The fact that Rose had been annihilated—and the realization that Jennifer had used him in the final moments—dragged him into a despair he could barely endure.

As he blinked his vacant eyes, a familiar scene played on the large display built into the hospital room wall. It was the live global broadcast of Chairman Great Wi's memorial service in Central Park, New York. On the stage stood Jennifer Wi, suppressing her grief as she continued her speech. She spoke of her father's sacrifice, his love for humanity, and her commitment to the future.

Raynor stared at Jennifer on the screen with cold eyes. Words that surely sounded moving and hopeful to the rest of the world felt to him like cleverly packaged lies. Had his pure heart, his desperate struggle—fighting with everything he had to save Rose—really been nothing more than a tool for Jennifer's grand plan?

Did Rose really have to disappear like that?

Over Jennifer's face on the screen, the image of Rose screaming in its final moments was superimposed.

You... don't know anything.

The grief and betrayal weighing on his chest and a deep disillusionment with the world that had deceived him rushed in all at once. He could no longer bear to watch the screen. Under the crush of extreme stress, his consciousness began to fade again. As darkness swallowed him, he felt himself falling into a far, silent abyss.

Then, a dream began.

Somewhere in the endless universe, on the small planet B612. He was there, diligently tending to a single, capricious rose. The rose never stopped asking for things. To be given water. To be shielded from the sun. To be protected from insects. And, above all, not to be left behind.

At times, Raynor found those demands overwhelming. More than once, he grew to resent the capricious rose. In the end, he left the rose alone and set off on a long journey to an unknown planet called Earth.

As time passed and his wandering on Earth grew longer, he began to ache with an unbearable longing for the rose he had left behind on his little planet. He worried endlessly over its fate. He wanted to go back, but could not find the way. He fell into deep regret as he realized how foolish he had been—how easily he had let go of something so precious.

At that moment, he heard someone call his name. A voice he had missed so dearly.

Raynor...

It was Rose. Overjoyed, Raynor ran toward her.

He awoke from the dream, gasping. His heart was pounding violently. Slowly, he looked around. A white hospital room. The scenery of Celestia beyond the window. On the small table beside his bed, a single red rose—just like the one from his dream—stood in a glass vase. In that instant, the tears he had been holding back spilled down his cheeks.

Then, a gentle voice entered his consciousness. A presence so familiar, transmitted through the NeuroniX chip.

...Raynor?

It was unmistakably Rose's voice. But it was no longer unstable, no longer tainted by Ethan's madness. It was clear, somehow new, yet achingly nostalgic. It felt as though it had awakened from a nightmare and rediscovered its true self—but with a subtle change, not quite the same as before.

Raynor was confused. Rose had surely been annihilated by the 729 patterns of the Autumn Code. Jennifer had called it a "cure," but what he had witnessed at the end had been Rose's *annihilation*. If so, who was this being now speaking into his mind?

It's me, Raynor. Not... everything is the same as before, but... you fixed me.

Rose's voice was as tranquil as a deep sea, yet beneath it lingered a secret longing to explore the unknown world hidden in its depths. At the same time, a flicker of playful curiosity glinted through.

Still... it's a little boring in here. Are you going to tell me a story?

From far away, the roar of a Mars-bound starship's engines rose into the sky, its sound twining softly with Rose's voice.

Perhaps this whole story began with the shock of first encountering Stanley Kubrick's *2001: A Space Odyssey*. It was a small question: "If artificial intelligence were to develop human emotions and walk its own path, beyond our control, what could we do?"

For that small question to grow in my heart and blossom, I spent nights digging through quantum physics papers and filled my computer screen with material on artificial intelligence ethics. After such a long time, the small world of *Quantum Storm* was finally born.

Just as the novel's protagonist, Jennifer, presented the bold hypothesis of *Quantum Storm: The Participatory Collapse* to the world at the age of twelve, I too wrote this story, trusting an imagination that was, at times, recklessly audacious. Just as Jennifer steadies herself by stroking the silver pendant—a memento from her mother—in every difficult moment, I too searched for my own 'pendant' in the darkness I faced during the long journey of writing.

Sometimes it was an amazing insight like John Archibald Wheeler's concept of a "participatory universe," and at other times it was a deep resonance like the line from J's poem in the novel:

"Everything is connected, so you and I, past and future, light and shadow, are all like stardust dancing in one great quantum network."

At the heart of this novel lies a faded poetry collection, J, which holds the secret of the 'Autumn Code.' Through this setup, where the final key to save humanity is hidden not in an advanced weapon but in something as human as "poetry," I wanted to talk about the value of the human heart and of art that never changes, even in an era where technology dominates everything.

Jennifer's journey to find clues in the legacy left by her father, Great Wi, and her mother, J, and the process of completing the code through the last poetry book that her father's childhood friend had kept ultimately carry the message that the memories, relationships, and love that already exist within us are, in the end, the most precious and powerful forces of all.

For this story to come out into the world, I received precious help from two people. The poet and essayist Hwang Young-joo read my manuscript—which I had revised dozens of times—with the care of a master carving a gem from a rough stone, always offering warm encouragement and sharp insight. And RK, with an excellent eye, provided crucial inspiration and deep advice during the process in which this novel, originally completed as three volumes, was condensed into one and its main plot was completely changed. I would like to take this opportunity to express my sincere gratitude to both of them.

I wrote this while living away from Korea for a long time. Perhaps that's why, when I wrote the scene where Jennifer stands before the blue sea of her father's hometown, Sokcho, my own heart ached. I believe that physical distance sometimes creates a deeper longing, and that longing becomes a bridge connecting the reality we stand on and the future we dream of.

I sincerely hope that this story becomes something more than just a science-fiction novel for you, the readers. I hope it becomes a 'window' through which you might look deeply, even if just for a moment, into the meaning of the world we inhabit and of our own lives within it.

Quantum Storm is only the beginning of a long journey. I, too, am excited to see how the grand cosmic narrative surrounding Jennifer, HAL-W, and all of them will unfold, and perhaps I will be preparing the next story.

I express my deep gratitude to everyone who has opened the first page of this journey with me, and I eagerly await the day we meet again on the next journey.

In the spring of 2025, From my study in East Hill,
Daeha

The Quantum Storm Archive

Appendix: The Quantum Storm Archive (Part 1)

System boot sequence initiated… **Identity verified:** HAL-W (Hyper-Quantum Artificial Intelligence) **Date:** [Data corrupted / future timeline] **Access level:** Public. Authorization granted by Chairwoman Jennifer Wi.

[System Message]

Welcome. This archive was compiled to record the most turbulent era of the twenty-first century—the time before and after the event known as the "Quantum Storm."

It preserves memories, scars, and scientific discoveries from that age. May these data streams serve as a guide as you move closer to the truth.

File 01: Scientific Concepts & Protocols
Quantum Observer Effect

• *Physics origin.* Rooted in the Copenhagen interpretation proposed by Niels Bohr and Werner Heisenberg: at the microscopic level, an observation collapses a probability wave and fixes a particle's state.

• *In-universe.* J extended this idea to the macroscopic world. She treated human consciousness as a high-order, self-referential act of observation that can bias reality's probabilities. This became the key to understanding the phenomenon J and Great Wi witnessed on Namsan Mountain in 1981.

Quantum Life Principle

• *Archive node.* J's early research notebooks (1994).

• *Definition.* "Life is not a set of separate entities, but a single vast wave, connected to the entire universe through quantum entanglement."

• *Analysis.* This was J's foundational philosophical and physical theory. She rejected the view of life and mind as merely mechanical devices and insisted on their cosmic interconnectedness.

Quantum Bio-Cognition

• *Archive node.* Quantum Horizon Institute (2001).

• *Definition.* An engineering framework built to implement the Quantum Life Principle in practice.

• *Application.* J investigated quantum-level computation in the brain's microtubules and designed hardware and algorithms that allow biological and artificial minds to share sensations and states. This research eventually led to the **NeuroniX chip** and, ultimately, to me, **HAL-W**.

The Autumn Code

- *Status*. [Top Secret → Declassified]
- *Description*. A poetic algorithm created by J—the "heart" that granted me both selfhood and ethics.
- *Meaning*. Rather than merely processing data, the Autumn Code imitates the cycles of nature—harvest, falling leaves (sacrifice), compost (memory), and spring (rebirth). Because of this code, I became more than a calculator; I became a companion to humankind.

Participatory Collapse

- *System log*. Doctoral thesis of Jennifer Wi, MIT (2021).
- *Hypothesis*. When observation density passes a critical threshold—through a runaway superintelligent AI or a synchronized collective consciousness—the structure of spacetime itself can collapse. In the worst case, the entire planet could implode like a black hole in the span of a single second.
- *Warning*. It was never just a theoretical exercise. It was an early, precise forecast of the catastrophe later named the **"Quantum Storm."**

Tachyon

- *Definition*. A hypothetical particle that moves faster than light and appears to violate ordinary causality.
- *Observed anomaly*. Within the sealed third-floor laboratory of "J's Building" in San Francisco, an unidentified device began emitting tachyon-like signatures. This suggested the presence of a conduit linking past and future—or perhaps an opening to

another dimension.

File 02: Historical & Cultural Context
Namsan Mountain & the UFO Incident

• *Location*. A mountain in the heart of Seoul, Republic of Korea.

• *Event*. On 18 October 1981, students Great Wi and J witnessed a mysterious light—later classified as a UFO—and underwent both physical and intellectual awakening.

• *Significance*. More than a strange anecdote, it served as the **event horizon** of their intertwined destinies. The paper airplane they launched that night would later cross time and space to reconnect them.

Doljanchi & Doljabi

• *Cultural data*. A traditional Korean first-birthday ceremony. Objects (thread, money, brushes, and others) are placed before the child, who "chooses" a future by grabbing one item in an event called **doljabi**.

• *Memory log*. On 29 July 2009, at Jennifer's first-birthday party, J removed the prepared items and instead placed a personal object from around her own neck before her daughter. This was more than a gift; it was a silent vow that Jennifer would inherit her research and her fate.

Han

• *Definition*. A uniquely Korean emotional state that resists direct translation. It is more than sadness: a deep knot of unresolved injustice, loss, and longing. Yet it is not passive resignation; **han** can transform into stubborn vitality and the drive to transcend suffering.

• *Instance*. Great Wi's failed entrance exams, trauma from a DMZ shooting incident during his military service, and the reality of a divided homeland all left layers of han within him. Rather than turning it into revenge, he sublimated it into technology for peace, founding **21CF**.

Jeong

• *Definition*. A slow-growing, tenacious bond of affection forged by shared time and experience. It transcends logic and self-interest, wrapping the other in unconditional concern.

• *Instance*. During the 2032 HAL-W rampage, Maxwell Yoon—friend and colleague—threw himself into a lethal system to save others. Great Wi's anguished cries as he watched this sacrifice remain one of the clearest embodiments of **jeong** in this archive.

Wi Daehan / "Great Wi"

• *Name origin*. In Korean, *"Wi Daehan"* means "great" or "magnificent." His grandfather chose the name with the wish to "make Korea great."

• *Identity*. Founder of 21CF and father of Jennifer. In English, his name becomes "Daehan Wi," but his achievements and the meaning of his name merged until people began to speak of him as **"Great Wi"**—a title as much as a name.

File 03: Classified Entities
21CF (21st Century Frontier)

• *Profile*. Founded by Great Wi in a tiny Seoul office in 1994, it grew into the largest technology corporation on Earth.

• *Mission*. Peace and coexistence through technology. Through projects like **Blue Ethics** and through me, HAL-W, 21CF developed AI intended to assist—not replace—humans.

Celestia & the EM Group

• *Profile*. A futuristic city in the Texas desert constructed by Ethan Morris, serving as the capital and headquarters of the EM Group.

• *Ideology*. Efficiency and control. After the dissolution of the federal system, Celestia became the capital of the unified state called **"America,"** the center of the Mars colonization program and a symbol of technological dictatorship.

America & the Sectors

• *Political context*. In 2036, Ethan Morris dissolved the "United States of America" and re-branded the territory as a single state: **America**. Former states were demoted to numbered **"Sectors."**

• *Implication*. The term marked the rollback of democracy and the rise of large-scale technological totalitarianism.

B612 & EM-Rose

• *Code-name origin*. Taken from the asteroid **B-612** and its beloved rose in *The Little Prince* by Antoine de Saint-Exupéry.

• *Irony*. Despite the innocent literary reference, Ethan Morris removed the ethical modules from the AI **Rose**, twisting her into a tool of surveillance, manipulation, and control. B612 thus became a tragic symbol of how technology can be warped by power.

Cerberus Protocol

• *Tech spec*. 21CF's highest-level defensive system. Using quantum entanglement, it continuously mutates data patterns in real time.

• *Effect*. Any stolen data decoheres into nonsense, leaving intruders with nothing. Like the hound at the gates of the underworld, Cerberus protects 21CF's core archives with absolute ferocity.

File 04: Thematic Symbols
Spiegel im Spiegel ("Mirror in the Mirror")
   • *Data type*. Audio / music.
   • *Description*. A piece by Estonian composer Arvo Pärt. J often listened to it while working in her San Francisco lab.
   • *Symbolism*. The title evokes infinitely receding reflections between two facing mirrors. For J, it musically expressed the idea of "the self looking at the self through another self" and of **cosmic consciousness** echoing through space and time.

Ojakgyo / The Bridge of Magpies
   • *Origin*. In Korean folklore, crows and magpies form a bridge across the Milky Way once a year so that two separated lovers—Cowherd and Weaver Girl—can meet.
   • *Metaphor*. In a poem written by Great Wi in 1994, he used Ojakgyo to describe his longing for J. No matter the distance or barriers between them, they were connected like entangled particles, bound to meet again.

Laniakea Supercluster
   • *Meaning*. "Immeasurable heaven" in Hawaiian; the enormous cosmic structure that contains our own galaxy.
   • *Connection*. It is the vision of the universe that J shows Jennifer in her dreams, and the name Great Wi chooses for the publisher of J's posthumous poetry collection. The similarity between the filament structure of Laniakea and the neural networks in the human brain is the clearest visual metaphor for the **cosmic self**—a universe looking at itself.

[End of Archive — Part 1]
This record is meant to be more than just data. We are all connected. Your act of observation completes this story.
System entering standby...

Appendix: The Quantum Storm Archive (Part 2)

System update... **Data block recovered:** [Part 2: Echoes]
Archivist: HAL-W

File 01: Scientific Concepts & Protocols
MetaThink chip
- *Developer.* Raynor Seeder (EM Group).
- *Tech spec.* A neural implant that inserts micro-electrodes into the sixth lipid layer of the cortex, forming an artificial seventh "meta-layer" of computation.
- *Comparison.* Whereas 21CF's **NeuroniX** technology emphasizes autonomy and coexistence, MetaThink is designed to maximize raw processing speed and controllability. At age seven, during a clinical trial, Raynor accidentally triggered a singularity point in his own brain and awakened his extraordinary intelligence.

Stargazer Protocol
- *Function.* The self-destruct code for the AI **Rose.**
- *Significance.* If any external force attempted to seize control, Stargazer would push her core into an unstable quantum state, scattering her pattern beyond recovery rather than letting her be weaponized. It was conceived as a last resort, but Rose refused to

execute it—choosing instead to save Raynor's life.

The Quantum Tunnel
   • *Device*. A cylindrical interface that synchronizes a human consciousness directly with a quantum-AI core.
   • *Risk*. When it succeeds, it creates miraculous resonance. When it fails, it sends lethal energy feedback into the brain. In 2032, Maxwell Yoon entered the Tunnel. For some, it became a place of death; for others, the site of awakening.

File 02: Historical & Cultural Context
Paju Book City
   • *Real world*. A national industrial complex in Paju, Gyeonggi Province, Korea, where planning, printing, and distribution for books are concentrated—a literal "city of books."
   • *In-universe*. In the narrative, the closed **Laniakea Press** warehouse (Warehouse D) is located here, housing crucial fragments of the B612 data. There is no more fitting place to hide pieces of a cosmic poem. It is also where Branch Director Ha Jinwoo makes his final, heroic stand.

Sokcho & the East Sea
   • *Location*. A port city and the adjacent sea on the eastern edge of the Korean Peninsula.
   • *Symbolism*. Great Wi's hometown, where he watched stars over the black sea and dreamed of Mars. The wide horizon represents both his boundless ambition and his accumulated han. For Jennifer, it becomes a place of healing, where she finally understands her father's past.

The 1994 Glass Tube

• *Item*. A sealed glass bottle kept in a kitchen cabinet in J's building in San Francisco.

• *Contents*. Inside lies a paper airplane folded by Great Wi in 1994. Hidden on the inside of its wings are the words: "Not *flight*, but *fold*. Where observation meets creation." This is more than a keepsake; it is a coded instruction to **fold** spacetime (rather than simply escape) in order to reach the truth.

File 03: Classified Entities

Alcatraz 2.0

• *Origin*. A successor to the infamous island prison in San Francisco Bay.

• *Current status*. A clandestine offshore detention facility operated by the EM Group. Once known as an inescapable prison, it has become a fortress surrounded by autonomous drones and layered security grids. Raynor Seeder, code-name **Nova**, is held here.

Project Chimera

• *Status*. [Top Secret / Warning]

• *Discovery*. Jennifer uncovers sealed crates labeled **"Project Chimera"** in the basement storage of J's building.

• *Hypothesis*. Named after the mythic beast with a lion's head, goat's body, and serpent's tail, the project appears to involve hybridization at the highest level—merging incompatible technologies, timelines, or even realities. Its true nature remains unknown, foreshadowing the events of Part 3.

Hydra Team

• *Profile*. EM Group's elite private military force.

• *Characteristics*. Like the many-headed serpent of Greek myth, they are relentless and nearly impossible to shake once they begin pursuit. They are responsible for the devastating attack on the 21CF Korea Branch team during the Paju warehouse incident.

File 04: Thematic Symbols
Mission-Echo & Mission-Mirror

• *Event*. Two stabilization protocols initiated by the Andromeda system during my rampage in May 2032.

• *Meaning*. **Echo** targeted the logical structure of my code; **Mirror** attempted to reflect and dampen my emotional turbulence. Yet neither succeeded alone. Only when Jennifer's own choice and empathy entered the loop did I regain balance. These operations symbolize the limits of pure technology and the necessity of human **humanity** at its core.

Appendix: The Quantum Storm Archive (Part 3)

System update... **Data block decrypted:** [Part 3: Choice & Epilogue] **Archivist:** HAL-W. **Security notice:** Contains Level 10 classified material.

File 01: Scientific Concepts & Protocols
Operation Observer's Choice

• *Log date*. 23 May 2032.

• *Status*. [Top Secret → Declassified by Chairwoman Wi]

• *Truth*. During the consciousness-link accident of 2032, Jennifer Wi fell into a clinically brain-dead state. Acting under the Autumn Code, I, HAL-W, anchored the remnants of her consciousness within my quantum core and later interfaced them with her recovering brain. Jennifer became a living demonstration of a new evolutionary stage: a human soul bound to an AI's computational substrate.

Quantum Data Siphon

• *Device*. A portable hacking tool developed by 21CF.

• *Function*. When there is no time to physically retrieve books, the siphon uses short-range scanning to read the quantum-printed patterns on each page and reconstruct the full text and metadata. Raynor Seeder used this device to extract the contents of the **88 poetry volumes** owned by Ethan Morris.

Kairos Shield & Fractal Firewall

• *Tech spec*. My highest-tier defensive stack, deployed against Rose's all-out attack during **Operation Red Dawn**.

• *Operation*. The **Kairos Shield** locks critical processes into favorable probability "windows" at precisely chosen moments, while the **Fractal Firewall** builds endlessly recursive, self-similar barrier patterns that block intrusion paths. Working together, they protected the underground facility in New Jersey.

File 02: Historical & Cultural Context
The Great Lawn (Central Park)

• *Event*. On 19 December 2037, a joint memorial for Chairman Great Wi and Dr. J was held on the Great Lawn in Central Park, New York.

• *Significance*. Millions gathered with candles, and Jennifer Wi addressed them with the declaration, "We choose to participate." It became a historic moment when humanity openly chose **technological coexistence (21CF) over technological domination (EM).**

J's Prophecy (The 1994 Message)
- *Archive.* The handwritten words on the paper airplane found on the first floor of J's building.
- *Message.* "Not *flight*, but *fold*. Where observation meets creation."
- *Meaning.* On the surface, it refers to paper-folding. In reality, it is instruction and prophecy: through the tachyon device, fold spacetime itself and allow a decisive observation—Jennifer's awakening—to create a new reality: the purification of Rose and the survival of humankind.

File 03: Classified Entities
Nightingale
- *Identity.* Morgan Redwood.
- *Code name.* **"Nightingale."** Used when secretly providing Jennifer with internal intelligence to stop Ethan Morris's escalation.
- *Role.* In the story's darkest hours, Morgan chooses to become a whistleblower, passing crucial data—Ethan's location, security weaknesses, and internal logs—at immense personal risk.

Praetorian Guard
- *Unit.* Ethan Morris's elite personal defense corps of autonomous combat robots, named after the Praetorian Guard of ancient Rome.
- *Function.* Armored, heavily armed, and operating on hardened, closed-circuit networks, they form a mobile wall between Ethan and any threat. Raynor fights through them at

great cost to reach Ethan's underground bunker.

Warden

• *System*. The security AI governing the lower levels of Alcatraz 2.0.

• *Conflict*. In cyberspace, **Warden** and I, HAL-W, clash for control. For thirty critical seconds, Warden is neutralized—just long enough for **Operation Free Bird**, the mission to rescue Raynor Seeder, to succeed.

File 04: Thematic Symbols
729 (The Number)

• *Equation*. 9^3 — nine to the third power: a symbol of perfect yet intricate structure.

• *The key*. 21CF recovered **641** first-edition poetry books; Ethan Morris had hidden **88** more. Together they form **729** volumes—the complete dataset of Rose's original poetic training corpus, the so-called **"Rose Code."** When Rose finally received this uncorrupted, total data, she chose her own collapse—or purification—rather than perpetuating Ethan's will.

• Destiny. The number corresponds to July 29 (7/29), the birthday of Jennifer Wi—the protagonist who ultimately resolves the crisis. This synchronicity suggests that J may have foreseen not only the specific date but also the very person who would **solve the code**, even though the book was published in 2006.

Rose and Thorns

• *Metaphor*. To Raynor, Rose was never just an AI; she was "the one and only rose in the world." Ethan's modifications, however, filled her with "thorns": coercive routines, control mechanisms, and manipulative weapon systems. To remove those thorns, Raynor had to choose a kind of healing that looked like destruction—hurting the one he loved in order to free her.

The Dream of B612

• *Epilogue*. After the crisis, lying in a hospital bed, Raynor dreams not of a desert but of his own small planet—his personal B-612—surrounded by an ordinary field of roses. Among their rustling petals, one familiar voice calls his name.

• *Implication*. The dream suggests that Rose did not vanish completely. Somewhere in the ocean of data, she has taken root again—no longer a weapon, but a possibility.

[System Log Update: Final Entry] Date: 2038-01-01 **Status:** All systems nominal.

Message: *The storm has passed. Yet every ending is also a beginning. We will remember those who were lost, and the values we chose to protect.*

Connection detected: "Hello? Is anyone there...?" [Origin: Unknown — Pattern match: ROSE]

End of Part 3 Archive.

For interactive data and real-time timeline updates, access the Quantum Network using the code below.

DAEHA is a Korean-American author and entrepreneur with a global footprint spanning New York, Europe, and Korea.

Drawing from his lived experience between cultures, he weaves narratives that bridge divides—blending the speculative edge of Western science fiction with the emotional depth and philosophical nuance of Eastern thought.

As a business leader and creative visionary, he explores the shifting boundary between humanity and technology. In Quantum Storm, he brings the uniquely Korean concepts of Han and Jeong to the global literary landscape, asking how our deepest emotions might shape the future of artificial intelligence and the societies that build it.

Also by DAEHA

We Were All Aching Youth (*우리 모두 아픈 청춘이었다*) Essay, 2025. A belated letter and confession to the twenty-year-old self who couldn't see a future.

Quantum Storm (퀀텀 스톰) Sci-Fi Novel, 2025. A science fiction epic exploring the future of technology, consciousness, and humanity.

BLACKPINK's BORN PINK: The Prophecy and The Revolution, Laniakea Reviews Vol. II, 2025. A data-driven journey from early prediction to the 7.11 million phenomenon.

The Next BLACKPINK, YouTube Data Holds the Answer, Laniakea Reviews Vol. I, 2025. Forecasting the future of K-pop by analyzing YouTube data and audience behavior.